SHE STARTED IT

A Novel

SIAN GILBERT

WM
WILLIAM MORROW
An Imprint of HarperCollinsPublishers

SHE STARTED IT. Copyright © 2023 by Sian Gilbert. All rights reserved. Printed in the United States of America. No part of this book may be used or reproduced in any manner whatsoever without written permission except in the case of brief quotations embodied in critical articles and reviews. For information, address Harper-Collins Publishers, 195 Broadway, New York, NY 10007.

Designed by Kyle O'Brien

Title page art © Chansom Pantip/Shutterstock, Inc.

ISBN 978-0-06-328629-0

For my granny, Marie Blackmore.
Your love of books inspired my own.

SHE
STARTED
IT

Robin

MAY 22, 2023

There's only the bride waiting for me, and she's covered in blood.

Normally at the end of a holiday on this island the whole party is ready with their suitcases, sunburned but cheerful. As I power across to them in my deck boat, they're often not looking at me but taking final glances around the island: its white sandy beaches, clear water, palm trees.

It's a perfect day to be on the sea this morning. The sun is warm on my back and the tide is on my side.

But the bride waiting for me has changed everything.

I wouldn't call myself an easily shaken person. When you run a private island, you prepare for every possibility. Just thirty minutes by speedboat from the mainland, I'm always there if something does go wrong. The guests have the island to themselves, but I've not left them stranded. There's an emergency phone, flares, and a fully stocked first aid kit.

Crises have happened before, of course they have.

Someone thought they'd climb the edge of the cliffside and ended up breaking their leg. Another woman insisted her pregnancy wouldn't be a bother and went into labour on the first night. I guess I thought I'd seen it all.

I haven't seen this.

The boat reaches the pier and I'm able to cut the engine and secure it before the bride hurries over.

"What's happened?" I ask, amazed by how forceful my voice sounds. "Is everyone okay? Do I need to call an ambulance?"

Now that she's reached me, the bride seems to be in a state of shock. There are deep gashes in her hands, but I'm not sure they're enough to cause the devastation on her thin white dress. All across the front are huge blood stains, grown dark with time. Scratches cover one side of her face. A slight bruise is forming underneath her left eye.

I reach out a tentative hand and she jerks backwards.

"Sorry!" I look around, trying to find signs of the others.

It's too quiet here. I think back to only days ago, the happy loud group of women I took to this island, leaving them ready for the hen party of a lifetime. Nothing seemed out of the ordinary.

"Where are the others?" I ask.

The bride's eyes finally focus on me, wide and fearful.

"Your bridesmaids?" I persist. "Where are they?"

"It all went wrong," she says.

I'm about to speak, but the bride isn't finished. She draws herself into a hunch, grabbing both arms, wrapping herself in an embrace despite the scorching weather.

Her next words leave me cold.

"She started it."

ONE

Annabel

I take out the invitation again, its creamy thick card with embossed lettering somehow more impressive than the first-class plane ticket to the Bahamas. There are a few minutes before my taxi arrives for the airport, so I sit on the velvet armchair by the window and study everything once more.

Dear Annabel, it reads. *I hope this invitation comes as a pleasant surprise. I am getting married in the summer next year, and would love it if you could be a bridesmaid. I have organised the hen party to take place on a completely private island in the Bahamas, and you don't need to spend a penny. Further details will follow about the wedding when you all arrive! Please write back to me to let me know you can make it. Full instructions are underneath and I have included your plane tickets. Love, Poppy Greer*

Poppy Greer, of all people. The invitation was a surprise, that was for sure. I haven't seen her in almost ten years, haven't even spoken to her. Not since the end of our A levels. Nor was she my favourite person. It's safe to say the four of us—that is, me, Chloe, Esther, and Tanya—didn't like Poppy that much and teased her for it. Harmless teasing, nothing serious. But still, it's a shock that she's invited us, let alone asked us to be her bridesmaids.

"I'm not going to turn down a free first-class flight and stay on a private island," Chloe said, when we all discovered we'd had the same letter. "Especially if it's all four of us."

There's a brochure in the envelope with the invitation and plane tickets. The island is called Deadman's Bay, an ominous first impression but easily forgotten at the sight of the clear ocean water. There's a small wooden whitewashed pier that peeks out into the waves, showcasing a strip of the faraway mainland and the blue skies above. Inside the brochure, there are a couple of photographs of the island itself. Through lush thick greenery is a tended lawn; palm trees are dotted about like streetlamps, some curving and others rod-straight, bound together by hammocks, and a fire pit sits in the middle surrounded by deck chairs. In the background there's a glimpse of the white beach, sun loungers and a small red-and-white-striped open gazebo. The beachfront home, the biggest accommodation ahead of four tiny huts at the rear of the island, is hidden behind four large palm trees that fight for space, a small single-storey white building with pink windows and a pink front door. Next to it, almost out of sight, a decking area complete with barbecue.

It wasn't hard to say yes. I didn't even have to change any of my plans; I had none, and I don't work. Andrew, my husband, didn't have a problem with me being away for four days either.

The other three all have jobs. Esther Driscoll is an investment banker at a top firm and had to beg, borrow, and steal to get the time off. She's much more serious than the rest of us. Even when out of work she's constantly on her phone, responding to emails. It's a far cry from the wild spirit she was at school and university, always the last to leave a party. But I know her mother got her the interview for her current job and she feels under a lot of pressure to perform, although she'd never admit that to us.

The last one to leave a party these days is Tanya Evesham, but that's because she's the one who organises them. She's an events planner, from arranging celebrity features to high-class birthday parties. When she first started, she used to invite us along to whatever bash she'd put together that night, guaranteeing us free cocktails and the ability to rub shoulders with the social elite. There's a certain charm to Tanya. She can capture a room's attention and thrives on it, always leaving people wanting more. Tanya's events were the social occasions everyone put on their calendar.

Until they suddenly weren't, a few months ago. Tanya stopped inviting us to parties, and we stopped hearing about them, though that hasn't stopped her throwing them and she seems busier than ever. She and her boyfriend, Harry—a professional bodyguard to a politician—bought a place last year on the outskirts of London and she's been busy redecorating, so the three of us have barely seen her, nor has she invited us for a housewarming.

For Chloe, this trip counts as work. She's the most delighted of us all. Chloe Devine (real name Chloe Smith, a hopelessly ordinary surname she never could have done well with, she tells us) is an Instagram sensation: just fifty thousand followers away from one million. Inundated with various sponsorship deals she advertises in different posts, Chloe loves nothing more than an opportunity to flaunt her wealth to her followers. But a first-class flight to a private island is a whole new level, and she's bought seven different bikinis for the occasion. Something as simple as a photo of her sipping coffee in a café gets hundreds of thousands of likes.

If I'd known all it took to get rich and famous was a nose job, I'd have done it before her. But I'm not jealous. Chloe is still single, despite the numerous relationships she's had. If you can call them relationships.

I'm happily married. I'm the lucky one.

As if he's read my mind, Andrew comes into the living room and finds me curled up by the window, slotting everything safely back into the envelope and then my Prada handbag. Chloe isn't the only one who has nice designer gear.

"Have you seen my keys?" Andrew asks, picking up the sofa cushions and flinging them back down. "I swear you always move them."

I sigh. Andrew loses his keys every single time he is about to go out, and every single time it's my fault. "Have you checked your coat pocket?"

"My coat pocket?" he echoes, as if I've gone mad. "Why on earth would it—" The rest of his sentence disappears along with him through the door, and I hear a jangle of keys. He comes back in with a frown on his face. "Did you put them in here? I could have sworn I took them out after work yesterday."

"Why would I move your keys?" I try to laugh and make light of it, but Andrew's expression darkens.

"You're always moving my things." He stands in front of the fireplace, adjusting his tie in the mirror that hangs above.

"Have you got something on at work today?"

He startles at my voice, but the tie is finally fixed into place. "Nothing in particular. Why do you ask?"

"You just seem very preoccupied with your tie today. And you've shaved."

This makes him sigh. "Honestly, Annabel, don't you have anything better to do than observe my morning routine?"

"Well, it's my trip today," I say, because he doesn't seem to be mentioning it. I wasn't expecting him to drop me to the airport, that would be ridiculous. But I had expected perhaps an early wake-up, breakfast together, some morning sex to say goodbye. Instead, Andrew pressed the snooze button and I had avocado on toast on my own in the kitchen. "I'll be gone for four nights."

"Right, your hen party," he says. "What time do you leave?"

"Any minute," I say, checking my phone. "The taxi should be arriving soon."

"You look like you're all ready to go." He nods at the suitcase next to me, then checks his watch. "I can't be late, babe."

"No problem." Because it's not a problem. He has to work, he's the one who earns the money around here, though he can be quite stingy with it, rarely allowing me to go shopping as much as I would like. But I have my ways around that. I stand and walk over to him. "I'll miss you."

"You'll be having too much fun," he replies, removing himself from the embrace I wrapped him in.

I fasten a smile on my face. "I love you. Hey, give me a kiss goodbye."

He laughs. "I'll be seeing you in a few days."

I'm about to plant a kiss on his lips before he can protest any further when my phone rings, the sudden noise breaking any romantic moment we might have had. Thinking it's the taxi, I hurry to answer it without even checking the caller.

"Hello?" As I put the phone to my ear, Andrew gives my shoulder a squeeze and heads out. The front door shuts behind him before the person on the other end is even able to respond.

"Annabel, darling, is that you? I can't believe you've actually answered one of my calls. You're normally so *busy*."

My mother.

I groan inwardly. Perhaps it's not too late—I can just hang up now and pretend there was a signal issue.

"Mum," I say, deciding to get it over with.

"Well, how are you, for God's sake? It's been months since I last heard from you."

To say I have a fractured relationship with my mother would be putting it delicately. There was no dramatic fallout, no deep dark secret for why I moved to the other side of Bristol and never came back. It's natural, really, that after university I would want to reinvent myself a bit. I became a better person, not someone content with working in a shop like Mum. The tiny two-bedroom house on the edge of Hartcliffe where I grew up is where she's always been, even after Dad left long ago. When I met Andrew, and he introduced me to his own parents—his father an ex-MP and his mother a dermatologist, living in their five-storey Georgian mansion in the centre of Clifton—it felt natural to break away from Mum.

Andrew's only met her the once, at the wedding, when I had to invite her. I spent the whole day in a state of constant panic that she would say something ignorant, repeatedly talking over her and laughing immediately whenever she tried to crack a joke so the attention would come off her. She had tried, she really had, but her too-tight dress from Next and the potted plant wedding present couldn't compete with Andrew's family's sophistication. Not when Andrew's mother arrived in a Givenchy dress with Chantilly lace and gifted us not only a diamond decanter and glasses "so there was something for you to unwrap" but also a seven-night stay in a five-star spa resort in Iceland. Their taste is just more elevated. I was relieved when Mum left, and Andrew hasn't asked to see her since, so I assume the feeling is mutual. She's better off in Hartcliffe and we're better off here, in a Georgian house identical to the one Andrew's parents live in a couple of streets away.

"I'm actually about to go on holiday," I say, hoping the taxi will pull up at any moment and give me an excuse to get off the phone. "I'm going to a hen party."

"Who's getting married?" Mum asks, always straight to the point. I wonder when the last time she went on holiday was. We certainly never went when I was a child, because I was always jealous hearing about everyone else's fantastic summers.

"That's the funny thing." For a second I'm not sure whether to tell her, but what harm can it do? "It's Poppy Greer's wedding."

"Poppy Greer?" Mum says, sounding surprised. "Poppy Greer from your school?"

"Yeah, that Poppy," I say. "It's a bit strange, isn't it? But she invited us to join her on a private island in the Bahamas. We couldn't exactly say no to that."

There's a sigh on the other end of the line. "That would be hard to refuse, I agree. You've seen her recently, then?"

"Uh—no," I admit, realising that sounds odd. "She sent the plane tickets with the invitation. But we've seen her on Instagram, posting about her wedding. She followed us all a few months back."

"Who's this 'we'?"

"Me, Chloe, Esther, and Tanya." Why does it sound weird now that I'm explaining it to her? Mum always has this way of twisting things to seem worse than they are. "We're all going to be her bridesmaids."

"But I thought . . ." Her voice trails away.

"What?"

"Never mind, I must have been mistaken." She clears her throat. Her tone lightens. "Well, this will be an opportunity for the four of you to make it up to Poppy, after everything. I hope you're thinking of that and not just a free holiday. How lovely that she's getting married."

This again. Whenever there's a chance to have a dig at me, she's straight in there with a shovel.

"We don't need to make anything up to her," I say. "That was all ten years ago. And it was silly teenage stuff, nothing serious. I'm going through more problems right now than she ever did!"

"The problem with you, Annabel, is you've always felt like the past doesn't matter because it's over. You don't think about how actions always have consequences. You're too focused on yourself and not focused enough on other people."

It's the same old message. As if I don't have enough going on.

Maybe she senses me drawing away, because she continues without waiting for a response.

"I mean it. Take this opportunity to make it up to Poppy for the past. You'll regret it if you don't. Perhaps that's what she's intending with this trip, a chance to clear the air." She sighs again, a deep exhalation. "I do worry about you, love. But not because your social schedule is packed, or Andrew is too busy at work. I worry that you're not living up to your potential. What happened to those degrees of yours? First in our family to go to university and you haven't even used them."

The taxi finally, mercifully, pulls up on our drive, and I can see the driver getting out, calling my phone. I give him a wave in the window and start gathering everything together.

"I have to go now, Mum, the taxi driver is here."

"Think about what I said. I miss you. It would be nice to see you more often than at Christmas. Maybe after your holiday you could come and see me for a few days?"

"Maybe," I say. "Bye now."

"Bye, darling. I love you. Have a great hen party."

She waits for me to hang up. She does it every time. I'm not sure why, when she has the last word. But I end the call and shove my phone in my handbag, doing one final check of everything before heading out the door.

It's nothing I haven't heard from her before, this insistence that I have to do something with my education. It's also not like I haven't thought about it. I chose to do Psychology because, at the time, I was passionate about understanding the human mind, and I still am today. When Andrew isn't around, I'm often at his computer researching different studies I find interesting. It's a side of me I don't show anyone, not since Mum used to sit on the end of my bed and listen to me waffle on about my revision for my A levels.

But there's no reason to use my degrees now. Yes, degrees, plural. I did a master's degree in Psychology too, specialising in the biological side. There's something so fascinating about the way several psychological disorders can be seen through scans and tests, physical proof of the genuine impact they can have. I'm not one for Freudian psychology—discussing feelings and connecting them to past trauma seems a load of rubbish to me.

The taxi driver helps me with my bags as I knew he would after I flashed him my brightest smile, and he even opens the car door. I know he's after a big tip because he's seen the size of our house, but it still makes me proud, knowing he's gone to that extra effort.

As he pulls out of the drive, I take a last look back at our home. It's in Andrew's name, and it's his money that paid for it, but I still call it "our." From the outside it reminds me of my childhood dentistry, which had converted a huge Georgian house to suit its needs. The inside had been hollowed out, each room turned cold and clinical, white-washed with awful linoleum floors.

I check my phone, but Andrew hasn't sent me a goodbye message even though he's never off his mobile, a constant presence near his right hand whether he's watching television or in the shower.

To take my mind off Andrew, I open the envelope with the tickets and brochure inside again, leafing through the pictures of the island once more.

I don't feel guilty about the past. Mum hasn't got to me. There's nothing to make up for with Poppy, and this invitation proves it. We're going to have a brilliant time and forget about the real world we've left behind.

If Poppy's still harbouring any grudges she wouldn't have invited us.

I can just relax now.

This is going to be fantastic.

TWO

Chloe

Okay, I think I might finally have enough pictures. This plane journey is *insane*.

I wasn't going to go until I saw Poppy was paying for it all. Since when is Poppy Greer of all people a rich bitch? I would say I'm not jealous but that would be a complete lie. If I had her money I'd be on a plane at least twice a week, enjoying all of this luxury. Who knows, though? If my sponsorships continue to do well and people enjoy the pictures from my holiday . . . oh, what's that? A high-end airline company like—I don't know, let's say Emirates—wants to sponsor you to enjoy first-class travel anywhere you want in the world? It's such a tall order, but you know what, I'll do it.

Simply arriving at the airport lounge was unreal. We had our own area where breakfast was being offered. Proper breakfast, complete with fresh fruit smoothies, and a whole variety of pastries, yoghurts, cheeses, and granola. Even though Esther ended up eating most of it I created the most beautiful plate of everything on offer, even the high-end wine with nuts and olives to the side. There were a few businessmen eating a small breakfast near us who certainly didn't appreciate the impromptu photoshoot next to them but this is work too, sorry, gentlemen.

I'm so close to a million followers now, it's within touching distance. My agent, a thin woman called Carla who I'm pretty sure lives on a diet of celery sticks and stress, has told me if things keep going the way they are it could happen within the month. She was delighted when I told her about Poppy's little getaway and insisted I take photos of every step of the journey. I wish I could have brought my proper lighting kit with me, but some of my followers have already said they prefer the "natural" look I have going on right now.

Meeting up with everyone again was actually a bit awkward at first. It's been so long since it's been the four of us all together. And I'm somewhat avoiding Annabel lately, for obvious reasons. Nor is it much fun seeing Tanya at the moment.

She's not looking much better. She didn't even make an effort for the plane journey—I mean, we're in first class, for God's sake, at least try and look like you belong—just wearing leggings and an oversized jumper. I think she was trying to hide how thin she's gotten, but you can't hide it in your face. There's a gaunt expression to her now, and these huge bags under her eyes. Maybe I should give her some tips on how to cover that up, because she's doing a pretty terrible job at hiding that there's something wrong.

Not that Annabel or Esther seemed to notice. Annabel gave a great big squeal when she arrived, rushing around and kissing our cheeks and telling us all how beautiful we looked. Annabel at least can be counted on to look the part, though how she can afford a Prada handbag when she doesn't work I'll never know.

"How long has it been since the four of us were together like this?" Annabel asked, in that stupid breathy voice she has when she's putting on a show.

"We all met up to discuss the invitations," Esther pointed out with a grin.

Come to think of it, Esther's dressed like she's hiding something too.

Esther enjoys exercise (which if you ask me is something super-fit people say just to have some superiority over normal people like us who suffer through it just to have a nice ass) so really she should be showing off her toned legs and arms, but instead she's completely covered up with baggy trousers and a long-sleeved turtleneck. While we were waiting for Annabel to arrive at the airport, she barely spoke to me and Tanya, instead distracted by constant messages on her phone from her boyfriend. She's chewed her lip so much she's broken through the skin, and there's a fleck of lipstick on her teeth, but I'm quite enjoying guessing how long it will be until she notices so I've decided not to tell her.

Annabel waved her hand dismissively at her. "Oh, you know what I mean. Not just a short lunch or whatever. We're all spending time together. Isn't it great?"

"Oh it's just *fabulous*," I said, but she didn't seem to realise I was making fun of her because she beamed at me in response.

We were escorted to our seats on the plane, and when I say seats, I mean suites, which is pretty incredible. There's a separate bed and sitting area, all in these cool neutral greys and whites, with a statement orange pillow on the leather armchair. With six suites on the plane, we've taken up four of them. Out of the last two, one is empty and the other is at the back, containing a rather stern-looking man in a suit with a shining bald head that made me giggle and Esther roll her eyes at me.

I'll admit takeoff made me a little nervous, that slight dip as the plane levels off never failing to send me into a panic that we're about to fall. There's something wrong with people who enjoy takeoff; it's not natural for us to just be floating around in the sky and any minute now I'm certain the laws of physics are going to remember and send us plummeting.

Orange juice and a hot towel helped take my mind off my fears. I pressed the towel into my face, knowing I had my backup makeup in a bag near my feet, and closed my eyes. When we finally levelled and the seatbelt signs went off, I sighed with relief.

Now, everyone is gathered in my suite. All of us are still in disbelief, I think, that we're here and about to join Poppy Greer on an island in the Bahamas. A part of me wondered whether our plane tickets would scan through and come up as duds when we first arrived, a final bit of payback for before, and the airline staff would laugh at us and send us away.

Esther said as much when we all went to lunch together a few months ago, when the invitations first arrived. We'd all brought them and laid them out on the table alongside our Caesar salads, taking in the exact same information Poppy had given us, the only difference being our names.

"I don't think we should go," Esther had said, shaking her head at the thought of it. "This seems a bit suspicious to me."

"How is it suspicious?" I asked, twirling a piece of chicken on my fork. My followers, my "family" as I like to call them (which is easy to do when your own family are a dad in prison and an alcoholic mum), love how into healthy eating I am (I got over a hundred thousand likes for a picture of this meal). "She's the one paying for it all." This, I felt, was the most important point.

Esther wasn't convinced. "But why *would* she pay for it? For us? Why has she chosen us to be her bridesmaids when she hasn't even seen us for however long?"

"On that note," Annabel said, frowning, "we don't actually know anything about the wedding yet. Like, where is it? *When* exactly is it? All we have is the invitation to the hen party and a promise of further details."

"So we'll find out when we get there. No biggie. She clearly wants to see how we're all doing." I shrugged, taking my phone and scrolling to her Instagram. "Ever since she followed us she's been liking all our pictures. In fact, she's even liked the photo I just took of this salad."

We were all stunned when Poppy followed us on Instagram a while back. First it had been me, obviously, but soon enough she had found the others' accounts and liked our pictures and stories whenever we posted them. Even Esther's, and Esther is hopeless at Instagram and only posts a photo about once every three months and has less than a thousand followers. Poppy's account isn't much better than hers in terms of followers, but she has plenty of posts. The first few were mainly of London nightlife, blurred images of cocktails and clubs, and then of course there were some of what must have been her artwork or ones she admired (Poppy is an art nut), but we all saw the one of her left hand with its sparkling diamond ring.

It was Annabel's idea to follow her back, just for a laugh. I mean, I only follow celebrities but the other three all did and we were able to see what she was doing. I know I wasn't the only one insanely jealous of that ring—how did Poppy Greer of all people bag herself a man with that kind of money?

After that it was a flurry of bridal pictures, from dresses she was trying on to her exploring various potential venues. Her shortlist for her wedding dress was fun. We all got drunk one night at mine and voted for which dress we liked best out of her posts. I went for a clingy silky Versace number personally, but everyone else preferred her more traditional options. It actually turned into a bit of a game for us—what has Poppy posted next, and would any of the photos show us what she looked like now? Because not one of these many wedding posts had her face in them.

A couple of months before we got our invites, Poppy had posted a story in front of some fancy-looking wedding invitations wondering about who to include in her wedding.

It's been so many years since I've seen some people, she wrote. Wouldn't it be fun to have some kind of school reunion?

"She'll be calling you up, Tanya," I joked at the time. "You'll be her maid of honour."

"As if she'd ever include us," Tanya had replied, rolling her eyes. "I'm shocked she's even thinking of inviting people from school."

Imagine our surprise then when the invites for the hen party came through the door. Not just for Tanya, but for each and every one of us.

I grinned at them all as we discussed what to do. "Hey, if she's willing to pay for holidays to the Bahamas, I think Poppy Greer can finally be one of us."

Annabel smiled at that, but even she was still reluctant. "I'm not sure any of us would be quite as generous with each other if it were our own hen parties."

"Mainly because she wouldn't be invited to them!" I laughed.

Tanya, who up until this point had been lost in thought, frowned. "Maybe it's not about that. Maybe we should think about going to . . . you know, see how she is. After everything."

"Is someone missing their old friend?" I teased. "Trust you to be feeling bad for her."

"I'm just saying." Tanya pushed her half-eaten plate of food away from her. "We were pretty rough to her, especially at the end. This could be our chance to wipe that slate clean. Not carry anything around with us anymore."

"Who's carrying anything around?" Esther asked. "I'm not."

"We should all go," Tanya said. "I think it's important."

"And even if Poppy is still a weirdo, the four of us will be on a private island living the life of luxury for four days," I added, ignoring Tanya's irritated sigh.

Esther gave in, holding her hands up in mock surrender. "Fine, fine, I'll come. We'll all go."

Annabel nodded. "Yes, alright. But I'm going for the sandy beaches and cocktails, not the childhood therapy session."

"Hoorah!" I lifted my glass of wine. "Let's toast to that."

"As long as I can get the time off," Esther muttered, but she grinned and raised her glass too. "To the Bahamas!"

"To the Bahamas!" we chanted.

Now, conversation returns to Poppy. I'm sitting in the armchair, whilst Esther and Annabel sit on the bed and Tanya stands near the opening. A flight attendant comes over and offers us all coffees after the meal we've just finished, and we accept. After she leaves again, coffees delivered, we can talk properly.

"I wonder what she's like now," I say, remembering the Poppy from long ago. "Her Instagram never had any photographs of her."

You know how there's always that one child at school who never seems to fit in, despite by all appearances being quite an ordinary kid? Nothing majorly wrong with them, no laughable features. And yet they are always on the precipice, never quite able to join the group and get what the joke is about, because odds are the joke is on them.

That was Poppy Greer. Sure, she was a bit overweight, and we all never hesitated to call her on it (I remember one time back when we were about twelve or thirteen Poppy Greedy was her nickname for months and months), but there was just something about her that meant no one wanted to be her friend. She had this odd, obsessive personality, where she'd fixate on certain topics and never shut up about them, like *Star Wars* or even *The Great British Bake Off.* Most weird of all were her creepy paintings. She loved art and was constantly putting hers on display at school. She still wore braces even when she was sixteen. She actually got on with the teachers and consistently came top of the class. You know, one of those kids.

I never imagined she'd be successful, because as much as the world wants to pretend otherwise, it rewards confident, attractive people. I mean, look at me. I flunked out of sixth form with three Ds but it doesn't matter because my double Ds make me thousands every month through bikini pictures. Look at Annabel too: beautiful, blonde, a better nose than me even though I've had mine done and she's with the delicious Andrew and doesn't need to earn anything. Meanwhile Esther's much more average, though she dresses well and has a killer body, so she has to do her boring banker job. As for Tanya, the less said about her the better at the moment, but she's not a dog. It's why her job in high-end events worked. You can't be the life and soul of a party and look like the back end of a bus.

"She was always brainy," Esther says. "Maybe she's in investment banking too."

"Maybe she actually earned her way there without connections," Annabel says with a grin.

Esther chooses to ignore the jibe, sipping her coffee. "I don't even know what happened to her after sixth form. Didn't she and her family move away?"

"I remember something like that," I say. "Wasn't her younger sister even smarter than she was? Maybe they moved so she could go to some swanky sixth form out in the country for geniuses."

"It's going to be so strange seeing her," Annabel says. "My mum tried saying it would be a good opportunity to make amends, if you can believe it."

"I didn't know you still spoke to your mum," Tanya says, and Annabel blushes.

"She managed to call me just as I was waiting for the taxi this morning," she mumbles. "I didn't realise it was her on the phone, I thought it was them getting lost finding the place."

"Easy to do with all those magnificent houses," Esther concedes. "What does she mean though—make amends? Amends for what?"

Annabel and Esther in particular have a tendency to pretend like nothing ever happened at school. I take a more honest approach. I mean, we're all twenty-eight this year, and if we can't acknowledge something as little as what happened with Poppy Greer, I think that's a bit immature.

"I tried saying this at the lunch. We could say we're sorry for how we acted," Tanya proposes. "That we're excited to be her bridesmaids."

"Who apologises for something that happened ten years ago?" Annabel says. "No, I think we just don't mention it. That's always easier."

"Agreed," Esther says. "Don't mention anything at all. Especially you, Chloe."

I frown. She would be stunned if she knew some of the things I'm hiding from them.

"The real question is who she's getting married to," Annabel says.

"True," I say with a giggle. "Who on earth would marry Poppy Greedy?"

We all laugh and the tension is broken.

Poppy is meeting us on the island itself, so I'm not sure if she's been out there longer or taken a different flight. It feels like she's deliberately adding an air of suspense to us seeing her after all these years, but I don't blame her. It would have been a bit awkward if we'd all shared this nine-hour flight and the journey to where we're staying.

I also think, not for the first time, that maybe we're her bridesmaids because she doesn't have any other friends. We might just be the closest she ever got to them.

And that's quite sad really.

The others go back to their own suites, Tanya proclaiming she is going to sleep the rest of the way and not to disturb her, whilst Esther plans to catch up on some work emails and respond to her boyfriend, Brad, who has already texted her a dozen times. Only Annabel and I actually enjoy the flight the rest of the time; I can faintly hear her watching a film and ordering more food, and I plan to do the same after I've finished uploading another photograph of myself.

I'm lying on the bed and holding the phone far above my face, seeing my hair has spread sexily around my head like a bleached halo. Much nicer way to join the Mile High Club than the airplane bathroom, I write underneath, knowing it's borderline too cheeky but also knowing these occasional posts get me a lot more likes. Sure enough, there are already hundreds, along with desperate comments from sad old men about how they'd like to join me up here. As if.

After a film and another ridiculous meal with a few glasses of wine, the attendant comes round with a final drink and cake.

"We should be arriving soon," she says to me, as I admire how tightly put together her bun is, the dewy freshness of her makeup despite being on her feet nonstop this whole time. "I hope you've enjoyed your flight."

"It's been magical," I tell her, but as soon as the seatbelt signs come back on for landing I get that tight, nervous feeling in my stomach once more.

THREE

Tanya

MAY 18, 2023

The brochure Poppy included with the invitations couldn't capture the beauty of this place.

Even just standing on the mainland pier puts into perspective how much brighter and sharper everything seems to be over here. Far out across the ocean I can see the island where we're going to stay, a small dark space on the horizon amidst all the blue. The journey from the airport has taken almost an hour, the four of us crammed in an uncomfortably hot taxi, and I spent most of it with my eyes closed trying to avoid the onset of a migraine from the stuffiness. Not to mention how rough I feel anyway. Now that I'm out, the air seems much fresher, vastly different from the fumes and pollution back in England.

Part of me still wants to go home, not wanting to face the inevitable. But another part of me wants to stay here forever, living an island life away from everything and not having to think about what's waiting for me when I get back. It's hard though. Every so often my heart beats in my chest like it's trying to escape, and my hands keep shaking. Constant reminders, determined to make me crack.

At the end of the pier, standing next to a boat, a middle-aged woman raises her hand in greeting, gesturing us to come forward. She's not quite what I imagined, picturing some gorgeous leggy athletic blonde dressed in hippie clothes with sun-kissed skin. Instead she's rather ordinary, in floral-patterned leggings and thick boots, her mouth breaking into a wide smile and revealing wrinkles.

"Not coming to help us with our bags then," Annabel murmurs, hitching her handbag up onto her shoulder. "So much for first-class service."

We're barely twenty metres from her, I want to say, and you've got wheels on your suitcase. But I hold my tongue, which is often the best thing to do with Annabel.

As we approach, I wonder what the woman thinks of us, four over-dressed women struggling along with our cases in our high heels. I'm the most dressed down out of any of us in my big jumper, but even that feels too much, especially in this heat. Not the best idea for someone who is trying desperately not to sweat as it is, but I can't exactly take it off now. She's immensely more practical, and I think I catch a hint of amusement in her expression once we're in front of her.

"You must be the hen party," she says, and her voice is unexpected too. Seeing her up close, leathery and shiny from the sun, hair pulled back into an unflattering low ponytail, I thought she'd sound gruff, almost manly. Again she surprises me, with a soft, lilting Welsh accent. I hadn't realised she wasn't native. "Welcome. I hope your journey here was okay."

"Wonderful," Esther says. "It's so beautiful here."

"You never get used to it," the woman says with a nod, allowing us another moment to take in the scenery. "I'm Robin, by the way. I'll be getting you safely to where you're staying." She lifts her hand and points across to the dark shape on the horizon I'd spotted before. "That's the island you'll be on. Deadman's Bay."

The name still gives me shivers. Robin notices and sends me a small smile.

"Don't worry, the name makes it sound spookier than it is," she says.

"It's a historical site, first settled on by a sailor who got shipwrecked. He married a woman from the mainland and they built a house together, though it hasn't survived. The owner's new house, where you'll be staying, is built on that same site. No scary deaths, I promise you."

"You don't own the island?" Chloe asks, finally listening after snapping a picture of the end of the pier.

Robin laughs. "I wish. Just the glorified taxi lady between the mainland and island. But the owners live in America, so I'm here running the day to day."

Sounds like a nice job to me. I study Robin, this pleasant and polite woman who clearly used to be from Wales. Why has she moved all the way out here?

Maybe I need to stop imagining everyone is getting away from something. But I feel like I've been running my whole life.

She steps forward to help us out, taking each of our bags in turn and loading them onto the boat. She does it expertly; one foot on the pier, the other on the boat, no fear or imbalance as the boat shifts with the gentle tide. Once the bags are loaded, she offers a hand to each of us to help us in.

"I get horribly seasick," Annabel says uncertainly, hovering at the edge. "How long is the journey?"

"We've got a good tide this afternoon," Robin tells her. "It shouldn't take more than half an hour, forty minutes at most. If the wind's against us it can take double that time."

"That long?" Annabel glances back at us, face pale. "And we'll be all alone out there?"

"There's an emergency phone connected by landline," Robin says, "and if that fails there are flares that are easy to spot from here. But no one's ever had to use them."

Brusque, she offers her hand again. Annabel admits defeat and boards the boat, teetering in her heels until she sits down on the long seat at the back. Esther goes next without complaint, joining Annabel and even giving her hand a squeeze to comfort her.

Chloe seems eager to get going; she doesn't even need assistance but instead steps into the boat and gets herself seated. But just as I'm about to take Robin's hand, Chloe pipes up, as if the thought has just occurred to her.

"What if there's a storm?"

"A storm?" Robin pauses to consider this, leaving my hand dangling. "At night there's often thunder and lightning, but it's nothing to worry about."

"But would you still be able to get out to us if there was a bad one?" Chloe persists, a glint in her eye that tells me she's just trying to scare Annabel. It's working; Annabel is gripping Esther tight.

Robin holds her hands up in surrender. "I'd have to get some outside help if that happened, I'll admit. If the storm was that bad. But again, that's never happened. You're going to be fine. This is a holiday, remember, ladies! Not a boot camp!"

I look across at the island, taking in how far away and small it seems. The sky above is clear, not a single cloud. The wind is calm.

Still. I turn my head towards the mainland, the comfort of knowing help should be immediate.

"It's Tanya, isn't it?"

I startle at my name. Robin is waiting for me.

"I was given an information docket with all your names," she says by way of explanation. "Are you ready to come aboard?"

Something about that makes me uncomfortable, but I shake the thought away and take her hand.

The four of us finally settled, Robin takes to the front, the roar of the engine being woken from its doze making Annabel and even Chloe jump.

As the boat pulls out into the ocean, picking up speed, the wind pushes us backwards, the breeze much more powerful out here. I'm glad to be moving, inhaling the fresh air. My head feels heavier than Chloe's suitcases and before we set off I was worried I was going to be the one throwing up over the side.

"I should warn you," Robin calls over the sounds of the engine and the waves. "In about five minutes you're going to lose any Wi-Fi connection. There's signal on the island, but it can be patchy. I'm afraid Deadman's Bay hasn't reached the twenty-first century in terms of easy internet access quite yet."

Now it's Esther's turn to look horrified. "No Wi-Fi? I can't rely on mobile data getting me through the next four days."

Chloe protests as well. "How am I meant to upload photos and videos of my holiday if there's no internet?"

"It's an adventure!" Robin says. "You're here for the bride anyway."

Chloe's already urgently uploading to her Instagram, Esther typing away at her phone.

Here for Poppy. It's what I tried saying to the others, but it's strange now that it's actually happening. All these years, and we'll finally be face to face again.

For me, all I can think of is the girl we left behind ten years ago. It seems strange to think of her as an adult like the rest of us, living a life independent of our influence.

Has she forgiven us? Forgiven me, in particular?

Sometimes I look at the others and I want to scream in their faces. Do they even care what we did in the past? Do they ever still think about it? Because there are days, especially since receiving the invitation, when I find that's all I can do.

There's no one else out on the water as we power towards the island, just the big empty expanse of ocean to surround us. I think of my tiny flat, the mould in the bathroom because there's no window and an extractor fan will never do a good enough job no matter what the landlord says.

I'm starting to wonder if Robin wouldn't mind a job share.

"How are you feeling, Annabel?" she shouts, the only one of us to remember that Annabel is supposedly seasick.

She does look a little pale, but there's no obvious signs of anything. She gives a weak thumbs-up. "Fine. It was worse just before we set off and it was still all wobbly."

"I knew you'd be alright," Robin says. "You're going to have a wonderful hen party. When's the wedding?"

This comment throws us.

"The wedding?" Annabel asks. "My wedding?"

"You're the bride, are you not?" Robin says, keeping her gaze straight ahead. The dark shape of the island is becoming more visible, a larger mark on the horizon now. "One of your bridesmaids came earlier to set up for your arrival."

How has she got this wrong?

Despite what I said to the others, I too had my reservations about this trip right from the start. The moment the invitation arrived, actually, three months ago. That I even got something through the post was the first warning sign. No one sends me letters or cards, not anymore. So when I saw something on the floor by the door that wasn't a bill the hairs on the back of my neck stood up, a primal sense of danger: something is wrong here.

And then for it to be an invitation to this island in the Bahamas. To be Poppy Greer's bridesmaid. I had no idea then the others were invited. I thought it was some kind of sick joke, and I very nearly tore up the invitation, brochure, and plane tickets there and then.

But I didn't tear them up. I sat with them on my lap for a while, and then I thought about those first-class tickets. What they might mean. A few hours later, Annabel had called us all asking if any of us had received an invitation too. This wasn't just about me.

It's still hard to think about the past. Part of me wonders if everything that's happening to me now is some kind of punishment for it. The

universe telling me that I deserve what I've got. I'm a terrible human being. Perhaps it's still selfish of me, in a way, to see this as a chance to seek
forgiveness.

The others are so excited to see what Poppy will be like now.

I'm more concerned with what she'll think of us.

"I think you've got this wrong," Esther says to Robin.

But Annabel finds the mistake hilarious. She throws back her head
and laughs. "Right. I'm the bride. Aren't I, guys?"

"Right." Chloe grins, but something about it still makes me uncertain. Why would Robin think that?

Robin nods. "Just the five of you. A small hen party but perhaps just
right."

"Are you feeling better, Tanya?" Chloe whispers to me, that gleam in
her eye again. "Poppy's not got herself a new friend."

The three of them have never let me forget that Poppy and I used to be
good friends. Best friends, I guess. We went to the same primary school
together and spent every day in one or the other's house, content with
talking and making up imaginary stories to pass the time. But once we
got to secondary school and I made friends with the other three, Poppy
and I drifted apart. It was just one of those things. That's what I told myself, anyway.

Occasionally, they all like to remind me that I was very nearly like
Poppy. Left out of everything, always on the sidelines.

"Shut up, Chloe," I say sharply, but she smiles at me.

Robin continues, ignoring our bickering. "We'll be there before you
know it."

The rest of the journey passes without further conversation. A peace-
fulness has taken over the boat, the four of us settled into the hard white
seats but off in our own worlds. Just like Annabel said at the airport,
it really has been a long time since the four of us did something together
like this. There's been the occasional lunch over the past few months,

though never all together, but they're quick and easy—in, order food and drinks, short catch-ups from everyone's lives, snippets of what we've all been doing, and then split the bill and be on our way.

So it's awkward right now, a bit fresh, the four of us spending more time together than we have in years. It's been easier to hang out one on one, with Annabel in particular, as much as I feel guilty about it. Esther always seems reluctant lately. As for Chloe, I try and avoid her as much as I can so she can't keep staring at me with such horror all the time. She was even doing it at the airport, those judging eyes that seemed to scream to the world that something was wrong with me. I'm sure the other three must meet up without me. I can be somewhat prickly at times, I know that. I'm not blind to my faults. And I've certainly been more difficult lately.

But I'm not entirely to blame.

We're nearing the island now, and even though we're much closer up, I can appreciate just how small it is. I say so out loud and Robin nods, cutting the engine as we approach the pier, a matching twin to the one on the mainland.

"About twenty acres all round," she says. "But it packs a lot in."

Unlike the mainland, there isn't a white beach connecting the pier; instead, it backs straight onto the earth, surrounded by trees and bushes but a dusty path in between. Behind this, further back on the island, there's a small mountain, visible cliffside paths snaking their way up to the summit.

After Robin secures the boat with a rope against a post, she helps us all out again and notices my gaze. "I call that Deadman's Peak, but it doesn't have an official name. It looks much more intimidating down here than it actually is. Children can walk up those paths quite easily, you just have to be mindful once you're up there that you don't fall." She allows herself a grin, nodding at our footwear. "I hope you've packed more than just high heels if you are planning to go up."

"No fear, I'll be staying on the beach," Chloe says, though she looks unimpressed. "There is a beach, right? It's not just this muddy patch?"

"Not to worry, we'll head through that path now and you'll see," Robin says. She heaves our suitcases out onto the pier and makes sure we're holding them. "Don't want them to roll off into the sea! Although at least we'd be able to see where they fell."

It's true; the water is even clearer over here, and not that deep. The sand is only about a metre down.

"Oh!"

Chloe's little exclamation makes us all turn to look at her. She's pointing ahead, towards the path that leads through to the main part of the island. "Is that Poppy?"

A woman is heading towards us.

"Here we are," Robin says. "She must have heard the boat. Your bridal party is now complete."

FOUR

Esther

MAY 18, 2023

I t's alright for the others. When this trip came up it wasn't a question of the impact of taking four days off, it was whether they had enough bikinis.

For me, it involved a lengthy conversation with my boss, a man who still treats professional women my age like we're about to pop out children at any second and hunts for a reason to get rid of them before they confirm a dreaded pregnancy. He wasn't happy, but he's friends with my parents and I haven't taken a day off in over a year, so there wasn't much he could do other than voice how disappointed he was that it was at such short notice (three months in advance) and at a critical time (when is it ever not?).

There are so many unread emails I'd planned to get through on my phone during this trip. I hold on to my favourite necklace as a stress release, a gold chain with "Esther" in cursive writing, grabbing my name against my neck.

Annabel's comment about connections on the plane is still bothering me. She's always liked to imagine she's better than us, more intelligent, more capable—and it takes everything in me not to point out how shallow her life has become. At least I'm doing something with mine.

Her husband was, of course, fine with her taking four days away without her. My boyfriend, Brad, on the other hand, took it as another sign I wasn't committing properly to our relationship, even after three years together. The night before I left he made it quite clear how miserable he was with the whole thing. I'd talk to the others about it, but they're all so consumed with their own worlds I'm not sure they'd even pretend to listen.

I don't know why I'm still friends with any of them, to be honest. It's a bit sad really, isn't it, the four of us clinging on to each other since school? Most people I know have moved on, couldn't imagine still being friends with their school mates. Even at university, when I went off to Warwick, I couldn't manage to shake them. All three had stayed put, Annabel at Bristol University, Tanya at UWE, and Chloe in one of her short-lived apprenticeships before she discovered Photoshop. That was my chance to break away, but the truth was, making friends at university turned out to be harder than I thought. Sure, I made them, but come graduation they all disappeared off to London and lived their own lives, happy in bubbles that didn't include me.

So I ended up drifting back to those three, and we've been stuck together ever since. Even after Tanya moved to London for her new job, she came back so often it felt like she was always here. I look in the mirror sometimes and see the beginnings of frown lines and wonder where the years have gone.

I'm so busy in my own thoughts it takes Tanya nudging me to realise everyone is distracted by something up ahead. I look up, and then I'm also transfixed at the woman coming towards us.

"That can't be Poppy," Chloe says, mouth left hanging open.

"That's Poppy," Robin says, oblivious to our shock, and none too confused that we don't seem to be sure.

Poppy Greer was a fat awkward girl with braces and greasy mousy hair. She had a slight hunch in her shoulders when she walked, probably because she always faced the ground. There was an air of desperation about her that followed her like a bad smell, and on warm days there could be an odour of that too.

This isn't Poppy Greer walking towards us, tall and lithe and smelling of cinnamon, her perfume so strong it drifts to us even though she stops about a metre away. She's wearing flat sandals but still stands at least a head above us, even me, and an open knit halter dress barely hides her tanned athletic body in its bright orange bikini. It's not just her appearance, even though that's so different—she's definitely plumped up her lips and changed her nose, her eyebrows shaped to frame her angular face—but the way she carries herself is like she's a new person. Her shoulders are back, her chin is lifted, and there's an ease about her, a calm yet strong presence that makes it clear she isn't afraid to be standing in front of us anymore.

God, do we hug her? What's the protocol here? Annabel seems to think about it, half-heartedly raising her arms before they turn into a stretch when Poppy doesn't move.

Any other scenario and I'd be barrelling forward, wrapping whoever it was into an embrace whether they liked it or not, because I'm just that kind of person. But this isn't any other scenario. It's Poppy Greer. And not the Poppy Greer we knew either—a new, confident, attractive Poppy that sets my entire body on edge.

"Hello, everyone," she says. Even her voice has changed. Before she always had this slight tremble, a giveaway of how nervous she was. Now it's deep and controlled. "I'm so happy to see you all."

It's in her eyes that I still see the same old Poppy. The bright blue, her best feature, and now that she's closer she still has the smattering of freckles from one cheek to the other, travelling across her new nose. Her hair is the same too, though rather than wet with grease she's been in the sea, the mousy strands slicked back into a ponytail that hangs onto one shoulder.

"I can't believe it's really you," Chloe says, to the point as always. "You look so different!"

Poppy laughs at that, a short tinkle that reads false to me. "I'm afraid so. Shall I take that as a compliment?"

"Definitely." Chloe has no sense of tact. "You will have to give me the name of your personal trainer."

"This is all my own effort, actually," Poppy says.

Just as I'm wondering whether we'll stand forever on this pier enduring Chloe's rude comments about how much better Poppy looks, Robin takes charge.

"Let me take you on a tour around the island whilst I'm still here," she says. "We can drop your bags off at the accommodation along the way."

She leads the way up the trail, the rest of us following behind. We've broken off into natural pairs. Annabel with Robin, clearly enjoying pretending to be the bride for a few moments longer, Poppy and Chloe in the middle, Tanya and I bringing up the rear. Tanya raises her eyebrows at me as we walk, indicating her head towards the front.

"What do you think of Poppy?" she whispers. She rubs her nose with her fingers, seemingly unaware of her distracting gesture. Her lips are chapped, made more obvious by the glaring sun.

"Crazy," I hiss back, trying not to get too much dust on my heels but realising it's a futile effort. "She looks like an entirely different person."

"Almost," Tanya says. "I can still see her underneath it all. Do you really think she's changed that much?" She seems in awe of her, hardly able to stop staring. I think her hands are even shaking.

"Haven't made my mind up yet," I say. And Tanya smiles.

We make our way through the path and it opens up onto the main lawn we saw in the brochure. A little gecko scurries past us in the grass and I hear Chloe shriek. As we reach the house there's a wind turbine hidden behind, and the array of deck chairs and random bits of outdoor furniture make it seem more scattered than the brochure led us to believe. But the decking area is beautiful, the light hitting the stone floor and bouncing up again, a huge sun trap. There's a large object hidden under some tarpaulin in the corner I'm convinced is a hot tub and I can't wait to try it. The whole area is quite large, the palm tree leaves whispering in the breeze, and I can see Poppy has been sunbathing on the freshly cut grass because some towels are on the ground, held firm by pitchers of what looks like Pimm's.

"So this is the main area, and that's the central lodge there," Robin says. She opens the front door and we all step inside, even Poppy, who must have had the tour this morning. The door opens into a deceptively big dining space, with orange tiles and white walls and a modern kitchen. "All the mod cons are in here, don't worry. We have a wind turbine and solar panels for electricity. I also brought all of the food Poppy requested with me this morning, so the fridge is fully stocked. There's a pantry as well and that's full. You certainly are planning quite the party."

Is there a wistful tone there? Has Robin ever stayed on the island?

"All the mod cons except Wi-Fi," Chloe comments.

Robin doesn't stop smiling, but it's starting to look a little strained. "Unfortunately so."

Past the living area are two bathrooms, each with full standing showers. Finally there's a bedroom in the back, still with the same orange tile that runs through the whole house, the linen and curtains looking like something from the seventies. The double bed, king sized, is the statement feature of the room, otherwise quite bare besides the garish accessories. Right above the bed is a large painting, but before I can look at it properly Poppy starts talking and we all turn to her.

"I took this room, I hope you don't mind," she says.

"It's the most modern accommodation," Robin says. "Although the huts have en suites, the bathrooms are quite temperamental, shall I say."

Temperamental? Chloe and Annabel exchange horrified looks, which makes me grin.

We continue on the tour, Robin taking us round to the huts at the back of the house, which are down a short path lined with trees and bushes. These open straight up into the bedrooms, more tastefully decorated with peach rugs and baby blue sheets, leading to tiny bathrooms with just a shower, toilet, and sink, the same colour as the greenery outside. It's basic, but at least there's proper running water and air conditioning. I was a bit worried we were going to end up looking like we'd been on a survival show. We each choose a hut, dumping our bags down on the beds, and Robin takes us to the beach.

"Oh my God," Chloe squeals, hurrying onto the sand and getting her phone out to take pictures. "Someone take a photo of me with the sea in the background! This is insane!"

It is. It looks like something out of a postcard or a film, a long, luxurious white strip of sand parallel to hopelessly clear water, the tide pushing small waves in and out. Sun loungers line the area closest to the path, and further along there's the gazebo from the brochure but also an added bar area that must be new, complete with various bottles of wondrous alcohol. The beach stretches quite far down too, at least a mile or so in one direction. Down the right-hand side leads back to the mountain. I'm pleased that I've brought my running trainers with me. This is the perfect new track to test out.

"There's another smaller beach along the other side, but it takes some getting to through the trees," Robin says. "I'd stick to this one. If you go along far enough, there're rock pools, which are great for fishing."

"I'm not sure we'll be doing that," Annabel says. "But this is amazing."

Even Tanya, who looks like she's been suffering from a bad cold ever since we all arrived at the airport, can't help beaming at the view. She takes her shoes off and settles her feet into the sand, and we all start doing the same. The afternoon is starting to wane away, the slightest hints of pink and orange beginning to form in the sky, and there's a heat to the sand that brings a wave of comfort over me.

"I've shown Poppy where the emergency phone is, but it's next to the wind turbine for your reference," Robin tells us, though only I seem to be listening now. "The flares are stored under the kitchen sink, and there's a first aid kit in both of the bathrooms in the main lodge. Do you have any final questions?"

"You don't want to stay for a drink?" Poppy asks.

"I wouldn't intrude." Robin shakes her head. "I'd better get going then, before it gets dark."

"We'll come see you off," Poppy says. "Thank you for everything."

"No problem. You've got everything you need?"

"Now I do." Poppy nods at us when she says that, which shouldn't make me frown but does.

"Let's go, everyone," Poppy says, and we end up trailing after her, feeling too polite to say anything.

Chloe mutters to us as we walk back along the path. "Since when is Poppy Greer telling us what to do?"

"She is the bride," Annabel reminds her, and Chloe sticks out her tongue. "Not that our tour guide seems to be aware of that!"

"Are you going to tell her she got mixed up?" I ask.

"Nah." Annabel chuckles. "What harm did it do? It was rather nice being the centre of attention."

"We'll have to ask Poppy about her fiancé," Chloe whispers. "Once that Rachael is gone."

"Robin," I correct her. "Her name is Robin."

"Whatever." She shrugs.

Without us to worry about, Robin's already in the boat by the time the four of us catch up, engine started and pulling away. Poppy stands close to the end of the pier, calling out a goodbye. We feel very detached from her right now, so I take a few steps forward and shout a farewell myself.

It's going to be very strange without Robin, that's for sure. With her gone, we'll have to spend time with Poppy. And there's no escape.

Although I think it's almost as much of a task as it is just spending time with Annabel, Tanya, and Chloe. It's been so long I've forgotten their irritable quirks, like Chloe's brashness, Annabel's remarks, and Tanya's intensity.

Robin gives us a final wave as the boat starts to pick up speed. The five of us watch her go, until eventually she's nothing more than a dot in the distance, heading back towards the mainland that now seems very far away.

"Well, then," Poppy says. She's holding a couple of bottles of champagne, one in each hand. "Shall we get this hen do started?"

"No time like the present," Chloe says.

Robin has disappeared amidst the distraction; when I turn back to look at the ocean we're entirely alone.

What are you thinking, Poppy?

How does it feel to be the bride at this hen party? To be the one in control of everything?

Maybe it's liberating. You finally have the tiniest grip on some power.

Even just arriving on the island with everyone, I could sense the atmosphere changing, the subtlest of shifts, as we all took this into account. That for once you were the one leading, not following. All that guilt I've been feeling for what happened; with this I should be able to move on.

There's something about this place. Endless possibilities.

I know deep in my heart that moving on isn't one of them.

I came here for a reason. Not that the others have the faintest of ideas.

It's time to settle the past once and for all.

One thing's for sure: not everyone is going to be leaving this island alive.

FIVE

Annabel

MAY 18, 2023

F irst thing's first," Poppy says. "I'm going to need all your phones."

We've barely sat down with our champagne, all together on the decking area that overlooks the beach. It takes us a moment to even register what she's saying before Chloe speaks for us all.

"What do you mean, you need our phones?"

Poppy smiles at her obvious discomfort. "It's not like there's great signal here anyway, but rule one of my hen party is I want there to be no technology. This is an island, and I want us to be completely in the moment. No texting, no calls, no distractions. And if you want to take pictures you can do it with this." She brings out, to our astonishment, a small digital camera, last spotted back in the noughties.

"I don't think you understand," Chloe says. "My phone is my job. I need to take pictures of this holiday and upload them."

"You can do that after." Her smile holds steady. She was expecting this. She knew we weren't going to give them up easily but she doesn't care.

I check my phone, but there's no signal anyway. Would it hurt to hand it over?

"Go on then," I say. I pass mine to her, and this seems to do the trick. Tanya shrugs and hands hers over too after checking it's switched off.

"I'll keep them safe in my room," Poppy says. "No one is going to be snooping, don't worry. But as it's my hen party, and I'm the bride, I think you owe it to me after bringing you all here on this luxury getaway to do this one small favour."

Esther sighs. "I am meant to be taking time off work, not still checking my emails. So—whatever. Take it."

With three phones in her possession now, Poppy raises an eyebrow at Chloe. "You're not going to upset me before the hen party has even begun, are you, Chloe?"

Chloe shakes her head. "God, whatever, fine. Take it. I can always claim I was having a social media detox."

"Perfect." Underneath her chair, Poppy brings out a decorated wooden box. Once open, I can see a deep blue velvet lining, and she places our phones within, shutting it with a snap and even going so far as to lock it with a tiny key. Chloe opens her mouth to protest at this, but Esther grabs her arm to silence her. "No going back now. I'll put this in my room and be back in a moment."

"I don't know about this," Chloe mutters as we watch Poppy walk away, confidence in her stride and ponytail swishing back and forth. "Why does she have such a hang-up about technology?"

Far away, a bird calls out, then flies off, making the trees rustle. As the early evening sunset starts to settle on the ocean behind us, the wind picks up, so we're grateful for the gentle heat of the climate.

"It feels right to not be relying on our phones here," I say. Plus it will be nice not to keep checking for messages from Andrew and finding nothing. "Look at this place."

"Annabel's right," Esther says. "It's not a big deal. It's four days. And I say this knowing I'll have at least two hundred emails when I return. It's quite freeing really. This could be a good thing."

Chloe rolls her eyes. "You're all mad. But whatever. I'm not going to be the one that causes drama."

"That'll be a nice change," I quip, and the others laugh as Chloe's gaze darkens.

It does feel naked not having my phone in my bag. My hand absent-mindedly dips to search for it and flails for a second before I remember, taking out some lip gloss instead and reapplying so Chloe doesn't realise triumphantly what I've done. Poppy returns to us across the decking, heels clacking against the wood, bringing with her another bottle of champagne and some wine.

"More drinks, ladies?" she asks, refilling our glasses. "Let's toast to our reunion, shall we?"

I wonder how much everyone remembers about the last time we were all together. But I plaster a smile on my face and lift my glass.

"To our reunion," I declare, and the others echo my sentiment and down their drinks. The champagne slides down my throat easily, spar-kling and fruity.

"You must have a million questions," Poppy says, pouring us all a glass of the white wine, topping it up almost to the rim. "But first I want to say again how happy I am that you're all here."

Chloe, blunt as ever, asks the question we've all been wondering. "Why have you invited us in the first place? And to be your brides-maids?"

"You four are important to me." Poppy takes a sip of her wine, and I think I can see her hands tremble slightly, betraying her air of certainty. "I know that the feeling is not mutual, but I can honestly say that you four have shaped the entire trajectory of my life. I would not be where I am today without you."

There's an awkward pause as this sinks in. Even Chloe looks at a loss for words for a few seconds, a puzzled frown forming on her face.

"But why have you never reached out to us before?" she asks eventually.

"We all thought it was a joke at first, the invitations to the hen party, when we haven't heard from you in ten years."

Poppy shrugs at that. "It never felt like the right time before. It would have been so minor, just inviting you for a catch-up over lunch or something. This was the best moment. At an important time in my life. I wanted you all to be there to see it. And thankfully, you all agreed. I knew you would."

"What about all the stuff we did to you?" Tanya says quietly, earning her looks from the rest of us. She's still wearing her massive jumper from the plane journey, even though I can see she's sweating. Why doesn't she take it off?

Tanya has always overexaggerated the impact of our silly school pranks. And I guess Poppy did too, if she's talking about what an effect they had on her life. It's so trivial to me. The idea that anyone would hold on to anything that happened at school just seems ridiculous. We're adults now, not teenagers. None of what happened before matters.

"Tanya," Esther snaps, but Poppy laughs.

"That's the whole point," she says. "I want to let bygones be bygones. Move on from the past. All I wanted when I was younger was to be friends with you all. Don't you think that might be possible now?"

"You really think that?" Tanya whispers, but she's interrupted by Chloe talking over her.

"If you keep paying for private island holidays maybe," she says, but she grins to let us all know that even she, materialistic as ever, could possibly be joking.

"So who is the lucky groom?" Esther asks, eager to move away from the subject of the past. "We don't know anything about him."

"Ah, yes," Poppy says. "My groom."

The rest of us exchange uncertain glances.

"We'll talk about my groom later, I think," Poppy says. "When we've all had a lot more alcohol in us."

"I'm fine with that," Chloe says, downing her wine and pouring another. "So what do you do now, Poppy? I saw you follow me so you must know I'm pretty huge on Instagram. Almost a million followers."

Poppy raises her eyebrows as if she's impressed, but I sense she's play-acting. "Yes, I did see. You must be on it every day, even though you never managed to find the time to follow me back. Well done, Chloe. As for me, I'm a doctor at Great Ormond Street Hospital, actually. I'm currently training to specialise in paediatric cardiology."

That shuts Chloe up.

"Oh, that's great," she mumbles.

It is great. I mean, we all knew Poppy was smart but to have reached such a position when she's only the same age as us seems unbelievable. Even Tanya and Esther look impressed—a mixture of shocked and impressed anyway. It's like we all thought that, despite her brains, Poppy Greer would end up much like the rest of us, if not worse. Perhaps stuck in some dead-end office job dreaming of how she was meant to be someone.

"I knew you'd make it," Tanya says, and Poppy gives her a funny look.

"Are you still doing your art?" I ask.

Poppy nods, though she doesn't seem happy about it. "I've been lucky enough to display my work in galleries across the country. Loads of people are in love with it. I'm starting to make quite a name for myself."

"That's amazing," I say, though my stomach squeezes when I think about what we did all those years ago.

There's something off about Poppy's whole energy, but I can't place it. Maybe I'm just not used to the new Poppy, but it feels more than that. There's a smugness there, at announcing her job. She knows she has the rest of us beat when it comes to work. And she definitely leads the conversation.

"What have you all been doing?" she asks, but she's looking at me. "Annabel? How is married life? You'll have to tell me."

I frown. How is married life? I'm not sure. Andrew didn't even do the romantic proposal—we were walking past a jewellery shop and I mentioned what I liked, and he asked if we should "probably" think about getting married. I didn't even get one of those rings at the time. Instead, he gave me a prenuptial agreement to sign. But I was so in love—am so in love—that I didn't care. Now I think I would have insisted on that ring. Oh well. I went and bought one for myself later. Andrew gave me his credit card and told me to buy whatever I liked, so it's basically the same thing. Three years in and we have a brilliant marriage. We don't argue at all, like so many couples. And we go for dinner and drinks with Andrew's work friends all the time.

"It's good," I say, aware of everyone waiting for a response. "You'll enjoy it, Poppy. As long as you've picked the right man. Like I did."

"You certainly picked a good one," Poppy says.

"You've never met Andrew," Esther points out. "So how would you know if she's picked a good one or not? But you have, Annabel," she adds at my falling face. "Trust me, you have. Tanya too, with Harry."

"Well, the marriage has lasted three years, so he has to be good, right?" Poppy says. "Don't you think so, Chloe?"

Chloe looks startled. Clearly, she hasn't been paying attention and is probably still fussing about her phone being taken away. "Uh, right."

"Glad you think so," Poppy says.

I'm about to question Poppy when she gets in there first, turning her attention to Esther now. "And what do you do, Esther?"

"I'm an investment banker at Goldman Sachs," Esther answers, lifting her chin. "I'm doing very well for myself, thank you."

"That's fantastic." Poppy leans forward. "You must really value your job."

"I do," Esther says. She lets out a nervous-sounding chuckle. "Honestly, it means everything to me."

"I understand," Poppy says, nodding. "I'm the same with mine. You hold on to that job and make sure you don't let it go."

For some reason, Esther glances at Tanya, then down at her lap, blushing. Chloe seems to be looking at Tanya too. Am I missing something here? Why has it gone so quiet?

Poppy stands suddenly, stretching her arms above her head and revealing a toned stomach. "How about we move this party to the hot tub? There's a plug nearby for the CD player. I know, so retro. Chloe, why don't you help me bring the booze along, set up for a little party?"

"Um, okay." Chloe, unused to being told what to do, rises.

Esther, Tanya, and I can't help but laugh that someone has finally ordered that little diva around, and with such cool nonchalance.

We all stand to go, but Poppy does a double take which makes us stop in our tracks.

"I didn't ask Tanya what she was doing now!" she says. "Although of course I know a little bit. Who hasn't heard of Tanya Evesham's amazing social events? I just have to get myself invited one of these days."

Tanya looks caught out, her face reddening. "I didn't think you'd have heard about them."

"Well, and why not?" Poppy says. "Us Londoners have to stick together, no? We've escaped the drudgery of Bristol to new heights. Your parties used to be the highlight of the season. Obviously, I was too busy with my job to be able to go to any, worst luck."

"We used to all go," I blurt out, because Tanya seems to be frozen, mouth open. "The three of us, I mean. Tanya used to invite us to London and we'd make a whole weekend of it. I haven't been to any in forever. There was one six months ago but I couldn't make it."

"I think that's the one I heard about," Poppy says. "Wasn't it some heiress's birthday party, Tanya?"

"I can't remember," Tanya says, though she keeps flexing and unflexing her fingers. "I throw so many."

"You were there, Esther, weren't you?" Poppy says.

Esther looks surprised. "Uh, yes, I guess I was. Chloe was too."

"I haven't heard of any in a while," Poppy says. "You'll have to invite me to the next one."

"Sure," Tanya says, in a voice that implies she'll do anything but.

We head to the hot tub, where we start to make the area look ready for a party. Poppy explains to us where everything is, and then Chloe and I hang across the roof of the lodge and a palm tree over the hot tub some banners, which say "CONGRATULATIONS BRIDE TO BE!" in huge pink letters, and we even go to the trouble of blowing up some balloons and sticking them to the decking around it. Chloe, in charge of alcohol, has not only brought an ice box with ciders and beers to the side of the hot tub, but has also fashioned a makeshift bar out of a couple of deck chairs, a line of spirits and mixers and plastic cups ready for the taking. There's even a couple of pizzas on some high stools that Poppy says she cooked earlier and can be eaten cold. The CD player has been turned on, and although the selection isn't great, a *Now That's What I Call Music* is playing and no one can refuse a good Britney song. The atmosphere has lightened. Poppy strips off to her bikini and gets in the hot tub, which bubbles away invitingly. Am I the tiniest bit relieved to see she has stretch marks on her thighs, that she isn't absolutely perfect? Maybe.

"Go and get changed," she says. "I'll be waiting for you here."

Chloe walks into my hut whilst I'm getting ready. She's in her bright orange two piece, and sits on the bed trying to tie her hair into a complicated topknot.

"Poppy's had way too much plastic surgery," she says by way of greeting.

"You're one to talk." I'm not embarrassed to change around Chloe, we've been friends for years, so I take off my leggings and top and bra, desperate to be free of them after the long journey. If anything I'd quite like to take a shower, clear myself of the plane and taxi and boat to the island, but I know that'll keep everyone waiting, so I stick on the pale yellow bikini Andrew said he liked once. My suitcase remains open, waiting to be unpacked. Poppy hasn't given us any time to settle in—it's been one thing after another, leaving us little room to breathe.

Chloe fastens her hair together with a clip and stands to look at herself in the full-length mirror next to the wardrobe. She wriggles her nose and moves her eyebrows around. "At least I look natural. Poppy looks like me with my filters on, and not in a good way."

"All I'm hearing is jealousy!" I dodge the hairbrush Chloe throws at me and laugh. "Come on, Chlo, admit you're dying to ask who her plastic surgeon is."

She pouts, but doesn't deny it. As she goes to pick up the hairbrush, she stops in front of a painting on the wall next to the window.

"Huh, look at that."

I turn from the mirror at her tone. "What?"

"That painting." She laughs, but it comes out forced. "It just reminded me of Poppy's art in the past, that's all. You don't think she asked to have her old art put up?"

I stare at the painting. It's true, it does. She had a telltale sign to her art—sweeping brushstrokes that blended thick paint and blurred the lines between shapes even when painting something conventional. She often used harsh colours that stood out against delicate backdrops, and this is no exception. It's a version of *The Last Supper*, with the figures and Jesus in particular painted in garish colours that make them seem as though they're reaching out beyond the pale, diminished background.

It does look like her style. More accomplished, perhaps. Less obvious than when she was younger.

"Maybe they did let her put art up in all the rooms," I say, thinking of the one in her bedroom too. "It's a private island. They probably let you do almost anything."

"Weird though, right?" she asks. "Considering what happened."

I don't want to think about what she means. I shrug, pretending it's not a problem. "She was always a bit strange, we know that better than anyone."

"Yeah, you're right." It takes a concentrated effort for her to pull her eyes away, and she looks for a distraction. "Do you want me to tie your hair up for you?"

Pleasantly surprised, I nod. "Yeah—thanks, Chloe."

I sit on the edge of the bed and she sits cross-legged behind me, almost like when we were back at school at sleepovers. Without my phone, I have nothing to look at but straight ahead at the painting. The angry contrast of colours makes me nauseous. Every single figure is crying.

As she pulls it back into the same style she has, I feel her breath as she sighs.

"What is it?"

"Oh, nothing." But she's lying, I'm sure.

I wait for her to finish, then turn around, eager to avoid looking at the painting for a second longer. "I think you just need more alcohol in you."

"You know," she says, "that's not a bad idea."

SIX

Chloe

Poppy's nose job looks wonky.

I'm sorry, but it does. Now that we're squashed up next to each other in this hot tub, which by the way is incredible, I'm right opposite to her and I can still see a bump on the left side. It's tiny, but noticeable. What a shame to have spent thousands of pounds on that travesty.

We've eaten cold pizza and drank about four bottles of cider each, and now we're finally moving on to the spirits that I set out in such a pretty fashion on some chairs. Esther does the job of pouring everyone a vodka lemonade, and then we all toast again to Poppy's hen party and her future wedding.

You know, I wasn't particularly keen at first, especially when she demanded I help her lay everything out. I almost decided to just take a bath in the main lodge and go to sleep. But I'm happy I came out, because we're actually starting to have some fun. Poppy is much more enjoyable to hang around with now, and everyone seems to be loosening up a bit.

"You four must have holidays like this all the time," Poppy says. "It must be nice having girlfriends to do things like this with."

I exchange a glance with Esther. Does this mean Poppy really doesn't have any other friends? There's a moment of awkwardness, so I start blabbering to move on.

"Not like this, but we went to Morocco a couple of summers ago at a five-star resort, and that was fantastic."

"Morocco?" Annabel frowns, and I know in that second I've fucked up. Her threaded eyebrows knit together in confusion. "Who went to Morocco?"

"You were busy with Andrew, I think," I bluster, aware of my cheeks turning pink. "It wasn't anything too special."

"The three of you went without me?"

Tanya clears her throat. "We didn't think you'd be interested."

"But why not?" God, she actually looks upset. No—angry, even.

"Like Chloe said, you were busy," Esther puts in smoothly. "It wasn't deliberate. We're sorry. You know how it is."

Poppy laughs. "Oh dear, I didn't mean to start something there."

A vein pulses in Annabel's temple, and she turns on Poppy. "And where are *your* friends?"

"Ouch!" she says, but there's a lightness to her tone, and she chuckles again. "You got me. Poor old Poppy Greer—friendless and having to resort to you four for her hen party, I bet that's what you're all thinking."

Well. She's the one who said it.

She nods at our faces. "I had a smaller celebration with my friends from work, but this is for you four in particular. I didn't want any outsiders ruining this special occasion. And hey, with me you're *all* invited."

Annabel's smile tightens, as if it might snap at any moment. I knew we should have told her about Morocco when it happened, but Esther insisted we shouldn't.

What is Poppy on about though? She's always been a bit of an oddball. I didn't say anything to Annabel earlier, but to be honest I was a little freaked out about staying in my room for any longer than I had to. I had a creepy piece of art hanging on my wall too—some weird re-creation of

The Scream, except with a woman this time, tears streaming down her cheeks. Proper depressing stuff, not exactly happy holiday displays. I was going to talk to someone about it but in all honesty I didn't realise it was Annabel's hut I'd walked into. I was hoping for Tanya, or even Esther. Anyone but her. It's still so uncomfortable around her at the moment, trying to avoid any mention of what I've been doing so I don't give myself away. But I think I did a pretty good job of hiding my thoughts.

"Let's play Never Have I Ever!" Poppy suggests. "We'll catch up on what we don't know about each other so easily that way."

Esther groans. "I haven't played that since university."

Annabel knocks back the rest of her drink, then grabs herself another bottle. "Really, Poppy?"

"Come on, it'll be fun," she says.

"I'm up for it," I say. I love a party game. Even if it is a bit funny, like we're trying to reclaim our lost youth or something. Being all together like this just makes us revert back to the people we were ten years ago.

Well, hopefully not entirely.

It's weird, but I'm pleased when Poppy grins at me, like we're co-conspirators. Imagine that, me being pleased with Poppy Greer's approval. "Brilliant. I'll go first."

She looks around at each of us, thinking seriously about what she's going to say. "Never have I ever skinny-dipped in the sea."

Blackpool, four or five years ago. I was on a different hen night with a bunch of friends from an apprenticeship course I was on at the time, and we all did it, even though it was October. One of the bridesmaids ended up catching a cold and the bride's bracelet was stolen from the pile of clothes we left behind.

I take a sip, watching Tanya and Annabel do the same. Esther shakes her head.

Poppy laughs. "Okay, maybe that one was too easy! Never have I ever had a one-night stand with someone."

Is she for real? I look at her expression, but she's smiling innocently, waiting to see who will take a sip. To the surprise of no one, the rest of us drink. Maybe there's still a little bit of the old Poppy Greer there after all.

"You're so traditional!" Annabel says. "Bless you, Poppy."

"Chloe, your turn," Poppy says. "We'll go round in a circle. I can't keep hogging every round."

"Never have I ever . . ." It's hard to think what I haven't done, without making me sound easy. I like to have a good time and I'm not going to apologise for living my life to the fullest. But then I think of something. "Never have I ever had sex with a woman."

I'm expecting no one to drink. Annabel, Tanya, and Esther stay still. Well, Annabel half lifts her glass, then obviously realises what I've said and puts it back down again. But we all gawp when Poppy takes a big gulp from her plastic cup.

"When?" I ask. And then, because I can't help myself, "Does your groom know you have, Poppy?"

She chuckles. "I should hope so, because that was what I was going to tell you all. My groom isn't a groom at all. She's another bride. She's a woman."

"A *woman*?"

The others look at me, surprised by the outburst. Are they joking? I can't believe I'm the only one who seems bothered by it.

"Everything okay, Chloe?" Poppy says. "You don't have a problem with that, do you? It's okay to like both, you know."

"Congratulations," Annabel says quickly. "I'm glad you found someone."

Poppy ignores her. "Chloe?"

She should know I'm not one to back down. She asked for it.

"I don't normally associate myself with people like you," I snap. "Hardly a surprise though, is it?"

Tanya shakes her head.

"What do you mean by that?" Poppy asks. She's trying to sound serious but she can't hide the hurt behind her question.

"Desperate enough to be loved by anyone," I say. "You always were Poppy Greedy."

Something flashes across Poppy's face.

Everyone else has gone silent too.

Is no one really going to back me up? They're all staring down into their drinks, desperately avoiding any eye contact. How pathetic.

Look, maybe I've had too much to drink, but fuck it. I'm entitled to my opinion.

"What?" I say. "God, relax, everyone. I'm joking, okay?"

I'm not joking, but whatever. As long as she stays sitting opposite me and doesn't come close, I won't let it bother me. I bet she's fancied me for years. I wouldn't be surprised.

There's a moment when they all seem to stare at one another, and then their drinks. Poppy is still seething. Finally, Annabel cracks a smile and begins to chuckle, and Tanya and Esther join in.

"You haven't changed, Chloe," Poppy says. But she's smiling again now.

It's Esther's turn next in the game, but she's hesitating.

"Carry on!" Poppy says.

"Never have I ever cheated on someone," Esther says.

There's a pause as everyone considers how honest they want to be. My eyes can't help darting a glance at Annabel, desperate for her to drink, but she remains still. Fuck it. They can't question the when or where or most importantly who. I decide to take one for the team and drink first.

Tanya and Poppy sip. I'm curious about Tanya, but she's hurriedly taking her turn to avoid questions.

"Never have I ever got a tattoo," she says.

I have a small butterfly on my thigh, which I point to as I drink. It's a matching tattoo, actually, not that I would ever tell anyone that. My mum has a butterfly on her thigh too. We got them done together to celebrate her last drink and the start of her sobriety. Unfortunately, that wasn't as permanent. Now I tell people I got it done after a wild night out on holiday in Thailand; it's a much more exciting story. Poppy brandishes her wrist at us for a moment, a red flower with a dark centre, then drinks.

"A poppy?" Annabel says.

"It's a love tattoo to yourself, isn't it?" I say.

"Perhaps," Poppy says, but doesn't explain any further. "Never have I ever stood up a date."

There's an awkward silence as we process this one. Poppy remains cool, but I wonder what's going on behind her eyes, what she's thinking.

"Does showing up to a date and seeing what he really looked like in person and bailing count?" I say quickly. "Because I'll definitely have to drink if so."

"I'd say that counts," Poppy says. "If you're not showing up to someone for whatever reason, that counts."

I drink, painfully aware I am the only one to do so. There's a bit of a lull in the game at that moment as we wait for Annabel to come up with something.

"Isn't this island beautiful?" Poppy gestures around us. The hot tub stares out across the main lawn, the beach visible just barely in the background, a quiet hush of the waves drifting in and out, audible if you strain to listen. Mostly, though, there is silence outside of the pop music blasting out of the CD player, and a growing darkness that reminds us just how isolated we are. Above us, the sky is not covered in pollution but a thick blanket of stars.

Esther leans back to look at the moon, which hangs as a crescent directly above where we are. "It's so strange being here. It's so far away from everything we know."

"Are there lots of bugs on this island?" I pull a face. It can be as beautiful as it wants but, if I wake up to a massive spider on me, this place is officially a nightmare.

Poppy looks amused. "Not a fan of bugs, Chloe?"

I shudder. "Not at all."

"I think you'll be fine. But you never know with an island. Of course they'll be around."

Annabel takes a cautious sip of her wine. "I can't think of anything else for the game."

Honestly, she's useless. I'm about to suggest something when Poppy butts in.

"Never have I ever done something for charity."

Oh, great. She's going to be a preachy type. The four of us stay still for this round, not a drop of alcohol consumed.

"I lied," Poppy says. "I donate to three different charities monthly and I also volunteer every Sunday at a homeless shelter. I was just curious."

"Hey, that's not fair!" I protest. "You can't just make something up."

She downs her drink in one, then refills. "There. I've drank now."

"Well, that doesn't really count," Tanya says.

"None of you really give to charity?" she asks. "But you all make so much money."

I frown. I'm not sure why she's so judgemental. "It's my money, and I can do what I want with it. And when I'm young I plan on enjoying myself. I've got lots of time to help others in the future."

"Chloe's right," Tanya says. Of course Tanya is backing me up. She owes me big-time. "And anyway, there are more ways to help someone than donating to charity. I've heard a lot of donations just go to administrative costs."

"What do you do instead, Tanya?" Poppy asks.

"Well, uh, some of my events raise awareness of certain issues," she blusters.

"Annabel or Esther?" Poppy persists. "Not just charities. Do you do anything for other people?"

Annabel avoids answering by drinking her vodka.

"Nothing," Esther admits bluntly. "But some of us have our own problems."

The atmosphere is well and truly dead now. What was Poppy thinking? She catches my eye as I glare at her and to my surprise she returns it in full force, keeping that intensity until it is me who has to look away, defeated.

"Perhaps that one was a mistake," Poppy concedes. "Chloe's right, that wasn't fair. The rules are you have to say something you've never done."

"Oh, it's fine." Esther, always the peacemaker, tries to placate. "Let's just do something else. Maybe it's time for bed."

"Never have I ever done drugs," Annabel blurts out.

Oh, Jesus. I can feel Tanya's eyes on me, but I ignore her and take a drink. I don't care. Let them judge me.

Even Esther the fitness fanatic has to drink. "If a bit of weed in my first year of university counts," she mutters. Tanya and Poppy stay as they are.

I don't say anything.

"Tanya," Poppy says. "You haven't ever taken drugs either? Really?"

I feel as though I'm holding my breath, but Tanya stays firm.

"Never," she says.

Poppy makes a great show of surprise. "But you organise parties in London. Surely it goes with the territory. Not even a tiny bit of, say, coke?"

Tanya shakes her head, but she's scowling now. My heart is pounding.

Across the sky there's a loud boom of thunder. A minute goes by, and then there's another, even more threatening than the first. It's getting closer.

"I think that's our sign to call it a night," Poppy says. "Now that we're all acquainted again, I can't wait for the hen party to start properly tomorrow."

"What's the plan?" Esther asks.

"As long as we're not too hungover, I'm thinking we'll have a nice breakfast and then a walk up Deadman's Peak. As for the rest of the day, you shall see."

My head automatically turns to look at the cliffside, which looms behind the lodge and seems even taller than it did during the afternoon. A flash of lightning illuminates the scene and a bird flies off into the distance, scared by the sudden brightness.

"That's me out of the water," Tanya says, and we all follow suit, hurrying out of the hot tub and into towels.

Poppy's gaze is on the sky. "Robin said there were often nighttime storms here. You'd never know during the day."

"Just some overblown chairs and rolling bottles of cider," Annabel says. "I'm looking forward to the walk tomorrow."

Is she? The Annabel I know wouldn't be caught dead doing outdoor activities. That's much more Esther's cup of tea. Maybe she's just trying to suck up again, that charm she puts on for strangers that warms them to her. But Poppy's not a stranger, as much as she feels like one.

"I'll see you in the morning, ladies," Poppy says. "Would one of you mind putting the cover back on the tub? Thank you for the game, it was very interesting."

She departs, heading across the decking and into the main lodge.

"I don't think I like Poppy," Tanya says, and for once I'm in full agreement.

"I mean, that's nothing new," Annabel points out with a small smile.

"Oh come on, she's not that bad." Esther reaches for the cover and places it on herself, then switches off the CD player. "Just a bit of a superiority complex, that's all. As if you three aren't as bad sometimes."

"We're not like that," I say.

"Whatever." She yawns, covering her mouth with her hand. "I'm knackered anyway. Are we heading off?"

"In a minute," Tanya says. "I just want a word with Chloe."

The other two look puzzled, but don't argue, heading down the path towards our huts.

"See you tomorrow morning," Esther says as she leaves, and I know for a fact she's going to ask me what Tanya said.

It doesn't matter. I'm not going to tell her.

Now that it's just the two of us, the isolation of the island grows. The thunder and lightning continue to make their way towards us, and the first spatters of rain start to fall. A pit of nerves enters my stomach. I don't know what she's going to say.

But Tanya surprises me.

"Thank you," she mutters, barely able to look me in the eye.

Is this really the time to be bringing any of that up?

"Right," I say.

"Seeing Poppy," she says, "it's odd, isn't it?"

"Yeah."

"You're a good friend to me, Chloe, I don't forget that. And I've been a good friend to you, haven't I?"

Tanya's words are starting to slur, a glazed expression to her face. She's drunk.

"Get some sleep, Tan," I say. "You need it."

She reaches forward and grips my arm, her hold surprisingly strong. "I mean it. Thank you."

"I have no idea what you're talking about," I say, stressing each word. "But okay."

She releases me, slowly walking to her hut. I watch her go, making sure she doesn't stumble.

I need to keep her on my side, but she's starting to become more trouble than she's worth.

SEVEN

Tanya

For a moment I forget where I am.

Soft morning light eases into the room. I must have opened the curtains and the window before I went to sleep, the breeze a welcome coolness to my face. It still feels early, so I take my time getting ready for the day. I sit up and stretch my arms, enjoying the gentle clicks in my shoulders. From my position I can see through the forest the path that leads to Esther's hut, a vision of greens and browns.

This room, this island—it's a world away from what I know.

Chloe's puzzled face comes back to me from last night. Her embarrassment, trying to move the conversation along, not wanting to talk about it. Maybe that's for the best, pretending she doesn't know anything. Maybe that's how she's decided to deal with it. I need to too.

Perhaps Poppy really is genuine about wanting to forget the past. She seemed happy enough yesterday, other than her disappointment in us not doing anything for charity. Maybe I've been worrying all these years for nothing.

I'm about to heave myself off the bed when I catch sight of Annabel bursting out of Esther's hut, face like thunder. Esther soon follows, dressed in her running gear, trying to placate her. I'm aware that if the two of them dared to look over they'd see me sitting up in bed staring at them, so I lie myself back down and try to hear what they're saying.

"And for it to just come up last night, like it was nothing! Oh, we all went to Morocco. That Chloe. She's such a smug bitch sometimes." Annabel's voice comes out like a screech. Esther tries to shush her.

Is this really what they're arguing about? Bloody Morocco? It was two years ago. And it was Chloe who brought it up anyway. Why have a go at Esther?

"Annabel, you need to calm down. I couldn't exactly say no, could I? And I didn't want you to feel like you had to go."

"I'm sure that was it. You were doing it out of the goodness of your heart."

"Haven't the past two years proven just what I'm doing out of the goodness of my heart?"

I frown. What are they talking about?

"You can't keep throwing it back in my face. I'm trying, I really am—"

"It needs to end, Annabel. I can't keep doing this. You need to think about what you're going to do, because you're on your own."

"Esther!"

I sneak a glance up, and find Esther storming away from Annabel this time, presumably off on one of her runs. Annabel is left standing by the hut, and even from this distance I can see every muscle tense with anger, her brow furrowed. From somewhere else—Chloe's hut, perhaps—something clatters onto the floor, and it's as if a light has switched on, Annabel's features change that quickly. The fury has melted away, and in its place is an expression of calm, as if nothing took place at all.

What the hell was all that about? Annabel hurries away, probably anxious about the sudden noise and not wanting to be caught near Esther's hut. I sit up again, mind whirring. Clearly, the two of them are hiding something. It can't just be that Annabel is mad about us all going to Morocco without her.

I stand up and head to the small bathroom, grateful the shower only takes a few minutes to heat up.

Fluffy peach towel wrapped around me, I start to unpack my suitcase. I take my time, carefully transferring each folded item to the oak chest of drawers underneath the window, laying out my outfit for the day on the bed. Oh God, right, that bloody cliff walk. I take out my Doc Martens.

A quick dab of makeup, and I'm ready. I find myself staring at my face in the mirror for a fraction too long, observing my frown lines, my paleness, the bags under my eyes. Do I really look that rough, or am I focusing too much? My nose is congested, no matter how many times I inhale, and if I stay still for too long my hands start to shake. I don't think the others have noticed though.

"Knock knock."

Esther pokes her head through the door. "Can I come in?"

"Sure."

She sits on the bed. Her hair, slicked back, hangs to her shoulders and her face is flushed.

"Have you been for a run?" I ask, as if I don't know already.

"Yeah. Just along the beach front. It's been so nice not to wake up and check my emails, you know."

"How long have you been up?"

"Hours. I'm always an early riser." She stretches out her legs and reaches her hands across to grab her feet, folding forward. "It's a great beach to run on, though." She sits back up. "You know how Robin was saying there were some rock pools down the other end? I found them."

"I don't know how you get your energy."

"I love it here," she says. "I'm definitely going to go for a run every morning whilst I have the chance. It's my only respite from my emails. And messages from Brad."

"Aren't you going to miss texting him?" He'd texted her so many times already even before we handed our phones in, hers a constant array of beeps whenever we got signal. "He's so loving."

She pulls a strange face. "You could say that. No, I think I'm glad I'm having a break from technology. We're heading up the cliffside today, aren't we?"

"That's what Poppy said last night." I apply sun cream to my shoulders and arms. "It's a bit of an odd hen party activity. I'd have thought we'd spend the day on the beach, getting tans."

"The best thing we can do is enjoy it." Esther shrugs. "You were the one who convinced us to come, remember."

My own feelings of guilt stab at my stomach, and I land on the only thing that troubled me. "You don't think that whole charity thing last night was a bit holier-than-thou?"

"Sure. But I just don't let it bother me." She heads to the doorway, then turns back to me. "By the way, whilst I was coming back, Poppy was already up, cooking us all breakfast. I told her I'd let everyone know."

"Is that why you came to see me?" I say, before she can head off.

"What do you mean?"

"To tell me Poppy was making breakfast." I realise I sound strange, and try a lighthearted grin. "Or did you want to ask me something?"

"How long have you been up, anyway?"

Did she see me looking through the window when she and Annabel argued?

I shrug my shoulders. "Not long. About an hour, if that."

"Right."

Is that relief? I can't tell. And then I notice something. "Hey, your necklace is gone."

"What?" She touches her neck, then hurries to the mirror, seeing nothing there. "Shit. It must have dropped on my run. I'll have to look for it later."

"You always wear that thing," I say.

"That *thing* is worth thousands," Esther snaps. "God, maybe it fell off when I was asleep. That can happen sometimes. I'll look in my room too." And then she heads out without another word.

The smell of the breakfast hits me before I even see it, Poppy on the barbecue cooking bacon and sausages. She's set up the main table out on the grass in some shade, each place laid out already with cutlery and glasses of orange juice. There's a bowl in the middle full of croissants, and a plate next to it piled high with toast.

"I didn't realise an army was coming to visit," I say, trying my best to start the morning on a positive note with her. It still feels strange, being here with her. All of the unspoken business of the past still brewing beneath it all.

To my relief she smiles at my weak joke, waving me forward with her spatula. "Good morning, Tanya. It seems you and Esther have the others beat when it comes to early rising."

"You must have beaten us all."

"Ah, well, I don't count," she says. "I struggle to sleep, you see. Insomnia."

"Right. Well, thanks for putting on this spread." I gesture around to the table. "Do you need any help?"

The others materialise as if by magic just as Poppy and I have finished. Poppy sits at the head of the table, informing them all of the wonderful night's sleep she had, a direct contradiction to what she just told me. But despite her claims of insomnia, she does look well-rested, and also quite young. She's not wearing any makeup and her face has that rounded quality to it, a freshness that my own seems to have lost even though we're the same age.

"Have any of you seen my necklace?" Esther asks as soon as we're all seated. "I think it vanished on my run. I couldn't find it in my room any-where."

"The gold one in the shape of your name?" Poppy says. "Can't say I have. It's beautiful though."

Chloe shakes her head. "Me neither."

"Damn," Esther mutters under her breath. "Annabel? Have you seen it?"

She looks startled, then shakes her head too. "No, sorry."

It still feels bizarre. Especially after everything we went through to-gether. Seeing her now with her natural glow, I'm reminded of when we were little kids and we'd make mud pies in her mum and dad's back gar-den, telling each other we were witches but good ones, hiding from soci-ety to make sure tiny animals like frogs and snails had protectors.

The memory brings a smile to my lips, and Poppy catches my eye and returns it, as if she's read my mind.

"Can I have some more of the orange juice?" Esther asks, nodding at our side of the table.

"Of course." Poppy stands with the jug, bringing it over me, and it's as if I know it's going to happen before it does.

"Oh my God! I'm sorry, Tanya!"

Poppy has dropped it, spilling the entire contents on my lap, the jug falling to the ground with a thud but not breaking. Chloe and Annabel, near to me, leap up in surprise, while I career backwards in my chair.

"Jesus, are you alright?" Poppy takes my hand and pulls me upright, but the orange juice has made her grip slippery, and she lets go just as I'm about to stand up, sending me back down again. "Oops! Sorry!"

Chloe rushes around and helps me up properly. My top is ruined, huge orange stains across the stomach, and my legs and arms are sticky. Everyone else is untouched, though Annabel keeps peering around for any sign of it on her.

"I'm so clumsy," Poppy says. "I'll pay for a new top, I promise. I'm really sorry."

"Forget it," I snap.

Maybe it's because of the anger bubbling inside of me, but Poppy's words seem false. Since when is she clumsy, this woman who has single-handedly managed everything so far? Who I saw throwing a piece of bacon up in the air and catching it with her spatula half an hour earlier? But there's no shame in her expression. It almost looks like a challenge. Her gaze is saying: *Do something about it, I dare you.*

All my certainty, my good feelings from earlier, vanish.

"Your breakfast will get cold." Chloe looks around hopelessly. "Should we put it in the fridge for you to heat up later?"

"I'll eat it now. It's fine."

"You know, it almost looks like you've wet yourself," Poppy says, grinning.

There's a gasp from Chloe and it all falls silent.

She didn't just say that.

After everything, all her talk of letting bygones be bygones, all her positivity and wanting us to be friends, and she says that?

Everyone stares in agony at me. I've become hyper-aware of the juice, as though I've been drenched head to toe, and I can't bear it a moment longer.

I take the top off, grateful I put a bikini on underneath my outfit, and swap the chair out for a different one. It is still silent while I do this.

Poppy finally breaks the ice. "I was joking, everyone."

"Maybe we shouldn't bring any of that up," Esther murmurs, flushed.

"Not ones for looking back, are you?" Poppy says.

Everyone returns to their seats, casting glances at me when they think I'm not looking. I don't know what to say. Did she drop that orange juice on purpose, to make her point? Or was it an accident she took full advantage of? I'm not sure, and from looking around at everyone else, neither are they.

"Well," Poppy says, with a short laugh. "I was going to say what a lovely morning this was, but now I'm not so sure! Come on, let's cheer up. We have a hen party to celebrate!"

The others laugh along with her, and I'm aware I'm bringing the mood down, sitting in the middle like the grinch. But I don't care. Determined to ignore the fact my thighs are now stuck to the chair thanks to the stickiness of the juice, I shovel food in my mouth, barely appreciating the nice taste, and Esther fetches more orange juice from the kitchen. I'm on my second croissant when I feel a foot pressed into my own, and I look up to find Annabel opposite me offering an encouraging smile.

"Come on then, fill me in," Poppy says. "I want to hear all about what you've been up to these past ten years. It's been too long."

"There's not much to really talk about," Annabel says. "We've already told you about our jobs. Well, they have. I'm just a housewife."

"You were always so brainy." Poppy leans forward, food dangling on her fork. "What made you decide to do that? I hope it wasn't just to make your husband happy."

Annabel blushes. That definitely was the reason. "Oh, I don't know, I couldn't figure out what I wanted to do."

"Seems a shame." Poppy takes a mouthful of breakfast and chews thoughtfully before swallowing. "You were always my rival in terms of brains."

Charming. Esther looks just as annoyed as me.

"You never know, I might go back to work," Annabel says, even though she's never mentioned it before.

"What would you do?" Poppy asks.

"Psychology. Use my degrees."

Would she? Her face seems earnest enough, but I'm surprised she hasn't said it to any of us. I check with the other two but they look just as astonished as me.

"What do you do for hobbies?" Poppy persists.

For some reason this makes Annabel uncomfortable, her head dipping to avoid meeting anyone's eye. "Not much."

"I love running," Esther says, rescuing her. "I run every day."

"Yes, I saw you this morning." Poppy finishes her glass of orange juice with a wink at me that makes me want to punch her. "Very admirable. I'm more of a yoga and Pilates girl myself."

"Me too," Chloe says. She's barely touched her breakfast, eating a couple rashers of bacon and a slice of toast and stirring everything else around on her plate like a five-year-old.

"No partner, Chloe?" Poppy says. "That surprises me. You were always the one with the most boyfriends back at school."

Is that a dig? Chloe can't figure it out either from the puzzled look on her face, but she takes it in good faith. "Not at the moment. I don't have a lot of time for men."

"I'm sure that can't be true." Poppy reaches over and pats her knee. "You'll find the right guy if you look in the right places."

"Chloe isn't too great at that." The words come out of my mouth before I can help it.

She scowls at me, and I know I've gone too far.

"What's that meant to mean?" Annabel asks, frowning.

"Don't start," Esther says wearily.

Poppy looks intrigued.

"Never mind," I say to her disappointment. "I was just being a bitch."

"I'd be careful of that if I were you," Chloe snaps. "You've already made a scene of yourself today."

"Let's leave it there!" Esther insists, while Chloe and I glare at one another.

"What about you, Poppy?" Annabel says, to move the conversation along. "What have you been doing the past ten years? How is your family?"

It's funny; it's such an easy, typical question to ask of someone after a long time has passed, but Poppy seems to freeze up.

"All fine," she says with forced breeziness. "I've been keeping myself busy. You know, my job takes a lot of work. I'd barely been out of university before going straight into it really. Not much to report on my end. I'm more interested in you four."

"Oh, right." Annabel doesn't know what to say to this, so we end up eating the rest of the breakfast in what I hope is companionable silence, but seems to be more uncomfortable than anything else, the air thick with unanswered questions from the past.

"I think we need to work off that meal now," Poppy says once everyone is finished, ignoring Chloe picking at her croissant. "We'll give Tanya ten minutes to get changed, and then we'll head up the mountain and see the view Robin was talking about. Everyone agreed?"

"You're the bride, it's your decision," Esther says. "We can clean the plates and tidy everything away, seeing as you cooked."

Poppy smiles. "I'll relax myself on a sun bed and you can come and tell me when you're all ready to go."

Chloe opens her mouth to protest, but Esther shakes her head at her from across the table. At least there's some joy I can take from that. Chloe looks unimpressed as Annabel and Esther start clearing plates, and half-heartedly takes the bowl of croissants with both hands.

"Make sure you change, Tanya, you really stink," Poppy says.

She's lighthearted as she says it, but it feels like a dig. I'm suddenly aware again of the citrusy orange smell radiating off me, the stickiness of my skin.

No one else hears her comment. Poppy walks away towards the loungers and flops herself down on one, raising a hand to her face to shield it from the harsh sun.

"I know she's the bride, but she could help a little bit," Chloe grumbles as she passes me.

"It's her weekend." Esther, always easy, gives another shrug of her shoulders. "She's the boss."

It's an interesting power dynamic. An unusual one. I watch Poppy a moment longer, long after the others have headed to the kitchen with everything cleared from the table. And I catch her sitting up, looking around, checking that they'd done as told. She catches my gaze again but it's not like before, where I felt we might be remembering the same innocent childhood memory. She stares at me with the same challenging look as earlier, and then makes a wafting motion with her hand, as if the stench of me still reaches her.

EIGHT

Esther

There's a surprising freeness up here on the summit. It helps calm my irritation after losing the necklace. I couldn't find it on the beach, nor in my room. I know it'll turn up somewhere, it has to, but I feel oddly naked without it, and my hand trails to my neck in the hopes it will magically reappear.

The journey, like Robin said, wasn't too arduous, especially not for me, though Annabel and Tanya are sitting on rocks catching their breath. Beyond the huts, we took the path through the trees until we reached the sloping hill at the start of the mountain, gradually getting steeper and steeper until the path became a distinct upward battle. It narrowed towards the end, making us walk up in single file, until the summit opened out before us, a few metres wide. Someone, long ago from the look of rust on its surface, had traversed beyond the jagged rocks to the end point and placed a cross at the edge of the cliff. The grass at our feet is tall and free, with weeds sprouting everywhere. The surface isn't flat, like the lawn by the lodge, but quite bumpy, making me cautious where I step. A solitary tree stands in the middle, a couple of dandelions sprouted beneath it. The summit itself isn't very beautiful, a rather overgrown, small space, with rocks sticking up everywhere that the others are grateful to use as seats while I step closer to the edge.

Looking down, even though I would hardly call this a proper mountain, isn't for the fainthearted. I'd wager the drop is at least sixty feet, straight down to the ocean below, the waves facing a stronger current here and hitting across the rock face with fury. The sea is also less clear, perhaps the current making the sand kick up and blur the waters, so there's an added uncertainty about what lies beneath.

But I'm focusing on the wrong things. The summit, the drop below, the ocean—they're not what the true appeal is. Robin wasn't wrong. The view is spectacular.

From where I'm standing, I can see the entire island. The main beach stretches along one side, shining white, and a smaller beach runs across the other side, a tiny patch of sand all the way at the top of the island. Next to it is another hut, this one painted green to blend in with the trees around it.

"What's that hut for?" I ask, pointing. The others stand next to me, squinting in the direction of my finger.

"I can't see anything," Annabel says. "What are we looking at, exactly? What hut?"

"The green one." I point again. "Close to the small beach, right up the top there."

"I see it!" Chloe cries triumphantly. Then she frowns. "That's weird, Robin didn't mention another hut. Do you know what it's for, Poppy?"

Poppy is also frowning, brow furrowed as she studies the hut. "Perhaps it was here when this island was first built on. I doubt it's livable now."

"I'll have to try and investigate on one of my runs," I say. "It could be filled with old stuff."

"Oh—actually!" Poppy slaps her hand against her forehead. "Robin did tell me what it was for. She said it's where the power generator is kept. Said it was best to keep away as there's all sorts of electricals in there. It's practically blocked off from the rest of us as it is."

"That's a shame."

"This view though," Annabel breathes.

It's not Annabel's style, being outdoorsy. She's an inside girl through and through, much more comfortable with a day of shopping and afternoon tea than hiking and braving the elements. After our disagreement this morning, she's been steadily ignoring me, and even now focuses on the view outwards, as if I don't exist. Tanya, normally better at pretending she's having a good time, has been in a sour mood all morning after the orange juice fiasco, wearing an entire new set of jean shorts and top, accessorised with a scowl.

Chloe, meanwhile, who I thought would complain even more than Annabel and moaned that her shoes were rubbing the entire journey up here, has been in higher spirits than I've seen her since we arrived. She's taken the digital camera Poppy brought with her, taking several dramatic shots of the island view from one way and then the other, as well as many of the trek up, and now she's clamouring for someone to take a picture of the view with her at the centre.

"Please, Tanya!" she pleads, thrusting the camera in Tanya's hands. "Just a couple, and then give me a chance to check the lighting."

"God, fine." Only Chloe could make Tanya turn photographer. I can't help but chuckle at Tanya snapping away as Chloe poses.

"You're quite fit, aren't you?"

Poppy's voice next to me makes me jump. I hadn't heard her move towards me.

"I mean, I guess I would say so," I tell her. "I run a marathon every year. But I haven't got any strength."

"That's amazing. You have to be careful on your runs though."

"What do you mean?"

She points to my wrist, the bruising on it obvious now, three distinct marks. "You must have banged your wrist this morning when you went running?"

I shrug my shoulders. "I guess so. I'm not sure. I bruise so easily."

That, at least, is true. Even a small knock leaves me bruised for days. I wrap my hand around my wrist. I hadn't realised my sleeves had rolled up, exposing my arms to the world. As hot as it is, I'm better off this way.

"I'm impressed by your dedication."

"Really?" Chloe's crass comment to Poppy last night still rings in my ears. I shouldn't have laughed along; that was weak of me. "Hey, I'm sorry about Chloe last night," I say now quietly.

Poppy looks surprised, both eyebrows raised. "I've heard worse. And anyway, you're not the one who said it."

"No, but I wouldn't count on an apology from Chloe."

This seems to amuse her. "Trust me, I won't."

"She can be difficult," I say, trying to be conciliatory.

"I hope you find your necklace soon," she says, as if we've been talking about that all along.

"Let's have a group picture!"

Chloe's excited squeal distracts us, and she gathers us together for a selfie. Poppy stands to the side at first, not sure if she's included in this request, before I pull her in and put her between me and Tanya. Chloe holds the camera high, getting us all in, and we smile broadly.

"Everyone say 'hen party!'" she shrieks.

"Hen party!" we echo, and there's a real sense of togetherness. We're all grinning at each other, and even Tanya cracks a smile.

"This was a great idea to come up here," Chloe says as we break apart.

"Let's have a look at the picture, then." I take the camera from Chloe and study the image of the five of us. We're all smiling, Chloe's broader than anyone, but there's something not quite right about it. Chloe has her hand gripped around Tanya's shoulder as if she might fall over at any moment. Annabel is detached on the edge of the group, and isn't quite looking into the camera. And Poppy being between me and Tanya just seems odd, as if she was always meant to be there but still somehow stands out like a sore thumb. My bruise is hidden behind Tanya's back, thank God.

"It's lovely," I say, when I realise everyone is waiting for a response. I hand the camera back to Chloe. "It's nice to have a picture of all of us."

"And no phones necessary," Poppy adds, triumphant.

Tanya goes to sit on a rock, while the rest of us return to looking at the view. Even Annabel has braved it, stepping closer to the edge.

"Not missing yours?" I ask Chloe.

"It's alright." Chloe puts the camera away and takes in the view properly.

Poppy walks beside Annabel. "Do you remember the last time the five of us were together like this?"

"At school?" Annabel says, frowning.

"More specific than that," Poppy says.

It takes me a second to realise what she's getting at.

"The art exam," I say.

Poppy nods. "That's it. Does anyone remember the exact date?"

"The twenty-second of May," Tanya says, surprising me.

"That's almost ten years ago exactly," Poppy tells us. "A whole decade between now and then. Could you believe in ten years' time from that moment that we'd all be together again?"

Why is she bringing it up? We all exchange an uneasy glance, knowing what happened.

Poppy darts forward and places her hand on Annabel's back. She's so quick none of us have any time to react. Annabel turns her head towards Poppy in horror, her mouth open, her hands rising in defence.

Poppy pushes her.

Annabel stumbles forward, but she's too far away from the edge for it to do any harm. She lands on her feet and steadies herself.

It was a gentle push. A push designed to tease, not harm.

We're all gawping at Poppy in shock as she bursts into laughter.

"What was that?" Annabel shouts, backing away from the ledge and standing behind me. Tanya steps forward and Chloe also moves around to join us so we're standing in a line facing Poppy, who is still chuckling, wiping a tear from her eye.

"That wasn't funny," I say. "Annabel could have died."

"Oh, come off it, Esther," Poppy says, grinning away at us as if we're having a normal conversation. "She was about a metre away from the edge. One tiny push wasn't going to kill her."

"Are you alright?" Chloe asks, as Annabel starts to tear up. "You're fine, you didn't get close to the edge, I promise you."

"How could you do that?" Tanya says.

Poppy throws her hands up in the air. "It was a *joke*. You remember those, don't you? The four of you? I seem to recall you used to like jokes a lot."

She does remember. I knew it.

"I know you were joking, but don't do anything like that again." I try to nod at Poppy, but she looks straight through me.

"If anyone should be afraid up here, it's me," she says. "After all, I know what you're all capable of."

NINE

Poppy

Dear Diary,

Oh my God. First day of secondary school! It's as big and scary as everyone says. Even though I'm practically an adult now, just turned eleven, it didn't matter how much Mum and Dad tried to convince me it was all going to be fine. I've already made a total idiot of myself.

Sorry, this isn't how diaries are meant to start, are they? Oh well! It's my diary and I can do what I want. But maybe I should introduce myself, because Mum's always telling me it's polite when meeting new people. Not that you're a new person, but you know what I mean. If anyone in the future, like a hundred years from now, discovered this diary hidden underground, they'd be like, oh wow, if only we knew who this was and we could make her famous across history? So I'm not taking any chances! Even though I'm definitely going to become famous anyway. I'm going to be a famous artist, you wait and see. And then this diary will be even more amazing because it'll be the diary of a famous person. Imagine if they found the diary of Picasso or Van Gogh or Leonardo da Vinci. It's basically the same.

I'm getting ahead of myself again, aren't I? My name is Poppy

Greer, I'm eleven years old, and I live in Bristol. And today was the first day of secondary school, and it was a TOTAL DISASTER.

I'm talking absolute-embarrassing-face-red-mortal-humiliation level. And I want to put on a brave face about it and try and get over it but what if this is it now? I'll always be known as that loser girl who embarrassed herself on the first day.

Thank God I have Tanya. She's my best friend, has been ever since that first day when we were tiny little kids in reception. I was reading a book in the corner when she came over to me and asked what it was about, and we've been together ever since.

Now we're both in Year Seven, it's crazy to think how grown up we are. I'm going to love all of the different subjects that are on offer compared to primary school (but Art will still be the best of course!). The welcome assembly, filled with over two hundred other Year Sevens, had the head teacher explaining to us our curriculum and what kinds of things we'd be doing. It all just sounds amazing, and I got to sit next to Tanya while we were listening because she's in my tutor group, thank God. I squeezed her hand when they started talking about the Drama department. Tanya loves acting and says she wants to be a famous actress when she grows up and I know that most people never get to achieve their dream but I really think Tanya will.

Tanya can star in Hollywood films and I can be displayed in all the famous art galleries of the world. My primary school teacher said I was the best at art she'd ever seen, and she could be quite mean when she wanted to be. She never made up praise for the sake of it, so I know she was telling the truth and I am talented.

Anyway. Let me get to the HORRIFIC INCIDENT, because that's what I really want to focus on.

We were on a tour of the school in our tutor group with our tutor leading the way. (Oh my God, our tutor! Totally a distraction from the main point but I think he might be the cutest man alive ever in the history of men. And I'm definitely not the only one who thinks so!) Most of the girls were at the front of the group, following him eagerly, whilst the boys kind of sauntered along in the middle. Tanya and I stuck to the back, enjoying taking in the view of the school and trying to make sure we remembered the way round to things so we didn't get lost. There was another group of girls hanging towards the back, even further than us, acting as though they didn't care at all. Even though Mr. Edwards said we had to be silent, they were whispering to each other constantly.

One of them let out a loud snort of laughter. I glanced back at Mr. Edwards, worried he'd think it was me and Tanya, but he hadn't even heard, continuing the tour and describing the History department now, as we entered a corridor filled with posters about the world wars and the suffragettes.

I shouldn't have looked at them. I know, I know! But they saw me staring and got up close to us.

"I'm Annabel," the middle one said. "And this is Chloe and Esther."

Chloe was the one who had laughed really loudly, and she was still giggling. Looking back now it was so obvious she was holding something behind her back, but I was too busy focusing on Annabel, okay?

"What are your names?" Esther asked, and yes, she had something behind her back too.

I told them my name, but I was really nervous, and when Tanya said hers I couldn't help thinking how much more confident she was than me.

"I didn't realise the two of you were so frightened of history," Annabel said. She pointed to one of the displays we were walking past. "I know it looks pretty graphic, but it's important to learn about. You shouldn't be scared."

"We're not scared," I said. At the time I was totally confused. I loved history, I wasn't afraid of a stupid poster. I got the top prize in my primary school for my project about Roman women.

Tanya saw it before I did and managed to jump backwards. I was too busy frowning at the displays and trying to figure out what I was meant to be afraid of when Chloe and Esther revealed a Capri-Sun each from behind their backs and squirted them onto us, aiming for our crotches. I was soaked, but worse, it looked like I wet myself. Esther and Chloe threw the Capri-Suns in a bin close by and started shrieking with laughter.

Yep. I basically looked like I had just wet myself in the middle of the corridor.

But don't worry, it gets worse.

"Oh my God! Sir!" Annabel called. "This girl has just wet herself! Poppy has just wet herself!" And then she burst into laughter too.

To my horror, the entire class stopped in their tracks and turned to look at me as Mr. Edwards hurried from the front of the group, taking in the scene. Me, with my wet trousers and warm face. The puddle of liquid on the ground between my feet. The three girls pointing at me, making the others join in, everyone roaring with laughter and me the butt of the joke. I couldn't even look at anyone.

"Are you okay, Poppy?" Mr. Edwards asked. He turned to everyone else, and his voice rose. "That is enough! I will not have you all laughing at her. Go and wait down the end of the corridor for me, and if I catch you misbehaving you will all have detention even though it's the first day! Is that clear?"

I can remember it word for word, because all I was thinking was, oh my God, Mr. Edwards thinks I have wet myself. He's trying to protect me. He's making it worse.

"I didn't wet myself," I said weakly, too late. "It was Chloe and Esther—they—"

Annabel walked past then, and she shook her head at me.

"Chloe and Esther?" Mr. Edwards said. "What did they do?"

I couldn't be a snitch on the first day. I just couldn't.

"Nothing," I said.

Mr. Edwards frowned at me but decided to let it go. "Let's get you cleaned up, and I'm sure there will be some spare trousers from PE. I'll get someone to take you to reception, and they'll sort you out, okay? And if you need a medical note from the doctor about your bladder . . ."

"Sir, no," I whispered, knowing how pained I must have looked. "I didn't wet myself. I promise. Please don't say anything about it."

"Well, alright." Another student happened to be walking past, and he called them over. "Are you able to take one of my Year Sevens to reception?"

"Yes, sir," the student said, eyeing me up and down curiously.

Mr. Edwards smiled at me. "I'll see you later. And don't worry, I'll make sure no one mentions this again."

As he went back to the rest of the class, I couldn't help wondering how he was going to manage that. Even I'd be talking to Tanya about the girl who wet herself on the first day, and I wouldn't believe her no matter how much she insisted she didn't.

It's going to be a story forever now. I'm going to be that girl.

And to add to my humiliation, a cleaner showed up with a mop and bucket just as the other student and I made to leave. The corridor was empty by this point, but it was still awful, and I was terrified at any minute another Year Seven group was going to come down here on their tour.

The other student turned out to be a Year Ten girl, who kindly didn't ask why I was standing there with wet trousers and instead took me to where I needed to go. The reception staff gave me spare trousers, which didn't look too different from the ones I had on, and a plastic bag to take my other ones home in. By the time I got back to my tutor room, lessons had started, and Mr. Edwards had to escort me to my maths class. I ignored the looks and whispers as I came in, trying to hide the carrier bag behind my legs.

Fortunately, Tanya had saved a seat for me and when I sat down she reached over and squeezed my hand.

"What happened?" she whispered.

"They gave me some spare trousers. That was it."

"You didn't tell Mr. Edwards it was Chloe and Esther?"

At the mention of their names I looked around, trying to find them. Chloe, Esther, and Annabel were at a table of four, the other seat occupied by a boy with his head already on the desk. They caught me looking and grinned, miming holding their noses.

"No," I mumbled to Tanya. "I didn't want to be a snitch. But I should have. And why didn't you help me?"

"I'm sorry." She squeezed my hand again. "Really I am, Poppy. It won't happen again. We'll stick together from now on."

It's not the first day I wanted. Tanya kept to her word, ignoring the three girls when they tried to talk to her, and even telling Esther to be quiet when she tried to bring up what had happened earlier. But once I got home, holding that stupid carrier bag, I was exhausted.

I pretty much just wanted to come straight upstairs and write this all down in here, but there was no getting past Mum and Dad that easily.

Ugh, parents, right? I know they mean well and whatever but sometimes you just want to do your own thing and they're always bothering you. Making you stay downstairs and spend time with them. Eating every meal with them and you better make sure everything is off your plate! Even if you're upset. But don't tell them you're upset because then that's all you're gonna talk about all night.

Look, I love Mum and Dad, I really do. They can just be a bit much, alright?

They were cooking dinner when I walked through to the kitchen, dumping my bags by the island counter and hopping on a stool. I knew there was no point in going straight upstairs, because one of them would be after me, asking what was wrong, why wasn't I coming in to say hello, especially as it was my first day. Mum was peeling potatoes while Dad watched a saucepan, but they both stopped what they were doing and gave me a big hug when they saw me. Even my little sister, Wendy, normally stuck in her own imaginary world, heaved herself off the sofa in the corner and joined in the embrace. Seeing her in her uniform, my primary school's colours, made me wistful and a bit emotional.

I wish I could go back.

No, I don't! I'm not going to cross that out because it'll make the page look messy, but I don't mean that. I don't even know why I wrote it. Honestly, I'm getting ridiculous over one stupid moment.

"How was your first day of secondary school, lovely?" Mum asked, returning to her potatoes. "We're making you your favourite tonight to celebrate, homemade chips and Dad's macaroni cheese."

"Delicious," I said automatically. "Thank you both."

Nothing gets past my parents though.

Dad gestured his wooden spoon at me. "You didn't answer the question. How was school? Were the teachers nice? Did you make any new friends? Did you get to see the Art department?"

Embarrassing moment number two incoming.

"What's this?" Wendy picked up the carrier bag and peered inside. "Why do you have a smelly pair of trousers in there?"

"What?" Mum came to check and I wanted the stool to swallow me whole. "Poppy, what's this?" She took a proper look at me and realised. "You're wearing different trousers. What happened?"

"Some Capri-Sun spilled on me, that's all," I said. "So the school gave me trousers from PE."

"I can still smell it!" Mum took the trousers out, letting the carrier bag fall to the ground, and sniffed hard. "They're even still a bit damp. Just how much spilt on you? This looks like the whole packet!"

Wendy raised her eyebrow. She's getting good at it. She always likes that she can do something I can't. "How do you spill a Capri-Sun?"

"My thoughts exactly." Mum put the trousers in the washing machine, then leaned over the kitchen island to focus on me. "Someone hasn't done this deliberately, have they?"

"No, Mum!" I snapped, hating seeing her eyes widen with hurt. "I told you it was an accident. That's it. My day was fine, okay? Just fine."

"Poppy—" Mum reached across for me but I stood, pushing the stool out.

"Just leave me alone." I ran from the kitchen, hurrying up the stairs and into the safety of my bedroom.

And that's where I am now, writing in you, diary. I know they'll come in soon. I know they'll comfort me, make me laugh, make everything a bit better. But I just want these few minutes to myself.

It's silly. Everything will be fine.

Oh God, that's them knocking now. Here comes the comfort brigade.

JUNE 27, 2007

Dear Diary,

First of all, I know it's been practically a whole year since I last wrote in this. I'm sorry, okay? Things have been . . . hard.

And when things get hard, what do I do? I paint. I'm not some writer. This was meant to be a notebook for writing in about all the cool things about secondary school. All the parties I was going to be invited to. All the amazing friends I was going to make.

Yeah, that didn't happen.

So I've been doing a lot of painting. And hey, at least that's going well. I'm definitely the best at art in my year and to be honest probably in the whole school. And I'm not bragging, this is what my art teachers have said to me, and I've seen my artwork on display next to some of the older year groups and I'm sorry but mine is better.

Does that make me seem totally arrogant? I don't mean to be. I promise it's just this one thing. Art is the only thing making me happy right now, so let me brag about it just a little please. Otherwise I think I might go completely mad. Maybe I already am? This entire diary entry so far has been nothing but craziness.

The art department is this area on the ground floor of the school tucked at the back, so unless you're going there for a lesson you'd totally miss it. But as you start walking down the corridor towards it, you see all these amazing paintings and sculptures that other students have made over the years. One of my paintings is there now too, next to some sixth formers, which makes me feel pretty special. It's definitely one of my more tame ones, just a nice field and some girls playing in the grass. The teachers have already told me I go a little bit too experimental on some of my pieces, but I can't help my mode of expression, or so I tell them, which I think sounds very grown up and important, like I'm a real artist.

There are three art teachers, but my favourite is Miss Wersham, because she's young and pretty and is always so impressed with anything I do, even if she also tells me to calm it down sometimes. She showed me how to do shading with an ordinary pencil so that it looks really realistic, and I've been practising ever since. The other week I drew a picture of a baby bird fallen from its nest and the mother bird looking for it, and she told me although I had really started to get the technique down, it was a bit too sad to put up for display. Which, I mean, honestly! Isn't art meant to be about emotion?

She put Ollie's attempt up, his silly little drawing of a rocket ship blasting off into space. He was there when she was showing me the pencil technique and of course had to have a go. Ollie Turner is a boy in my art class. He's alright, he's definitely really good at art too, but he's not as good as me. I'm the best. He has to settle for being second and I think it really annoys him, because he looked so smug when Miss Wersham put his up and not mine. I couldn't help telling him that was because although mine was "brilliant" (which I promise Miss Wersham really said!) it was too emotional and sad for display. It would upset people.

I quite like that idea, that my talent would produce an emotion from people. Don't the best artists do that? Make people sad.

And anyway, I am sad! I'm replicating my truth onto art! Which is the whole reason why I'm writing in here again.

So. The big news. The horrible news. The reason why I haven't been writing in here because I kept waiting for her to turn around and come back to me, because surely seven whole years of friendship means more than some stupid girls who poured stupid Capri-Sun all over me on the first day.

But I know for sure now. So there's no hiding it anymore.

Tanya and I aren't best friends. She's gone off with Annabel and Chloe, and Esther. And I have no one.

It was so gradual I didn't even notice at first. Tanya got moved to sit by Annabel in the seating plan for loads of our subjects, because their surnames are close together in the alphabet. So obviously they had to talk to each other because they were doing the same work.

As the weeks went by, though, Tanya started being busy after school, when we used to hang out every day. It became once a week, once every two weeks, and then not at all, with her saying her mum told her she had to take school more seriously now she was in secondary so she didn't have time to go out.

I'm not stupid. I suspected that wasn't true. I thought maybe some kids at school had invited her to things and she felt too bad to tell me about them. We still hung out every break and lunch, until after Christmas I caught a bad cold and had to be off for three days. When I came back, expecting Tanya to be bored to death without me, I found her having fun and gossiping with Annabel, Chloe, and Esther, and she very reluctantly came back to sit with me.

That lasted a couple more weeks, and then she stopped hanging out with me at all. And worse, that was when she started to join in with all their teasing.

Yeah. That hasn't stopped. That wasn't just a first day joke. Every day they make fun of me. Sometimes I pretend to be sick to stay home from school just to get away from them, but Mum is starting to get suspicious now.

At lunchtimes I often tried to stay in Miss Wersham's room, and she was okay with this at first, but when it started to become every day, even she got tired of me. It didn't help that Ollie and some of the other arty kids thought I was getting extra help and that it was some kind of art lunch club, so she had to tell us all to leave.

Anyway. Let's get to the reason I'm writing in you now. My birthday disaster.

When my birthday rolled around, in late June, Tanya and I had stopped talking all together. But the problem was my parents didn't know that. You're not going to tell your parents you've suddenly become a total loser, are you? It was better for them not to know. But that meant that despite my best efforts at pleading with them, they insisted on inviting Tanya to my party.

"You have to invite Tanya, she's your best friend," Mum said, picking up the phone to give Tanya's mum a call.

"Please," I begged her. "I just want it to be family. Me, Wendy, you, and Dad. That would be nice."

"Nonsense," she replied, and that was that.

Which was why, when we sat at the kitchen table with my birthday spread, waiting for Tanya, I couldn't bear it. The time ticked by and soon she wasn't just ten minutes late, she was half an hour.

It's embarrassing for me to even write this, but part of me did think she might just show up. It was my birthday. She didn't have to tell anyone. I wouldn't. It could have been like old times.

Last year we went to a water park together and then had a sleepover at my house, eating takeaway pizza as a massive treat. We made friendship bracelets and said we'd be best friends forever.

Spoilers, but she didn't show up.

"This isn't like Tanya," Mum said with a frown, checking her watch for the third time. "I wonder if something's happened."

"Tanya hasn't been here in forever," Wendy muttered.

I haven't told Wendy any of what's been going on, but she's perceptive. I know that Mum and Dad think she's some kind of child genius, and they're forever stressing that they aren't doing enough for her when she already has private lessons in violin, Mandarin, and advanced maths. She snuck a sandwich when Mum wasn't looking and stuffed it in her mouth, shrugging her shoulders at me.

It was true, though. The last time Tanya came round was in the Easter holidays for a sleepover, and that was only because Tanya's mum had a work event that took her to Manchester. It was awkward the entire time, especially when Annabel, Chloe, and Esther teased me about my house later that week based on what Tanya had told them.

"Let's just eat," I said. "I don't want all of this to go to waste."

Mum and Dad had gone to maximum effort to celebrate me turning twelve. There was enough there to feed an entire kingdom.

As if it couldn't get worse, Mum decided to choose chaos.

"Well, hold on now, I'll just give Jane a ring."

Tanya's mum.

I tried begging her to stop, honest I did. "Mum, don't! It's fine."

She ignored me, taking the house phone and dialling Tanya's home number. She knew it off by heart, that's how close we used to be. She'd always have to ring there to ask whether I'd be home for tea.

"Hi, Jane, is that you? It's Sue, Poppy's mum." She turned her back to me as I mimed for her to hang up. "We're just at Poppy's birthday party and were wondering if Tanya had left yet. We've been waiting for her, you see, and—what's that?"

I closed my eyes.

"When was she meant to do that? No one has called the phone this morning." Mum looked back at me. "Right. I see. Well, thank you, Jane. No, thank you, I'll pass that along. All the best." She hung up the phone and sighed.

"Well?" Dad said. "Is Tanya coming?"

"No." Mum put the phone back in its place and sat down. "Apparently there's been some kind of mix-up. She can't make it today after all. But Jane told me to tell you she wishes you a happy birthday, and there's a card in the post for you. Now, let's get started, shall we?"

I don't know what Jane said, but later, when I checked Facebook, I saw the truth for myself.

Having the greatest time today with my best friends!

Tanya had posted a photograph, tagging Annabel, Chloe, and Esther, of the four of them hanging out together at the park eating ice creams. They were all beaming at the camera, arms round each other, the sun shining behind them.

It was such a simple day out. Nothing special. Just ice creams in the park. And Tanya couldn't even give that up for me on my birthday, after everything.

I got under the covers and cried. I didn't think it would be fine in the end. I just cried and cried and never wanted to face the world ever again.

Sorry about the smudges. I didn't mean to cry writing this. I thought writing things out was meant to be good for you? That's a total lie, then.

Still. At least I can pretend you're my friend, diary. It reminds me of Anne Frank's diary, her dedicated and much more sophisticated writings to "Kitty." I don't think I want to name you though.

That will just make me feel even more alone.

TEN

Annabel

I can't believe she'd push me like that, right near the edge of the cliff.

The atmosphere is awkward on the way back down the mountain, but Poppy seems determined to pretend there isn't a problem. I don't care if there was no way I'd fall—she was tempting fate, making me scared. All the way down she kept chatting in this loud, obnoxious way, as if she had no idea I was still upset, and now we're out on the beach, it's as if the whole morning has been forgotten about.

"It's the perfect time to sunbathe, don't you think?" Poppy says, as we gather by the sun loungers. "I'll make us some margaritas, and we can just relax here for an hour or so before lunch."

I plaster a smile on my face, knowing it must look forced. "That sounds great." I'm not going to be the one who ruins the hen party. I'll just suck it up and chalk it down to her warped sense of humour. "I'm going to go and have a shower. I'm all sweaty from the climb."

"I'll walk back with you," Poppy says. "I need to come make the drinks anyway."

Great. We leave the others to flop down on the sun loungers (Chloe repositioning hers out from under the shade of palm trees onto the open sand) and head back towards the main lodge. It's much warmer than this morning. I'll be grateful to get in the shower. My face feels slimy and my hair is beginning to stick to my temples.

At first, I think we're just going to walk along in silence, which would be preferable, but Poppy reaches out and grabs my arm, giving it a squeeze.

"How are you doing?" she asks.

"Fine. Like I said, I'm just feeling a bit sweaty." I try to shake her hand off my arm, but her grip is firm.

"You're still upset about that push, aren't you?" She runs her free hand through her hair, then releases me. "I was messing around. I'm sorry."

Walking side by side like this, I can't catch her eye to see if she's being genuine. But she sounds sincere enough, so I weaken. "No, I'm sorry. I'm being silly about it. How were you meant to know I'd take it so seriously?"

"I should have realised. We can't joke around like we used to. It's been ten years, after all."

My breathing becomes shallow. It's not the first time she's brought up the past, even though she keeps insisting she wants to move on from it.

"You're right," I say. "It's been a long time. We're getting to know each other again."

We reach the decking, and she stops, ready to head inside the main lodge and make the cocktails. No one seems bothered that it's barely midday, but I suppose it is meant to be a hen party.

"Don't take too long, Annabel," she calls as I walk away. "I don't want you to miss out on a single thing."

In response I wave my hand at her. I'm grateful for the shade the lodge brings as I head round the back towards my hut. Part of me wants to turn round and ask Poppy for my phone to look through, just to see if Andrew has sent me any messages, but something tells me she wouldn't be so receptive about that.

Reaching the little porch of my hut, I realise the front door is open. Barely noticeable, the tiniest of cracks, but open all the same.

I definitely closed it when I went out this morning.

Didn't I?

I try the door, opening it wide and then shutting it, just in case it doesn't close properly. But it closes with a distinct snap, a noise I'm sure is familiar from earlier. There's nothing out of the ordinary when I head inside, no sign that anyone else has been in here. It looks just as I left it, hair products and makeup strewn about on the chest of drawers, and my clothes piled up in my open suitcase, waiting to be unpacked properly. The painting still looms over the room, reminding me I have to ask Poppy if she painted it after all.

The shower splutters as I switch it on, none of the power from this morning. A slow trickle is all that comes out, occasionally coughing out large splashes. It also doesn't get any hotter than lukewarm at best.

"For God's sake," I mutter. I know we're on an island in the middle of the Caribbean but you'd think five-star luxury would lend you some basic facilities. Perhaps the supply works on a timed basis, giving more in the mornings. How am I meant to know? I deal with it as best I can, the water painstakingly making its way down my body, and end up coming out feeling cold in this tropical heat.

It's taken so long I'm surprised Poppy hasn't come searching for me. But this time to myself has been desperately needed. It's odd to go from spending so much time by myself at home to being surrounded by four women every second of the day. I miss Andrew as well, even though he's hardly ever home.

There's an awful dark blue sequined top Andrew bought me last Christmas that I packed with me. Don't ask me why I brought it. I've worn the thing once at Christmas drinks that very evening, it's not my style at all. I guess it reminds me of him. Maybe I'll put it on just to feel a bit closer to home.

I put back on the white shorts I was wearing earlier, and swap out my boots for some matching sandals, then rummage around for the top. I know it's in here somewhere, but I end up taking out all my clothes and putting them away in the drawers to find it. Eventually I reach the bottom of my suitcase, and I'm left with some tights and an old nightie.

The top isn't in here.

I check again, going back through the clothes I've already put away, and even look around the room and under the bed in case it's magically ended up there. But there's nothing, not even a forgotten sock from a previous guest. The room is spotless, and my suitcase is empty.

My mind goes back to the open door when I first arrived. Did someone come in? But why would someone—and it would have to be one of those four—come in and take nothing but a blue sparkly top that's quite frankly hideous? They'd have to have gone digging through all my clothes to pull it out. There's just no sense to it.

Surely Esther wouldn't do something as petty as this, no matter what argument we had earlier. It's not her style to be childish. She's much more upfront about things when they bother her. Hence why we had the disagreement in the first place.

No, I had to have not packed it after all. Even though I remember putting it out on my bed at home, ready to bring with me. Maybe it fell out at some point before I zipped up the case. It's probably lying on the bedroom floor, Andrew walking past it every morning and evening and not realising he has the ability to bend down and pick it up.

Still though. I frown, and pick out a different top.

I'm heading past the main lodge again when I see Chloe and Tanya on the lawn, standing together clutching towels.

I thought they were all sunbathing? Their heads are close, expressions serious.

They're so distracted I manage to catch the tail end of their conversation, freezing when I hear my name.

"Annabel doesn't know still, so if you would stop making it obvious—"

"You have to tell her."

"Think about what I could tell her about you, why don't you?"

"That's not fair." Tanya turns at this, and catches me. Her face flushes. "Annabel!"

Chloe barks out a high-pitched laugh, but she's fooling no one. A muscle twitches in her jaw and she can't quite meet my eye. "What are you lurking about for?"

Their expressions are filled with worry. They don't know what I've heard. They don't know how long I've been standing there.

"What are you two talking about?" I ask, as if I'm none the wiser. "You didn't even notice me coming up behind you."

"Nothing," Chloe says, but she's too quick, too guarded.

"We were talking about Poppy, if you must know," Tanya says, to which Chloe nods. "We're not sure about her."

They're lying, but I take the bait. I'm not getting an answer from them right now. "What do you mean, you're not sure about her?"

"This whole trip." Tanya shrugs. "I don't know. The way she acted on the cliff earlier, that push. And then the whole orange juice fiasco this morning. Are we sure she's not doing these things deliberately?"

"We've got to stick together," Chloe says. "The four of us against only one of her. Even if she is messing with us, she can't do anything too bad."

I wonder if Poppy stole the top from my suitcase. But why? What would be the point?

"The four of us against only one of her," Tanya echoes, as if we're in some kind of cult.

"I don't know," I say. "She did apologise to me when I was coming back here. I think she just doesn't know how to act around friends."

"Are we friends with her?" Chloe smirks. "Would any of us have shown up to this if it was a weekend in Brighton?"

"Come on." I'm irritated by the pair of them and can't bear to be in just their company a second longer. "Poppy will be wondering where I got to."

"I'll be with you in a second," Chloe says.

Poppy and Esther are lying in the sun when we get back to the beach, clearly not concerned about my whereabouts at all. Two pitchers of margarita, and a couple of plates of fruit, are nestled in the shade. The two of them sit up when Tanya and I come and join them, the harsh glare of the sun hitting the back of my neck and making me wish I'd put more sun cream on.

"Feeling better?" Esther asks, and I nod.

It's good to lie here in the sun, forgetting about everything. But I can't shake this uncomfortable feeling in my stomach, and I'm not even sure what it's for. Poppy's odd behaviour, pushing me on the summit? The missing top? Chloe and Tanya having some kind of secret conference about me? I place a hand on my tummy to try and calm myself, but it doesn't work.

And then the four of us hear Chloe scream.

ELEVEN

Chloe

MAY 19, 2023

My makeup is ruined. Destroyed. Every bottle of foundation, smashed onto the floor and spilled. Even my eyebrow pencils have been snapped. My expensive eyeshadow palette has fallen face-first, each section ruined. Behind the table, the window is wide open, and the curtains twitch in the breeze.

I can't believe it. I've never been so stupid in my life. All of this, hundreds of pounds' worth, ruined because I put them on the end table near the window, and a strong breeze must have blown them all over.

"Chloe?" Esther comes rushing in.

Even though I know what happened, I can't help but shriek at her. "Did you do this? Which one of you did this? Everything is ruined!"

"What are you talking about?" She looks past me and sees the mess on the floor. "Oh my God."

"What the hell am I supposed to do now? This is all I brought with me. All that's left is some mascara and powder. That's useless!"

"You can borrow our makeup," Esther says, bending down and beginning to pick up the pieces. "Or we can salvage some of this."

"Don't bother," I snap, knowing it's not her fault but past caring.

"There's no point. Might as well just burn some money too, while I'm at it."

"How could this have happened?"

"Either one of you decided to ruin my life, or it must have been the stupid window!" I point to it, then sink down on the bed, tears streaming down my face. "The wind must have knocked them all off. I'm such an idiot."

"The wind?" Esther places the smashed pieces back on the table, then studies the window with a frown. "It hasn't been that windy today, has it?"

Now that she's mentioned it, it hasn't. The makeup was definitely still in place this morning, I bloody put a load on. And the weather has been calm all day.

"Maybe the wind gets funneled here somehow," Esther murmurs, more to herself than me. "It creates a stronger force and that's what knocked your makeup off."

"Maybe." But now I'm doubtful. Would one of the others really smash my makeup?

I'm thinking of Poppy instantly. She didn't like that bi comment I made yesterday, I know it. She's too sensitive, as most people are nowadays. And it's hardly my fault she is what she is.

Esther heads out, then returns a couple of minutes later with a wet sponge and some kitchen towel. "Here," she says, getting to work cleaning the floor. "Not much we can do now, but I'd shut that window if I were you."

"Right, thanks." I close it tight, then sit on the bed again as Esther cleans my floor. "You don't need to do that."

"I wanted to talk to you anyway," she says, which makes me nervous. She finishes the floor, then comes and sits on the edge of the bed, face solemn.

"What is it?"

"You'd tell me if there was something going on, wouldn't you?"

What does she know? I try to keep my face impartial, but I know I'm a shit actress. My heart starts pounding.

"What are you talking about?" I say. Even I can hear the false lightness in my tone.

"With Tanya. I think there's something wrong."

Tanya. She's talking about Tanya. It takes everything in me not to breathe a sigh of relief. Thank God.

"I haven't noticed anything," I say, lying to her face.

"You two have been talking a lot lately." She peers at me, and seems on edge herself. Does *she* know something about Tanya and is wondering whether I do too? Are we both thinking about the same thing? "She hasn't told you anything?"

"She's been a bit off recently, but I don't know if I can talk about that."

"She's been going through a lot. And she looks so ill now, like she's really struggling." Esther shakes her head. "Never mind."

Damn.

"I think you do know something," I venture. "I might know something myself. Related to how ill she is."

She frowns at that. "Is this about six months ago?"

Six months ago? Is she talking about the party?

She sighs. "Don't worry." Is it just me or does she sound relieved?

"We can talk about it if you want," I say hopefully.

But she's firm. "No. It's better unsaid."

She's frustratingly vague, but I can tell I'm not going to get anything else out of her. "You seem stressed yourself, you know."

She looks up, startled. "I'm fine."

I meant it as a throwaway comment, but the more I think about it the more I realise it's true. She's been standoffish and odd, not like the normal Esther at all. Not that she's particularly friendly to start with, but she's often the one member of the group who likes to make sure everyone is okay. The secret keeper. It must be annoying her to no end that I know something she doesn't about Tanya.

But I'm not about to blab. Tanya knows secrets of mine as well, and I can't have her spilling those in revenge.

"You'd say if there was anything wrong, wouldn't you?" I pull what I hope is a sympathetic-looking face.

"Of course." She shrugs, then seems determined to change the topic. "Are you going to tell the others about what happened with your makeup?"

"No point." It's not like they had anything to do with it. And even if they did, they're not going to come right out and say so.

"It could have been Poppy," Esther whispers, looking around her shoulder at the open doorway to check no one is listening. "She could have come and knocked them over. She was making margaritas for ages."

"Don't be silly," I say, even though I had the same thought. I lean in closer, my voice a whisper too. "She is odd, isn't she?"

"She was talking about what she had planned this afternoon. Sounded very excited, but wouldn't give us specific details."

"I think she's enjoying making us uncomfortable, you know."

"I agree. God, come on, they'll all start coming over if we're here any longer. I said I'd check on you after you screamed so they're probably wondering if we've both been murdered now."

"There's no one else on the island," I point out. "It'd have to be one of them."

"True." Esther laughs. "But I wouldn't put it past them. Let's go."

We head out the door, giggling, and collide straight into Poppy, who is standing just outside. She doesn't look caught out, even though she's clearly been eavesdropping. Instead, she stands there brazen as anything, arms folded, a smile on her face.

"Jesus, you frightened the life out of me," I say. "Have you been listening to our conversation?"

"I was just coming along to see if you were alright," she says. "What was all that screaming about?"

"My makeup was smashed all along the floor," I tell her, watching for her reaction.

She raises her eyebrows, but there's no real shock there. "Oh dear, how did that happen?"

"Must have been the wind," I say. "No one would have done it deliberately."

"Must have been."

"Lunch, then?" Esther says. She massages the back of her neck with her hand, and I notice some horrible ringed bruises on her wrist, as if someone has grabbed her too hard. She catches me looking and drops her hand immediately.

Poppy stands there pleasantly enough. I can't believe how assured she is. She's been caught out snooping on us, but she doesn't seem bothered at all. If anything, she's challenging us, begging us to confront her, and for some reason we're too afraid to. Which is so odd. It's Poppy Greer. Confronting her is our old pastime. It's funny how things change.

She grins at us. "I can't wait to tell you guys what I have planned this afternoon. It's going to be a day to remember."

TWELVE

Tanya

MAY 19, 2023

Lunch lasts forever. The five of us are sitting around the same table where we ate breakfast, and I find myself sitting as far away from Poppy as possible to avoid a repeat of the orange juice incident. Annabel has been off since we came back down from the cliff, and even Chloe is in a bad mood. Poppy keeps up the pretence that we're all having a fantastic time, chatting about funny anecdotes from her times at work, and all of us respond with just enough enthusiasm.

Finally, Poppy disappears into the main lodge and comes back with a huge, expensive-looking bottle of gin and a couple of envelopes. Her eyes are lit with excitement. This must be her fun scheme for this afternoon that she's kept referencing.

"Are we doing shots until we pass out?" Chloe quips. "That's a game I could get behind."

Poppy laughs. "Not quite. Though this gin is incredible. I've only had it once before because it's so costly, but trust me, ladies, when I say it is worth it."

"What are we doing then?" Annabel leans forward and tries to look at the two envelopes. One is peach, the other baby blue, but otherwise they're blank.

Poppy claps her hands together. "As part of my special day, you're all going to take part in a scavenger hunt."

"A scavenger hunt?" Esther looks unimpressed. "Like we're part of the Girl Guides or something?"

I'm as doubtful. Out of all the things I was expecting Poppy to say, that wasn't it. All of us traipsing around this island looking for things?

"I'm sure I don't have to explain the rules to you." Poppy beams a megawatt smile, choosing to ignore our lack of enthusiasm. "But whoever comes back with the most items will win this fabulous bottle of gin here, and also their choice of activity for this evening's entertainment."

"Can we win our phones back?" Chloe asks.

"Oh, don't be silly!" Poppy laughs again, a short bark that shuts Chloe up. "Now, there are five items all together, so I thought I'd split you four into two competing teams. Won't that be fun?"

"You're not coming with us?" I say.

"Well, of course not. I know where all the items are."

Good point. I glance at the others. It would make the most sense to pair with Chloe, as annoying as she is. I don't want her spending too much one-on-one time with anyone else, not with what she knows.

"I guess Chloe and I will—"

"Oh, I've already chosen your teams." Poppy hands me the peach envelope, and the baby blue to Annabel. "Esther and Chloe, you're together. And Annabel and Tanya."

Oh Jesus.

Chloe masks her look of horror well as Esther turns to face her, shrugging. Meanwhile, Annabel offers me a raised eyebrow. I know I've been odd with her recently, but I can't help it. Really, I would have wanted anyone but her, considering what I'm not telling her. But I fix a grin on my face, as if I'm pleased.

"Inside the envelopes is a clue to your first item," Poppy says. "I gave you different clues so you wouldn't all end up following one another. Another clue will be next to the item when you collect it. Be sure to look everywhere, and most importantly, have fun!"

She takes in our reluctant faces, and shakes her head in amusement. "Honestly, look at you four. You're on a private island, it's a beautiful day, and I'm giving you the chance to go exploring. What more could you ask for?"

"Another few hours of sunbathing," Chloe mutters. She's trying to catch my eye but I ignore her, opening the envelope with Annabel instead.

The clue is written in the same neat handwriting as the invitation.

> *I'm near the height of a dead man,*
> *Nestled within a bush,*
> *Come and find me if you can,*
> *I'm a delectable treat for a crush.*

"Nice rhyme," I say.

It comes out more sarcastic than I intended, and a flicker of something crosses Poppy's face. Anger? Irritation?

"I'm going to make this place look amazing for tonight," she says. "The four of you need to be on your way now. And no sharing clues!"

"Fine, fine." We wave goodbye to Chloe and Esther, who head off in the opposite direction back towards the beach. Annabel and I head down the path that leads to the cliff. We don't turn back, but I'm certain Poppy is watching us go.

"The height of a dead man," I say as we round the main lodge and disappear out of sight. "Well, that's a pretty easy enough clue. Robin called the mountain here Deadman's Peak. It'll be around there somewhere, put in a bush."

Annabel nods. "Right. Whatever. Let's head there."

She's much less enthusiastic than this morning. Walking with her now, I realise just how little time we've ever spent together as a pair. Chloe has been to lots of my events solo for her Instagram career (for better or worse, considering what we now know about each other) and even Esther is easy enough to talk to, always wanting to make you comfortable. Annabel and I are the most distant of the four of us, and being put together now seems to really highlight how little we're able to talk to each other. At school I used to be afraid of Annabel. She had such a queen bee energy about her, so much confidence, style, and brains all wrapped up in a pretty exterior that she wasn't afraid to brag about. Every little scheme, every little plan of ours or event—that was Annabel, making sure everything went her way.

And when things didn't, we all knew about it. It's so easy to remember. Something about being on this island with Poppy has brought back memories of the past I don't really want to think about, but they're all flooding back now. I can imagine Annabel's temper if she finds out what I've been keeping from her. What Chloe has done.

Maybe Chloe and I aren't the only ones who will face her wrath. I still don't know what she and Esther were arguing about earlier. That's an odd one for sure. Esther is so amenable. What did Annabel do that got even her riled up? Something about Esther doing something for two years. What on earth is that about?

It's dark under the cover of the trees like this, walking towards the cliff. Although there's a path created either deliberately or through many footsteps over the years, the terrain is still bumpy in places, and at one point Annabel almost trips over, having to steady herself against a palm tree.

"This bloody island," she says. "It's not what I had in mind."

I know what she means. But the white sandy beaches, the clear ocean, all of that is breathtaking. We just didn't expect to be traversing through the rest of it, on some pointless mission.

"We might as well try to enjoy it," I say.

Annabel frowns. "Well, you are Poppy's biggest fan."

"It's been so long since we were together," I say, in an attempt to warm her to me. "We should meet up more often just the two of us."

"You seem off lately."

Because I can't bear you not knowing the truth. "I've been distracted." This, at least, is true as well. If Annabel knew what I'd been through in the past six months, we'd be having a very different conversation right now.

"How's Harry? London?" she asks, the dreaded questions.

"Oh, you know. Fine. How is home?"

"Fine."

We're both lying. Our answers are plastic, cheap and readily available without any prior thought. If I imagined Poppy's little getaway bringing the four of us closer together again, I imagined wrong.

The path begins to slope upwards, heading towards the summit, but a large bush on the right stops me in my tracks.

"This has got to be it."

I'm weirdly invested in this scavenger hunt, my heart thudding as I reach my hand into the bush, ignoring the brambles scratching at my arm.

"Is there something there?"

"Yes! A box. Look."

It's quite big, the size of a shoebox, but gift wrapped with a bow. There's a label on the front that says "Open Me" with a kiss, so the two of us sit on a stone nearby and unwrap the bow and lift the lid.

I almost drop it.

Inside, amongst pink tissue paper and another envelope, this time golden brown, is some lipstick. A very expensive brand.

We don't have to look underneath or open it to know what colour it's going to be, but we do it anyway.

Bright red.

"What the hell is Poppy playing at?" Annabel says, standing and running her fingers through her hair, a common nervous habit of hers. "Why would she make red lipstick of all things part of the scavenger hunt? She knows what we'll think when we see this."

The images come back to me as if it happened yesterday. The lipstick. Our laughter. The teasing that followed. Her humiliation.

"She's sick." Annabel's voice is tight with tension. "She's trying to get a reaction out of us. Well, it won't work."

"You're right." Fingers trembling, I open the envelope for the next clue.

"What are you doing?"

I look up to find Annabel's face white with anger. "What do you mean?"

"You're not seriously carrying on with her stupid game?"

"What other option do we have?" I take out the new clue. "We're on this island for three more days whether we like it or not. We might as well go along with it."

"If she's going to start dredging up the past when she claimed she was fine with it . . ." Annabel sighs, but the fight has gone out of her. "Alright. What does it say? And put that damn lid back on. I don't want to look at that stupid lipstick a moment longer."

Neither do I. I put the lid back on the box, glad it's out of sight. I have a bad feeling about the next clue.

Carry on through the trees,
Head towards the secret beach,
A beautiful scene that will please,
But don't be spooked if you hear me screech.

"She should stick to art and being a doctor," Annabel says, and I can't help smirking, the awkwardness between us easing a little. "Right. She must be on about that second beach we saw this morning from the cliff.

It might be carrying on down this path instead of heading up the mountain. Come on, and you can carry the box with the lipstick inside."

The walk through the middle of the island doesn't take long. Robin wasn't kidding when she said this place was tiny. But it's less travelled than everywhere else as plants sprout up in the middle of the path and several more bugs crawl around. Eventually, the path opens up again and, instead of squeezing through in single file between the trees, we're able to walk as a team as the smaller second beach becomes visible. It's nowhere near the size of the one we've been sunbathing on. Each end is easy to see, a hundred metres at most. In the middle of the sand, half submerged, is another gift box.

Annabel picks it up, but hesitates in opening it.

We both know the lipstick is scratching the surface.

"What do you think the other two have found?" I ask, knowing that must be playing through her mind too.

"She wouldn't use the art exam, would she?"

My breath catches in my throat. When Poppy brought it up on the climb this morning I thought I was going to faint. She's planted it in our minds, and this scavenger hunt is like a sad tribute to everything leading up to that moment.

"Okay, maybe she wants us to apologise," I say. "Maybe that's what she's getting at here."

"But she said—"

"I know what she said. But then she gave us red lipstick in a gift box. If that isn't a direct hint, I don't know what is."

"What if she wants something from us? Like money?" Annabel looks panicked now.

I shake my head. "She's a doctor, she makes more money than us."

"Because I can't." She chews her lip. "I mean, Andrew controls the finances. I have no money of my own."

"Annabel, this isn't about money." Why is she so worried about that?

The thought seems to have come from nowhere. "Just open the box. Poppy is simply making a point. We'll go back and apologise, and that will be that."

She nods. "Sorry. I'm a bit all over the place. The push this morning, when I was already angry after—"

I wait, but she stops. "After your argument with Esther?" I say eventually.

She blinks, startled, and then her gaze hardens. "Esther told you about that?"

"I saw you from my hut," I admit, embarrassed. "You were, uh, pretty loud."

Her fingers play with the bow on the box, unravelling it. "What did you hear?"

It's hard not to pretend I heard more, but there's no way I can bluff something I have no clue about. I shrug my shoulders instead, hedging my bets. "Not much. You were upset about Morocco. Esther mentioned something about helping you for two years."

She studies me for a long moment, concern etched in her features. "That's right, I was upset about Morocco. I'd told Esther for years that I'd always wanted to go there. I was upset you'd all decided to go without me."

She's not telling the truth. It's her voice, higher pitched, as if she's at ease, when she's panicking inside. I'm not brilliant at reading people, but Annabel is an open book. She keeps pressing her lips together for something to do, and she stares straight down at the scavenger hunt item.

"It seemed like more than that," I venture. "Why would Esther be angry at you too?"

"Drop it, Tanya."

Above us, the sun is unrelenting, making us sweat. We need to get in the shade. I give in.

"Alright, forget I said anything. Open the next item."

What is it going to be? I watch as Annabel tosses the ribbon to the ground, and opens the box. For a second all I have to go on is her reaction. A look of confusion.

"She's fucking with us," Annabel says, and throws the box on the sand as well.

The item clatters out as the box lands. A green envelope sits waiting to be read.

Annabel is right. Poppy is messing with our heads.

Because this one is personal to me. I know it. She remembers what I did to her when she turned twelve, ignoring her and hanging out with the others.

"A party hat, like from children's birthdays," Annabel says. "Just what is Poppy doing?"

That's what I'm starting to wonder.

She invited us all here for a reason. We're not just going to enjoy a holiday and then go home. I think we all knew that really.

The question is, how far is she willing to go?

THIRTEEN

Esther

A scavenger hunt. Like we're children again.

At the end of the beach, past the rock pools, is a large cave opening. It takes some getting to—hopping across rocks covered in lichen and seaweed, and at one point I think Chloe is going to slip and fall into the sea—but we make it onto the sand. It doesn't go too far, so only the very recesses of the cave are dark, and without our phones there's no hope of a light. There's something claustrophobic about being even this far in, still with an easy view of our escape route. I've taken my shoes off to avoid them getting wet, and I'm grateful I did now I'm over here, because the sand is wet and stodgy. A clear indication that the tide covers this place when it gets dark.

We don't have to search long. There's a rock a few metres in that sits at a high enough height to still be dry, and on top of it sits our second item for the scavenger hunt. It's in another gift-wrapped box, an odd sight amidst the stark wilderness of the cave surrounding it.

The acoustics in here are strange. Every step we take, particularly those by Chloe, who's still wearing her boots, is echoed back, as if someone is following us. It's cold in here, and from above some kind of water drips down in various places. The cave is a world away from the hot paradise of the rest of the island, and even though I'm grateful for the respite from the sun, the longer we're in here the more I worry that the tide is creeping behind us, ready to catch us unawares and strand us.

We're already uncomfortable enough as it is. The first item, hidden behind the sun loungers on the beach, was an empty Capri-Sun wrapper. Anyone else looking at that would think it was a bit of rubbish, not part of the game at all.

We knew better.

"What do you reckon this is, some red lippie?" Chloe says. She doesn't waste time, tearing the box open and tossing it on the sand, not seeming to care that the tide will sweep it away into the ocean.

Conscious of this, I pick it up, ready to bring it back with us. Chloe is holding the object out in front of her, confused.

"Well, I don't know what this is meant to mean. Do you?"

The cave echoes her last two words back at me: *Do you? Do you?*

She's holding a hand mirror, but the mirror part has been smashed and broken, a few shards remaining. It seems expensive. There are diamantes down the handle, and it's made from real wood, painted white.

"Maybe she's referring to when we—"

"This is stupid." Cutting me off, Chloe hands me the mirror and I put it back in the box. "If she's going to be playing games like this I think we should just double down."

"Double down?"

"Get back there and pretend like we just enjoyed it. Like we have no idea what she was trying to do with this shit."

"I don't know." I'm torn. Would it just be easier if we apologised after all, even if we still think it was a bit of fun that ended up going too far?

We head for the destination of the final item, which seems to be in the main lodge itself, where Poppy is staying. As we walk back out of and across the rocks, the harshness of the sun hurts my eyes for a second. It's amazing how dark and damp that cave was in comparison.

"Deadman's Bay was a bit of a giveaway," Chloe says as we walk down the beach. "Do you think she chose it deliberately?"

"She's hardly going to make us dead men."

Chloe laughs. "Relax, Esther. We need to enjoy this for what it is—a game. And if Poppy wants to play one, we'll show her she messed with the wrong women."

I think about Poppy now. She's changed so much. Strong and sure of herself, words I never would have used to describe her in the past. After everything we put her through, I don't think any of us have appreciated just how brave she is to see us all again, all by herself, in this isolated location. Of course she's been odd; how could she not be?

"I'm tired of playing games," I say, and for once I'm telling the truth.

Chloe notes the seriousness of my tone and raises an eyebrow. "What's going on with you, anyway? You refused to tell me earlier."

I'm not as good an actress as I thought. Not as good as Tanya, anyway. "Nothing really."

"Well, that's not true," Chloe says, blunt as ever. "You've been acting odd since we got here. No, since before we got here. You barely talk to any of us anymore, and don't say it's because of work, because you've managed just fine without your phone today and yesterday."

I can't breathe properly. "It's nothing."

Chloe rounds on me, stopping me in my tracks. For once, her expression is concerned. "You know, you can talk to me about it. I won't tell the others."

I'm almost about to tell her. Something about getting it all off my chest seems so relieving. But then I see it, the hint of excitement behind her eyes, the idea that she might know something the others don't.

She sees this as gossip, pure and simple.

I close up again. "Leave it, Chloe. We need to get moving and find this last thing."

The contrast in temperature after being in the cave is starting to take its toll. Sweat sticks to my upper lip no matter how many times I wipe it away. Poppy is nowhere to be seen as we hurry across the lawn, but she's decorated the place for tonight. More banners are up, balloons are littered everywhere, and the table is set up with drinks and canapes. The prize for the winners of the scavenger hunt, the bottle of gin, is in pride of place at the centre of the table. The CD player is also on, old nineties tunes adding some home comforts to the island.

The door to the lodge is already ajar, so we think we've been beat, but when we get inside the final item is still sitting on the kitchen table, untouched.

It's huge. So big, in fact, a sinking feeling hits my stomach and I can hear my heart in my throat.

"Jesus, that looks like . . ." Chloe can't finish.

"Get it over with."

Tanya's voice startles us both from behind. She and Annabel walk through the door and shut it behind them. All four of us are in the kitchen now. I realise that ahead, Poppy's bedroom door is closed, and wonder if she's in there right now, listening to us.

"Poppy is round by the cliff," Annabel says, as if reading my mind. "We bumped into her on our way back."

"What's she doing out there?" Chloe asks, frowning.

"Does it matter? Look at this thing." Tanya folds her arms. "What did you two get on your little scavenger hunt? We had a birthday party hat and red lipstick."

Shit. So there was lipstick. Chloe widens her eyes at me.

"A Capri-Sun wrapper and a broken hand mirror."

Annabel sighs. "I knew it. This is all about what we did to her."

We all stare at the box in front of us.

"So this has to be—well." I start undoing the bow, aware of my trembling hands. "I think we all know what it is."

Tanya makes a groaning sound. "God, just get it over with."

I open it up, and we have our fears confirmed.

It's a canvas. There's a painting on it, but it's hard to see what exactly. It almost looks like the four of us—there are definitely four distinct figures with similar hair.

But it has been destroyed. Someone has thrown black paint over the top of it, and punched holes in the fabric.

I think I'm going to be sick.

"Dredging up the past is so unnecessary." Annabel waves her hand. "She thinks she's being clever here, but it's just pathetic."

She sounds confident enough, but there's a shake to her voice that betrays her act. I cover the canvas with its wrapping again and we stand awkwardly, not sure what to do next.

"I guess we'll go find her now," I say.

Chloe shrugs. "We could just sack this all off and head to the beach. Grab some of the alcohol and food along the way and have our own party."

"That's a bit awkward." Tanya rubs the back of her neck again and again, a stress response. "Maybe we *should* just talk about it. She wants to."

"She wants to fuck with us," Chloe says. "This isn't how you start a conversation. It's how you start a war."

Typical Chloe, always heading for the nuclear option. She's always been the most reckless of the four of us, never one to plan ahead. Back in school she was the one who'd do the most impulsive things to Poppy, like tripping her up in the corridor, offering to hand out work from the teacher and then making sure Poppy's was dropped, or scrunched up, or lost. She didn't have the brains, or the energy, for anything more thought-out. Even in her adulthood she still makes stupid decisions.

The others surprise me though. Tanya grins, as if she agrees, and even Annabel has perked up. I'm the only one who sees this as what it probably is—a callout, but nothing too dramatic. We're just getting a taste of what we did to her, a reminder of our actions.

"Let's calm down a bit," I say. "It's a game at the end of the day."

"What's that saying?" Annabel says. "Play stupid games, win stupid prizes."

"Whatever happens, we'll stick together," Chloe says. "It's four against one. As it's always been."

Annabel nods. "Right. We're a team."

Are we? Even standing together right now, we're not quite united. Annabel is keeping secrets from Chloe and Tanya. Tanya is keeping secrets from Annabel and Chloe. I'm keeping secrets from them all. And I'm damn sure there are more secrets I'm not even aware of. We claim to be best friends, but I'm not sure that's true anymore. If it ever was.

In reality, we all stick together because we know no one else would ever understand what we did in the past. And the trouble is, we've all become so convinced that what we did was alright that we've accepted an invitation from the very woman we did it to.

"Esther?" Chloe presses. "You're with us, right?"

"Of course," I say.

I might not be a good actress, but I am an accomplished liar. I wouldn't trust these women with anything, and I don't trust them to have my back if it all goes south.

"Oh, brilliant!"

Poppy's warm voice makes us all jump. She's standing in the doorway; none of us heard her come in.

"You've found all the items." She claps her hands together. "Shall we quibble about who got here first? I think you're all winners."

"Poppy," I say. "You know what these items mean. What are you playing at?"

She smiles, unperturbed. "All will be explained soon enough. Come on, it's time to start the party. I want us all looking our best!"

"But, the painting . . ."

"I said you're going to have to wait." Poppy puts up a hand to stop me from saying anything else. "It's been ten years, after all. You can wait a short while longer."

Annabel chews her lip. "So this is all going to mean something?"

"Obviously." Poppy looks at her as if she's stupid. "I wouldn't have gone to all that effort otherwise."

"Why can't you just tell us now?" Chloe says. "This is all becoming a bit uncomfortable. I thought we were here for a good time." Her bravado from before has dampened somewhat. I don't know what it is, but Poppy seems to have a strange effect on us all. It's as if we're in awe of her, despite everything. Like we can't believe she's standing in front of us telling us what to do, and because of that we have to obey.

"And we are! That's why I want us to focus on partying tonight. We're going to give my hen party the celebration it deserves. There's alcohol of every variety for us to enjoy. Not to mention all the party food."

"If we're all winners, who decides what we'll do tonight?" Tanya asks.

"I think I've already decided what we're going to do tonight. And because I'm the bride, none of you can say no."

"We've figured that out already," Chloe mutters.

Poppy nods. "Yes, I see you have. And it's about time. Now come on, I want you all looking your best. Go and change into your best outfits."

For a second, I'm tempted to tell her no. Just give up on the whole thing and go to bed and refuse to participate. But there's a glint in her eye I don't like.

It's been ten years since we last saw Poppy Greer. We don't know what she's become in that time.

The others can sense it too, the shifting tide of the day's events.

We're at the whim of whatever this bride wants.

And maybe we deserve it.

FOURTEEN

Poppy

Dear Diary,

JULIAN DAVIS ASKED ME OUT!!!

No, really. As in, actually asked me out. On a date!

I'm going on a date!

I know what you're thinking. Me, going on a date? Poppy Greer, the biggest loser in the whole of Year Ten? The total saddo with no friends whatsoever, who spends most of her days walking around the corridors at lunch and break pretending she has somewhere to be instead of staying still and running into those four?

Well, it's true. I'm not kidding.

I've always wanted a boyfriend. It's been so unfair watching everyone else pair up and look so happy. The other day I was walking home and this older guy accidentally bumped into me and he was so tall, with this sweepy blond hair and bright blue eyes and for a second we stared at each other and I was convinced he secretly liked me. But then he carried on and didn't look back, even when I stopped at the end of the road to give him a chance to return and talk to me.

Those four have all had boyfriends. Yes, even Tanya. Well, why wouldn't they? They're so pretty. Annabel wears her blonde hair in all these complicated plaits with different clips that glitter and catch your attention, and she wears her skirt so short, showing off her tanned legs. Every boy watches Annabel when she walks down the corridor. And then Chloe is so bouncy and bright and obvious—I don't know how she gets away with unbuttoning her shirt so far down and wearing pink and black bras that can be seen so obviously underneath. She wears a ton of makeup too, even though we're not allowed, insisting happily to the teachers that she's all natural and rolling her eyes when their backs are turned. She's had three boyfriends this year alone! Every week there's a story about Chloe making out with one guy or another, and I'm so jealous I want to scream.

They're all so thin and gorgeous. Their hair is always in place, never looking greasy, and they just know how to act around boys. I make a total fool of myself.

Tanya walks past me now as if I don't exist, unless she's joining in with the other three teasing me. She wears her skirts short too, barely covering her bum, and she's started going to dancing classes so her legs look really toned. She used to be practically the same size as me.

I'm so fat. I tried shortening my skirt once but it just displayed my flabby legs even more and the four of them laughed so hard I had to tie my jumper around the back just to avoid everyone staring. And they weren't staring for the right reasons, let me tell you.

The only boy who ever speaks to me is Ollie from Art, and that's only when he wants some help. Now that we're both doing GCSE Art he's much more open to hearing my ideas because he knows that I get good marks. But he's not interested in me, not like that. I think he'd rather die than have people think that about us. I think most boys would.

I thought I'd never get a boyfriend. But I was wrong! So wrong.

I can't wait to shove it in everyone's faces at school on Monday!

They're not going to believe it when Julian and I walk in hand in hand after our amazing date tonight. Oh wow, I'm just thinking, what if his hands are sweaty? What if mine are sweaty? Everyone will be looking at us and I'm definitely going to go bright red. But surely we'll hold hands before then. Maybe even tonight.

What if we KISS?

I'm not sure I know how to do it. I've watched films obviously, and it always looks pretty gross to me, very wet and hard to breathe properly, and I've read in magazines what you're meant to do. But I've never actually done it. I bet Julian has done it dozens of times. Hundreds. Thousands.

We sit next to each other in Maths. All hail Mr. Holmes! He put us together as we're the top two and he said we should help each other get the best marks possible so we're ready for our GCSEs next year. I thought it was just me who enjoyed our chats in lesson, thinking he must have viewed me as the same gawky chubby weirdo everyone else does.

I have tried hard though. No more short skirts! That's not me. But I have new heeled shoes that those four haven't made fun of yet, and even though they told me my new haircut makes me look like a thrown-away Barbie doll, I think it looks quite nice. I've bleached my hair and it's cut in layers so it frames my face really well, hiding my round cheeks and double chin. I've also got new glasses, large black ones rather than the red small rectangular ones I had before that made my face look wide. I've even started wearing foundation, though I'm not sure I've got the colour right yet because Chloe said I looked like an Oompa-Loompa.

Esther and Annabel are in the same maths class too, and Esther even sits on the same table as me and Julian. She broke up with her boyfriend Aaron a month ago and she's definitely been trying to get with Julian ever since. She laughs in this stupid high-pitched voice at *all his jokes, even when he's not really trying to be funny, and because she sits opposite him she does this thing where she leans forward on her elbows, squeezing her boobs together to make sure he's looking at her cleavage. It's so embarrassing, but I definitely thought Julian liked it, because he never failed to stop what he was doing whenever she did that.*

He did tell her to stop once when Esther told me I was a know-it-all. He was quite sharp about it too, looking so disappointed in her.

He's always been nice to me, despite everything. He's not like the other boys, who ignore my entire existence and never invite me to parties. I overhear everyone on Mondays talking about the crazy activities that went on at the weekend, the drinking and wild antics, and I burn with jealousy. I always thought, when is it going to be my turn? I want to have fun too.

Well. My turn has finally arrived!

He texted me! Mr. Holmes encouraged us to swap numbers so that when it came to revision we'd have a buddy, but I didn't expect Julian to ask me for mine when Mr. Holmes moved on to help someone else.

"You actually want my number?" I said, dumbfounded.

"Sure," he said, so calm and casual, as if it was nothing. He has this amazing crinkly smile that shows off his dimples and he did it then, practically making me swoon like some heroine in a Jane Austen novel. "Why not? You kick my ass at algebra. I could use some help down the line."

Esther's face was in shock, mouth hanging open. She definitely fancies him. Pretty much everyone does, myself included! Who can resist those green eyes?

It was so satisfying to agree to his request in front of her. "That would be awesome. I mean, cool." I recited it to him twice to make sure he got it right.

"I'll put my number in your phone now," he said, reaching his hand out.

For a second his fingers brushed against mine, and oh my God when I tell you I think my heart took off like a rocket.

"Oh, no!" I said. I must have squealed it I was so nervous. "I mean, I'll just put it in. Just tell it to me like I did for you."

I couldn't let him see that my Contacts list held a grand total of five people: Mum, Dad, Wendy, Nan, and Tanya, whose number had gotten in only because she'd accidentally sent me it after informing all her contacts she had a new phone. It was too humiliating for anyone to know about. Not even any of the people in my GCSE Art class asked for my number, even though I knew they all hung out with each other on the weekends.

He raised his eyebrows (did I tell you he has a slight scar on his right eyebrow that breaks it up at the arch? it's so cool) but shrugged his shoulders and nodded. "Sure, no worries."

And now I have six contacts, and one of them is the best-looking boy in the whole school.

So when the text arrived yesterday, that name Julian *appearing on my screen, my heart started thudding, going into overdrive when I read the message. Here, let me write it out in full, because I still can't believe it:*

Hey Poppy, I thought you looked beautiful in Maths the other day. I can't stop thinking about you. Do you want to be my Valentine? Meet me at Greville Smith Park, in the dome, tomorrow night at 6pm.

Beautiful! Julian Davis thinks I'm beautiful! And look at how he texts. Like he's writing a love letter! It's so amazing.

And he wants to meet in the dome!

The dome is part of the children's playground at the park, but tucked towards the back. Normally, it is full of teenagers who want to have somewhere quiet to make out, because it is totally private. Inside, the dome opens up so you can stand quite easily, decorated with blue and white tiles that make me think of swimming pools.

I've been in the dome once before, during the day when little kids were about, just to see the fuss. Standing on my own in there it didn't feel special, especially when there was an empty bottle of vodka left behind. But I did pick it up and put it in the bin, earning me a judgemental glare from a mother with a pram who must have thought I'd been drinking in there.

If only! But it was nice even for a second to have someone believe I could be that kind of person. Someone who had friends and did daring things.

I texted back almost immediately saying I would love to, knowing I couldn't play it cool no matter how hard I tried. But he responded basically straight away! Look!

It's a date. See you tomorrow. Don't message me again. I like the air of suspense around our relationship.

A date? Our relationship? You better believe I blushed. It was so hard not to text him back and ask if this meant we were boyfriend and girlfriend. Don't worry, even I know that's completely crazy! We have to see if we like each other first.

Oh, I hope he likes me. Because I like him.

I told Mum and Dad and Wendy at dinner that evening.

"A date?" Dad growled, putting on a typical ferocious overbearing father voice, then grinning. He thinks he's so funny! "My daughter on her first date! Though I'm not sure I like the idea of you two

just hanging around in a park together. Can't he take you to the cinema or something?"

"That's just where we're meeting," I said, though I wasn't sure myself if that was going to be it. What did it matter though? "I'm sure we're going somewhere after."

"You be careful," Mum said, though I could tell underneath she was delighted. "I want you back no later than nine, you're only fourteen."

"Nine! That's so early."

"Ten then. But that's final."

"So what is this Julian like?" Dad asked. "Are you going to be as lucky as your mum was when she met me?"

"Dad," I groaned. "He's great. Really."

Wendy leaned forward. "He is smart too, Dad. He's in all the top sets. And he's super sporty, he's captain of the football team but also part of the basketball squad. He seems nice."

"That's wonderful," Mum said. "And of course our Poppy is worth ten of him, but I'm happy she's been asked out by someone so lovely."

"He's very popular with girls though." Wendy frowned, and I knew what she was thinking. Blunt as always, she had to voice it. "Why has he asked you out, Poppy? You're not exactly . . ."

"Not exactly what?" I challenged her.

"Wendy," Dad said, a warning tone in his voice.

"I was going to say popular," Wendy said with a pout. "It just seems a bit odd, that's all."

"Well, he doesn't judge people by how popular they are," I said. "Maybe you should learn the same lesson."

"Let's not argue over the dinner table," Mum said, ever the peacemaker. "We've got an apple crumble for dessert."

"I'll fetch it," Dad said, gathering the plates up. "Just consider me your waiter for the evening, ladies."

Wendy and I scowled at each other from across the table. It's not easy, having a sister like Wendy, let me tell you. She's only twelve but she's already surpassed me in pretty much everything. We're total opposites in how we look. I'm more mousy, she's dark. I have too many freckles, she barely has any at all. That includes height. I've inherited Mum's tiny legs while Wendy is like Dad, tall and graceful, and worst of all she's slim despite her eating the same as me. I could forgive the fact she's better looking than me, with straight white teeth while I suffer with braces, but the fact that she's smarter than me too is just unfair. She has loads of friends, and they're always in her room singing karaoke at the top of their lungs and just having fun.

So maybe now she's finally a little jealous that there's something I've done first. And with the best possible guy. I've had a guy show interest and ask me out. She hasn't had that yet for all her pretty dark hair and popularity.

But after dinner, she stopped me.

"You'll be alright, won't you?" she asked. "You won't do anything stupid?"

"I am capable of looking after myself." I sighed, determined to just ignore her when she grabbed me by the arm and made me look at her.

"I mean it," she said. "Don't do anything he wants just because he wants to, right?"

"Who's the older sister here?" I laughed. "I'll be fine. I'm used to being the butt of a joke anyway, so if he tries anything I'll recognise it in a second."

Wendy still looked worried. I know she sees most of it; we go to the same school. She knows I hide a lot of the truth from Mum and

Dad. They know I don't have any friends, of course they do, it's been years now. But they don't know just how badly I'm bullied, how every day it's a miracle if I'm not crying myself to sleep. Wendy sees the ostracisation, the laughter, the pranks. But, as if by unspoken agreement, she doesn't tell Mum and Dad about it.

As much as I'm jealous of her, she's still my little sister, and I love her to bits.

Anyway, I must rush off now. I have a fabulous date to go to! Will report back later how it all went.

LATER

Dear Diary,

I want to scribble out everything I wrote before.

No, I want to tear it up and throw all the little pieces in a bin.

I'm so stupid.

Of course no one is ever going to love me. Of course I'm never going to get a boyfriend. Who would want someone so ugly, so pathetic?

I hate myself. And I hate them.

I HATE THEM. I wish they were dead.

In the end, I arrived at the park too early. Of course I did, I'm the desperate sad one. I was never going to be late and play it cool, was I? My phone said it was a quarter to six, so I tried to slow my pace as I got to the dome. I couldn't see anyone else around, but he might have already been in there, so I ducked my head and made my way inside.

There was a small box with a note on top. The box was bow-wrapped with red silk, and there was no hint to what was inside, but the note had my name on.

Poppy, *it read, in neat handwriting I didn't recognise,* Wear this tonight to make yourself even more gorgeous. I'm taking you to a nice restaurant with my savings! Love, Julian x

Love! Julian wrote "love"! With heavy breaths, I unwrapped the bow and took the lid off the box, thinking it might have been a necklace or a bracelet. And he called me gorgeous, so I was ready to wear anything!

God. I need to stop crying and just write this. At least angrily stabbing the pen to paper makes me feel a bit better, because I can pretend the paper is them.

It wasn't jewellery. It was lipstick.

Proper lipstick, the kind in actual shops that adult women wear and that Chloe tries to sneak into school, though she keeps to nude and pink shades.

When I opened the cap it showed a bright, scorching red. Thick and matte. Practically the colour of a chilli, or a double-decker bus in London.

I should have known even then. That's not me. I haven't ever even worn lipstick before, let alone a shocking red one like that, like all the film stars. Like a sexy pinup model. And I'm definitely no pinup.

But Julian said I would look gorgeous. There was a public toilets nearby, and I could use the mirrors in there to put it on. I'd pucker my lips like they do in films and blow kisses and transform suddenly: weirdo schoolgirl into supermodel.

I grabbed the box, sealing the lid back on, and tucked the note into my jean pocket. As I emerged from the dome I took another look around, to see if he'd arrived, but there were just some girls far away chatting on a bench that I could hardly make out. I hurried to the toilets, eyes blinking in the sudden bright light against the dark backdrop of the park.

Toilets are never the most pleasant places, especially public ones, but I set the box on the sink, taking the lipstick out and hovering it towards my face. I wasn't sure exactly how you were meant to put it on, but it couldn't be harder than drawing or painting, and I was good at that. I would just apply the right amount of pressure, probably a lot to make sure it didn't come off, and I'd look amazing.

Yeah. Makeup and painting are very different, if you haven't learned that already.

It came on very easily—a lot easier than I imagined. All of a sudden my lips were bright red. And not just my lips either—even with my steady hand there was some that smudged above my lip, giving me what looked like a much bigger upper lip than lower. I tried to correct it by doing some more underneath, but that just made me look like I'd suddenly had filler injections. When I pursed my lips out, like I was kissing someone, the centre of my lips was still stubbornly pink, so I had to put even more on.

When I smiled, imagining a beautiful Hollywood grin, instead all I saw was flakes of lipstick on my two front teeth.

Did I look grown up and sophisticated, or did I just look like a five-year-old who had got into her mother's makeup?

And then there was a flash.

"Say cheese!"

Annabel, Esther, Chloe, and Tanya appeared in the doorway. Annabel was holding up her phone, and the flash went off again. They were taking pictures of me.

"Stop it!" I shouted.

They were in the toilets by then, laughing and surrounding me.

"Oh my God," Chloe said, practically doubled over with how much she was screeching at the sight of me, "is this really how you think lipstick is worn? I knew you were useless but this is another *level. And to think we just thought we'd get some funny pictures of you posing in the mirror! This is priceless."*

"How did you even know I was here? What are you doing?" I asked.

I tried removing the lipstick, rubbing the back of my hand against my lips. Sure enough, some of it came off, staining my hand as if I had painted it myself, but when I looked in the mirror most of it was still there, except now loads of it had smeared across my chin and cheek.

Annabel took more pictures. "You look like such a freak!"

"Please stop!"

"You didn't really think Julian wanted to go out with you, did you?" Esther said.

It's horrible remembering this. Writing this down. But I need to. I need to get this out of me before it eats me up inside.

"Julian plays football after school on a Friday and has to leave his phone in the changing rooms," Tanya said. Even now, after years, it's awful how much she enjoys tormenting me, just like the other three. Does she really not look back at when we used to be friends and feel bad? Or is she just glad it's me and not her? "We snuck in there and texted you from his phone. It was Esther's idea. It was so funny."

"Of course he's not interested in you, you idiot." Esther smirked.

"God, you look so ridiculous!" Annabel said, taking another photo. "Like a horror movie!"

It wouldn't come off, no matter how hard I scrubbed. I even started running the taps and wiping it that way, and that just made it worse, creating an entire circle of red around my mouth, dripping down my chin.

I couldn't bear it. Pushing past them, trying to ignore their laughter and jeers, I ran home, unable to hide my tears, slamming the front door behind me.

"Poppy?" Mum and Dad came out of the living room straight away, clearly anxious. "What happened? Are you okay?"

"Leave me alone!" I shrieked.

They saw the lipstick then. It was so hideous and obvious, how could they not?

"What's happened to your face? Has someone hurt you?" Dad practically sounded hysterical. He grabbed hold of me by the shoulders to look at me closer. "Did this boy hit you?"

I was so confused, and then I realised. I'd made such a mess of the lipstick, such a state of myself trying to clear it all up, that it looked like a wound, an injury, a smear of blood all around my mouth.

It hurt just as much as if it really had been an attack.

"It's lipstick!" I shouted. "He didn't hit me! He didn't even show up! He didn't even know there was a date!"

"Oh, Poppy." He hugged me then, but I wrenched myself free and ran upstairs.

"Just leave me alone!" I said, slamming my bedroom door.

"Please open the door." Soon enough the whole family was outside.

"Poppy," Dad said. "Come downstairs and we can watch a film with popcorn. You don't have to talk about it if you don't want to."

"I'm sorry," Wendy said. "I'll kill him at school, just you wait."

"Please leave me alone," I said. "I just want to be by myself for a while."

Eventually, after more begging, they did leave, and I was left sobbing into my pillow. But after a while, I lifted my head up, and found the pillow stained with red. There was no way that was ever going to come out.

"Fuck!" I screamed. I never swear. It feels weird even writing down the word, as if I'm going to get into trouble when these are my private thoughts. But it was all I could think of saying at the time.

The lipstick was still in my pocket, so I took it out and threw it across the room, watching as the cap flew off and rolled under my desk. What looked so expensive and beautiful before, a way to turn me into someone I wasn't, now just looked tacky and cheap. I picked up what was left and crushed it into the desk, watching the insides crumble and fall apart against it. Another stain. Another mark that would always be there to remind me of what happened.

"Poppy." It was Wendy, knocking at the door.

"What part of 'leave me alone' don't you understand?" I snapped.

"I'm sorry, but you have to see this."

When I opened the door Wendy was standing there holding her laptop to her chest, face grave.

"What is it?" I asked.

"You're, uh, on Facebook."

I knew. When they took those photos. I knew they'd do something with them. I just didn't know what exactly, or how fast they'd act. But I should have realised that they wouldn't even let me have a moment's peace.

Wendy came into my room and sat on the bed, beckoning me to sit beside her. I saw her glance anxiously at the stained desk and pillow, but she didn't comment. After I sat down, she passed the laptop along.

Facebook was open. It was logged into Wendy's, not mine, but even on hers I was the top attraction, the first post that came up. A photo album of me in those toilets, staring at the mirror, then desperately trying to remove the lipstick, then turning towards them all.

I'm crying in the photos, but the lipstick is the worst. It looks even more horrific than it did in real life. I can still picture each image now, as if my brain has decided to play a little slideshow just to entertain me.

One of the captions read: Poppy Greer's New Art Project. *That hurt the most.*

I was a clown. It was smeared all over my face and even on my teeth.

"It's not that bad," Wendy said. The liar.

I barely listened to her, scrolling through all of the various comments.

Do you think she's ever even heard of the word "makeup" before?

LOL! Obviously not! She looks so ugly in school she never wears it.

Makeup wouldn't save her anyway!

What the hell does she think she's doing? I knew she was a saddo but this is so tragic.

I feel sorry for her, she has no friends and has to pretend she has a boyfriend on Valentine's Day.

What a loser.

OMG she's such a clown! This is so funny!

This actually should be her art project. I can't stand the way she shows off about her work. She's not even that good. Stuck-up bitch.

Remind me tomorrow to show her how lipstick is really meant to be worn! Like, hello, not on your teeth!

She thinks you have to eat it!

She eats everything else so no wonder! HAHA!

Another post popped up. A relationship status update.

Julian Davis is now in a relationship with Esther Driscoll.

Of course. Why would he ever have been interested in me? When he could have her?

Wendy took the laptop away and closed the lid. "Don't look at it anymore."

"How am I going to go to school on Monday?" I whispered, fresh tears streaming down my cheeks.

"You can and you will," Wendy said. "Don't let them beat you. You're the best person I know."

The best person she knew, dumb enough to believe Julian asked her out.

After she left, I took a final look at myself in the mirror. I still looked a state. I have some face wipes on my bedside table, and it took three of them to finally scrape the remaining red away, leaving my face sore and pink. As the wipes fell into the bin I couldn't help thinking how gruesome they looked. How ruined.

Without really thinking I punched the mirror hard. I'm hardly strong, so I was surprised when it cracked at my hit, one shard falling to the carpet stained with blood from my knuckle. When I picked it up, I stared at it for a long time before taking the jagged piece and scratching it across my arm.

There was a sharp pain that made me gasp, nothing for a moment, and then an angry rush of blood that looked exactly like the lipstick that had been smeared around my mouth. The skin was warm and prickly, and tears fell from my eyes, but I was weirdly excited by it. By the pain.

Fingers trembling, I did it again, smaller this time, cutting next to the original mark. The sharpness came again, making my heart thud in my throat.

And then I stopped, putting the jagged shard in my bedside drawer, wrapped in tissue. I sucked on my arm until the blood settled, then panicked, staring at the vicious red cuts left behind.

What had I done? And yet I felt better. Horrified. But better.

Later, when Mum came in to say good night, bringing a hot

chocolate with whipped cream and mini-marshmallows, I told her I was sorry. I had smashed the mirror in anger. I wore a long-sleeved pyjama top to avoid her questioning the marks on my arm.

"That's alright, you were upset," she said. "We'll remove that mirror tomorrow. Don't go near it in case there are bits of broken glass on the floor."

I didn't tell her I'd kept one for myself, tucked away in the bedside drawer for if I decided I wanted it again.

I hate them all. They deserve to die. If a bus came and knocked them down tomorrow, the world would be a better place.

Maybe I should give you a name after all, diary. Because you're the only friend I'm ever going to have. It's pointless to imagine any different.

I'm always going to be alone.

———

FIFTEEN

Annabel

Chloe comes into my room just as I'm finishing getting ready for the party. We've both gone over the top with our makeup and clothes. I'm wearing a tiny tight dress and my favourite pair of black open-toed heels, and she's wearing short purple dungarees to go with her black vest. Both of us have false lashes and heavy eyeshadow, and looking in the mirror it feels like we're eighteen again.

"War paint," Chloe says, which makes me smile. "Poppy is messing with the wrong bitches. Even if I did have to borrow Esther's makeup to get myself looking beautiful."

"Isn't that the truth." I put the finishing touches to my hair, scraping it back into a high ponytail. I'm surprised Chloe didn't just ask to borrow my makeup though. She's been so off with me recently. In the mirror, I catch her looking at me strangely, biting her lip. She clenches and unclenches her hands and it's clear she wants to say something. "What's up?"

"Just thinking," she says. "Isn't it funny that Poppy is a respected doctor now. I never would have thought that about her ten years ago."

"It is strange." I think back to the Poppy we knew.

"I wonder what she thinks of us," Chloe says. "I bet she thinks we haven't changed at all."

"I hope we have," I say. "We weren't the best to Poppy before. As she's so keen on reminding us. But we're better now."

"She's just mad none of us bothered to find out what happened to her after she moved away."

It never even occurred to us to find out what Poppy was doing after sixth form. We finished our exams and had our own celebration, and that was that. That was normal, though, to not care what happened to people in your class after school finished. I don't know what happened to anyone else either.

"Maybe it's good after all we're back in touch," I say, thinking of my mum's words.

Chloe seems lost in thought.

"Chloe?"

"Sorry." She shakes her head. Worry floods her features. "Look, Annabel, there's something I need to tell you."

There's something serious about her tone, so unlike her.

"What is it?" I ask.

She rubs her hand against her forehead, ironing out her frown. "I don't know where to start."

There's a knock on the door and Esther pops her head through, holding bright pink sashes with red lettering that say "Bridesmaid." "For you two, courtesy of our bridezilla! You look incredible."

"So do you!" Chloe grabs the sashes and puts hers on. The moment's gone. She seems grateful for the interruption and keen to get away. "Come on, Annabel!"

I oblige, putting mine on as I take in Esther's outfit. She's dressed for the occasion too, her pink sash clashing with her baby-pink jumpsuit and white sandals. Her hair is tied up into a bun, and tendrils frame her sharp face. She looks stunning. She knows it too, wriggling her eyebrows at Chloe's compliment.

We follow her out and down to the beach, where Poppy and Tanya are already waiting, and the three of us can't help but laugh at Poppy's outfit. She's gone full bride: white floaty dress and her hair bouncing in mousy curls to her waist. A long veil is pinned to her head and falls down the back of her hair, and to finish the look she has long white gloves up to her elbows.

The uncomfortableness of the day is somewhat forgotten as we all down a shot of tequila and suck on some lime. Then Esther pours everyone a glass of vodka coke, and we're sitting in a circle, a spark of excited energy between us.

"Never Have I Ever was just the beginning last night," Poppy announces, brandishing her glass high in the air.

"Oh, God!" Esther says.

"Let's have a toast and put today behind us."

We exchange glances between the four of us, uncertain.

"Really, ladies," Poppy says. "I just wanted to give you all a fright. And it seems I succeeded. We still have lots of hen party left to enjoy, and I plan to spend the majority of that time now drunk or on the beach. Not to mention all the fabulous wedding details I am going to reveal to you tomorrow morning. Who's with me?"

She sounds genuine enough, so we shrug and concede, lifting our glasses in the air.

"To a good night and a great hen party!"

"To a good night and a great hen party!" we chorus.

Poppy claps her hands together. "And now for the main event. Tonight we play Truth or Dare!"

I reach for the vodka coke again and take a long sip, my stomach clenching in anxiety. Another game.

"I know, to make it fair we'll spin a bottle to decide whose turn it is," Poppy says. She takes a bottle of cider from the side and downs it, impressively not stopping for air once as the liquid vanishes down her throat. She leans into the middle of the circle and tests the bottle on the bumpy sand and rug, and it spins fine. "Perfect. Are we all ready?"

"As ready as we'll ever be," Tanya mutters.

Poppy ignores her comment, and spins the bottle. She's done it too strong, and we're waiting almost twenty seconds for it to stop spinning. It slows further, and further, before finally stopping on Esther.

Relief hits me, and I let out a breath.

"I choose dare," Esther declares. It's a change for her, the sensible one. The mood of the evening must be having an effect on her. Or the alcohol.

"You were the only one who hadn't skinny-dipped out of the four of you," Poppy says. A gleam in her eyes tells us all what she's thinking before she says it. "I dare you to strip naked and run into the ocean for ten seconds."

"Oh, bloody hell." Esther shakes her head. "I wish I'd chosen truth now."

"Too late." Poppy is gleeful, and the rest of us start chanting for her to take off her clothes.

"I'll just go in fully clothed," she says. "That's practically worse. I'll be in wet stuff for the rest of the night."

"Nuh-uh." Chloe grins, wide as the Cheshire Cat. "That's cheating. Come on, everything off!"

She stands, but doesn't seem happy about it. Her arms wrap themselves around her body, and for a moment I'm worried she actually looks scared.

"Hurry up!" Poppy says. "We can't spend all night on you."

"Fine. Whatever."

She strips naked, even pulling a sexy pose at us, one hand behind her head and the other on her hip. She has a mark on her stomach, I notice. Some kind of bruise. She catches me staring and covers it with one hand.

"I slipped in the shower the other night," she explains. "The day before coming here. I'm so clumsy."

She doesn't give me time to question this. We hear her scream as she dashes into the water.

"Fucking hell! That's cold! So much for a tropical island!"

"It gets warm if you stay in there!" Chloe calls. She smiles at us. "At least that's what I assume."

Esther returns and wraps a spare towel around herself, plonking down on the cushion still naked. "Jesus." Her teeth are chattering. "My turn to spin the bottle."

She flicks it expertly, and it rotates a few times before coming to a clear stop in front of Tanya.

"What'll it be, Tanya?" Chloe asks.

"Truth," she says.

Esther puts her clothes back on, squeezing her ponytail and releasing sea water. "Hmm, I can't think of anything to ask."

Poppy clears her throat. "I have one."

"Go on," Esther concedes.

"Why did you and Harry break up?"

A shocked silence follows. Tanya gasps at Poppy's question. The rest of us are just confused. Tanya hasn't broken up with Harry. They only bought their London flat last year. She was talking to us a month or so ago about their new kitchen. They've been together ages.

"I think you've made a mistake," Esther says. "Tanya and Harry haven't broken up."

Chloe glances between Tanya and Poppy. "How do you know Harry, anyway?"

"We broke up because of work." Tanya finishes her drink and pours herself another one. "There, are you happy?"

"What?" Now I can't help getting involved. "Why didn't you tell us? When did this happen?"

"It happened months ago." Tanya drinks more. "Leave it, Annabel."

"Months ago?" I echo. "But how? I don't understand."

"I just didn't want to tell you all. That's it."

She reaches forward and spins the bottle. It careers off to the left, losing control, and hits into Chloe's knee.

Another pause follows, and Chloe rescues the mood, scooping up the bottle with a short laugh. "I guess that means it's my turn. Give me a truth."

Tanya doesn't offer one, sticking to draining another glass and pouring a third. "God, I have a headache."

Before we can say anything, Poppy jumps in. "What is your deepest fear?"

It's an odd question.

"Do you know," Chloe says, "I was about to say flying, because I hate it. But actually, I think the most scared I've ever been was last summer. My flat was burgled. I woke up to find my laptop was gone. The police thought it might have been a crazed fan, so I had the locks changed and everything because there was no sign of forced entry. And I couldn't sleep for weeks."

I remember Chloe after that. She came to stay at mine and Andrew's, convinced that some stalker was going to come and murder her. She ended up staying with us far longer than the one night originally agreed, but even Andrew seemed okay with her staying, telling me she'd gone through something traumatic and to have a bit more sympathy.

"It's the fact I was fast asleep and they were in there," she says. "They could have done anything."

Poppy has both eyebrows raised. "You wouldn't want someone to take advantage when you're at your most vulnerable."

Chloe doesn't know how to respond to that.

"Anyway!" She spins the bottle, and it lands on Poppy.

"Dare," she says.

Chloe drinks the rest of her glass, then grabs the bottle of vodka to refill. "I know, I dare you to shave your eyebrows."

Esther spits out most of her drink. "You can't get her to do that! That's too far."

"Chloe always likes to take it too far." Poppy stands, brushing sand away from her legs. "But I'll still do it."

"Is she really going to?" I ask, as Poppy strides away from us.

"She's bluffing," Esther says. "Chloe, that was harsh even for you."

"That's what she gets for making us go on that scavenger hunt," Chloe says. "It's a dare, she has to do it."

Poppy returns with a razor, and to our astonishment shaves a part of her eyebrow off. A clear line break appears just at the arch, and she repeats this on the other side.

"There." She throws the razor down, and turns her face towards us. "You didn't say how much of my eyebrows I had to shave. But I've shaved them."

There's something about it. She looks wilder, more dangerous. It suits her.

Chloe scowls; she wasn't expecting Poppy to outsmart her, nor to look good as the end result. But she can't complain. Poppy did as dared.

I'm starting to feel tipsy. The rest of them are getting drunk too. Tanya's eyes are glazed over and Chloe's pouring herself yet another drink. Even Esther is drinking away and giggling at Poppy's antics. It's just Poppy who has a modicum of sobriety.

Poppy spins the bottle but it's a weak attempt. It barely does one rotation before it ends up back at Esther, who groans at it being her second turn already.

"Truth this time," she says. "I'm only just dry!"

"Is it true you got your job because your mother knows your boss?" Poppy asks.

Esther is stung; it's her sorest subject. I should know, I like to make jibes about it even though I know it bothers her. Why do I always like to pick at people's insecurities? I know I'm doing it, in fact that's almost why

I do it in the first place. There's something about watching someone's face fall and know you're the one that caused it, that you're in the stronger position.

It's what used to make me gravitate towards Poppy so much at school.

"My mother got me the interview," Esther says sharply. "I still had to prepare for it. I still had to prove I was worthwhile enough for the job. And I am. I'm amazing at it, no one can deny that. I should be answering a million different emails right now but I can't because I'm stuck on this island and you have a stupid phone rule, so don't talk to me about not being worthy of my job!"

"I didn't say that," Poppy says. "That was you."

"Maybe we should just leave it now," Chloe says nervously.

"Oh, it's bloody true, Esther, and you know it." Tanya lifts her head from her drink and scowls. "Think of the thousands of applications they wouldn't have even looked at. You bypassed that whole part. You think you're better than everyone?"

Oh God.

Tanya is not a nice drunk. She gets mean very quickly, homes in on a target and attacks, even if we're all meant to be on the same side here. How much has she had to drink? She's shaking as she grabs another bottle and pours the contents into her glass, and she almost misses her mouth.

"Oh, because the people you work with are so much better!" Esther snaps. "How much does it cost to hire you to run an event again?"

"That's the point. I know what I'm talking about."

"And how's Harry?" Esther asks. "Did he cheat on you? Is that why you kept it quiet? I wouldn't have expected it from Harry, but why else would you not say anything?"

"Esther." I place a hand on her shoulder. Tanya's face is fuming. "Don't do that."

"Why not? She started it! And she's got a bloody cheek talking to me about job competency, let me tell you."

"No one started it!" Chloe shouts. "It was a stupid game. Just leave it."

The outburst leaves us in silence. Esther and Tanya can't even look at each other, and Chloe is shaking her head at both of them. Poppy is an avid audience member, eyes wide, hints of enjoyment crossing her face.

"My turn!" I declare wildly, taking the bottle and pointing it at me. "Ask me something. I pick truth."

Esther takes a deep breath and closes her eyes for a moment. When they open, her posture relaxes, and I can see she's decided to let it go. Thank God for that. Tanya still looks upset, but she's returned to her drink, nursing it with both hands.

Poppy takes advantage of Esther being distracted and asks a question of her own. "When do you want to start a family?"

Not that question. Why is it a woman in her twenties can't go more than five seconds without someone asking that dreaded question?

"I'm not sure I want to."

Poppy lets out a noise of surprise and we all turn to her. "Sorry," she says. "I just thought you were like, number one housewife."

"I'm not sure what I am," I say.

"But you love Andrew," Poppy says. "Right?"

"Right." Of this, at least, I am sure.

I lean forward and spin the bottle.

It lands at Chloe.

"Dare." She grins. "But I'm not having you get revenge on me by telling me to shave my hair off. No repeating dares!"

"I dare you to down the rest of the vodka."

There's still at least enough for four shots in there. It's an insane idea.

"She can't do that," Esther says. "Poppy, you're a doctor. You should know that."

Poppy holds her hands up in surrender. "Fine. *Half* the remaining vodka. Is that a fair compromise?"

"I don't compromise," Chloe says. "Shut up, Esther, you're always too much of a goody-goody." She grabs the bottle and chugs it back, her face squirming in discomfort. Some of it spills outside her mouth, dripping down her chin, but she succeeds, the vodka finished. She places the bottle back on the table but it slips from her grasp and crashes down onto the sand, mercifully not breaking. "Jesus." Her voice is slurred; the effects are instant. "There!" she cries.

"I think it's time we all had some more drink." Poppy pours the rest of us some wine, then gives herself some cider. "Come on!"

It's getting more difficult now. I find myself holding my hand to my mouth to keep everything in.

Is my hand shaking? Things are starting to become blurry.

"Sorry for what I said about Harry," Esther blurts out. "That was rude of me. Are we okay?"

Tanya sighs. "No, I'm sorry for what I said about your job."

Chloe chooses that moment to barrel between them both, wrapping an arm around each of their shoulders. "Are we friends again? Hooray!"

"Piss off, Chloe," Esther says, but she smiles.

"It's hard keeping secrets from one another, isn't it?" Poppy says.

"We don't keep secrets," Chloe says.

"Now we both know that's not true."

"Hey." Chloe struggles to her feet again, pointing a finger outwards. "Don't pick on me. What about Tanya, she's—"

"Chloe!" Tanya snaps.

Poppy nods. "No, no. You're right, it's not just you. It's everyone."

"Everyone?"

It's the last thing I remember saying. The rest of the night passes by in a blur, vague shapes of us getting up and dancing at one point, singing at the top of our lungs, being supplied with more drinks. This seems to go on for hours, coupled with reaching for handfuls of party food. We become united as a five, for the first time ever, partying and chatting, but I can't remember the conversations.

At some point there was an argument. I remember raised voices. Tanya? Tanya was angry at someone, I think. Was it Poppy?

I don't remember going to bed, but I must have eventually, because I wake up to a sudden bang in the night, followed by some rustling. My head is pounding and my mouth is dry.

"Hello?" I mumble, but when I turn over to look there's nothing, just the empty room around me and silence. Turning over is enough of an effort to make me groan, the room spinning.

I listen out, but the noise has stopped.

Something must have dropped, that's all. I debate whether or not to go and investigate when the heaviness of sleep overwhelms me again.

SIXTEEN

Chloe

MAY 20, 2023

I wake up boiling in a puddle of my own sweat. Above me, the air conditioning has stopped working, a stubborn orange light on display.

"Jesus Christ." I reach my hand for the bedside table when I remember my phone isn't there. From the view outside, the sky is bright blue, indicating I've slept in.

No matter. I take my time in the shower, giving my hair a long time to condition, and shriek when I take my towel off the rack and find a spider on the wall next to it.

"Fucking island!" I shake my towel out again and again before drying myself with caution, checking every five seconds that the spider hasn't jumped on. I can hear the others now, chatting and eating, so I leave my hair to drip dry and throw on a sundress and sandals. Not like I can do my makeup anyway.

They're over by the decking, having breakfast. Someone has gone to the trouble of offering a full spread, a mixture of croissants and toast and hot food for those with stronger stomachs, and yoghurt and granola and fruit for those like me who can't face eating a huge meal right now after last night. Esther is looking the most fresh and ready for the day, while Tanya sits vacant and tired. Annabel is nowhere to be seen, and Poppy is at the head of the table with sunglasses on so it's hard to see how she's recovered from the night before, but maybe that's an indication. She's also overdressed for the occasion, wearing a sparkly long-sleeved top that would do better on a night out than the morning after.

Poppy nods at me as I sit down. "Good morning, Chloe."

"What time is it?" I ask, spooning myself some yoghurt.

"Late." Poppy pours me some juice without incident, though I find I'm holding my breath until she's done. "Almost eleven. I was about to come and wake you."

"Sorry." I take a sip. "You lot have been up for a while then?"

Esther can't resist an opportunity to brag about how much of an early riser she is, nor how fit and active. "I was up since seven, which is late for me. Had a long run, then a swim in the sea to cool off. It's been a nice morning. Quite peaceful, actually, by myself."

Tanya rolls her eyes, but Esther's facing me so she can't see. I have to hide a smile, though looking at Tanya is enough to make me serious again anyway. She looks even worse than she did yesterday, kind of sweaty and pale, as if she was the one who went for a run. And she keeps sniffing, though I don't think she realises it.

"Sorry I'm late!"

Annabel comes hurrying across the decking, flip-flops clacking against the wood. She's wearing a floaty sundress with amazing floral patterns on. A dress I know for a fact costs almost two grand, because I wore it in a campaign I was in a few months ago.

How the hell is Annabel affording that? Andrew barely gives her enough to buy food shopping, let alone a luxury wardrobe.

It's pretty impressive. Maybe there's a bit more to Annabel than meets the eye, some of her old self still in there and not just the boring housewife she's become.

I'm about to ask when Annabel starts speaking again. "What a night, right? I remember us dancing to Britney."

"Hard not to do." Esther laughs. "We need to take it easier tonight."

"You've all got your wonderful gin to share," Poppy says. "Don't think I've forgotten."

"Oh, God," Annabel groans. "I don't think I can handle another night. We're not eighteen anymore."

It's a harmless comment, but I cringe thinking about it. We're not eighteen anymore, and with Poppy sitting at the table with us, I don't want to be reminded of what we did when we were that age.

"What's the plan for today, Poppy?" I ask to move the subject along quickly.

She lowers her sunglasses. "You'll see. First, enjoy your breakfast."

We spend the next hour or so making conversation. Even though I was feeling rough this morning, I've perked up, and help myself to a croissant. There's a more relaxed atmosphere to us all now after the awkwardness of yesterday. It feels like we might just enjoy this hen party and have some fun.

I keep on thinking this, oblivious when Poppy says she'll be right back, unquestioning when she brings the wooden box with our phones in it to the table.

"Oh, brilliant," I say. "I have so much I need to catch up on. And loads of pictures I want to take. What made you change your mind?"

"Well, I guess I can see how many emails I can try and download without Wi-Fi," Esther says. She bites her lip. "And reply to Brad."

Poppy shakes her head. "No, that's not why I've brought your phones out."

"Well, why then? Is something wrong?"

"It's time the truth was laid bare," Poppy says. "I've spent a couple of days with you all now, and you're the same as ever."

An uncomfortable feeling begins to prick itself across the back of my neck. "What do you mean?"

"I figured I should give you all a chance." Poppy unlocks the box with her key and opens it up. "But there's no change. You're all petty, selfish, and materialistic. As you always have been."

Tanya sighs. "I knew it. I knew there was a catch."

Annabel looks confused. "But this is a hen party. What were you expecting from us?"

"If you think that about us, why bother inviting us?" I snap. "Why go through with this whole holiday, to a private island no less, if you were just checking to see if we were the same as when you knew us before? What's the point?"

"That is the right question, Chloe." Poppy smiles at me, removing her sunglasses. There's a wildness to her expression, something she was hiding well before. "My four dearest friends, the women who made me what I am today. Why would I invite you all to this private island when a weekend somewhere nice in England would do?"

"We don't have to listen to this," Tanya says.

"The problem is you do, because you have nowhere else to go," Poppy says. "And I'm going to make sure you all listen, because you know why I've brought you here."

"Jesus Christ." I stamp my foot on the ground. "This isn't because of something that happened *ten years ago*, is it? You can't still be harbouring a grudge over all of that. The pathetic scavenger hunt was bad enough. This is just a new low, going into our phones. I thought this was meant to be a technology-free holiday. You're insane."

Her face darkens, and there's a moment when I think she may come for me. Aggression spikes her features, then a second later she's relaxed again.

"Annabel," she says, choosing to ignore me. "Do you remember when you told me I'd end up sad and alone?"

"Don't listen to this shit," Tanya says.

"That would have been when we were kids," Annabel says. She folds her arms across her chest, unperturbed. "Trust you to remember something like that."

"Kids!" Poppy laughs. "Technically, you were eighteen and I was seventeen. That makes one of us a kid, I suppose. You told me I'd end up sad and alone, and when I died no one would bother to mourn me at my funeral apart from my mum and dad and—" Her voice breaks, betraying her true feelings, and she has to clear her throat. "And my sister. That no one would ever love me. You must remember. Chloe even brought it up this very holiday that she thought I was so desperate to be loved I'd go with anyone."

I want to hide behind something. It was a joke. Sort of.

Poppy continues, even though Annabel is staring at the ground, cheeks blushing. "So I thought to myself, how can I get back at Annabel Hannigan? Well, you're not Annabel Hannigan anymore. You're Annabel Dixon. And therein lay an idea. Andrew is very good looking, isn't he?"

Annabel jerks her head up, stricken. Even Tanya has lost her scowl and looks stunned.

Poppy isn't saying what I think she is, is she?

She's enjoying herself now, clicking Annabel's screen on and off. Annabel's background, a picture of her and Andrew on their wedding day, seems to add to the torture. "He was so easy. He drinks at the same bar after work every night. You know he finishes at five and not seven, don't you?"

"Are you making a point or just rambling?" Annabel asks.

"Getting there," Poppy says. "I was going to sleep with your husband, Annabel, I'll be blunt. Or, well, I was going to make you think I had. Bring him up to the hotel room I'd booked above the bar, take a photo of us together, send it to you. But by the time I got there, he was already with another woman. He was with another woman every single night I tried."

To my surprise, Annabel doesn't collapse at this. She remains steady, eyes on Poppy, as if she's simply telling her about the weather.

I want to tell Poppy she's wrong, but I can't. Just like I can't ever tell Annabel that Andrew tried it with me once, at one of Tanya's parties a year after they got married. I was coming out of the women's toilets in a club that has long since shut down due to a drugs bust, and he was leaning against the wall waiting for me, grabbing me by the hand and pulling me close to him as I walked by. I still remember his hot and sticky breath on my neck, his insistence we find somewhere quiet, that he knows I've always wanted him too.

Poppy glances at me, and I'm convinced it's all over. She gives me a small smile, then turns back to Annabel, and I exhale with relief.

"What's your point?" Annabel says.

Poppy looks startled. "What do you mean?"

Tanya doesn't know what to do with herself, face agog. She keeps trying to catch my eye and it takes everything in me to ignore her.

"Is this all you've got?" Annabel says. "Evidence of Andrew cheating on me?"

"So you knew?" Esther says. "Annabel . . . is that why you've been . . ."

"Shut up, Esther," Annabel snaps.

What's that about?

She turns again to Poppy and smirks. "I'm afraid your little game has backfired. I already knew about Andrew. Typical man. But what do I care? He's wealthy. He was my ticket out of my depressing life. He still comes home to me at the end of the day. I'm the one he married."

She can't know everything. My stomach feels like it's about to flip over I'm so nervous. Still, though. I can't help but admire her. There's still Annabel Hannigan in there somewhere, queen bee of our school and not someone to be messed with.

Poppy is uncertain, watching Annabel closely. Annabel's phone is still in her hand, and I'm sure there's going to be something awful in there.

"You might have been aware," Poppy says eventually. "But what about everyone else? How would you feel if they all knew about Andrew's dirty little secret?"

She throws Annabel's phone to her then, a quick movement that gives Annabel barely any time to react.

"Thankfully, you all have great data plans on your phones, so the lack of Wi-Fi wasn't an issue," Poppy says. "Of course, with the signal being as patchy as it is, I had to spend a long time uploading everything, but it worked. It's a shame that meant all your data has run out. But I've taken screenshots of everything I did so we don't have to worry about you not being able to take a look."

"What have you done?" Annabel asks, opening her phone.

"I'd have a look at screenshots from your Instagram, your Twitter, and your Facebook," Poppy says. "A lot of family members on your Facebook, aren't there? The kind of people you don't want to see your dirty laundry. Or Andrew's dirty laundry."

Annabel actually laughs. "Jesus Christ, you're crazy."

"What has she done?" Esther grabs the phone and then gasps and covers her mouth with one hand. Her tone shifts to pure venom, aimed at Poppy. "You absolute psychopath."

Tanya, panicked, hurries to take a look, and in the commotion, I'm able to get close enough to peer over Tanya's shoulder and see for myself what Poppy has done.

Annabel's profile page. There's a new photo album, entitled: My Darling Husband.

Oh, Jesus.

The caption is worse.

Andrew and I have been married for three wonderful years. And in those three years I have been fortunate enough to find out that he has shared this time with me and at least fifty other women. Enjoy a little slideshow of Hubbie Dearest.

The photo album makes me sick. How did she even get these photographs? Andrew in bars, his hands on women's thighs and smiling seductively. His face buried in their necks. Kissing them in hotel lobbies. Leading them to hotel rooms, hand on their asses. I scan through each picture, panic in my throat, but each image is a stranger, a smiling curvaceous blonde or brunette. I didn't know. I didn't know he was seeing all these women.

"So what?" Annabel says. "Was it you who took all these pictures? You realise all you've done is turn me into the innocent victim? Andrew is the bad guy here, not me."

She keeps flicking through the screenshots; the images never seem to end, and finally Poppy smiles again.

"I'd finish looking through everything before you continue being so cocky," she says.

Oh shit. Why is she looking at me?

Annabel carries on, still confident, and then all of a sudden she drops the phone in shock, sending it clattering to the ground, screen cracking right down the middle.

"Annabel?" Esther bends down and picks it up, then she recoils too at what she's looking at.

"You bitch!" Out of nowhere, Annabel darts forward and slaps me in the face. "I should have known! Of course you did!"

I reel back as a sharp sting floods my cheek, clutching at it.

"Annabel, don't!" Esther cries. She and Tanya rush over to pull her off.

"Annabel!" Tanya steps in front of her as she tries to go for me again. The breakfast table is abandoned, the five of us all standing now, half on the decking, half on the lawn.

"Feisty as always, Annabel," Poppy says gleefully.

"You slept with him! You slept with Andrew!" Annabel screams.

Esther thrusts the phone into my hands and I can see what they've all seen. Shit. It's worse than the others. Me and Andrew at restaurants.

In bars. In hotels. And then, last of all, kissing on the doorstep of their house, his hands in my hair and my arms around his waist.

Oh God.

"She's been fucking your husband, Annabel," Poppy tells her. "Remember that time Chloe was burgled and came to stay at yours? She brought it up on this very trip. Well, she and Andrew have been fucking ever since."

"How do you even know that?" I whisper. Has she been *spying* on us? What else does she know?

"Oh, that's what you're worried about, is it?" Annabel shouts. "Not the fact that you've been screwing around with my husband when you're meant to be my friend?"

Everyone is looking at me in horror.

I have to try and explain. "It was a mistake. I didn't mean for it to happen. We were alone in the house one evening, and it just . . . we . . ."

"My God." Annabel shakes her head. "In my *house*? When I was being kind and letting you *stay*? You jumped into bed with my husband?"

Esther's eyes widen. "Oh, Chloe, you didn't."

Annabel keeps pacing back and forth, and any second I think she's going to go for more again. "How many times?"

God, hundreds? Andrew is pretty fantastic.

"I don't know," I say instead.

"Fuck." Her face screws up in pain, and for a second I do actually feel bad.

"I'm sorry. I really am." It's not my fault he kept messaging me, calling me, telling me he couldn't bear to go a week without me in his arms. How was I meant to resist?

"But you didn't stop it, did you?" Annabel says. "When was the last time?"

I might as well be honest. She'll probably find out from Andrew. "Before the hen party. Last weekend."

"Jesus Christ. That's sooner than Andrew was with *me*." Annabel throws her head back and laughs. "My God."

"I'm ending it. I'll end it when we get home." Will I? I don't know, but it's probably the right thing to say.

"Oh, don't bother. You've always been a selfish bitch but this is a new low," she snarls over her shoulder. "You couldn't just let me have someone, could you? You've always been pathetic. Always been an attention seeker. You couldn't bear it that I had him first. Couldn't bear that someone might find me more attractive than you."

Here we go. "That's not true."

"I bet you were much more shocked than I was to find out he'd been sleeping with a load of women," she says. "I bet you thought you were the only one. Special."

Well. I didn't know he was. But I'm not about to tell her that.

She must see something in my face though because she grins triumphantly. "I thought so," Annabel says. "Should that make me feel better? That you're even dumber than I am when it comes to Andrew? Because it doesn't. You're my friend, Chloe. Or at least you're meant to be. And this is how you treat me?"

"Oh, because you've always treated the rest of us so well!" I snap. It's about time she heard it. "Kindness and being caring, that's what you're known for, is it?"

"Don't even try it, you pathetic little—"

"This has gone far enough," Esther says. She moves in front of us both, holding her palms out. "We can sort this mess when we get home. Stop it. And you." She fixes her stern gaze on Poppy. "Give the rest of us our phones back and we're calling Robin and getting the hell out of here."

"Yes, give me my phone back," I say.

Poppy opens the box again, taking another phone out.

Mine. I recognise it immediately, the white case with stickers of my Instagram handle on the back. I reach for it, but Poppy pulls away.

"I'm surprised the rest of you haven't figured out the obvious," Poppy says.

"What do you mean?" Tanya asks.

"If I've done that to Annabel, what on earth have I done to the rest of you?" She waves my phone in the air, grinning at me. "And Chloe, seeing as you've already had quite the starring role, we might as well continue with you. You're up next."

SEVENTEEN

Tanya

MAY 20, 2023

Chloe, to her credit, tries to defuse the situation rather than freak out and attack Poppy, which is what I'm debating doing. Every bone in my body seems to hurt, or I'd grab the box from her now. My head is pounding even more, an incessant drumbeat this entire holiday. Annabel is still furious, full of rage not only for Chloe but Poppy too, no doubt for wounding her pride. Esther and I exchange glances, trying to figure out what to do.

Maybe we deserve this. This punishment Poppy is dishing out, whatever it is for each of us. We had it coming.

"You've already gone far enough with Annabel," Chloe says. "You don't need to hurt anyone else."

"I think it's you that's gone far enough!" Annabel snaps. "Go right ahead, Poppy! Fuck her life up too."

Poppy grins. "If I just hurt Annabel that wouldn't be fair, would it? That would just be targeting one person, and that's quite vicious, wouldn't you say?"

"You haven't answered why you're doing this." Esther looks to me in support, and I nod, though I keep my mouth shut. "So tell us. Maybe we can put this right. Surely that's why you invited us here? Why bother with all of these dramatics if you didn't care what we thought?"

"The four of you made my life a living hell," Poppy says. "And the worst thing is, not one of you cares. Not one of you tried to find out what happened to me after school."

"We're sorry!" Chloe says. "There, I said it. I'm sorry, Poppy, for how I treated you. Everyone else is as well, aren't you?"

"I'm not sorry," Annabel says, still sitting down. "There's a difference between being a teenager and doing stupid things, and being an adult and destroying someone's entire life. Nothing we did was even that bad!"

"Annabel!" Chloe snaps. "Just say it."

"I think you've opened your mouth enough, don't you?" she hisses.

"I think this will please you, Annabel," Poppy says. She presses something on Chloe's phone, then holds it up for us all to see.

"I don't have a boyfriend or a husband, so there's nothing you can hurt me with," Chloe says. "And I don't know how you got into my phone."

"I know what can hurt you," Poppy says. "For example, I'm so happy you're finally showing your family of followers, as you call them, what you're really like."

The colour drains from Chloe's face, her confidence gone. "What are you talking about?"

Poppy turns the sound on Chloe's phone, and we hear it. "This is your Instagram story right now," she says. "I figured I'd save the video to your phone as well so you could view it whenever you wanted."

It's the first night we got here. I can see us all in the hot tub; the camera shows everyone except Poppy.

"Never have I ever . . ." Chloe's face is lit up by the light on the roof of the lodge. There's no question that it's her. "Never have I ever had sex with a woman."

The camera doesn't show it, but we can hear someone drinking.

"What the hell?" Chloe says. "How was there a camera filming this? None of us had our phones."

"Now that's not true," Poppy says. "I had my phone. I just made sure you didn't have yours. Had quite a nice little vantage point. On both nights."

Chloe's mouth falls open.

I'm equally as horrified. What else has she uncovered?

The video continues, oblivious to our shock.

"When?" Chloe asks. "Does your groom know you have, Poppy?"

Poppy chuckles off screen. "I should hope so, because that was what I was going to tell you. My groom isn't a groom at all. She's another bride. She's a woman."

I cringe as the camera shows us Chloe's disgusted face. "A *woman*?" And then she laughs, this awful awkward laugh where she seems to understand she shouldn't be so bothered by it but can't help it.

"Everything okay, Chloe?" Poppy says. "You don't have a problem with that, do you? It's okay to like both, you know."

Chloe's face darkens further, as if she can't stand to even breathe the same air as Poppy.

"Congratulations," Annabel says, her attempt at trying to defuse the situation. "I'm glad you found someone."

"Chloe?"

And then the worst part of all. Chloe knows it too, because she tenses, hands balling into fists, no doubt praying the video will cut off before we get to it.

"I don't normally associate myself with people like you," Chloe snaps. "Hardly a surprise though, is it?"

Tanya shakes her head.

"What do you mean by that?" Poppy asks.

"Desperate enough to be loved by anyone," Chloe says. "You always were Poppy Greedy."

The final shot is of her laughing at her own joke, face lit up with joy and arrogance. Then the Instagram story ends.

"Oh dear," Poppy says. "I don't think your followers like the real you, Chloe. You're down to six hundred thousand just in the past couple of days."

"What the—I don't—" Chloe can barely speak. She's pale, and there are even beads of sweat at her temples. "That's my job, Poppy. Oh my God."

"All the comments under your latest photos are all just calling you homophobic, and encouraging people to unfollow," Poppy continues, as if Chloe hasn't said anything. "Your agent has called you a dozen times and she's left some furious messages. Apparently PrettyLittleThing no longer wants to use you in their campaign? And your other sponsors are pulling out as well."

Chloe is going to faint. She wobbles where she stands, and Esther gets to her, grabbing her by the sides and holding her up. Annabel cackles with laughter.

Poppy hands her the phone. "You said those things, not me. I just let the world know who you are."

I'm stunned when Chloe accepts the phone into her hands without comment. She tries to call her agent to no avail, tapping out desperate messages instead that probably don't go through. Tears arrive, coming thick and fast down her cheeks, leaving her face red.

"My life is ruined," she mumbles. "I'm done for. All over a stupid joke."

"It's not a joke," Poppy spits.

"This isn't real, right?" Chloe has a hand to her mouth, muffling her words. "I'm dreaming. I'll wake up tomorrow and I'll be at home."

Poppy leans over and pinches her, none too gently, making her shriek. "What the fuck!"

"This isn't a dream, and this is far from over." She takes another phone from the box.

I'm positive it will be me next. After all, we were friends for years. If she's got a grudge against us all, I must be the one she hates the most. I wonder if she knows what that guilt has done to me. Even now I'm desperate for at least a drink to mask this awful pain.

Instead, it is Esther's phone she pulls out, and I know then she is leaving me until last. Her pièce de résistance.

Can I stand here waiting around for her to tell me what she's done?

Pinpricks of nerves dance along my arms and legs, sending goose bumps everywhere even though it's boiling hot, the decking starting to burn at my feet.

Chloe is still transfixed on her phone, trying to get in touch with her agent.

Esther is different from those two; she's more like me, capable of thinking and assessing a situation. She frowns at Poppy now, not rising to the bait, but a pulse jumps in her neck and that's how I know she's terrified too.

"What is the worst thing you've ever done to me?" Poppy asks her.

"You mean the exam?" Esther says. "That wasn't meant to go down the way it did."

Poppy holds up a hand to stop her. "Not you, plural. You, singular. Esther, what is the worst thing you've ever done to me?"

Her frown deepens. "I don't understand."

But I do. I know what Poppy's getting at, and from the gleam in her eyes as she nods at me I have my suspicions confirmed.

"Esther," I say quietly. "She's talking about Julian Davis."

"Julian Davis?" Esther's eyes widen. "But that wasn't just me. It was all of us."

"Your idea," Poppy says. "Your boyfriend."

Esther laughs nervously. "But surely you haven't. I mean, you couldn't have." Panic sets in, as she starts to understand like I do just what Poppy may have done. "Oh shit. The dare last night. Poppy, you *haven't*."

"I thought it was brilliant, actually."

Esther snatches her phone from Poppy, but I can tell Poppy wasn't trying to hold on to it.

Too late, I realise that's because she's already done everything she is talking about. There's no way to stop her. These posts, these stories, they've been up for at least an entire day, and whilst we've been here on the island everyone back in England has been seeing these in real time.

Esther gasps. "You *bitch*," she hisses. Her entire demeanour has changed, her shoulders rise up and her fists clench, scowling. She throws her phone to the ground, not seeming to care when the screen cracks.

Poppy stays relaxed, a confident smirk that challenges Esther to approach.

I bend down and pick up Esther's phone. It's open to a screenshot of her work emails, a message from her boss informing her she's fired for inappropriate conduct and sexual harassment. Then I scroll through, finding pictures of other emails, confused responses from colleagues about what she's sent them, some angry, some ignored entirely, others telling her she's being reported to Human Resources. Dozens upon dozens of emails of Esther posing naked, her running into the sea, her coming back out drenched, water dripping down her naked chest. Each email comes with a message propositioning her colleagues in personalised tones. There's even one to the CEO of the company.

This is the worst. Chloe can lose her Instagram following, Annabel can lose her husband, but this is calculated cruelty. The fear I was feeling before has ramped up to a whole new level, and now I'm concerned.

I can't let Poppy reveal whatever it is she's done to me.

But before I can do anything, Esther has slapped Poppy full in the face, the smack so loud I'm sure I'd have heard it standing on Deadman's Peak.

"You're fucking dead!" she screams. "Do you hear that, you bitch? I will kill you. I'm calling the police, I'm suing you, you'll lose your precious doctor job and end up with nothing."

"Esther!" Chloe grabs her by the arm. "Don't give her the satisfaction!"

I remain where I am. It's surprising—Chloe, who is usually the impulsive one, calming down Esther, the level-headed one. There are sides to them I'm learning even now, perhaps their true selves when the going gets tough.

"How could you?" Esther cries. "How could you do this?"

"You're all a bunch of hypocrites," Poppy says, though her voice trembles slightly. She's backed off, holding her hand to her cheek. Even I can see the redness underneath. Esther is strong. That had to have hurt. Are her eyes watering? "You know how I could do that. Think of all you've done to me. Think of what you did, Esther."

"You're a psychopath," Esther says. "And I'm done with this."

"Why don't you think about what you did?" Poppy calls. "I don't remember you being so upset when something happened to me."

"This bitch is going to pay for what she's done," Esther snarls. "I won't take this, the second we get back to the mainland I'm getting in touch with a lawyer. There will be a way to prove Poppy did this rather than me, and they'll have to give me my job back. They can't just be able to fire me like that."

She turns on her heels and walks away, heading towards the main lodge.

"Don't run away, Esther," Poppy shouts after her, sickeningly cheerful. "We're on a tiny island, there's only so many places you can go."

"Go fuck yourself," she yells over her shoulder, and carries on. One of the balloons from the other night is still stuck to the ground, and she stamps on it as she goes past. In that second I realise where she's going. The emergency phone. I jump up and hurry across myself, just as she reaches it and steps back, on her face a look of horror.

"Esther?"

The emergency phone is within a phone box, quite old fashioned. I follow her horrified gaze to what is inside and put a hand to my mouth.

The wire has been cut.

This has been broken for hours. Days, even. The actual phone itself has vanished. Someone has even gone to the trouble of smashing the buttons, breaking a few of them off, just in case.

There's no way to call the mainland now.

"Shit!" I'm furious, rage boiling inside my body and setting my skin alight. We return to the others.

"Why would you smash the emergency phone?" I shout at Poppy. I'm so mad I'm tempted to slap her too. But my body is still betraying me. Sweat emanates from my armpits and nausea swells in my stomach. Instead, I'll have to use my words. "What if there's an actual emergency on the island, like one of us has a heart attack or something? Or falls from the cliff? That's just insane. You realise there's still two days until Robin comes back?"

Esther is just as furious. "You're a stupid bitch. Look at what you've done."

Poppy shrugs. "Was that me? I can't remember."

"Do you not care if one of us gets hurt?" I say. "Because that someone could very easily be you."

"I like the sound of that," Esther says.

Chloe and Annabel are united in this: eyes gleaming, we all turn to Poppy, a new idea forming in our minds.

"Careful now, Tanya," Poppy says. "Anyone would think you were threatening me. And you don't need to lose your head. There are still the emergency flares, if there was a real issue. Calm down."

"But we can't use those just to call Robin back!" I snap. "You know that. They'd send out the coastguard. You've stranded us."

"You've endangered us!" Chloe cries. "My entire livelihood is at stake because of you. My whole life."

"You did that," Poppy says. "With your homophobic comments. Not me. My original plan for you was to just leak some naked photos, like I did with Esther."

"I want to leave!" Annabel says. "I want to get off this stupid island and back to the mess of my life and try to sort out what you've done, because you're not getting away with it. I will make sure that you pay."

"And what about Tanya?" Chloe asks, causing the rest of us to fall silent.

That woman. I could strangle her. "Forget about me. I don't want to hear it."

Annabel looks perplexed. "But you must want to know what she's done. She could have ruined your job."

"Leave it, Annabel," I snap.

"No, she's right," Poppy says. "I didn't get to talk about you, Tanya." She waves my phone in the air, full of glee. "Last one."

"Don't do it," I say, in a low voice, aware of how menacing my tone has become.

It doesn't faze Poppy. She tosses my phone back at me, and once it's caught between my hands, she begins speaking.

"Tanya has already lost her job."

"What?" Annabel stops in her tracks.

"You heard me," Poppy says. "Tanya lost her job months ago. Have none of you bothered to notice she hasn't organised an event in half a year? Just like none of you noticed Harry left her around the same time, I suppose."

I open my mouth to try and argue against this, but I can't. It's true. I haven't done anything for months. I tried to make the others think I was just throwing private parties, not grand public events with invitations open to people.

They all stare at me, gobsmacked, and I know I've gone very still. My knuckles turn white from how hard I'm gripping.

"But why?" Annabel says. "How could you have lost your job? I don't understand. Is that why Harry left you?"

"It's hard to know what to do to someone whose life is already ruined." Poppy is enjoying this now. I want to wipe that smug grin off her face. "But then I found out how you lost your job. And I have to admit I was surprised."

Esther gasps. I can't bring myself to look at anything other than the ground.

"I messed up at work," I say. "The heiress's birthday party six months ago. I should have known when you mentioned it. The entire event was a disaster."

It had been a huge event, a boat cruise down the River Thames for a sixteen-year-old daughter of a Russian billionaire. She was something of a minor celebrity herself. Everything should have been planned down to the last detail, but I was distracted. Busy with my own issues. One of her friends managed to sneak some drugs on board because I hadn't hired enough security for the event, and the birthday girl ended up in hospital getting her stomach pumped.

"And why was it a disaster, Tanya? How did that poor sixteen-year-old end up in hospital for three days straight whilst her parents were furious with you?" Poppy persists. She's enjoying this. "Well, drugs are a terrible thing, aren't they?"

"Christ, Tanya," Annabel says. "She overdosed? How could that happen?"

"I wasn't focused. It shouldn't have ever happened."

"Oh, Tanya knows all about drugs," Poppy says. "I wouldn't have been surprised if you'd supplied them to her yourself. Thank goodness you at least had some sense there."

"What?" Annabel looks perplexed.

Chloe is biting her lip so hard it's starting to bleed. She knows what's coming.

I can only brace myself for impact.

Poppy continues. "Did you all know that Tanya has been addicted to cocaine for the past two years? Because everyone else does now. I made sure to update all your social media with your confession."

Oh God. Everyone now knows.

All of the aches and pains, the constant congestion and flu and nausea, seem to dial up to their maximum capacity. Staring at Poppy it's as if she's underwater, everything around me a sickening blur of shapes and colours. I've tried so hard to hide it. I know I've been grumpy and distant. I know I look like shit. But as long as no one questioned it, or pointed anything out, I was fine. I could get by. Now it feels like there's a neon sign pointing to me: addict, addict, addict.

The only person who knew, besides Harry when he broke up with me for it, was Chloe, who caught me taking it at this very party.

She covered for me. And I covered for her.

That was our agreement.

"London is such a hotbed for that kind of thing." Poppy sighs, as if this upsets her. "You'd be surprised at some of the children that come in due to drug issues. It's a terrible world out there. But Tanya kept it very under wraps."

"That's not why I was fired," I say, finding my voice. "It had nothing to do with that. They fired me for incompetence. They didn't know I was . . . I took drugs too. I've hidden that part of myself."

"Oh, Tanya." Poppy shakes her head at me. "You're smarter than that. You're an independent contractor. Why do you think no one has hired you since? One bad gig and that's it, you're finished? Unlikely."

I'm starting to doubt myself. "But they didn't know. They didn't know the reason things went wrong was because I was high."

"Someone made sure they did know. Someone wanted to protect client friends of theirs."

"No." I turn to Chloe, furious. "Did you *tell* them?"

She looks like a deer in headlights, mouth open. "No! Tanya, I didn't!"

"When I think of what I did for you!"

"I didn't, I promise!"

"It was me."

Everything falls silent. We all turn to Esther, who is red-faced and beginning to stutter.

"You have to understand," she says. "A lot of people at that party are clients of mine, and I'd booked you for the event. It was embarrassing. They wanted more of a reason than that you were incompetent. So I told them the truth. I tried to sell it as a sob story, that you were struggling. It backfired."

"Oh, wonderful," Poppy says. "I didn't have to tell you myself. Look at Esther playing the good girl."

My head is swimming. "But how did you even know?"

"I was at that party too," she says quietly. "I saw everything."

"Oh my God." I can't believe it. "All this time, and you didn't tell me? And then you got me fired and made sure I never got another job again? How could you?"

"Please." She tries to reach for me, and I back away, disgusted.

"Get away from me."

"So now you all know why I brought you here," Poppy says. "I wanted to see whether the four of you had changed and become better people, or whether you were still the same shallow self-centred girls who left me behind at school in pieces and never came back. And what did I find? More of the same. If not worse. I had to punish you all. You deserved it for what you did to me."

"You're pathetic," Annabel hisses. "You won't get away with this."

Chloe holds her phone in the air. "As soon as I get signal, we're calling Robin or whatever her name is and getting the hell out of here. And you will regret this."

"I'd hurry up with getting signal if I was you," Poppy says. "Because your phones only have so much battery left, and I've thrown all your chargers into the sea."

It's the final straw. Already enraged, I step towards Poppy and push her with both hands into her chest. She stumbles backwards, but manages to catch herself from falling. I'm about to go for her again when Esther pulls me away.

"Don't, Tanya," she says. And then, under her breath: "Not right now anyway."

"Get off me!" I snap. "You've done enough to me. You're almost as bad."

Poppy smirks, and it takes everything in me not to launch myself at her once more.

"I don't know what you're smiling about," I say. "You won't be smiling by the time I'm finished with you."

She mocks fear, clapping a hand to her mouth. "I'm shaking where I stand."

The rest of us have closed ranks against her, standing as four against one. We're in no fit state anymore, destroyed by the endless revelations. Poppy seems to sense this too, because she folds her arms, relaxing her guard.

"I'm taking a walk," she says. "You all need to think about what you deserve. Because there's more to come. We'll talk later."

"More to come?" I say. "Who do you think you are?"

Chloe's hands are trembling. "Haven't you done enough?"

Annabel bites her lip, and Esther is shaking her head.

"Poppy!" I call. "Tell us!"

But she ignores me now, turning from us and walking away.

Esther scowls. "What the fuck are we going to do?"

I hate her. But I hate Poppy more. I turn to Annabel and Chloe, who are steadfastly ignoring one another.

Poppy vanishes from sight.

"She's trying to fuck with us," I say. "She wants us arguing. She wants us divided."

Chloe nods. "Should we go after her? What did she mean by 'later'?"

"No." Esther still seems shell-shocked by it all. "I have no idea what she meant. But we can't think about that right now. We need to get out of here."

"Do any of you have signal to call Robin?" I ask.

They shake their heads.

"Well, keep checking. We'll get off here soon enough." But the battery on my phone is at ten percent, and I'm not holding out much hope.

"I'm drinking this fucking gin," Annabel says, taking it from the table and opening it up. "Who's joining me? Let's drink our prize from the scavenger hunt."

"You're on," I say.

"You're drinking at a time like this?" Esther says. "After everything that's just happened?"

"When else is there a better time?" Annabel snaps. "Our lives have been ruined. I say we drink."

She pours enough for a double, then passes me the bottle. I pour one for everyone else, even Esther, and each of us drink it straight back, needing the alcohol to numb our feelings to everything that has just happened. The gin is surprisingly bitter and hard to get down, but that just makes me more determined to drink it.

"This tastes like shit," Annabel says. "Some prize."

"Fuck her," Chloe says. "Let's wreck this place."

"Let's get fucked ourselves," I say.

My rage is focused on Poppy Greer. For now, everyone else seems to be in agreement.

"She's dead," Annabel says. "I'm going to kill her."

"Not if I kill her first." Chloe raises her glass in the air. "To sending that bitch to hell."

We all toast, our faces solemn. From catching my reflection in the glass I can see I'm pale, white with wrath.

"What are we going to do?" Esther says. "Shouldn't we talk about what happened?"

"I think you've done enough talking," I say.

"I'm sorry. I didn't think you would be blacklisted like that."

"Did you all know?" Annabel asks. "You all knew about Tanya's cocaine addiction and didn't tell me? Just like Morocco?"

"I didn't know that Esther knew. She kept that all to herself." A bottle of unopened tonic sits on the side and I add it to the gin. "It's hardly comparable to a fucking holiday, Annabel."

"No." At least she has the grace to look a little ashamed. "I know that. I just don't know why you didn't try to get some help."

Maybe because I didn't feel like I deserved any.

"I thought I could handle it," I say instead.

"My career is over," Chloe says. "All because I made one stupid joke."

"My career too." Esther sighs.

"You deserve it," Annabel says to Chloe. "It was your own fault. Look at that. Your actions have consequences."

"Annabel," Esther says in a warning tone. "Leave it. We have bigger problems. We need to deal with Poppy."

"Were we really that bad?" Chloe asks. "At school, I mean. To Poppy. Did we deserve this?"

Esther's response is instant. "No. We were kids. Yes, we could be harsh at times, but that's nothing compared to what Poppy has done now."

"What she's done now is unforgivable," Chloe says, ignoring the scowl from Annabel.

The alcohol is finally masking some of my withdrawal symptoms. "So what are we going to do about her?"

"She's the one who should be frightened," Esther murmurs.

We all look at one another. Do we dare?

"She's all alone on this island with us," Chloe says. "I don't think she thought that one through."

"She needs to watch her back," Annabel agrees.

"Could we do it?" I whisper. "Would anyone even care if she . . . never came home?"

There's a pause, and then we drink some more. We're all still on edge, but the thought has burned into our minds now, that glorious idea: revenge. After all, it's not the first time the four of us have banded against her. It'd be like stepping into old comfy shoes or returning home after a long time away; sure enough, it'd be like we never left.

As we carry on drinking, losing ourselves to the rest of the day and night, our phones drain of battery.

Esther's is the last to go. A final dark screen that sends us all over the edge and into a determined drunken stupor.

We're stranded on this island now, but maybe that's a good thing after all.

Because that bitch is going to pay.

I'm just not sure which one of us is going to get to her first.

EIGHTEEN

———

Esther

MAY 21, 2023

The hangover hits me as I sit up, making me moan and close my eyes again. The throbbing never seems to subside, crashing against my skull. Did we really drink that much? Even holding my head gives me no comfort, my vision blurring and refocusing a number of times before it settles.

Maybe this is just the after-effects of yesterday reaching me. Part of me wishes it was all just some awful fever dream, but the dry mouth and aching kidneys remind me all too well it wasn't. I've really lost my job. Everyone at my work has seen me naked.

For a second I think I might throw up there and then on the bed, and I have to lean over the side and take deep breaths. There's no telling what is going on back home. My office might have been packed up already, my stuff in little boxes in a dreadful back room somewhere waiting to be collected. Oh God, and I'd have to walk through to get them too. Past everyone whilst they look at me in horror. Actually, would they even let me in after that? I'm not sure what's worse. Facing everyone again or being humiliated waiting in the foyer for someone to come and bring me everything.

I won't let it happen. There will be a way to prove it was Poppy who sent the pictures. Surely they can't get rid of me so fast.

I wonder if my parents have found out. My mother, who got me the job interview in the first place. Jesus.

The room feels hot and stifling. I need to get out of here.

As I fling the covers off, I gasp.

My stomach is red. I think I've been injured when I realise it's from the red lipstick. A word, written on me. No, an insult. *BITCH*. When the hell did that happen? Was it Tanya? Poppy?

I try to rewind my brain for last night's events but come up stubbornly blank. Only a few key memories stick in my mind. For a second I think I must have overslept, a first for me, but then the sunrise starts to filter through the window and I realise it's dawn.

My hands fly to my phone, which now sits on the bedside table. The black screen reminds me that there is no charge; the crack reminds me how shattered our lives have become. Those emails come flooding back to me again, and even though it achieves nothing, I turn the phone upside down so the screen no longer faces me.

It's very quiet. Despite how I'm feeling, I can't imagine not going for a run. It's like breathing for me, as natural as other people who desperately reach for caffeine in the morning. There's a moment as I stand up when the world seems to tilt on its axis and I think I'm going to fall, grabbing the bedpost. Mercifully, it rights itself, and I take slow movements. The lipstick lies on the floor, cap missing. I shove it into a drawer, desperate not to see it. As I change into my gear, scrubbing the horrible lipstick away, I can't even hear the ocean. It must be very calm out there this morning.

One look in the mirror tells me all I need to know about last night. Bags are heavy under my bloodshot eyes, my lips are dry and cracked, and even staring for too long gives me a headache. I tie my hair up into a messy bun and head outside, sunlight making me groan.

First: water. I walk past the other huts, all lights switched off. I think I can even hear Annabel snoring. Tanya's door is half open, and I'm tempted to go and close it but don't want to scare her. Outside Chloe's hut, the Capri-Sun wrapper from the scavenger hunt is stuck under one of her boots. Why does she have one of the items too?

As I round the corner to the main lodge, I can see a puddle of sick on the decking. Nice. There was no rain last night, so it's remained, the smell getting worse in the heat. I swirl my tongue around my mouth, conscious that I could be the culprit, but I'm clean. If morning breath and forgetting to brush my teeth last night can be considered clean. But at least I haven't thrown up.

When I open the lodge door, there's a smudge of something wet on my hand.

"Gross," I say, thinking it's vomit. I rush over to the sink and wash my hand under the tap.

It's then that I see what I touched is red, coming off my hand down the plughole.

Blood?

I snap my hand back, but all traces are gone, and when I go to the doorframe there is the slightest of smudges now. Stained. Dark. As if in the shape of fingers wrapping around.

I lean closer and smell, but the fresh air outside interferes and I can't be sure.

Did one of us get a nosebleed or something?

I drink gratefully from the tap, filling and refilling one of the glasses from the cupboard. My throat feels like it's on fire and even now my hands are still shaky. We aren't young anymore, clearly. We can't just bounce back.

The door opens and Chloe heads inside. She looks even rougher, clutching her head.

"When the hell did we go to bed last night?" she asks, filling her own glass of water and taking a long gulp. "I feel like death. Like actual death."

"Haven't got a clue. Did you wake up to anything strange?"

"No. What do you mean?" She sits down at the kitchen table, and I do the same. We're careful to keep our voices quiet, aware of Poppy in the room just next door. "How are you feeling?"

"Rough," I say. I omit the fact I woke up with *BITCH* scrawled in red lipstick on my stomach. "It feels like I've been run over by a bus carrying cymbals. You're up early."

"Couldn't sleep. I still can't believe what happened yesterday."

"We should have seen it coming." This is the thought I keep coming back to. We knew things were awkward, that things were starting to turn when we did that scavenger hunt. And yet we persisted. Why? Because we wanted to prove that we weren't that bad? Because our egos were too great to admit that Poppy might still have a problem with us?

We were fools.

Chloe indicates the door with her head. "Is she up?"

"Haven't heard from her."

"Maybe we should wake her up by pouring our water over her face."

This finally makes me smile. "Don't tempt me."

Chloe holds her water out in front of her, considering. "I'm not joking." As she leans forward, her face is caught in the light and I can see scratches down her neck.

"What are they?"

"What?"

"On your neck. Did something scratch you?"

She looks baffled. "Scratch me?" Her fingers touch the marks on her neck, and she realises what I'm talking about. "Huh, that's weird. No idea. Maybe it was from the bushes on that bloody scavenger hunt."

"Are we planning a coup?" Annabel walks in, followed by Tanya close behind.

I hold my breath at the sight of Tanya, but at the moment she seems content to ignore me, passing right by me to get herself a drink of coffee as if I don't exist.

"Tanya," I say, but she pretends she hasn't heard me.

The four of sit around the kitchen table, but there's no easy conversation to have. We know things about each other now. Annabel's husband's cheating not only with random strangers but with Chloe. Tanya's drug problems. Chloe and I have lost our jobs. It feels intimate. We don't discuss these kinds of things. Not as a group, anyway. I'm very aware that there's more Poppy didn't uncover, something I'm relieved about.

"Does anyone else feel like they've been hit by a lorry?" Annabel asks, rubbing her forehead with her fingers. "I've never been this bad after drinking before."

Chloe nods. "Same here. No matter how much water I get down me, nothing is helping."

"I wasn't asking you," Annabel says.

Tanya stays quiet, but from her closed eyes and pained expression I'm sure she's feeling the same.

I need to make it up with Tanya somehow, but now isn't the time. Same with Annabel and Chloe. If we're going to be united in this, we need to actually be on good terms. Right now, it's like we're a group of mines, ready to explode at the slightest touch. We pick at toast, focused on the closed door of Poppy's bedroom.

Half an hour goes by before Chloe stands up, impatient. "We should just go in. She doesn't get to hide in her bedroom all day. She needs to face the consequences."

"Chloe's right," Tanya says. "She's a coward."

We walk to the bedroom door, but hesitate.

"What if she's just asleep?" Annabel asks. "I don't want to spend another second in her company."

"Poppy is the one who is going to set off those flares and get us home,"

Tanya says. "I'm not going to be the one who gets in trouble for it. She can take the blame. She's the one who cut the landline in the first place."

There's something sinister about the closed door and the silence it brings. Why hasn't Poppy come out at the sound of our voices? Every other day she's been up at the same time as me, a fact that surprised me to no end. Every time I went for a run she would be there, either on the decking or on the beach, watching me go.

"What's that?" Annabel says sharply. She's staring at the floor.

We all look down, and at first I'm not sure what she's talking about. But then I see it, the rust-coloured marks, spilling out from under the frame. Hastily wiped away.

"Is that—" I can't finish my sentence.

"Jesus." Tanya steps back. "That's blood, isn't it?"

Annabel bends down and rubs her finger at it. "Someone has tried to clean this," she says. "It's just the stain left."

"Old then?" Chloe says, eyes darting around the room to see if anywhere else is contaminated. "Not from this trip?"

Annabel stands up, brushing dust from her jeans. "What do I look like, a forensic scientist? I don't know. I don't remember seeing it before though."

"There was blood on the front door," I say.

"What?" The others stare at me in shock.

"I just thought one of you got a nosebleed or something and wiped your fingers on the frame." I walk over and demonstrate where I found it, the remainder still there but easy to miss. "Like someone had blood on their hands and touched it accidentally."

Everyone looks at their hands, but they are clean.

"Does anyone remember much of last night?" I say.

They pause to think, then shake their heads.

"So anything could have happened," I conclude.

"Then . . . the blood?" Annabel walks back towards the bedroom door, to that suspicious large stain on the floor that leads under the frame and could carry on further for all we know. "What caused the blood?"

"Maybe Poppy is dead," Chloe says, and we all laugh.

"That'd be like all our wishes coming true, no?" Tanya says.

But then we look at the blood again.

"Why isn't she coming out?" Chloe asks uncertainly.

Tanya seems to feel the same, because panic flits across her features. "We need to go in."

I nod. We're all at the door within moments, knocking several times.

"Poppy!" Annabel calls. "Poppy, are you in there? We're coming in!"

Without waiting for a response, Annabel pushes the door open. It swings back violently, clattering all the way against the wall on the right.

The light is off, but it doesn't matter. Sunlight streams through the dual-aspect windows, flooding the room with brightness. Everything comes together with horrific clarity.

Poppy's bed has been slept in, the sheets tangled. The covers are thrown off, half hanging to the ground. A glass of milk she must have brought to bed is lying in pieces on the floor, the milk mixing with the puddle of blood. The bedsheets are covered too. Angry, violent blood stains that have transferred onto the quilt and ground, even above on the wall in a dreadful splatter. The drawers have been opened, as if someone has been searching for something, objects thrown about without care onto the ground.

The bed is empty. Poppy isn't there.

On the wall above, she has her own gruesome painting. It looks familiar, like a re-creation of something I have seen before, but I can't place it. A woman stands, half naked, a cracked and barren landscape behind her. The sky is dark. She wears a flowing white skirt but her top half is exposed, only thin white straps around her waist and shoulders, almost like a straitjacket. In the centre, her torso is split and a broken heart is visible. She is covered in scars, from her wrists travelling up her arms and even on her stomach. Tears stream down her cheeks.

It is a self-portrait. Poppy's eyes stare in anguish at us from the canvas, but there is an unapologetic defiance about the pose too. This is who she is, take her or leave her. Even though she is injured in the painting, there isn't any blood. Not like what is directly below it.

An unsettling trail leads to where we are standing. Swathes of blood in smeared solid stains. Drag marks.

"What the . . ." Annabel claps both hands to her mouth, and wobbles on her feet. "I think I'm going to be sick."

Tanya steps forward, but I pull her back. She turns to me, expression dark. "What the hell are you doing?"

"We can't touch anything," I say. "This is a—this is a crime scene."

"A crime scene?" Tanya echoes. "This has to be some kind of joke."

The windows are closed and the stench is overwhelming. Something musty hits my nostrils and now that I've noticed it I can't escape. This is real.

"Where is Poppy?" Chloe whispers.

Someone needs to take control. Annabel's face is still pale, Chloe stands frozen, and Tanya looks puzzled more than anything else.

I take a deep breath. "We need to look for her. Search the island. Just in case she's hurt somewhere."

Chloe nods, eagerly. "Yes, she must be somewhere. This is a tiny island. She can't have vanished."

"Unless someone put her in the sea," Tanya says.

"Christ, Tanya!" I snap. "That is not helping. No one has put her in the sea. What an awful thing to say."

Annabel's face falls. "It would be so easy to do. She would wash away."

"There's only us on this island," I say. "So that *can't* have happened. Got it?"

Their silent responses give me no comfort.

"We need to look around." My voice sounds much more confident than I'm actually feeling. Any minute now I think I'm going to faint.

A headache forces itself into my forehead. "Annabel, you do the huts. Chloe, you do the general outside area like the lawn and the trees. Tanya, you do the cliff. And I'll take the beach. She can't have . . ." I struggle to finish. "She can't have got far if what we see here is to be believed, but we have to check."

We leave the lodge together, but separate immediately. I'm grateful for the break from them, allowing my breath to come out in the gasps it desperately needs. I head for the beach without hesitation, praying beyond all hope that I won't find anything sinister.

The beach stretches out for over a mile, but even from here there are no obvious shapes in the distance, no clear indications of Poppy sunbathing or going for a walk that would ease everyone's worries. Not that I expected that. If anything, I'm relieved her body hasn't washed up on the shore, the tide turned against her assailant.

Calm down, Esther.

My pulse continues to race as I stride down the sand, taking care to look out in the ocean as well as in the ditches that lead to the trees and overgrowth on the opposite side.

By the time I reach the rock pools, I'm convinced there's nothing to be found here. I happen to glance upwards and spot Tanya standing atop the cliff. She isn't looking at me. Her hands are burying her face.

Is she crying? Has she found something?

But no. She wipes her eyes and turns to head back down. There must be nothing there either.

I'm almost at the start again when I see it.

Drifting in and out with the tide, snagged on a jagged rock that pokes out of the sand a couple metres into the sea.

The top Poppy was wearing yesterday. The sequins that made it sparkle at breakfast have gone into overdrive exposed to the sun like this, glittering more than the ocean. Taking my shoes off, I go into the water and grab it to safety.

The collar is covered in blood.

"Oh my God," I say out loud.

For a second I'm tempted to throw it back in. What good would it do for the others to see?

But I'm too late.

"That's Poppy's top!" Annabel shrieks. "It's covered in blood, oh my God!"

Chloe and Tanya aren't far behind, coming running when they hear Annabel. They stop dead when they see what I'm holding.

"Did you find anything?" I ask them. "Any sign of Poppy?"

I already know the answer from their expressions, but disappointment hits me when they shake their heads anyway.

"Where did you find that?" Chloe asks.

"It was caught on that rock there." I point. "Pure luck that it happened to stay. Anything else would have . . ."

"So she was in the sea?" Tanya says.

"How did her top come loose?" Annabel asks, horrified.

I study the garment, finding a large tear down the side. "There's a rip here. Maybe from where it caught on that rock it came off. I don't know."

"Or someone removed it," Tanya whispers.

"She's dead," Annabel says. "Poppy is dead, isn't she? All that blood, there's no way she survived that."

"We need to call the police," I say.

"How?" Tanya says. "Poppy cut the phone line, remember? And our phones have no charge, and no signal anyway."

"Do we want to?" Chloe runs her fingers through her hair. "I mean, this could still be a joke. Right?"

"We all wanted her dead," Annabel says.

"Jesus, Annabel," I say. "We were speaking figuratively."

"Were we?" She walks around us, pacing. "I don't know. We were all so angry. And so drunk. I don't remember last night."

"This is insane," Tanya says. "You can't seriously think that one of us..."

"It has to be a sick game," I say. "She's playing with us somehow. She's messing with our heads."

Chloe nods. "Poppy pretty much told us she was going to do something to us. What if this is it?"

Annabel is still staring at the bloodstained top in my hands. "But if this is a game, how do you explain all the blood? This shirt? The fact it was in the sea?"

All too aware of what I'm holding, I try to bundle the top into a ball to hide the blood. "I don't know. Maybe she cut herself?"

"Cut herself?" Tanya rubs her temples with both hands. "Impossible. It was like a bloodbath in that bedroom. There's no way you could cut yourself that much and not bleed out and die. And we've searched the island! She can't have gotten far with that many injuries."

"Then it's someone else's blood?" Chloe says, almost hopefully.

"We're all here. And none of us are injured. How can it be anyone else? There's no one else on this island."

"Do we know that for sure?" Annabel whispers.

The thought terrifies us. We gaze round at each other, faces pale.

"That's impossible," Tanya says firmly. "The pier is so close to our huts. We would have heard the engine of a boat if it came by. We can hear the sea from our bedrooms for goodness' sake."

Chloe isn't comforted by this. "They could have had a rowboat or something! We never would have heard that."

"A rowboat all the way out here?" Tanya shakes her head. "Impossible. We're talking about crossing the ocean, not the River Thames."

"We were so out of it, maybe there was a boat and we just didn't hear it," Chloe persists.

Could that be possible? We all look half dead, a mixture of stress and exhaustion. There's a nervous energy around the four of us, which isn't helped by Chloe looking to check that no one is around.

There can't be anyone else.

"It doesn't make sense," I say. "Why would someone come to the island just to harm Poppy? What about the rest of us?"

This makes them pause.

"Esther's right," Annabel agrees. "There's no reason why a stranger would come and just hurt Poppy."

Chloe frowns. "But then, if it's not a stranger, and Poppy is still missing . . ."

"The flares!" I remember. "We can use the flares. They're under the kitchen sink. This is an emergency now. We need help."

"Of course!" Tanya starts to hurry towards the main lodge.

"Wait—" Chloe starts, but I'm in no mood to listen, following after Tanya and hearing the others coming too.

The flares are our last beacon of hope, quite literally. The moment we fire one of those into the sky, someone will come and get us.

But when I open the kitchen cupboard I'm met with an empty cardboard box.

They're gone.

"What the fuck?" I shout. "Where are they?"

"They were here!" Annabel says. "Robin told us."

"Poppy must have moved them when she cut the phone line," Tanya mutters. "That stupid bitch."

"No." Chloe looks as if she might cry. "She said at the time she didn't touch them, remember? Said if there was a real emergency we still had them to use."

"But then what?" Annabel says in disbelief. "How can they be gone? Are you saying one of *us* moved them? Because we've just established that there can't be anyone else on this island, right?"

I don't know what to think. My head is spinning. "If one of you moved the flares, now is the time to say."

"Well, I certainly didn't!"

"How can you even *say* that, Esther?"

"You don't trust us!"

"Shut up!" I shout. "Just shut up, all of you. What the hell are we going to do?"

"I'm not sure what we can do," Tanya says. "Everyone's phones have no charge. The main landline is cut. The flares are gone. Robin doesn't come here until tomorrow morning. I think we're going to have to wait."

"But Poppy is missing," Annabel says. "We can't just wait."

Missing is a kind way of putting it. All that blood. I'm sure she's dead.

"Unless you're thinking of swimming across to the mainland," Tanya says. "But I wouldn't try it."

"So we're just stranded, until tomorrow?" Annabel says. "No help, no nothing?"

Tanya nods. "That's what it looks like."

"But the flares." Annabel shakes her head. "That's deliberate. Someone moved them so that we couldn't get any help. So that we couldn't get off this island. What does that mean?"

We all regard one another in silence.

It means that someone on this island doesn't want us to leave.

Someone on this island is a killer.

Question is, which one of us?

It is quiet in here. Dark. Not yet near morning, the moonlight through the window illuminates the scene in front of me. My heart pounds, my mouth is dry. I want to deny the blood, the still corpse lying on the bed, but I know I can't. This was always going to happen.

Poppy is dead. Her face is still energetic, eyes and mouth open as if screaming, tears still stained on her cheeks. Her hair fans out behind her head like the halo of snow angels we used to make together as children.

My hand clasps around the handle of the knife even further, as if it might become one with my palm. The blade is steeped in Poppy's blood, as are my own clothes, covered in sweeping red stains that scream the truth.

I'm embarrassed and angry when my own tears come. This isn't about me. This is about her.

I want to scream.

What have I done?

It's all my fault. I've killed her, and this is the result.

What do I do? One quick glance at the window tells me morning is creeping closer. I have to act fast. I have to hide her, so no one else can ever see her like this.

Hide her, and hide the knife.

NINETEEN

Poppy

Dear Diary,

I just applied for my absolute dream. A place at the Slade School of Fine Art in London.

We were talking about universities during an art lesson a few days ago. We have all of Monday and Wednesday afternoons in the art rooms, working on our portfolios. The sixth form group is quite small, only eleven of us, so we're able to chat as long as we get on with the work.

"I'm going to study Biology," Sally, a girl who is obsessed with drawing in this animated style that is definitely copied from the various manga she reads, said.

"Biology!" another girl (our art class is hopelessly populated with girls—there are only three boys) called Jayla said in horror. She's actually quite good; she does these small sculptures made out of wire that look like different things depending on the angle you're looking at them. "Absolutely not. I'm going to do Art for sure. I'm applying for Oxford, Slade, Goldsmiths, and Newcastle."

Ollie sighed at that. "Imagine getting into Slade! That's my total dream." He looked at me. "Where are you applying, Poppy? You're doing Art in the future, right? I've already applied to Slade."

It felt like I was copying him if I said Slade was my dream too.

"Oh, I don't know, I think so," I mumbled instead.

"As long as you don't try to be too out there like you did in your GCSE," Sally said. "Even if you still got an A*, which I think was totally unfair."

Miss Wersham cut in at this point. "Poppy and I had a long conversation about her Art GCSE, and thankfully things were able to be sorted out in time. But Poppy, you absolutely should pursue Art at university. You're incredibly talented." And then, probably because she felt she had to, she added, "You all are."

I almost got in trouble with my Art GCSE. Our portfolios had to incorporate at least two different mediums of art, and at first I wanted to argue against that. I had been painting and drawing my whole life up to that point—it was what I was good at. I had this whole plan for a series of self-portraits that got increasingly more abstract and it would have been so great just as a series of paintings, but Miss Wersham told me I had to do what the curriculum asked.

"But isn't this really good art?" I asked at the time when she pulled me in to have a conversation about it. "Why can't I just do this when you know it's good enough?"

"It's about what the exam board wants," she replied, as if that settled it.

Look, I'm not pretending I know everything. I definitely don't. But when it comes to art—I know what's good and what's not. And it felt so silly to add some sculptures into my portfolio (I wasn't going to add photography, for God's sake) when it worked as it was.

I did my best to argue against it. It was only when Miss Wersham invited not only me but my parents in for a chat and said I'd *fail my whole portfolio if I didn't get my act together that I finally gave in.*

When I started the A Level Miss Wersham had a quiet word with me again.

"We're going to follow precisely what the exam board wants, aren't we?" she said.

"Right," I said, but I rolled my eyes.

"I'm being serious, Poppy." She frowned. "You have such a talent, and you just need to get the grades that show that. When you get to university, I'm sure you'll be free to experiment how you want then. But right now this is about making sure you have the fundamentals understood and demonstrated. I'm sure you'll still have an amazing portfolio."

"Not as good as I could make it though," I muttered.

It was true. The Art GCSE portfolio was fine—but it wasn't as good as my original plan. And even then Miss Wersham wasn't particularly happy with it, even if she did give it the highest grade possible.

"It looks awfully sad," she observed when she saw it for the final time. "Don't you think?"

I supposed she was right. But I was sad. After everything that had happened with Julian, what else was my art going to represent? I moved from more cheerful pieces to harsher swathes of reds and blues and blacks with abstract backgrounds and forceful depictions of myself in the centre. It was how I was feeling.

"Are you alright, Poppy?" she asked me, concern in her eyes. "If there's anything you want to talk about, you know I'm here for you."

"I'm fine," I lied. "I just like painting this kind of stuff. It doesn't mean anything."

And I am fine. Mostly.

I didn't have the heart to tell Miss Wersham the teachers hadn't been doing the best job of being there for me, but at least since Year Eleven and sixth form things had calmed down.

Annabel, Chloe, Esther, and Tanya didn't pick on me anymore. Not really. Not since our GCSEs meant things had to get serious, and then our A levels. Sure, they might occasionally make a passing comment or laugh at something, but they did that with most other people, that wasn't exclusive to me. I could breathe a bit better these past few years, because every day wasn't a torment. And I had the art group, at least. I tried not to let it bother me when they all walked home together or hung out after school and never invited me. I just think they're jealous of my talent anyway.

It has been so much nicer. To exist in the same space as those four and not feel terrified of my every move, worried about the scrutiny I'd get. Instead, okay I'm alone, but I'm happier.

And I've found ways of coping with the loneliness. It might mean I have to always wear long sleeves, but it's something.

When I got home from school that day after everyone talked about where they were applying I spent all evening researching all the different art schools across the country. There were lots of amazing ones, but I knew my heart was set on Slade.

Imagine! Me going to London. The capital. I've only been to London once before and that was for a birthday trip to all the main attractions when I was really little, so I barely remember it. I could be like all those professionals with their fancy clothes and a nice handbag, sitting on the Tube. In the evenings I'd have lots of friends from university so we'd all go out drinking and clubbing and not come home until dawn.

And yet, when I went to apply, my fingers hovered above the mouse, too terrified to click to start my application.

What if it was just like school? What if no one liked me? And worse, what if they were all much better at art than me and laughed at me and then I didn't even have that?

What if I didn't even get in at all?

The stress of it had me reaching inside my bedside drawer for my piece of mirror, but just as I was about to cut myself and feel some relief there was a knock at the bedroom door.

"Poppy, are you busy? Mum says dinner is almost ready."

It was Wendy.

I jumped up, slamming the bedside drawer shut, and opened the door to her. "I'll be down in a minute."

"What are you doing?" she asked, already looking past my shoulder. She saw my computer screen and let out a squeal of excitement. "Oh my God, you're applying to universities! Which one have you picked?"

Without waiting for permission, she pushed past me and sat at my desk, clicking through the various tabs I had open.

"Slade School of Fine Art?" she said. "Wow, this is in London. It looks amazing!"

I went over to her, hovering behind her nervously. "It's one of the best art schools in the whole country."

"You will definitely get in," she said. "Why haven't you started your application yet?"

"I was just looking," I told her. "I'm not sure if I'm even going to apply. I'd never get in. I don't think I'm good enough."

She looked at me as if I'd grown another head. "What are you talking about? Of course you'll get in. You're the best in the whole school!"

I wish I could have Wendy's confidence. She's always been so sure of herself. She's so smart she could do whatever she wants in the future. I didn't know how to tell her that I wasn't so brave or intel-

ligent. Art was my only option, and the idea of putting myself out there for the world to judge me suddenly felt like too much, especially when I got judged enough as it was right now. The thought that I'd apply and then not get in, and that those four would somehow find out . . .

Wendy softened when she saw the doubt in my face and turned to me, grabbing my hands. "Hey, you only need to look around this room to see how talented you are."

Paintings I did for fun at home decorated the walls of my bedroom. I tried to keep things lighter here, but even then, looking around, I could see the marked difference in pieces I had done when I was eleven or twelve compared to one I had completed only a few months ago. The paintings were better—I got better every year—but they were darker too.

"I know you've had a tough time," Wendy said, surprising me. "But it's been so long since everything happened with . . . Julian and those stupid girls. You smashed your GCSEs. You're going to smash your A levels. And you deserve to go to the university of your dreams and go be that famous artist you've always wanted to be."

She clicked on the "Start Application" button, and began filling in my details.

"Wendy!" I said, but I didn't really try to stop her. One of her hands was still holding mine.

"There's no going back now," she said, grinning. She gave my hand a squeeze. "You deserve this, Poppy. Go to London and be happy!"

"As long as you don't follow me in a couple of years." I laughed. It felt good to laugh.

"Hey, London is a big place!" Wendy protested with a smile. "You'll be too busy with all your new London pals to have time for your silly little sister anyway."

Seeing her there, helping me get my application started, suddenly brought tears to my eyes. I managed to wipe them away while her back was turned but gave her a big hug.

"What was that for?" she said. "You're not off to university yet, you know! You still have practically a whole year here!"

"I'll always have time for my silly little sister," I said. "Thank you, Wendy. For believing in me."

"Any time," she said. "What are sisters for?"

She stood up and nodded, satisfied, when I sat in her place and continued with the application.

"Shall I tell Mum you'll be a little late?"

"Yes please."

After she left, I finished off the rest. Again, my fingers hesitated at the "Submit" button.

This was really it.

I might have no friends. I might turn and run at the sight of Annabel, Chloe, Esther, and Tanya walking down the corridor towards me. I might spend my evenings listening to sad music and relying too much on an old, jagged piece of mirror to give me any kind of feeling beyond being lonely.

But I am definitely good at art. And I definitely deserve a place at Slade.

I'm going to get out of here and make my dreams come true.

And so I pressed "Submit."

Now it's a waiting game. I have to produce a portfolio and send it to them, but that will be easy. I have so many paintings to choose from. I just have to believe in myself.

A couple of days later, on the Wednesday, I told everyone I had applied for Slade.

"You applied for Slade too?" Ollie said, looking a bit put out.

"It's my dream as well," I said. And it felt so good to say it out loud.

It didn't matter that when I was walking home a bus drove past me through a puddle and splashed mud all up my skirt and tights. Or that of course the moment this happened Annabel and Chloe happened to be walking on the other side of the street and burst into laughter.

It didn't matter.

I still had a massive smile on my face thinking of the future.

MARCH 20, 2013

Dear Diary,

I DID IT!!!! I GOT INTO SLADE!!!

I can't believe it. I actually can't believe I'm writing this.

I got an email yesterday telling me my UCAS application had updated, but I had no idea what it was going to be. And then I saw it.

An offer from the Slade School of Fine Art. All I need is ABB in my A levels, including an A in Art, and I'll be there in September.

Me! I actually got in!

I was too scared to write in here before, but I was actually shortlisted and invited for an interview last month. It was terrifying. Mum came with me and I had to talk to all these super-posh people about my art and what I wanted to get from this university experience and even famous artists I knew and admired. I was so nervous I was sure I had messed it up entirely, so I didn't want to write anything in here in case I jinxed it. But I didn't mess it up! I GOT IN!!!

Mum and Dad and Wendy absolutely screamed when I rushed downstairs and told them.

"I knew it!" Wendy gloated, thumping me on the back. "I knew you'd get in! What did I tell you? You're amazing!"

"We're so proud of you!" Dad said. He was actually crying! "We're celebrating tonight!"

And we did. We went out to this mega-expensive restaurant in the centre of town that I've never seen the inside of before, even though it was a school night, and Mum and Dad even let Wendy and me have a tiny glass of champagne each when we toasted to my future. I had this huge steak for dinner and it was incredible, but the best part was the massive slice of cheesecake I had for dessert that I wouldn't share with anyone, not even when Wendy regretted her chocolate fudge cake and asked to swap.

It felt surreal walking into school the next day. I was absolutely buzzing with excitement to tell Miss Wersham and the rest of the class, but I managed to hold it in until the afternoon when it was our lesson. After we all got settled I told everyone I had an announcement to make.

"What is it, Poppy?" Miss Wersham asked, looking hopeful.

I couldn't wait a second longer. "I got into Slade! I'm going to go to London and do art and become a famous artist!"

"Oh Poppy, that's incredible!" Miss Wersham gasped.

Even the rest of the class are super impressed and happy for me.

"Poppy, that's amazing!"

"Wow, you actually did it!"

"London! You're so lucky!"

Only Ollie didn't look particularly pleased for me. I knew he had gone for an interview to Slade too. He'd actually been shortlisted before me, and I remembered how awful I felt when he came in bragging about his interview. I was so sure it was all over for me, but then a few days later I was invited for an interview too.

Once I'd calmed down and everyone had stopped talking, I

reached out to grab his arm and try to be comforting. "Don't worry, I bet you'll get your offer in a few days too."

He scowled at me and pulled his arm away. "Actually, I got my rejection two days ago. They didn't want me. My application was unsuccessful."

My face turned bright red and the class went deadly silent.

"Why didn't you tell us?" Sally asked. "We would have made you feel better!"

"Exactly!" Jayla added. "I didn't even get an interview with them, so don't worry."

He shrugged, but he was just as flushed as me. "I didn't want to. Who cares about Slade anyway?"

But I knew he did care. He was just as excited as me chatting about it. We'd even talked about living in the same accommodation together so that we had someone we knew in those first few weeks. It was almost like we were becoming real friends.

That wasn't going to happen now.

"They said I was being put on a reserve list if someone else dropped out or didn't accept their place," he said. "But who is going to do that?"

Not me, that was for sure. I don't know anyone who would give up their place at Slade.

"Well, there are plenty of other universities who would be lucky to have you," Miss Wersham said. "Well done, Poppy, and Ollie, I'm sure you'll get a place somewhere else soon and you'll like that one just as much as if you got into Slade. Getting into your first choice isn't always what's best. Things can work out in mysterious ways."

But I knew her words weren't going to mean much to him. I knew I'd be devastated.

I tried catching up with Ollie after the lesson ended.

"Hey Ollie!" I called. "I'm sorry about earlier. If I'd have known you were rejected I wouldn't have come in talking about it like that."

He wasn't in the mood though. He turned to me, scowling, and practically hissed at me. "Back off, Poppy! You're making it worse. I don't want to talk to anybody, and especially not you. Now go away."

It hurt, but I knew it was because he was hurting. And I knew from experience time to yourself could help.

I'm not going to let him dampen my mood though. I got into Slade! I'm actually achieving my dreams.

And do you know what I did when I got home from school?

The house was empty. Mum and Dad were still at work and Wendy had after-school revision. I went to my bedside drawer, took out that piece of mirror, wrapped it in some tissue paper, and put it in the kitchen bin downstairs.

Because I don't need it anymore.

I'm going to make the most of these last few months at home and school. I know I've been difficult lately, and moody, and okay, that's not entirely my fault, but I also need to move on. Annabel, Chloe, Esther, and Tanya won't be able to hurt me for much longer. I'll be free of them forever.

My A Level art portfolio is shaping up well. I'm sticking to the rules. Miss Wersham has approved all of it. There's just the final exam in May, a huge eight-hour-long creation of something completely new, and then I'll be done. I'll get my A grade, and I'll get out of here. As much as I would like to, I'm not taking any chances. Everything has to go exactly right, and then I can escape.

I can't believe it. I'm writing this diary entry with a big stupid smile on my face.

Things are finally looking up.

TWENTY

Annabel

MAY 21, 2023

I t has to be one of us," Esther says. "One of us did this."

Tanya opens her mouth to protest this again, then closes it. We're all starting to think it. There are no other options. We're on a private island in the middle of the ocean with the mainland miles away. No one else is here, and there's no way off until Robin comes tomorrow with the boat.

My mind strains to remember last night, but it remains a stubborn blur of images. Why did we get so drunk? What were we thinking? To drown our sorrows, I suppose, after everything. What a mistake.

But then we were also discussing what we were going to do to Poppy...

"If someone confesses to murdering Poppy, maybe we can help you cover it up."

We all turn to stare at Tanya.

"What do you mean cover it up?" Chloe says. "Cover up a murder?"

Tanya juts her chin out, defiant in the face of our obvious disgust. "You can all look at me like that for as long as you want. You know it makes sense."

"How on earth does it *make sense*?" Esther spits. "You're talking about hiding the fact someone was killed. By someone here!"

"Well, you wouldn't know the first thing about hiding something, would you, Esther?" Tanya snaps. "You love to spill people's secrets, even if that means them losing their jobs."

Esther's face darkens. She glances at me, and I give a tiny shake of my head, begging her not to say it.

Chloe steps between them. "Now isn't the time for this. Look, maybe covering it up isn't such a bad idea."

"You got a confession to make, Chloe?" I say. It comes out more forceful than I intended, and she holds her hands up in surrender.

"I'm not saying that! It wasn't me. But we're on an island. We have time to clean the blood. We can tell Robin that Poppy went for a swim and never came back."

Esther shakes her head. "Cleaning blood is more difficult than you think. It's not as simple as giving it a wipe-down. That stuff stays. What if they did a full-blown investigation? The first place they'd check is the main lodge, and oh look, there's all her blood. And then we'd all be implicated. We'd all be proven liars."

"And how do we explain the broken phone and missing flares?" I say. This idea is complete insanity. "Not to mention the fact that back home right now, everyone is witnessing Poppy's revenge."

Tanya takes a deep breath. "So what do you suggest, Annabel? Come on, you were always the ringleader in our little schemes at school. Pray do tell us how we should proceed from here."

"Maybe Poppy is still on the island," I say desperately. "Maybe we're all jumping to conclusions."

"Ah, yes, she's just picked herself up after all that blood pouring out of her and taken herself for a nice little walk."

"Stop it, Tanya." Chloe starts to pace back and forth. "What is going to happen when Robin comes back? What are we going to say?"

"Whoever did this is going to have to come clean." I make sure to look each of them in the eye. "We were all angry at Poppy. We all had our reasons to hurt her. We'll understand it was just a moment of madness. But you need to tell the truth now."

"But it's like you said," Esther says. "We were all angry. We're all suspects. Why would whoever did it come clean now?"

I can't believe what I'm hearing. Esther faces me calmly, and shrugs at my expression.

"I'm just saying. *I* didn't do it."

It's awful, but I don't know if I believe her. Nor do I believe Tanya and Chloe, not after their discussion on whether we should just cover the whole thing up. My three oldest friends, and I don't think I trust any of them.

"Does anyone remember anything about last night now?" I ask. "Does anyone know the last time they saw Poppy?"

As I say it, a memory comes back to me. The four of us, sitting around the fire pit, and Poppy returning from her walk. She'd been gone for hours. She told us something about sunbathing, but we ignored her and pretended she wasn't there. And then she went inside the lodge, not turning to say good night. I think someone (Tanya?) shouted after her, calling her rude names. And we all laughed.

I tell the others what I remember, but I'm met with frowns.

"No, that wasn't the last time," Chloe says. "She came out again, remember? She stood on the decking and stared at us all."

Did she? I try to think back, but come up blank.

The others are nodding though.

"Yes, it was odd," Esther says. "Even considering everything that had gone down."

"What about the rest of the night?" I say. "Like, when did we even go to bed? Did anyone hear anything?"

They shake their heads.

"I have no clue." Esther folds her arms. "But I did wake . . ."

"Wake what?" I prompt, when she stops speaking.

"No, never mind." She waves her hand at me. "I don't know what I was going to say."

"Do we really all not remember?" I'm suspicious, but I can't help it. "All four of us got that drunk that we all blacked out and woke up none the wiser?"

"It is odd," Tanya concedes.

"The gin," Chloe says. "What if it was the gin?"

Esther frowns. "You think the gin was spiked or something?"

"Poppy didn't drink any. It was all us. Our prize, remember?"

Shit. Realisation dawns on our faces.

"But why?" Tanya asks.

Oh, God. Thinking back, I remember it tasting a little bitter, us all complaining it wasn't worthy of being called a prize. But we knocked it back, shot after shot, until the whole bottle was consumed. What if it was bitter because Poppy had put something in it?

"Poppy did say there was more to come," Esther says. "Maybe she was planning on something today while we all felt this rough, or maybe she was going to do something when we were out of it last night."

"Maybe she did," Chloe says. "Maybe she started doing something, going into one of our rooms, and whoever it was caught her and—and killed her."

We take this in with a beat of silence.

"No." Tanya shakes her head. "Poppy was in her own room. Not one of ours. Someone had to have come in to find her deliberately."

"Is it such a bad thing?"

None of us know how to take Chloe's question.

She shrugs her shoulders at us. "I'm just saying. We all wanted her dead for what she did, didn't we? We were all talking about getting revenge."

"Maybe we all did it and we just don't remember," Tanya says.

"Is anyone actually sad that she's dead?" Chloe says.

Jesus Christ. I'm already sick of the sight of Chloe's face, and this just gives me another excuse to showcase my disgust. "It's one thing to say we're going to get revenge, another entirely to actually do it."

"I'm not sad she's dead," Esther says. "If anything, we should be toasting to that. And whoever did it deserves a medal."

God. This would be so much easier if I trusted them. But I don't.

"Look, let's just . . ." I look around the kitchen wildly, then come to a decision. "Let's just take some time out, and we can calm down and figure this out later."

Half of me expects them to argue with this, so I'm surprised when they just nod, accepting my judgement.

We start walking out of the main lodge, broken off into pairs: me and Esther, Tanya and Chloe. Esther's breath is jagged, I can hear it walking next to her.

"You okay?" I murmur, then pull a face. "I know that's a stupid question."

She doesn't look at me, but reaches for my arm and gives it a short squeeze. "This is mad, isn't it?"

"Do you really think we should just be happy she's gone?"

Esther leans closer, indicating her head behind us, where Tanya and Chloe have slowed their pace. Their heads are close together too, whispering away. "I can't believe those two wanted to cover it up. That's suspicious, isn't it?"

I can already sense the battle lines being drawn, us versus them.

"Maybe they were just . . . looking out for us."

Esther snorts at that. "Maybe we should go along with what they're suggesting, is all I'm saying. And then figure out what to do from there."

We reach the lawn, the main lodge looming behind us. The scene no longer looks picturesque, postcard material. Remnants of our previous nights are scattered about, deflated balloons and even a puddle of sick on the decking. The banner congratulating Poppy hangs limply, one side fallen. Nothing about this place screams a celebration has taken place. If anything, the landscape seems to know, despite the scorching paradise weather, that something awful has happened. Everything looks too bright, too colourful, a sickly masquerade of a good time.

Esther wraps an arm around my waist as we survey the scene, putting her mouth to my ear. "Remember, you owe me, Annabel. Don't go getting any stupid ideas."

Fear grips me. "That has nothing to do with this."

"Even so." Esther releases me and tries to smile, but it twitches at the edges and I can see how nervous she is. "Me and you need to stick together, if this all starts going wrong."

"It's already going wrong." But Tanya and Chloe have caught up to us now, and Esther starts backing away.

"I'm going to go for a run," she says. "I can't think like this."

"I need to have a shower," I say, pressing my hand to my forehead and feeling nothing but sweat. "I'll be ten minutes."

Tanya and Chloe head for the decking area outside, but look uncertain of each other. The main lodge remains an uncomfortable presence. That closed door, the knowledge of what is behind it, will remain at the forefront of our minds.

After I'm done showering, I head back. Tanya and Chloe have set up at the dining table outside. Rather than sit opposite one another, they're sitting together in deep conversation.

I know I shouldn't. There have been enough secrets, and I'm not innocent. But I stay where I am, hidden in the shadows of the trees on the path, and listen to what they're saying.

"It could very well be," Tanya says. She's calmer now.

I'm still in shock that she's been on drugs the past two years. So many revelations, so many things I didn't know.

But it shows she can keep a hell of a secret.

Chloe is more panicked. She looks behind and for a second I think she sees me and I freeze, but then she turns around and carries on. "It's the only way."

"Don't worry. We'll stick together."

It's so similar to what Esther said to me.

We are drawing lines in the sand, making alliances.

"Hey both of you!" I call, making my presence known.

They break apart, guilty expressions on their faces.

If it weren't for Poppy revealing what a conniving bitch Chloe was, maybe I'd be leading the celebrations. We'd toast to her death, confess who did it, and make a plan to turn her death into an accident, a mysterious disappearance. We'd cover for each other and live happily ever after.

But I can't do that.

It doesn't matter, I want to tell them. Make your alliance.

I don't trust any of you.

TWENTY-ONE

Chloe

MAY 21, 2023

Look, when it comes down to it, Poppy deserved it.

Deserved to die such a bloody, brutal death? No, maybe not quite to that extent. I'm not a monster, for Christ's sake. But after everything she did, I mean she should have seen it coming. Talk about putting yourself in danger. And now here Poppy is, turned up dead. It could be any one of us. We all had our reasons.

I can't believe we haven't all agreed to just cover it up. Is that really so bad? Who really cares about Poppy, especially after what she did to us all? But no, she had to go and reveal that Andrew cheated with me. And then Esther had to go and blab that she's the one who turned Tanya in and left her without work for months on end. So Annabel hates me and Tanya hates Esther. The four of us aren't going to work as a team.

Which means I'm going to have to look out for myself and myself alone, no matter how much Tanya wants to side with me. Sorry, babes. I'm all about number one. And if we're not going to be covering this murder up, I need to make sure I'm not the one who ends up going down for it. My life has already been fucked up enough by Poppy's little video, even if I'm sure it'll all blow over by the time I get back. (Honestly, people are so sensitive these days, it's so pathetic.) I'm not having me tied to this as well, no way.

Claiming a bad headache, I leave Tanya and Annabel at the dining table, pretending I'm going to bed.

Not true.

I'm going on a little scavenger hunt of my own. Time to see what you've all been up to, ladies, and hopefully I'll find something that will mean I can walk away from this free and easy. I head into Annabel's hut first.

The place looks a mess, which is so unlike Annabel. Clothes litter the floor, the drawers all open. It's odd, as if someone before me has come in here looking around for something. Annabel went to have a shower earlier—was she searching for something then? Or was she making sure something was well hidden? I check the various open drawers, but other than some underwear and socks, there doesn't seem to be much of interest. I'm still baffled by the expensive quality of her clothes. Every single item has a high-class designer label, far too many for a housewife, no matter how much she pretends Andrew gives her a large allowance. It bothers me, but it's nothing to do with Poppy, so I continue. I go so far as to run my hands underneath the pillows on the bed—nothing.

As I'm about to leave, something in me tells me to check the bathroom as well. A towel lies discarded on the floor, and the air in here is hot. My foot steps on something under the towel.

The broken mirror from the scavenger hunt.

What's that doing in here?

Worse. The remaining shards of glass have vanished. Were those used to stab Poppy?

I drop the mirror and cover it back up with the towel, then hurry out.

It's not enough. I haven't found anything conclusive. Maybe Annabel just stood on it like I did and put the glass shards in a bin somewhere. I'm being ridiculous.

When I get to Esther's hut, I knock first, just in case she's come back from her run.

"Esther?" I call, opening the door. But she's not there, and the room is in a much more pristine condition than Annabel's. Even her clothes for the day, put out before we found out anything about Poppy, are folded on the bed, waiting to be worn. The windows are open, reminding me of my smashed makeup.

As I search, I start to doubt myself. What am I even doing? Looking for what—the murder weapon? Poppy's body, hidden under the bed? And what if I do find it? What then?

Esther's bottom drawer opens to the lipstick from the scavenger hunt, cap missing and most of it crushed, pieces of red staining the bottom.

What the hell is going on?

"What do you think you're doing?"

Esther's voice startles me, and I practically topple over from how I've bent down. Straightening myself upright again, I'm met with her accusing glare.

"I should ask you the same question," I declare, jutting my chin outwards to show her I'm not afraid. "Why is that lipstick from the scavenger hunt in your drawer? What are you playing at?"

"You sneak into my room and you're the one asking me questions?" She strides forward, and for a second I think she's coming for me, so I hold my hands up in defence.

Her face falls. "Christ, Chloe. You're scared of me, aren't you?" She sits down on the bed and kicks her trainers off. "Is that why you're in here? You think I killed Poppy?"

"No! I don't know." I take out the lipstick and throw it on the bed. It looks sordid, a disgusting reminder of how we tricked Poppy into thinking Julian liked her. It looks even worse on the bed like this, open and ruined. "Why was this in your drawer?"

Esther looks pained. She takes out her ponytail and lets her hair swing loose, scratching at her scalp. "It's going to sound worse if I tell you the truth."

"What does that mean?" Now I'm even more nervous. Are my teeth chattering? I clamp down on my jaw to prevent Esther from noticing.

"I woke up with the word 'bitch' written on my stomach in this lipstick. And the lipstick was on the floor next to me."

The shock of this makes my mouth fall open again. "How? Why?"

"I don't know." But as she says this, her face clears. "Oh my God. Yes, I do. Last night, when we were wasted, we got all the scavenger hunt items out on the table. Started messing around with them."

Something about this sparks my own memory. I was doing something with the Capri-Sun, pretending to squirt it all over Tanya. Did Annabel have the mirror, then? Is that why it ended up in her bathroom? Did Tanya have the party hat? I have a vague flash of her putting it on me and snapping it against my chin. Is that where the scratches came from? And then Esther—we were mucking about with the lipstick, putting it on, pouting our lips. Did one of us write on Esther?

I wonder what happened to that grotesque canvas, the symbol of the worst thing we did.

"I think I remember too," I say cautiously. "But why didn't you just tell us this morning?"

"I thought it was just a drunken mistake. Some kind of stupid game. And then things became complicated."

Of course. My nerves start to ease. I am jumping to conclusions.

Her gaze narrows. "What about you?"

"What?"

"You sneaking into my room like this." She makes a tutting sound with her tongue. "I'm disappointed, Chloe. I can't believe you doubted me."

"It's not you." Suddenly, I'm eager for her approval. Steadfast, dependable Esther. She'll help me. Annabel despises me, and Tanya is too unreliable. No one's going to believe a drug-addicted loser when it comes to police questioning. I have to pick my allies better. "I've looked in Annabel's too. I'm looking in Tanya's next. Come with me."

"I thought you and Tanya were buddies," she says.

Shit. Does she know what Tanya and I said?

I laugh, but it comes out sounding forced, even to me. "We're all friends, aren't we?"

"Do you think this is real?" she asks, avoiding my comment.

"What do you mean?"

"All of this. The blood, Poppy going missing." She wraps her arms around herself. "I keep convincing myself Poppy is going to come out at any second and tell us it was all a game, but that's beginning to feel less and less likely."

"There's too much blood," I say.

And we all wanted to kill her. We all had a reason.

She sighs. "Let me change into my clothes. I'll meet you in Tanya's hut."

She avoided my comment about us all being friends, but I can't challenge her on it. I hurry out of the hut and back up towards Tanya's, again knocking before entering.

The curtains have been drawn in here, so I turn on the light, but the bulb merely sparks, then dies. Sighing, I open the curtains and get the fright of my life.

On Tanya's window, which faces thick trees and isn't a route any of us would go down, is a splatter of blood.

I open it in an instant, leaning my head out as far as possible to see the ground below.

But there's nothing else. No body, which was my first thought, heart pounding, but no more blood either.

Hands trembling, I search Tanya's room. I can't find anything.

I'm about to leave when the door opens and Esther walks in.

"Jesus, Chloe, you look like you've seen a ghost. What is it?"

"There's blood on Tanya's window."

"What?" Esther's voice comes out half strangled. She hurries to where I'm pointing, then staggers backwards, hands on her head. "Oh my God."

"What do we do now?" Is it bad there's a thrill of excitement rushing through me? That I might just have stumbled on something after all?

"Sit down." Esther thinks I'm trembling with fear. "You're going to faint."

I crash onto the bed, enjoying playing the part of a frightened damsel, but something feels off about the landing.

There's something underneath the mattress. The weight is distributed wrong—what should be a flat surface tips upwards at this end, and even though I'm sitting on the corner, I'm still higher up than the rest of the bed. Esther notices too.

"Shit." I rise to my feet again, and we both shift the mattress off the bed to the springs underneath.

There's a bundle of sheets, wrapped in a ball.

I think back to the conversation Tanya and I had an hour ago at most, walking back from the beach together whilst Esther and Annabel hurried ahead, no doubt deep in their own.

"You and me, we owe each other," Tanya had said, her voice low and somewhat threatening. "You need to appreciate that."

"We're innocent," I'd replied. "So you have nothing to worry about anyway. Right?"

"Right," she agreed, linking arms with me. "But we're closer than Esther and Annabel, aren't we? We'll back each other up, especially when the police arrive tomorrow."

"Of course."

"Think how suspicious we're going to look. It's best we get our facts straight about last night as soon as possible. So shall we say we saw each other go to bed? But we don't know about the others?"

"You're on."

Oh Tanya, Tanya. Nice try.

Esther and I unfold the sheet in silence. We both avoid looking at one another, but I can hear her panting breath, a sign of nerves or excitement, I'm not sure.

There are two sheets tangled in this mess. We unwrap the first and see the second is stained with blood.

For a second, I panic, despite myself.

"Maybe we should just pretend we didn't see this," I say. "I don't know what I was thinking, looking around everyone's rooms. It was a mistake."

Esther stares at me, astonished. "It's too late to say that now! You're the one who dragged me into this. We can't just leave it. She'll know we were here. And there's the blood on the window too."

I know she's right, but it's all become frighteningly real now.

"Fine." In a fit of bravery, I unravel the sheet, and then have to force myself not to throw up at the smell.

Like a prize at the end of Pass the Parcel, a bloody knife sits in the centre.

TWENTY-TWO

Tanya

MAY 21, 2023

Before I even know what's happening, they come for me, screaming their way down the beach, yelling my name, brandishing something in their hands. Esther is carrying what looks like bedsheets, and Chloe is carrying . . . a knife?

I sit up straight from my sunbed. What the fuck is going on?

Annabel rises too, confusion in her face that turns to horror at the sight of Esther and Chloe, who have joined us now.

It *is* a knife. With blood, thick and dried on the blade.

What is Chloe doing with a knife?

For a mad second I think she and Esther have come to kill us both, and I stand, ready for a fight.

"No wonder you wanted to cover it all up!" she declares, as if this means something.

Annabel comes to my side, still puzzled. "Where did you get that knife?"

Chloe points her finger at me. "Tanya had hidden it under her bed, between the mattress and bedsprings. It was wrapped in these sheets."

Esther, apparently her fabulous assistant now, opens up the bedsheet she's holding, revealing a large bloodstain in its centre. But the wind is stronger down by the sea, and it whips the sheet from her hands before she can do anything about it. We watch it fly into the air and then land on the water, floating out with the tide.

It doesn't matter. We all saw the blood before it was taken.

And the knife is still in Chloe's hand.

"I have no idea what you're talking about," I say, trying to keep calm. "Why would I hide this under my bed? That's a bit stupid, isn't it? And what were you doing in my room anyway? I thought we had an agreement."

I catch Chloe's gaze as I say this, but she stares straight through me, unrepentant.

"Chloe was searching all the rooms," Esther says. "I found her looking around mine, so I said I'd help her out looking in yours."

"Of course you did." I have to resist the urge to slap her.

"Wait." Annabel frowns. "You looked in my room? What for?"

Chloe's cheeks redden, but she presses on, convinced of her own righteousness. "I wanted to see if I could figure out what had happened. If I could find anything."

"How dare you look in my room after everything you did to me?" Annabel says. "You've got a hell of a nerve."

"Why are you so bothered about it anyway?" I ask. "Since when were you Poppy Greer's number one fan?"

"You don't have to like someone to care about their murder!"

"I think you just want to make sure you're not to blame," I say, and watch Chloe's face reveal I've hit the nail on the head. "I knew it. You've always been a selfish bitch."

"You're just trying to turn it around on me now! You're the one with the knife in your room."

"And what about your own room? Did you search that?"

"Well, no, obviously not."

I smirk. "Obviously not. Bit of a biased search party if you ask me. How do I know you actually found this knife in my room?"

"I was there," Esther says. "I found it too. Stop trying to change the subject."

"And what subject would that be, Esther?" I'm not even hiding my anger now, my voice coming out in sharp bursts. "That I secretly killed Poppy last night, then had the marvellous idea to hide the murder weapon in my own room?"

"No one else would have had time to put it in your room last night," she continues. "Stop trying to make excuses."

"So I have time to dump Poppy's body in the sea but not the murder weapon?" I can't help but laugh at the ludicrous nature of their accusations. "Oh sure, that makes a lot of sense."

Doubt begins to creep into Annabel's features, to my immense satisfaction.

Esther is more sure. "Maybe you didn't dump her body in the sea. Maybe it's still here on the island. There was blood on your window. You could have moved her somewhere out there."

Blood on my window? A complication.

Annabel has separated from me now, moving closer to Esther and Chloe.

"Do you realise how insane you both sound?" I say. "You're going to accuse me of murdering Poppy? Really?"

"Well, one of us did," Chloe says, "as everyone keeps saying."

"Not me. You've got the wrong person."

"You had the most motive." Esther seems to be almost enjoying this. It's strange. I've never seen her like this before. "You were Poppy's closest friend, after all. Her oldest friend. She had more reason to hate you than anyone, and you had more reason to hate her. She exposed your drug addiction to the world."

This seems to be convincing Annabel. She nods, slowly. "And your drug addiction, the withdrawal symptoms must be bad. Maybe you lashed out without thinking, made a terrible mistake."

I knew they'd look at me differently with this out in the open. Poor Tanya, addicted to drugs. Always the life and soul of a party and then corrupted by the party itself. No job, no partner, barely any money as it's all spent on cocaine or booze or just a simple good time, and any savings I once had are being used up fast. And now there's no chance of getting any of that back, because everyone knows what my life has become.

Because of Poppy.

Yes, I was angry at the time. Okay, angry is a soft adjective for it. Furious. Incandescent with rage. And of course I'm on edge without the cocaine. Who wouldn't be when they've been on it practically every day for the past two years?

So if I had the chance last night would I have hurt Poppy? After everything?

Perhaps. But the others don't need to know that.

"It's okay, Tanya," Chloe says. "I get it. We were all angry. Just tell us what happened, and we can move past it."

"Let me say this once, to make sure it's nice and clear," I say. "I. Did. Not. Kill. Poppy. That is all."

Esther sighs. "You've been caught red-handed. This is pathetic."

"No, you're all pathetic. One of you has done this, and you're trying to blame me!"

Annabel takes the knife from Chloe, staring at it in amazement. It's one of those proper kitchen blades, always a prop in scary films. There's something farcical about all of this. Any second now I'm expecting a director to shout "Cut!" and for us to laugh about how realistic we made the scene.

I wanted to be an actress once, a long time ago now. It was my dream when I was a kid. I was one of those terrible "arty" children who waxed lyrical about playwrights and poets and thought I was something. In all the school plays as the lead role. Even went to loads of auditions for plays and television series.

Never got a single callback.

"Not convincing enough," they told me once. "I didn't believe your pain."

I wonder if they'd believe me now.

"Tanya, please," Annabel says. "Let's put this awful day to rest. Just tell us."

"You're believing Chloe of all people, Annabel? Really?"

It has the reaction I'm hoping for. Annabel looks back at Chloe and frowns.

"Don't listen to her," Chloe says.

"She slept with Andrew!" I say. "How on earth are you even giving her the time of day?"

Chloe smirks. "Funny how you're willing to say that now, but not before."

Fuck.

"What do you mean?" Annabel asks.

"She knew," Chloe says. "She knew about the affair. She's known for practically a year, and she's never said a word to you."

I found out by accident. In the summer last year, Annabel had borrowed a jacket of mine for an event and never brought it back. She'd been acting aloof about it too, pretending not to remember this had even taken place. I knew she was away for the weekend for a family wedding and decided to get it myself from Andrew.

What I didn't anticipate was Chloe's car in the driveway, and the two of them clearly expecting a food delivery when they answered the door half dressed and finding me there instead.

All this time, and I've kept it a secret.

Annabel seems to freeze for a few seconds, hand still clutching the knife. Perhaps not the best decision to tell her whilst she still has a literal murder weapon in her hands, and Chloe seems to realise the same thing, backing away behind Esther, raising her hands in the air as a gesture of surrender.

But Annabel sidesteps her, coming face to face with me. She is calm. I wonder what currents are swirling underneath.

"Is what Chloe said true?" she murmurs.

"Surely not," Esther says. "That's crazy."

"I'm not asking you." Annabel's voice is poison. "I'm asking Tanya."

Behind her, Chloe watches me triumphantly. This little bitch. She's planned all of this.

"Look . . ." I try to buy some time. "It wasn't easy. I wanted to tell you. But Annabel, I was just trying to protect you. I was messed up with my own stuff, as you've found out the past few days. I was in my own chaos. I kept telling Chloe to come clean."

"I can't believe this!" she shouts. "You as well? It's one thing Andrew fucking any random blonde he happens across, it's another for that bimbo to be one of my so-called best friends, and then another thing *again* for my other best friend to know about it the whole time as well! This is un-believable."

"I'm sorry—" I try to reach for her, but she shrugs me off.

"I can't stand the lot of you," Annabel says. "Stay the fuck away from me."

"Annabel!"

She's striding away down the beach and rewards Esther's call with her middle finger.

"Annabel, don't you dare do that to me!" Esther yells. "Or there are things I've been keeping quiet that could come out as well. Annabel! Come back!"

Despite Esther's threat, she keeps walking. Soon enough she's a figure in the distance, not once looking back at us.

"What secrets are you keeping, Esther?" Chloe says. "Deadly ones, perhaps?"

"Shut up, Chloe," I say. "She's never going to forgive me."

"Join the club," she mutters.

Esther steps between us. "Enough. We have more important things to worry about than Chloe's stupid affair with Andrew! We have the knife! It's covered in Poppy's blood!"

"Oh for God's sake!"

"You need to go to your hut and stay there," Esther snaps.

Even though her tone is serious, the line still comes out sounding comical, ill-fitting for the situation. "You're not my mother."

"Let me put it another way," Esther says quietly, in a voice I've never heard from her before. "Either you go there and stay there of your own free will or I'll make sure that you do."

I want to argue further, but there's a wildness to her eyes that I don't trust. Even Chloe looks at her, surely afraid herself of this new Esther that has emerged from nowhere.

Or has she always been hidden underneath?

She was the one who came up with the Julian plan, after all. I remember being surprised at the time, that that level of calculation was somewhere within her.

There's a bruise forming around her left eye, and more around her neck.

Are those marks from someone attempting to strangle her?

Who would do such a thing, except someone trying to escape? Using whatever force they can muster?

Chloe and Esther walk me back to my hut like they're my bodyguards, one on either side of me. I can still feel Chloe's seething anger, but it's not her I'm worried about. Esther's coldness radiates from her, and when they leave me in my room alone I find I'm breathing a sigh of relief at just being away from her.

They think they've solved this, but they haven't solved a thing.

If anything, they've made it worse.

Because we're all against each other now. I'm the one that wanted us all to come, to finally face the past. I didn't want things to happen like this. But if that's how we're going to behave, so be it. Let them all fall apart. It's what they deserve.

An hour or so passes, and there is a knock on my door.

"Come in," I call from my bed. I'm not getting up for them. If they've come to apologise, or to accuse me further—let them. They're all going to hell in the end.

Whoever it is enters silently, closing the door behind them.

"Tanya," she says.

I turn around—and see the knife.

TWENTY-THREE

Esther

MAY 21, 2023

Poppy sits up in her bed, hair wild, rubbing her eyes. "What are you doing here?"

She's not afraid, but she should be. She wears a flimsy nightie, the spaghetti straps falling off her shoulders. The curtains are drawn, revealing a sliver of night sky that illuminates her on the bed in a spotlight. When I step forward, she sees the knife in my hands. The moonlight from the window catches the blade, making it gleam.

Her eyes are wide, and she raises her arms to protect herself. "Don't hurt me."

But I'm not in a forgiving mood. "You should have thought about that before you got me fired. Before you ruined my life."

"I'll say it was me," Poppy says, pleading. The desperation in her tone brings me further satisfaction. "You don't have to do this."

"Too late." I'm stumbling forward, still under the influence of that gin, but I throw myself onto the bed and push the knife deep into her torso.

"Esther!" she screams, panicking, trembling, trying to get away.

I take the knife out and plunge it in again, watching her bleed out all over the sheets.

"That's what you get," I tell her.

"Please!" she begs, her voice now a high-pitched squeal. When she realises I'll do nothing to save her, she raises it higher, appealing for anyone else. "Someone! Help me!"

And then I laugh. I laugh and laugh and laugh, as the light vanishes from her eyes and she turns cold and still.

Jesus Christ.

I wake up, my body jumping forward as I gasp for breath.

What the fuck was that? A dream? A nightmare? A memory coming back to me of that night?

For a second everything is just a white blur around me, and then things come into focus. I'm sitting up on my bed in my hut, on top of the covers, which are now drenched in sweat alongside my clothes. My mouth is dry and my throat feels like it's on fire. Mercifully, there's a bottle of water on the side table, and I glug it down, barely pausing to take a breath before the whole thing is gone.

I went for a nap. It comes back to me now. After we put Tanya in her room, I went to my own, determined to rest, still feeling hungover.

That was all just a horrible dream.

That's what I'm going to tell myself anyway.

I stand up and go to wash my face, changing into a simple sundress. The sun is still high in the sky, but no longer surrounded by a never-ending expanse of blue. Instead, storm clouds are beginning to gather, dark and threatening, turning blue into grey. Soon enough, it will rain. Perhaps worse.

Has anyone seen to Tanya in the past few hours? As I exit my hut, I think I can see Chloe in the distance, sunbathing on the lawn. Did Annabel come back from when she walked away? Is she in her hut now?

Tanya's is quiet and dark when I get to it. I knock on the door loudly, then call her name.

Nothing.

"I'm coming in," I say, loud enough for Annabel to hear in the hut next over if she's in there.

It's worse than Poppy.

Tanya is lying on the bed, eyes glazed at the ceiling. There's no life in them. Blood has spattered on the wall above the headboard, but most is pooled around her, seeping into the sheets. The knife—the same knife, I realise wildly, its tell-tale chip in the handle visible for all to see—is sticking out of her chest.

She's dead.

I scream.

I've never screamed like it in my life, pure agony and terror escaping my body in one long howl. Even at home, when I'm scared beyond my wits, the pit of nerves that eat away at my insides every day when I walk through the door, even when those nerves are confirmed with the real thing—it's never like this.

Did I kill Tanya? The thought comes to me of its own accord, a horrific shock to my system. Was my dream actually real, supplanting Tanya for Poppy in my subconscious as a way to deal with what I did?

Annabel and Chloe are behind me before I even finish screaming. I don't know how long I scream for. Perhaps a minute. Maybe longer. My throat is hoarse, all previous efforts of easing its dryness vanquished.

Chloe lets out a shriek, both hands clapped to her mouth.

Annabel, surprisingly, is the one to take action, marching forwards and switching on the light so the full devastation is clear. She hurries to Tanya, pressing a hand to her throat, even though we know it's futile. And then with a trembling hand she takes the knife out of her chest and sends it clattering to the floor.

"She's dead," she says, as if this wasn't already obvious.

"Cover her up. *Please*." Chloe turns from us and walks back outside, grabbing at her hair. "I can't look at her like that."

Annabel takes a second, peering at Tanya's body. "She's been stabbed twice."

"Twice?" Mustering up some courage, I come and see what she's talking about.

Sure enough, there are two puncture wounds. The one that the knife had settled in, the centre of her chest. But also one at her shoulder. The sheets are tangled, and the bedside table has been knocked onto the side.

"There was a struggle," I say. "She fought back. Wouldn't you have heard that in your hut next door?"

Annabel shakes her head. "I wasn't in there. I came back from the beach ten minutes ago. I was trying to eat. God. I can't believe this. She's really . . ."

"Have you covered her?" Chloe shouts. "I can't go in there."

Annabel and I drape one of the sheets over Tanya's body.

"Why is she still here and not Poppy?" I wonder aloud when we're done, stepping back and surveying the scene.

"Poppy was killed at night," Annabel says. "Much easier to move a body under the cover of darkness."

"But if Tanya is dead now too . . ."

Annabel finishes my sentence. "Then we were wrong about her. She didn't kill Poppy after all."

"I don't get it," I say. "Poppy makes sense. But Tanya? Why kill Tanya too?"

Chloe and Annabel shake their heads.

"Poppy, we all had our reasons. She had done terrible things to us. None of us were really sad that she had died. But Tanya was one of our oldest friends. I don't get it."

"She kept my cheating with Andrew a secret," Chloe says to Annabel. "You were annoyed at her for that."

Annabel's eyes flash with something. Anger?

"That's not a good reason to kill her," she says. "What about Esther?"

She turns to me. "You had gotten her fired. She was furious about that. Maybe you had another argument, you got angry."

"You're right, these are all trivial reasons," I say quickly. "They don't make sense."

"But it must have been one of us." Chloe moves back outside again, and this time we follow her, keen to get away from the sight of Tanya's body under that sheet.

"Yes."

"It was alright when it was Poppy," Chloe says. "This is different."

We all regard one another then as a cloud passes over the sun, darkening the landscape and creating shadows across our faces. The wind has picked up, a whistling sound between the palm trees, and the waves are starting to churn in the distance, victims of the weather before any of us. I don't know what to think about the two women that stand before me now, women I've known since we were at primary school together. I've grown up with them, we've seen each other from where we began to where we are now.

And I don't trust them at all.

"What do we do now?" Chloe says. "What the hell do we do now?"

"We need to stick together," I say. "No one goes off on their own anymore. We stay together, down in the main lodge."

"The main lodge?" Annabel echoes. "But the bedroom is where Poppy was killed. You can't expect us to stay there."

"It's also the most central, and it has the kitchen and two bathrooms," I explain. "We won't go into the bedroom, of course. I doubt any of us are going to feel like sleeping anymore."

The sky illuminates with a flash of lightning, followed by the distant roar of thunder. As if on cue, the first droplets of rain begin to fall.

"We need to move." I close Tanya's door, avoiding one last look inside. "It looks like there's going to be a storm tonight."

The three of us hurry to the main lodge, escaping inside before the rain starts to hammer down, beating the earth like a drum, relentless in its strength. We can hear it even with the door shut, like a percussion band all around us. We make coffee, aware of Poppy's closed bedroom door, then sit around the kitchen table, mugs clasped between both hands like we're desperate for warmth in this increasingly humid climate. Chloe can't look at either of us, focusing on her mug as if it's the most interesting thing in the world, and Annabel seems in shock.

Even though my stomach is tight with anxiety and my pulse jumps in my throat nonstop, I try to calm the others.

"We just have to make it until morning," I tell them. "Robin is coming first thing. We just have to survive the night."

"Easier said than done, apparently." Chloe glances up from her cup, lip trembling. "I can't believe she's dead."

"I don't even know what to think." Annabel takes a long sip of her coffee. "Everything has changed in the space of a day. This time yesterday we were getting drunk off that gin, everyone still alive. We thought Poppy's revenge was the worst thing we were going to face. We had no idea."

"I just don't understand it," Chloe says. "They're dead. They're not coming back. Ever."

We sit like this for a while, listening to the rain outside. More thunder roars, and before long it's clear a huge storm is passing through our tiny island.

Everyone else has always underestimated me. They look at me and don't see a threat. Why would they, when it's so much easier to see me as the same girl in the past? Even though, as has been proven, I am very good at keeping secrets, and not just my own.

Tanya in particular. Oh, Tanya most of all. Out of everyone, she's the one I had to make sure never stepped off this island again. She knows why she had to die by my hand, the life leaving her eyes as she accepted her fate.

Maybe I'm starting to let my anger get the best of me. My emotions. This has certainly been a hen party to remember, even though the bride is now absent.

I'm sorry you had to die here, Poppy, but it has to happen this way. The past finally needs confronting, so that I never have to think about that day ever again.

Who knows what I'll do next? I'm past the point of no return now. And I don't want to go back.

TWENTY-FOUR

Annabel

MAY 21, 2023

With the kettle boiling and the storm outside, it's hard to even hear myself think. For something to do, I offer to make everyone a cup of tea, aware that one of us drinking at the table is a murderer. We sit in silence for a long time after I hand round the mugs. I haven't washed them since the coffees, and I can taste a weird mixture of the two in my mouth. It doesn't matter. Any kind of caffeine boost will do.

"It was the same knife that killed Poppy," Chloe says suddenly. "I don't understand. Didn't you bring it back, Esther? Where did you put it?"

Esther flushes. "What are you implying?"

"I'm just asking," Chloe says. "Don't jump down my throat."

"I didn't have it with me."

They don't remember that I was the last one with the knife. I'm not going to help jog their memory. Those two. They went and searched all our rooms. The thought still makes me anxious, wondering what they found. With everything escalating, I haven't had a chance to have it out with Chloe properly yet, and the idea she still went snooping to see if I was capable of being a killer, after everything she did to me, is astounding. And her room was never searched. She could be hiding anything in there. Or maybe she was the one who planted the knife in Tanya's room in the first place, then staged her little detective game. Since when is Chloe of all people interested in stuff like that?

Anger burns inside of me. She's been steadily avoiding my gaze, sneaking glances when she thinks I'm not looking. I try to study her, wondering what Andrew saw in her that he didn't in me. Is it her inviting eyes? That alluring smile? Or how easy she is, always available at the drop of a hat?

She's been my friend for over twenty years, and this is how she treats me? It's this, not Andrew himself, that tears me apart. That she could do this to me.

Not because she's been such a great friend. She hasn't. She's a selfish, stupid little girl.

But because I can't believe I have allowed this to happen and not realised. That I haven't been able to make her face the consequences.

"This is all Poppy's fault," Esther says.

Chloe, to her credit, looks as confused as me. "How is this all Poppy's fault? She's dead. Tanya is dead."

Esther slams her mug on the table, spilling tea. "If she hadn't invited us in the first place, none of this would have happened. We should have known, from the very start, that it was a mistake. You all convinced me."

"Oh, come off it, Esther," Chloe snaps. "We all wanted to go in the end. It was a luxury private island, all expenses paid, with first-class flights. We'd have been stupid not to."

"But that's just it, isn't it?" Esther sighs. "We *were* stupid. To agree to it. Ten years down the line after what we did, Poppy just treats us to an incredible holiday? All we cared about was the opportunity to go on the trip of a lifetime, not to see her."

I think back to when we first received the invitations.

"Tanya was the one who convinced us, really," I say. "She was the one who felt guilty about the past. It wasn't just about the free holiday."

"And look where that got her," Esther points out. "She's dead."

Chloe's eyes widen. "Do you think that might be why? She used to be Poppy's best friend, remember. Maybe whoever it is has it out for both of them. Maybe Tanya was on Poppy's side."

"I never should have come," Esther insists.

"You could have not come," I snap. "You could have said no yourself. You didn't have to join us."

"I wanted to get away," she says quietly, almost to herself.

"Well, there you go, then." But she seems distant, as if she's forgotten what we're even talking about.

"One of you planted the knife in Tanya's room," Chloe murmurs. "For me to find it."

"None of that makes any sense." I frown. "If the goal was to make it seem like Tanya was the culprit, then why kill her too? It ruined the obvious suspect. It threw doubt on the whole thing again." Which makes me think you put the knife in there yourself, I want to add, but I refrain.

"Unless there are two separate killers?" Chloe says. "Maybe Tanya did kill Poppy after all. And then someone killed Tanya."

"For revenge on Poppy's murder?" I shake my head. "That's even more crazy. Something isn't right here."

"Besides Tanya and Poppy being murdered, you mean?" Esther puts in.

It still feels unreal, as if I'm trapped in some awful nightmare. Any second now I'm expecting Poppy and Tanya to walk through the door, claiming it was some kind of elaborate prank, that they were pretending.

"What happened to the painting?" Chloe asks.

I'm struggling to keep up with her train of thought. "What painting?"

She gestures out the window, as if that will help. Outside, the storm has picked up. We can hear the rain in the pitch black, only visible when a flash of lightning sparks the whole island. Thunder always follows closely behind, louder than anything I've ever heard back home.

"From the scavenger hunt," Chloe says. "After last night, we all had things from the scavenger hunt. The Capri-Sun wrapper was outside my window. You had the broken mirror, Annabel. Esther woke up with lipstick on her stomach. I didn't find the painting at all. It's vanished."

"Maybe it just blew away," I suggest. "The winds were already starting to pick up earlier."

"Maybe." She isn't convinced.

The ruined canvas was the worst item in that stupid game.

Poppy's painting. Her final art project ten years ago.

We must all be thinking about it, because Esther brings the subject up. "Before she died, Poppy said there was more to come from the scavenger hunt. Do you think she was going to make us relive every moment?"

"I think so," I say. "But she never got the chance. That was the reason she brought us all back, wasn't it?"

"To make us talk about what happened at the art exam."

Chloe clears her throat. "Tanya always said we should have just brought it up at the start, apologised and dealt with it. We were the ones insisting it wasn't a big deal."

"Because Poppy was the one who said she was willing to let the past go!" My voice is raised, but I can't help it. "Why should we bother dredging it up? It really wasn't that bad!"

"About that," Chloe says. "I tried to bring it up at the time, but none of you would listen. It's about the burglary."

"The burglary?" Esther finishes her tea. "What does that have to do with anything?"

"Well, I told you, the thief stole my laptop." Chloe starts drumming her fingers on the table, a nervous habit. "And that was all they stole, so the police thought it was some kind of weird fan stalker thing."

"Yes, so?"

"It had the video."

My heart sinks.

"The video?" Esther's face falls. "You don't mean that video?"

Chloe nods.

"I thought you'd deleted that years ago," Esther hisses. "What the hell were you thinking, keeping that on your laptop like that?"

"I did delete it originally! It wasn't like I was watching it every day or something! It was an accident," Chloe insists. "It transferred over with my old files when I switched laptops. It must have been saved in an archive or something. I only knew it was there after the laptop was stolen, when I was checking my backup drive and found it."

Esther stands up and grabs Chloe by the shoulders, shaking her. "You stupid bitch. Why didn't you tell us?"

"I tried to! None of you would listen. None of you wanted to talk about the past. You all pretended like nothing ever happened."

"Oh, don't use that excuse. You should have tried harder to tell us. Too busy fucking Annabel's husband to worry about it."

Stung, Chloe shakes herself free of Esther's grasp, and stands up too. "But the point is, what if it was Poppy who burgled me?"

"Poppy?" Esther echoes. "But how?"

"She knew our addresses," I say, realising what Chloe is getting at. "She posted those invitations to us. How did she know our addresses? I never thought to wonder about it. I guess I just figured she'd found out somehow, but how? And when? How long had she been watching us? Making her plans?"

Esther's face has gone very pale. "If Poppy was the one who stole your laptop, then she had the video. She's had it for months and months. She knows for sure now exactly what happened that day and what we did."

"She's been planning this for a long time," I whisper, horrified.

Esther is less appalled. "Annabel, it's alright! She's dead. She never got to follow through with anything else. This is all just speculation."

The bruises on Esther's neck have turned green, large angry rings that wrap themselves around.

"What else was she planning?" I say. "What if she's already done it, sent something to everyone we know? She said there was more. What if her being dead doesn't matter because it's already been done?"

"No." Chloe buries her face in her hands. "No, no, no. She can't have."

"You idiot." Esther rounds on Chloe again. "And you, Annabel. You both need to calm down!"

And then everything goes black.

Chloe screams; I do too, I can't help it. We're plunged into darkness. Lightning flashes, and for a brief second I see Chloe and Esther, equally as terrified, and then it's black again. A loud growl of thunder rumbles over our heads, shaking the lodge, and then all we can hear is the hissing of rain, powering down on the roof in an unrelenting tirade.

"Shit, what's happening?"

"I can't see anything!"

"Fuck!" Esther collides with a chair and sends it smashing to the ground.

"What do we do?" I shout.

"There are torches under the sink!" Esther calls back. I don't know why we're shouting; something about the panic, the sudden blindness, seems to necessitate it. "I saw them while we were looking for the bloody flares. Fourth cupboard to the right of the fridge. If we could just get there."

I'm not sure whether the others are trying. I fumble my way along, feeling the cold walls with my fingertips. It seems to take an age, stepping like this, afraid at any moment something is going to trip me up, each of us aware that we're in a room with a killer and we won't be able to see where they're coming from.

My hands find a kitchen counter, scraping at the edge. Moving across, I find the fridge, a different material to the rest.

"I've found the fridge!" I yell. "Fifth cupboard along?"

"Fourth! I'm almost there too from the other way!"

"I can't move!" That's Chloe, shrieking from a short distance away. She clearly hasn't even stepped an inch, frozen to the spot. I don't blame her.

I count along, feeling the grooves of the cupboard doors to make sure I'm counting correctly, and then fling open the cupboard door I think is fourth. I collide with several random objects, hearing them spill out onto the kitchen tile, making crashing sounds.

"What are you doing?" Chloe cries. "What's happening?"

"Just feeling around for the torches!" On my right, something grabs my arm, and I scream again.

"It's me!" Esther says. "Let me help too."

A particularly close bolt of lightning crashes down outside. I'm sure it has hit the island. For a moment the ground seems to pulsate, reacting to the blow. But it's a blessing in disguise: illuminated finally, the cupboard becomes visible, and right at the back tucked between two cardboard boxes of cleaning products I can see four torches.

Esther and I reach for them at the same time, smashing our hands together. She even scratches me in what I hope is an accidental move. She grabs one and switches it on, just as we're plunged into darkness once more. I grab two, switching one on and keeping the other for Chloe.

I shine a spotlight across the room, and we find Chloe rooted to the spot, scared. Dodging the various things that fell out onto the ground in my search, we hurry around back to her and I pass her the third torch, which she switches on straight away, grateful for some actual light.

"Thank God they have the batteries already in," I say. "I don't know what we would have done. Good memory, Esther."

We're lit up like we're telling ghost stories, standing together in a circle.

"What even happened there?" Chloe asks, a little breathless.

"It's the storm." I direct my torch to the window, and we see nothing but darkness. "It's cut off the power."

"There must be a fuse box somewhere," Esther says. "This place has to get power cuts all the time."

"If there was one, it'd probably be round the outside of this building, where the telephone was," I say. "That would make sense."

Chloe bites her lip. "But that would mean going out in this weather."

"It's around the corner." My jacket is hung on the back of one of the chairs and I put it on. "I'll go and check. It's only flipping a switch."

Esther tries the light switch in here just in case, turning it off and on again, but nothing happens. "I figured it was worth a try," she says with a shrug. "I'm not going out there."

"I'll go."

Chloe puts on her coat too. "I'll come with you."

"No thanks," I snap. "I can do it without your help."

She looks disappointed, but doesn't argue. I open the door and am swept up in the wind, my hair flying everywhere, dress blowing up. Rain pelts down, soaking me without care, and the temperature is an awful mix of humid and freezing, all at once.

It takes my breath away.

"Jesus Christ," I gasp.

"Sure you still want to go out there?" Esther says.

"I have to. We can't spend hours like this."

"Rather you than me. Close the door behind you."

I step out and the wind slams the door shut anyway. Exposed now, I need a second to gain some balance, the force of the gale pushing me backwards. Even shining my torch isn't much help, the rain so thick and heavy my vision is impaired. But I press on, forcing myself through, striding round the corner towards the telephone box and moving the torch all around, trying to find sight of a fuse box.

Aha. There!

For one awful second I think I'm going to need some sort of key, as it's enclosed in some kind of storage box fixed on the wall. A ledge built above keeps it dry from most of the rain, but the wind travelling in all directions has still managed to soak it some. Thankfully, there's no key needed. I grab through a tiny hole with my finger and pull it out, and then the wind smashes the flap round to the wall on the other side, keeping it open and doing me a favour.

There's the mains switch, flipped to the off position. Thank God. I flip it on, expecting the outdoor lighting around me to come to life, but nothing happens, and after a few seconds it flips down again.

Shit.

"Is it working?"

I nearly jump out of my skin.

"Sorry!" Chloe is behind me, no jacket to speak of, drenched by the rain. "I needed to talk to you!"

"Can it wait?" I yell over the wind. "This isn't the best time."

"No!" She ducks under the ledge, which is hardly enough cover for one person, let alone two, and brings her face close to mine so I can hear her properly. "I need to tell you how sorry I am."

Oh, Jesus. "It's not important right now."

"It is! I'm sorry. I was a complete idiot, like Esther says. I'm selfish. I only think about me. And I guess I've always been jealous of you."

This stops me in my tracks. "Seriously?"

"It's true, I promise. I hated that you had the perfect husband, the perfect life."

"My life is nowhere near perfect, as you saw."

"I know. I'm sorry."

It's not enough for her to say sorry. She knows it. I know it. But we also know that we have bigger problems right now. We can deal with this when we're back home and safe again.

If we ever make it home.

"The mains aren't coming back on," I say. "I don't know what to do."

"I don't know either." Chloe leans close again. I think she's trying to be covert, but she has to raise her voice because of the storm. "Don't you think Esther is acting suspicious?"

Not more alliances. As if she'd ever think after what she's done I'd join sides with her. I shrug my shoulders. "I don't know what you mean."

"She's been so nonchalant about everything." A word I'd never expect from Chloe. "And she has all those bruises around her neck and on her body. Like she's been in a fight. Don't you think that's odd? The one on her neck looks like someone has strangled her."

I have thought it myself. The various injuries on Esther that no one seems to be bringing up, her strange attitude to all of this. But I'm almost positive some of the bruises were there when we arrived, as long ago as that seems.

"She had the knife last," Chloe says. "She pretends she doesn't know what she did with it. But how can she forget? It's the murder weapon! You don't just forget where you put the murder weapon."

"I did forget."

"Christ!" Chloe screams.

Esther is standing behind us. She switches on her torch to reveal herself. She's been standing in the shadows, listening for who knows how long.

"How long have you been standing there?" Chloe demands.

"Long enough," she says. "Come inside, and I'll explain."

"Explain what?"

"About the bruises. It's time."

We head back inside, teeth chattering from the rain. I sling my jacket back over the chair and jog on the spot to try and warm myself up a bit. Chloe and Esther sit down, dripping puddles onto the floor.

Esther sighs. "It's Brad."

"Brad?" I repeat.

"He did this to me. My wrist, my neck, my face. All of it."

I understand. "Brad *hurts* you?"

Esther nods, mute.

"Oh my God." I can't take all of this in. "Why didn't you *tell* us?"

She smiles at that, a wry smile. "I think if there's one thing we've proven over the past few days is that we are not a good group of friends. We can't rely on one another."

Chloe is astonished. "I had no idea. I saw the two of you together, and he seemed so attentive . . ."

"Brad on the outside world is a wonderful man," Esther says. "Brad on the outside world is my soul mate. Brad when he is alone with me is a different man altogether."

I think back over the past year or so. Esther's coldness, her moods, her reluctance to do anything with us. Her panic about the hen party. I thought it was because of her work, but maybe there was more to it than that. I think of Brad constantly texting and calling her, his persistent messages that I was so jealous of in comparison to Andrew's apathy. The way Esther flinched if you moved too quickly. The way she took herself off on her runs to unwind and escape her stresses, but I never thought to ask what she was unwinding and escaping from.

"The bruise on the neck is particularly bad," she says. "When he found out about the hen party he choked me, told me it would leave a mark that would remind me of him while I was away. There was no use trying to explain I was going to a private island, that there wouldn't be any other men. It didn't matter."

"Oh, Esther." I don't know what to say. "You have to leave him."

"I deserve him," she says. "Look at what we did to Poppy. I deserve everything he's ever done to me."

Chloe is stuck for what to say. "I thought . . . when the bruises came up . . ."

"You thought I'd gotten into a fight?" Esther says. "With Poppy? Well, you were half right. Just the wrong person."

"How long has it been going on?" I ask.

Esther ponders this. "Since the beginning, I suppose. Our first argument."

There's an awkward silence as we process this information.

"The fuse box didn't fix the problem then, I take it?" Esther asks, eager to talk about something else.

I shake my head. "I guess we're stuck like this until the morning."

"There was the generator," Esther says. "I remember Poppy mentioning one. When we climbed up Deadman's Peak, or whatever she called it. That little green hut?"

The climb up the mountain feels like a lifetime ago, a different time. Our stop at the top, taking in all the scenery, and then that small green hut in the distance. We had been so different then. All five of us together, taking that picture. I wonder where the digital camera is now. That's vanished too. That picture is the last image of Tanya and Poppy alive.

"It was all the way across the other side of the island," I say. "There's no chance of us making it there in this storm."

"I bet it would have some kind of backup system." Esther stands up and reaches for my jacket.

"What are you doing?" I say.

Esther senses the panic in my tone. "What's up with you? You went and tried the fuse box. I can try the generator."

"We have the torches." I reach for my jacket. "It's fine."

But she hangs on to it, tugging back. "I said I'll try."

"No." I'm firm.

Chloe sits between us at the table, puzzled. "We'll just stay here."

"See," I say. "Chloe agrees with me."

"Annabel, let me feel like I'm doing something useful. Please." She gives a final tug of the jacket, and it slips from my grasp.

Falling loose, something escapes the pocket, hitting the ground hard.

I don't want to look, even though I know precisely what it is. There's no time to grab it either. Both of them are about to see.

"What was that?" Chloe shines her torch in the direction of the sound, and we all stare at what has been spotlighted.

Esther's necklace.

My senses are dialled up to ten. Everything is on edge—heart rate, breathing, pulse, even movements. My fingers twitch but my legs are frozen. My mouth hangs open, desperate to offer an explanation but finding none that will make this okay.

Chloe stands from her seat, pushing her chair back until it clashes with the wall. "That's Esther's necklace. Didn't you lose that days ago?"

"After the first day," Esther says, remarkably calm, which makes me more nervous. "I always wear it. I couldn't believe it was gone."

"But then how?" Chloe turns and directs her torch on me, making me feel hot under its bright light. "I don't understand. What are you doing with it, Annabel?"

"That," Esther says, "is what I was going to ask."

I want the ground to swallow me whole. Part of me debates running, escaping out into the storm and not coming back.

"I thought Poppy had taken it," Esther murmurs. "I was so sure. But it was you."

"Esther," I appeal. "I'll explain."

"I should hope so," Esther says. "Because you need to start right now."

TWENTY-FIVE

Chloe

Why has Annabel got Esther's necklace? It doesn't make any sense. Being able to see only via torchlight is obscuring the situation further. I can switch my view to just one of them at a time, flicking my torch to and fro. The wind is getting even stronger outside now, howling and thrashing against the window, making us have to raise our voices even in here.

"Really? Me as well, Annabel?" Esther asks, full of venom. Her controlled calmness from before has vanished in an instant, making me question her true feelings if that's how easily she can change them. "Surely you wouldn't be so stupid to steal something from me, not when I *know* about you. Or maybe that is why you stole it? Did you plant the knife in Tanya's room too?"

"What?" Annabel exclaims. It comes out like a little squeak. "That's not it. You've got this all wrong."

"You're trying to make me look guilty." Esther turns to me then too, furious. "I heard both of you out there. Conspiring to make me the one who took the blame. Saying I looked suspicious. I thought explaining about the bruises would be enough, but this shows premeditation. Planning. Were you in on it too, Chloe?"

"No!" I protest. "I had no idea about any of this!"

Annabel raises her hands, tries to silence us. "Please, if you'll listen, I'll explain. It was after our argument, Esther."

"What argument?" I frown.

But Esther seems to know what she's talking about. "You mean about your . . . ?"

"Yes."

"Will someone please tell me what is going on?" I interject impatiently. "I have no idea what you're talking about."

Esther presses her lips into a thin line. "You need to tell her."

"Fine." Annabel sighs and sits down, beckoning us to join her. Once we're all seated, the necklace placed in the centre of the table, she continues, keeping her eyes on it instead of us. "Esther already knows about this, Chloe, but I'll explain it from the beginning so that you understand. I . . . I steal things."

"You steal things?" I repeat.

She looks pained. "Andrew isn't—well, you know him quite well, as we have discovered. I'm sure you'd agree he isn't the most generous man in the world."

Is she really trying to blame Andrew for her being a thief? I can't tell her Andrew bought me an expensive gold necklace when I complained all I had was silver jewellery, as tempting as it is, so I simply nod instead.

"Even though it was at his insistence that I stopped working, he didn't give me anything to do. I was stuck at home so often, bored out of my mind. So I started going shopping, just for something to keep me entertained."

There's a long pause now. I think about all of her expensive clothes, the ones I was so puzzled by. It's starting to come together.

I have to admit, I'm impressed. I didn't think Annabel had it in her.

"At first, I'd steal a couple of things," Annabel says. "Nothing major. A bracelet here, a scarf there. Things that if I was challenged I could easily claim I forgot about and apologise for. But then I started wanting bigger things."

Naturally. No one wants to walk around looking like a bargain bin.

"I'd ask the staff to let me try things on. And then when they got distracted with someone else—I'd walk out without looking back. I've nearly been caught so many times, but I can't stop. It's like a rush."

"Just how much are we talking here?" I ask.

"I don't know," she whispers. "Andrew doesn't even question it when I show up wearing something entirely new, even though it costs far more than he'd ever give me. I have credit cards too, loads of them, so even when I'm stealing something I'm buying something else on those. I don't even check them."

"How did you let it get so bad?"

"I couldn't stop." Even just from the light of the torch, I can see the tears welling up in her eyes, making them glisten. "It became so addictive. I was so sure that was what Poppy was going to expose when she started talking about secrets. But I guess I hid it well."

"And Esther knew about this?" I confirm.

"She started questioning my outfits. I had to tell her."

Amazing, the life-altering secrets we kept from one another. Annabel the little thief. My affair with her husband. Esther's abuse at the hands of her boyfriend. Tanya's drug addiction. And we're supposed to be friends.

"So you stole the necklace as well?" I say. I can't help but smirk, despite everything. "That was a bit stupid, wasn't it? When Esther knows about you? Surely she was going to suspect you had something to do with it."

Annabel finally looks ashamed. "Esther always goes on about that necklace. And whilst we were on the trip, she lost patience with me. Said I was on my own with this. It was my problem from now on."

"You showed up to this hen party in an outfit that costs at least five thousand pounds!" Esther snaps. "Of course I was mad. So what, you stole my necklace in revenge?"

"Yes."

Esther reels back as if Annabel has slapped her. "You really are incredible."

"I'm sorry. I was angry at you."

"After I kept your problems quiet!"

"It was a moment of madness. We had argued. I stormed off. I came back to talk to you again, only you were on your run. The necklace was just there on your pillow . . . I'm sorry. I would have returned it, after everything that's happened here."

"But you didn't, did you? It was still in there, tucked away for when you returned home."

"I don't know what I was thinking."

The expression Esther has is one of true disgust. I've never seen her this angry before; it almost frightens me. But then she slumps down in her chair, the fight gone out of her.

"Whatever," she says. "What's done is done. We have bigger problems now."

"Why didn't you tell me?" I ask.

"Because you probably would have encouraged me," Annabel says. "And besides, you were clearly too occupied with my husband to notice anything wrong."

Yeah, I reckon I deserved that one.

The two of them have turned away from one another, arms folded. We are all against each other now. Annabel despises me and Esther despises her. And me? I don't trust either of them.

How long is it until morning? How long must we sit trapped in this room, escaping the raging storm outside but facing a worse one inside? I don't think we're going to make it to dawn at this rate. The atmosphere is so thick, so wrought with tension that the knife used to kill Poppy and Tanya would be put to good use in here, cutting the air and releasing some of the pressure that is building up.

I might as well play the role of peacemaker, if it keeps me from getting stabbed to death. That would be nice.

"We all kept things from each other," I say. "And I know better than most that we can all do terrible things."

This isn't met with the reception I hoped.

Esther scowls and mutters something under her breath.

Annabel curls her lip at me. "Some worse than others."

God. I can't bear another second in here.

"I remembered something else about last night," Esther says suddenly.

The two of us turn to her.

"It's odd," she says. "It was late, could have even been the early hours of the morning, really." She frowns in concentration. "The four of us had gone to our huts—what we thought were our huts—and then I remember thinking all my stuff looked very unusual. I acted crazy, tearing out the drawers and trying to find my clothes. Turns out I was in Annabel's room."

Annabel's room. The image of it comes back to me from my search, everything chaotic.

"You were the one who trashed my room?" Annabel says. "I figured I'd done it in my drunken state and just hadn't remembered. I was so shocked when I woke up to it."

"I came to my hut," Esther says. "And it's funny, but I could have sworn someone was following me on the way there."

"Following you?" The thought gives me chills.

Esther clears her throat. "It was very unusual. But you know you can just sense things sometimes? It was like eyes watching me everywhere I went, a shadow at my back. Maybe it was just a delusion from the gin, I don't know. But it felt real. I ran to my hut. Annabel was inside, of course, we'd switched in our confused state. And God, it sounds awful now, but I was just so relieved to be inside, and thought that if anything was out there at least it would, you know—"

"Get me first," Annabel finishes, appalled. "Jesus, Esther."

"Well," she blusters. "Nothing happened to you. You must have stumbled back to your hut fine, because you woke up there the next morning."

"But it could have! Poppy was killed that night!"

"I didn't know that at the time, did I?"

The two of them bicker at each other like this for a while, as I lose myself in trying to think back to last night. It's all still a blur. I can figure out the main events: us getting together, drinking that gin, getting wasted, doing stupid things with the scavenger hunt items. But the details are hazy, and I don't like the idea that Esther felt someone was watching her. Because every time I think back to that night, an uncomfortable prickling feeling seeps over my skin.

And I think it's because I thought the same thing.

"Maybe we should each have something." Fear is making me speak. "Each carry a knife too, just in case."

"In case one of us decides to murder the other two, you mean?" Esther runs her fingers through her hair. "We're safer without them. We just need to stick together."

I don't know how to explain to them both that I'm going mad in here, locked in this small room with the two of them. Knowing one of us is a killer. Not knowing when they'll strike next. It's all very well and good pretending two against one will make a difference. What about the one they go for first?

And I'm not planning on that being me. I'll kill these bitches myself before I end up dead.

"I think it's better if we all split up," I say.

"Split up?" Annabel says. "No way."

"And there's the storm outside," Esther points out. "None of us could move even if we wanted to."

Something about the way she says it, that patronising tone of hers, breaks me.

"You both think I'm so stupid, don't you?"

"What?" They feign ignorance, but I know them.

"Airhead Chloe, always down for a laugh but not for a stimulating conversation," I say. "See? 'Stimulating,' that's an impressive word, no? I'm not completely braindead. I can see right through both of you. I don't trust either of you."

"Now isn't the time for you to get all insecure about your intelligence," Esther snaps.

"But you two have always lorded it over me. And Tanya, and even Poppy bloody Greer. Treating me like I'm some dumb blonde bitch without any substance."

"Well," Annabel says. "I mean. You are, aren't you?"

"Jesus, Annabel," Esther says. "Stop making things worse."

"I knew that's how you saw me." I stand up and head for the door.

Esther tries to reach for me. "Chloe, don't. It's not safe."

But the air in here is sticky and humid, and I'm sweating, the glare of torchlight making me hot. Through flashes in the dark I can see Annabel's stubborn expression, Esther's concerned one, but I don't care anymore.

"I can't spend another second in here with either of you," I say. "Don't follow me, or I'll think you're the killer. Just leave me alone."

"Chloe!"

I swing open the door, and before I even take two steps out it flings backwards at me by the force of the wind, knocking me in the side of my body and making me gasp.

"Are you alright?"

"Fuck off!" I shout. Despite increasing pain in my side, I push the door again, holding it open fiercely with all my strength.

The storm hasn't let up. If anything, it's worse than before. Projecting my torch ahead, I can only see a few feet in front of me, the tended lawn now filled with debris from around the island. Palm trees swing practically horizontal, and my hair has a life of its own, trying to escape being rooted to my head.

But it's better than in here.

"You're making a mistake," Esther calls.

"So let me make it!" I say. "I'm so done with this. Poppy deserved to die anyway."

"And Tanya?" Annabel says. "What about Tanya?"

I take one last look at them both. The torch shines across their faces, giving me a final snapshot of the women I thought were my friends. Annabel is furious, eyes blazing, standing with her own torch aimed my way. She's drenched from the storm, hair sticking across her face and obscuring her mouth so I can't tell if she's saying anything more. Esther is still sitting, calmer, a slight frown between her brows. She doesn't say anything. They're not the women I came to the island with.

I don't recognise them at all.

Leaving them behind, I head out into the storm.

TWENTY-SIX

Esther

MAY 21, 2023

Annabel and I are left standing in the dark, the door still open. The storm makes its way inside with greedy ambition, knocking our mugs and smashing them to the floor. Rain seems to come in sideways, drenching us without care. My ears start ringing, sensitive to the harsh elements. I flick my torch towards Annabel, and then the door.

She seems to understand, even if it is hard to speak over this force of nature. "We should go and look for her. She's just gone a little stir-crazy."

Haven't we all? Despite the storm's assault, there's something freeing about the rush of air that attacks us, fresher than the humidity in here. I'm also very aware that I don't want to be alone with Annabel right now, not here in the dark like a sitting duck. Better we go out and face the island than stay in here together.

It's hard to judge what she's thinking without shining the torch in her face, too much of a giveaway that I'm trying to figure her out. Her admission to stealing my necklace has twisted things for me. Before, if there was anyone I was going to trust, it would be Annabel. Now, I'm not sure. If she's willing to steal my most precious possession from me, what else is she willing to do?

"Let's go," I shout. "She can't have gone far."

Armed with our torches, we march out into the downpour. It's worse out here, unprotected, the gale careering us in various directions. Rain soaks my skin, making it difficult to breathe. We edge out, slowly, then stop, wondering which way to go.

"The beach will be dangerous," Annabel yells. "She won't have gone there."

"Where then?" I call. Even speaking is an effort. The storm seems determined to suck up our voices and carry them away like fallen leaves.

"She's probably gone to one of the huts," Annabel shouts. "We need to check."

"Maybe we should split up," I say. "Take two each."

There's a silence, and I wonder if she's heard me. I turn to her, and catch her struggling expression in my torchlight. Her hair is stuck to her face no matter how many times she tries to free it, and mascara drips down her cheeks. She looks vulnerable in this moment, and not scary at all.

I take pity on her. "Never mind. Let's carry on together."

We head around the main lodge slowly, sticking close to the walls. Every now and then lightning illuminates the way for us, crashing down into the sea nearby with a hiss that seems to crack open the earth, making the ground we move on shake, as if we're stumbling about drunk. I'm careful to keep my torch pointed forward on the path ahead, but Annabel seems more frenetic, the beam scattering across the general area, revealing shadows within the trees that look like people watching us.

"Chloe!" Annabel screams, straining to be as loud as possible. "Chloe, where are you?"

There's no response. Hard for there to be, when even the highest scream gets whipped away like it's nothing. The wind is the only reply, a great howling and whistling that starts up as if the sky is in agony.

We reach the first hut in gasps, practically falling on the door to open it. Automatically, I reach for the light switch, but of course it remains dark.

"Chloe?" I call.

Again, no answer. Our torches prove there is no one in here, not in the bathroom either after Annabel checks. But it is a relief to get out of the storm even just for a few minutes, and we sit on the bed and take the time to get our breath back. Even though we've been moving very slowly, very carefully, it's as if we've run a marathon.

"What should we do?" Annabel asks. Her voice is hoarse from screaming.

"This is the first hut. There are three others."

"Two."

I frown at her. "What do you mean?"

"She won't have gone in Tanya's."

Of course. I'd almost forgotten. It's unsettling to think of Tanya's body, lying there on her bed. It's even less of a comfort to think of Poppy's, vanished in the sea, currently whirring around due to the storm, perhaps sunken now far below the surface, so far it lies unaffected and decomposing.

My throat swallows of its own accord, preventing me from being sick.

"Well, two more then," I say with forced brightness. "She'll be fine."

"What if she isn't in there? Do we keep looking?"

As if on cue, thunder roars above our heads and something crashes down outside.

"We can't go out around the island in this," I say. "If she's not in the huts, there isn't much we can do right now."

Annabel looks downcast, but nods. "Yeah. I understand."

"Shall we carry on?" I rise.

None of us packed for a storm like this, expecting sunny beaches and blue skies all the way. Annabel and I are both in thin white dresses which offer no protection, and yet we're not freezing to death. Adrenaline pumps through our bodies, keeping us warm and alive. The air is pungent, like the smell of perfume, a sweet smell that contrasts with our sour breath as we gasp for oxygen.

Chloe isn't in either of the remaining huts.

We have ended up in mine at the culmination of our search, and all I can think about is how good a sleep would be right about now. I'm starting to go dizzy with exhaustion.

"She could be in Tanya's, despite everything," I say. "That could have been the one she had to seek shelter in. Or maybe she's back at the main lodge already."

"Maybe." Annabel squeezes her hair, creating a puddle of water on the floor.

The power is still out, the storm is still raging.

There's nothing more we can do.

"We should try to sleep," I say. "I'll stay in this hut, you stay in yours. I'll watch from the doorway and make sure you get in there safely."

"You don't trust me, do you?"

The question is like a slap, but I hold steady. "With good reason."

"I'm sorry about the necklace," she says.

"I just think we'd sleep better if we were apart," I say. "And we'll wake up in a few hours and Chloe will be back, you'll see."

"Right." She sighs and lifts herself off the bed. "I am tired."

"Me too."

"You'll watch me go to my hut? Make sure I get there safe?"

"Of course."

She heads out slowly, even more cautiously than when we were walking together. It's a short journey, not even twenty metres, but she takes her time, making sure not to stumble. I keep my own torch steady for her as she wobbles with her own, and after a painstaking few minutes she makes it to her hut and opens the door.

She's about to head in, then turns on the doorway, mouthing something to me.

"I can't hear you," I shout. "What?"

Her lips move again, but the wind swallows her voice whole.

When I make a shrugging gesture with my hands, she shakes her head. Finally, she goes inside, closing the door behind her.

It's a relief to close my own door, despite the increased isolation it brings. I turn the lock, a sense of respite at the sound of the click that tells me I can breathe normally again. Without taking off my dress I lie down on the bed, pulling the covers over me.

The emotions of the day at last hit me, spiking me in the heart, and I allow myself to cry.

Who am I crying for? Myself, mainly. Stuck here on this island without a way to escape, thinking about how two of the people who came here less than four days ago are now dead. Thinking about how I've lost my job, my entire livelihood, and now others know about Brad's abuse. I don't know what I'm going back to when I go home, if I even make it.

I try and calm myself down with slow, purposeful breaths. But the effort is futile. Sobs break out of my mouth, choked cries that soak my pillow with something other than rain. I stink of the island, of the storm. A mixture of rain, earth, and sweat. We must be in the eye of it right now, because the wind has suddenly died, leaving silence in its wake. It's still pitch black, but it's comforting to be able to hear nothing other than the ringing in my ears.

I can't sleep. I lie here fatigued beyond measure, more drained than I have ever been, and yet my brain remains switched on. My senses are alert. My body seems to know that danger is lurking around the corner, and won't let me relax. Perhaps I should thank it, for keeping me focused.

There's a flash of something outside my window. A torch? It disappears, and then appears again.

Definitely a torch.

Is it Chloe?

I hurry to the window with my own torch, ready to show her a way forward. My face falls when I see who it is.

Annabel.

What is she doing out again? Is she taking advantage of the lull in the storm?

Her torch flashes over my window and I have to duck my head. After it passes by, I watch her go. She's walking around the huts again, checking various places. Is this an innocent search for Chloe, or something more sinister? She seems in a world of her own, but every now and then her eyes dart left and right, checking no one is following her.

I'm not taking any chances. I move to my door, careful not to shine my torch so she notices me, and feel around for the handle.

There.

Still locked.

She can't come in here.

It makes me feel somewhat safer, but upon returning to bed, I'm still faced with the same problem. I can't sleep. I don't think anything is going to make me at ease on this night, not with Annabel wandering around in the dark and Chloe missing. Not when last night five people were on this island and now there are three.

TWENTY-SEVEN

Poppy

MAY 17, 2013

Dear Diary,

I went to prom! I went to a PARTY! I drank and danced and boys actually FLIRTED with me! ME!

This year so far has been the best in my entire life. First Slade, and now this. Are things finally turning out okay for me? After everything? Even Annabel, Chloe, Esther, and Tanya were nice. I went to Esther's house!

The prom started at seven o'clock. We all went through the rites of passage, even me: going dress shopping with your mum and having your mouth ache as she takes picture after picture of you smiling and insisting you look beautiful in all of them; getting your hair and makeup done in the hours before and then having to sit stiffly and avoid eating or drinking; and for others it means meeting up somewhere for your dramatic transport to the venue, in our case the Marriott Hotel on College Green. I missed out on that last stage, getting into a stretch limousine with other girls or even something more ostentatious like an old-fashioned double-decker bus. But Mum and Dad treated me to a proper London black cab, with Dad as my taxi driver, and when we pulled up outside it felt like it was a *conscious decision rather than one made out of loneliness. Mum and Wendy were sitting in the back with me, and for once I didn't care that they were there embarrassing me in front of everyone, making sure I looked perfect and taking more pictures.*

"You look so stunning," Dad said, after opening the car door for me and pretending to bow and doff his cap. "Have a wonderful evening."

The three of them were going to some science conference for the weekend with Wendy, now that she was seriously thinking about pursuing a career in medicine.

"I will," I said. "Thank you for everything! This has been amazing."

"And you look so lovely," Mum said, near tears. "We're so proud of you, darling."

As self-conscious as I felt, I was proud of my dress. With high heels to match so I didn't feel so dumpy, it was a long, straight dress with floating sleeves. It sounded plain, but diamantes had been stuck along the hem and up to the waist and they sparkled against the grey colouring. As for my hair, it had been tied into a complicated bun with strands framing my face. The hairdresser had said I looked chic, and I liked that word. Catching myself in the car window, I swivelled myself this way and that, watching the bottom of my dress twirl and my hair stay in place. I'd never worn makeup to this extent before either, and although the sudden amount of foundation was a bit shocking (and I secretly worried there was too much of an orange tinge), I definitely looked grown up. And so different.

But no red lipstick. It was a pale pink shade, but even so it made my heart thud when the makeup artist put it on.

Mr. Edwards, who still made me sigh wistfully, broke into a smile at the sight of me heading up the stairs to the front door.

"Oh, Poppy," he said. *"Don't you look lovely! I'm so glad you came."*

He knew better than most that I was doubting coming here. I'd even had a meeting with him a few weeks ago about it, where he convinced me that I had to attend this last school event, and he'd watch out for me.

"Thanks, Mr. Edwards," I said. "I'm glad I'm here too!"

"Head on inside now," he said. "I'll see you in there soon enough."

As we entered, hotel staff had been hired to hand us either a glass of champagne (if we could show our ID, but I'm underage) or a glass of orange juice (if we preferred or if it was our only option) and then we walked down a long red carpet through some double doors into the events room. It was a massive space complete with dozens of circular tables decorated with white cloths and elaborate centrepieces. There were little placemats with cards showing people's names. This year the seating plan had been done by random, which had proved controversial, but the teachers said we were all (or almost all) adults now, and could get used to chatting to people we didn't normally. I was pleased, of course, because it meant I didn't have to join a table where people didn't want me.

Across the other side of the room was a dance floor with a DJ and crazy sound system. There was even a disco ball hanging from the ceiling and strobe lighting. As most people weren't here yet, there was only prerecorded backing music playing, but some people from my art lesson were already standing in a circle on the dance floor, throwing their hands in the air and cheering whenever the beat dropped. Ollie Turner, brave in a turquoise tux, nodded at me when I waved at him, but didn't seem keen to invite me over to dance so I moved on.

In another corner, as part of the theme of this evening being Vegas, there was a "gambling" section. Everyone was given ten plastic coins to bet with, and the person with the most left at the end of the night won some kind of prize.

I was admiring the roulette wheel, currently unmanned, when I heard a gasp behind me.

"Oh my God, Poppy, is that you?"

I turned, and was met with Annabel, the last person I wanted to see.

Annabel was standing alone. Her outfit wasn't as incredible as I expected it to be. She had clearly done her own makeup, which, although impressive, didn't reach the level of a professional. Her hair too, blonde and shining as always, had been left to hang loose, straightened but nothing major. Finally, her shoes were the same ones she wore to the Year Eleven prom, white strappy sandals that were scuffed at the toes, and her dress was a skin-tight satin maxi. I would have expected her to go overboard, but this was quite a simple effort.

Before she could say anything else, a whole group of boys came in, loud and rowdy. They had tried hard with their gelled hair and suits, and as they came past us they stopped dead and wolf-whistled.

Annabel turned to smile at them, then flushed when she realised.

They weren't wolf-whistling at her. They were wolf-whistling at me!

"Poppy Greer, that can't be you!" One of them, probably the best-looking guy in our year now that Julian had left, came towards me with a grin. His name was Aidan and he had been Annabel's boyfriend for the past six months. "Bloody hell, you don't half clean up!"

The other boys were in eager agreement.

"She looks sick!"

"I would."

I couldn't help but be suspicious. After Julian, I couldn't trust boys. But they all seemed genuine, looking me up and down appreciatively. A few of them were nudging each other and whispering things I couldn't hear. I felt even more self-conscious, risking a glance towards my chest to make sure nothing was accidentally on show.

But there was nothing wrong. They really did just think I looked good. Looked pretty!

I've never been called pretty.

Aidan gave me a wink, then walked over to Annabel and kissed her on the cheek. "You look alright too, babe. Though couldn't you have worn something similar?"

"No." Annabel was scowling. I'd never seen her look so mad. Her entire face was red and she looked as if she wanted to slap him.

"Catch you later, yeah, babe?" Aidan said. He waved at me. "And you too, Poppy!"

"Come and dance with us later, Poppy!" one of the other guys called.

After they all left, Annabel and I were left standing awkwardly together by the roulette wheel. She was blinking furiously, as if she was trying not to cry.

And then it was like a light switch went off on her face because she broke into a smile and rolled her eyes. "Boys, right?"

Was she trying to joke with me?

"Right," I said uncertainly.

"You're the new shiny toy," she said, and I still wasn't sure if she was joking.

"Where are Chloe, Tanya, and Esther?" I asked, to try and get off the subject of Aidan and the other boys when she remained where she was, as if expecting a conversation.

For a moment she hesitated. "They're on their way in some ludicrous car. I decided to come a bit earlier instead."

"You didn't want to travel with them?"

"It was easier if I came this way. I live close, so I just walked."

"You live close to the centre?" I tried to imagine Annabel's home and pictured some arty loft apartment with a mother who held a cigarette between her lips and a paintbrush between her fingers and spoke with a French accent.

"Close enough, anyway," she said, then changed the subject. "Did you come here by yourself?"

I wasn't sure if it was a deliberate dig, or if she just wanted to talk about something else, so I gave her the benefit of the doubt and tried a joke myself. "It's not like I had many options."

"We're sitting on the same table, you know," she said, pointing to one of the tables at the far back corner of the room. "Maybe we could go sit down together?"

"Sure." I was suspicious of her intentions, despite the fact she hadn't done anything to me in over three years, but I walked along confident enough that nothing could go wrong in here with all the teachers around. As we went across the room, lots of people stopped me and complimented my hair and outfit, even people I'd never spoken to before.

"Poppy, you look amazing!"

"Wow, Poppy, you're actually so stunning."

More of the guys, who were mostly standing together in one big huddle, let out some gasps of surprise at me as I hurried by. I could even hear some talking about how they never knew I was hot, which shouldn't have pleased me so much but did, making me grin from ear to ear.

Annabel was sitting two places from my left on the table, but she swapped her placemat with Eric Smith's and sat next to me. It was so odd, the two of us sitting together as if we were friends, as well as all the attention I was getting. I felt like I had become a real person, the person I was meant to be. No more Poppy Greer the sad case, left in the background, but Poppy Greer the somebody, part of the inner circle and appreciated.

"You're getting so many looks," Annabel said.

I tried to play dumb. "They're looking at you, not me."

She laughed. "Oh, come off it, Poppy. You know I'm not stupid. I beat you in that mock exam we did the other week. Everyone is looking at you. And in a good way, for once."

Her last comment stung.

She must have seen my face, because she pulled one of her own. "Sorry, that was mean of me. I don't mean to be such a bitch all the time."

"You're not."

"I am."

"This looks cosy!"

I jumped. Esther, Tanya, and Chloe had arrived, each looking like a model.

Annabel's posture had changed straight away. She leaned away from me, and turned towards her friends, smiling wide. "You three are fashionably late."

"It's a shame you couldn't come in the limousine with us," Esther said to her. "My mum would have paid for you, you know."

"That's alright," Annabel said quickly. "Where are you three sitting?"

"Oh, we're all split up, worst luck," Tanya said. Then she seemed to look at me properly and her eyes practically fell out of her head. "Jesus Christ, Poppy."

"You look actually attractive!" Chloe shrieked with laughter. "Oh my God, look at you trying to fit in. It's worked! You're crazy hot tonight."

Esther raised an approving eyebrow at me. I could see the shiny silver piercing through it, which was not normally allowed during schooltime. "You do look pretty, Poppy. I think you're even beating Chloe."

Chloe, whose natural looks meant she didn't have to try as hard as everyone else, had opted for a dressed-down look similar to Annabel, but pulled it off better. She appeared as sleek as the rest of us who had spent hundreds, without seemingly needing to. But her scowl at Esther's comment made her look ugly. "I'm not sure about that."

"Right, everyone," Mrs. Hargreaves, our head teacher, shouted. "If we could all find our seats, we'll start this evening with a few announcements and testimonials and then we'll eat our three-course meal."

Annabel and I were left sitting together, joined quickly by others in our year. When our table was full, she leaned over and whispered in my ear.

"We're all thinking of having a party after this, do you want to come?"

"A party?"

"You know, somewhere where you can actually drink." She chimed her champagne glass with my orange juice, then shrugged her shoulders. "Think about it."

"No one will want me to come," I whispered.

"Of course they will. And anyway, it's at Esther's, so no one else will have a say."

Esther lives in a Georgian house with five floors in the heart of Clifton. I'm not sure what her parents do but she's ludicrously wealthy, and her party after the Year Eleven prom was apparently legendary.

"You really want me there?"

"Sure," she said, as if it was nothing.

"I mean, my parents and sister are away, so . . ."

"Great! You're coming then!"

I started hesitating, trying to back out of it. This was Annabel after all. I still remembered Julian. "I might be too tired from the prom."

"Poppy, calm down," Annabel said. "Relax and enjoy yourself tonight. It'll be great."

Amazingly, despite my doubts, I did enjoy myself. The meal was nice, and Annabel and I talked for ages about our exams and what we wanted to do. I was off to Slade, she was staying put in Bristol. Our table managed to come second in the quiz that was played during dessert, and we each won a book voucher, which the others groaned at but I was pretty excited about. Afterwards, the dancing commenced and the Vegas-style gambling section started up, headed by Mrs. Hargreaves to make sure no one was cheating. I lost all my coins betting red on the roulette wheel, and Annabel soon lost hers after risking a fifteen in a game of twenty-one. The others had joined us by this point but there was such a crowd around us that it didn't feel strange, hanging out with those four. Tanya seemed more awkward than any of them, and when she went out on the balcony to smoke I went and joined her.

One of the science teachers who everyone always said smelt of weed was out there too, but at a distance, off in his own world.

Other than that, the balcony was empty apart from the two of us, the DJ playing "Stronger" by Kelly Clarkson. Even from out here with the doors shut, we could hear the thumping music and the sounds of everyone screaming along to the words.

Tanya lit her cigarette, taking a long inhale, then leaned back against the balcony. "You don't smoke."

There was no point pretending with Tanya. Even after all these years, it was like she still knew me better than anyone. I remembered us making a daft pact when we were ten to never smoke or take drugs because we respected ourselves too much. We declared it out to the world (my garden) and sealed the deal by dipping our hands in a muddy puddle and shaking on it.

I wondered if she remembered. "You broke the pact," I said softly.

To my surprise, she grinned. "I knew you were going to say that."

"I just wanted to check you were alright," I said. "That's why I came out here. I wanted to ask how you were doing. What are your plans?"

She took another inhale, blowing the smoke out in rings. "I'm going to UWE. Not quite as impressive as Slade."

The teachers had announced my Slade offer in the school news-letter, which meant everyone knew. It had been so embarrassing, feeling the eyes of everyone on me, judging me, but I also felt secretly proud too.

"You're studying journalism, right?"

"That's right," she said, sounding astonished. "I didn't expect you to know."

"I think one of the teachers said," I mumbled, realising I'd given it away that I still kept track of her, despite everything. "I'm happy for you."

"Thanks." She took a final long drag, then put the cigarette out on the balcony's stone, flicking it off the edge.

"What happened to the acting dream?" I couldn't help asking it.

"Ah, that." She shrugged. "I gave up on that a long time ago."

"You shouldn't," I said. "I always thought you'd make it."

"Ah, well," she said, a small smile on her lips. "Remember when we used to dress up on the weekends and put on fashion shows for your parents?"

"I remember." We always did different themes each week. My parents, with patience rivalling a saint's, would sit on our old velvet sofa and clap and cheer as Tanya and I strutted across the room

thinking we were Tyra Banks. "My favourite was when we dressed up as high-fashion clowns."

Tanya burst out laughing, clapping her hands together. "Oh my God, I remember that. No, my favourite was when we decided that aliens would one hundred percent wear Uggs on their hands and gloves on their feet, and we had to hobble along when we tried to walk because we couldn't squeeze our feet into your old woolly gloves properly."

Then I was laughing too, and God, for a minute it was like no time had passed at all. It was me and Tanya again, close as we had ever been, and it was wonderful.

"Come on," she said, shattering the bubble of our old friendship. "We had better go back in, they'll be wondering where we got to."

That use of "we." I was finally included.

The rest of the night was spent dancing with everyone else, as if I had always been a part of them. When the lights eventually came on and Mrs. Hargreaves thanked us all for coming, I was a sweaty mess, but so was everyone. And then Esther said the magical words I had been waiting for, the confirmation I was truly in the in-crowd.

"Poppy, you're coming to the afterparty, right?"

"Of course," I said immediately.

On the way, I texted Mum and Dad, telling them I'd got home safely, even though that wasn't technically true.

There were about forty of us from the sixth form ball, but even this seemed a huge number. Esther's house wasn't small, but the place became crowded in seconds. She led us down to the basement, which was a huge open room complete with sofas and tables. Someone put on some music and it was as if we'd never left the hotel. People began dancing again, but this time we were all supplied with alcohol to liven the mood further, having stopped at the shops along the way back and stocked up with dozens of bottles.

I'd never drunk alcohol before. I know, a seventeen-year-old girl in the twenty-first century never having had a single drink. But it's not like I'd had the opportunity. This was my first party.

Aidan passed me a plastic cup filled only slightly. "Do a shot with me, Poppy. We haven't seen you drunk yet!"

He was so hot, and standing so close to me I was terrified he could hear my heart beating.

"Sure," I said, as if I did this all the time, even though I had no idea what was in there.

"On the count of three," Aidan said. "One . . . two . . . three!"

Both of us drank the liquid straight down. I couldn't help but gasp and choke slightly as the burning sensation hit the back of my throat, and Aidan laughed as he thumped me on the back.

"Maybe doing shots isn't the best thing for your first party!" he said. "Here."

He reached across and brushed his fingers across my lip. In that moment, I think time stood still. My stomach began swirling, and any second I was worried I'd faint.

But I knew I had to calm down. This was Annabel's boyfriend. I took a step back, adding some distance between us, and he seemed to understand.

"You had some around your mouth," he said. "Let me introduce you to some of my mates later. They'd love to get to know you."

"Sure," I whispered, barely able to get this single word out.

Was this what it was like for every other girl? A cute boy came up to you at a party and made a move? Or said he'd introduce you to his friends? Some of the other boys were nearly as good looking as Aidan. I wasn't going to be picky.

A first kiss would have been nice. That was all that was on my mind, and my lips still tingled from where Aidan had touched them.

"Are you having fun?"

Annabel appeared behind me, as if from nowhere, holding a drink in her hand. She held it out to me. "A vodka lemonade. A bit easier than a straight shot."

"Oh." I immediately felt awkward. "Aidan just came up to me, I didn't—"

"It's cool," she said. She shrugged her shoulders. "He's friendly. It doesn't bother me. He's just trying to make sure you have a good time. Now take it."

I hesitated.

"This isn't your first time drinking alcohol, is it?" she said.

"No!" I said, but it was too late.

"Oh, bless you." She raised her voice, letting everyone else hear. "Guys, this is Poppy's first ever alcoholic drink, excluding that shot she just did! Can we have a round of applause?"

Blushing furiously, I took my first sip and had to train my face very carefully not to flinch at the shock of the taste. It was even worse than the shot somehow. Sharp and strong and awful, even a little bitter. Annabel muttered something to a few of the guys standing by her, and they all laughed. But the crowd cheered at me.

"Down it, down it!" they chanted.

"Oh, God," I mumbled, but I did as they said, choking it back despite its making my eyes sting.

"Is it meant to taste like that?" I said to Tanya, who had been standing near me, taking part in neither the cheering nor the laughter.

She frowned. "Taste like what?"

"Odd. Like there's something awful?"

She leaned over and sniffed my drink. There was nothing left of it now, so she shrugged her shoulders at me. "I can't smell anything. But it shouldn't have tasted too bad if it was just vodka in there." The attention off me for the moment, she poured me another one and handed it over. "Try it again."

This time, the drink seemed to go down easier. There was still the distinct sense I was drinking something alcoholic, but there was no strange bitter taste to it.

"That one was fine," I said.

"Maybe Annabel just gave you too much for your first go," Tanya said, but the frown remained. She went over to Annabel and although I couldn't hear what they were saying, it looked serious until Tanya was eventually won round, smiling and shaking her head.

The party carried on. I remember dancing, I remember some of the guys in my year with their hands on me as they tried to dance next to me, everyone cheering and having a fun time. It was like my senses were dialled up to ten, but I figured that's just what being drunk felt like. Everything was bright and colourful and I felt more confident than I ever had before, like nothing could ever bother me again. I kept being supplied with drinks from the girls, and when they giggled I giggled too, in a stupid high-pitched voice.

One amazing moment was on my way back from the toilet, when Chloe's boyfriend, Elliott, cornered me. He didn't actually go to our school and had shown up at the afterparty an hour or so in. He was so different from the boys at school. He even had a nose piercing, which was definitely not allowed at ours.

"Here's my favourite girl," he said, putting an arm around me.

Even though I giggled, I still thought of his girlfriend. "Isn't Chloe your favourite girl?"

He grinned at that. "Of course. Doesn't mean I can't have more than one though, right?"

He leaned forward, and I'm sure he was about to kiss me. My heart started pounding, and I leaned towards him, even starting to close my eyes.

But then Esther walked into the hallway and he sprang away from me, laughing.

"We were wondering where you two had got to," Esther said. She didn't seem bothered, but she was mainly looking at me. Had she seen that we were about to kiss? I couldn't be sure.

"I was just helping poor Poppy back," Elliott explained. "She's drunk as anything."

"Well, maybe go dance with Chloe," Esther said.

After he walked away, I expected her to say something to me.

"He really was just helping me," I blurted out when she stayed silent.

"I'm sure," she said, then went to the toilet herself.

The rest of the night I danced with lots more guys, but I didn't come close to a first kiss again. And when Aidan offered to walk me home, Annabel came out of the toilets saying she'd thrown up and needed Aidan's support, so he didn't get the chance.

But walking home by myself didn't bother me, not after the amazing night I'd had. When I got home, I hung up my prom dress as carefully as possible, not wanting to wrinkle it any further so it held the memory of that night forever.

I really think I'm finally becoming someone, diary. Imagine what I'm going to be like in the future!

No one is going to recognise me.

TWENTY-EIGHT

Annabel

MAY 22, 2023

The storm is starting to weaken.

What was once heavy rain, the kind that prevents you from barely taking a single step, is now pathetic spitting, and even the thick clouds have started to drift away, their work done. The stars begin to peek out from behind them, hidden all along, and finally bring some light to this place.

How is it still night? It must be almost dawn soon, surely. It feels like this night is lasting forever.

Maybe it is. Maybe we're trapped on a magic island where time has no laws, and we're doomed to be here until only one of us is left.

God. No wonder I didn't sleep.

I didn't even attempt it. I lay in bed for ages, and then the moment the storm seemed like it was clearing, I was up searching for Chloe again, not caring what a battered state I looked. But she wasn't in any of the huts, not even Tanya's, which I checked on with some trepidation, or the main lodge.

I emerge from my hut somewhat cautiously, the hairs on my arms standing on their ends.

Across the lawn, puddles have formed, revealing the area isn't as straight and perfect as I first thought. It's muddy too, brown marks gathered everywhere. My sandals become drenched with it, but I don't care. The final efforts of the storm finish, and at last the moon appears from the clouds, crescent-shaped but strong enough to brighten the whole island.

I head for the main lodge, and find Esther sitting alone at the table, drinking more coffee. She has that wired, too-much-caffeine energy about her, gripping the edges of her chair with her jaw clenched. She jumps when I walk in, but masks it well, composing her expression into one of calm.

"You couldn't sleep either?" I say.

She shakes her head. "I tried. It was pointless."

We both look out at the sky, which seems to taunt us with its perpetual nighttime.

"Where's Chloe?" Esther asks.

My heart drops. "You've not seen her?"

"No."

"We need to go and find her properly this time," I say. "She could have just become stranded due to the storm. We told her she was an idiot for going out in this weather. You know what she's like. Impulsive."

Both of us can picture Chloe then. Her vibrant energy, but also her reckless behaviour. Her tendency to act first, think second. She'll have just got lost, stumbled somewhere in the dark and stayed there until the storm passed. That's what I need to keep telling myself. Or maybe she has been hurt, but in an accident of some kind. I can't think about the alternative, because there's only me and Esther left.

Esther stands. "We'll look together again. We still have our torches. They'll be better now. We weren't able to get far before. Let's go."

She strides out the door without looking back. I hurry to the kitchen drawer and pull out a knife, just in case, and slide it down my bra strap, wincing at the cold metal against bare skin. I have to be prepared for whatever scenario, that's what I tell myself.

Despite the improved lighting out here, we're clumsier somehow. We stick together, walking as a pair, but it doesn't help my nerves. The trees are shrouded in shadow, and every now and then I'm sure someone is out there watching us, following our every move. At one point I stumble over a branch and go crashing to the ground, my knees and palms now slick with mud and leaves.

Esther doesn't help me up, but she does stand and wait for me to rise again. Neither of us wants to get too far ahead of the other. Neither of us wants our back turned. Assuming Chloe would have sought shelter, we trek through the muddied path underneath the palm trees, heading past the cliffside, which stands out harsh and angry against the moonlight, and shine our torches into bushes. Everything has gone quiet since the storm, the whooshing of the black ocean to remind us of the force of what happened. The ground is littered with its reminders too: twigs, leaves, even scattered remnants of our hen party have ended up here. An old balloon is nestled in a thorny bush, and somehow one of Esther's running shoes is wedged between a couple of rocks.

"Chloe?" I shout. "Where are you?"

There's no response, no sign of her. She has to be somewhere.

Poppy's missing body, that puddle of blood she left behind, springs into view in my mind, as if laughing at me. I shake the thought away and press on.

Eventually, we reach a small fork in the path. We stop, considering which route to take.

"The one on the left leads back down to the main beach," Esther says, holding her torch at it. "It's not far. Chloe could have gone this way."

"But the other way leads to that smaller beach." This route seems less travelled, weeds growing on the path, but I remember it from the scavenger hunt, going with Tanya. It's hard to believe that was only two days ago. That Tanya is dead now.

"Right," Esther says. "It has the green hut with the generator."

"If Chloe remembered there was a hut around here, she might have tried to find it for shelter."

"It's a possibility," Esther concedes. "But I don't think there's any point in checking. Chloe won't have known the way. That path is more difficult. It was the middle of the storm. She could barely see as it was."

She turns to head down the path that leads to our usual beach, but something in me hesitates. "Wait."

She looks back. "What is it?"

"I really think we should go down this path." Something about it is calling out to me, like a beacon.

Esther doesn't look pleased, but she can see I'm not in the mood to argue. "Fine."

It doesn't take long. The path opens out very quickly, and the beach is a small clone of the main one. Driftwood has washed up on the shore from the storm, as well as a lot of seaweed. Up ahead, the green hut is perched on the end, along with a small motorboat.

The sight of it sends my heart to my mouth.

"Esther, there's a boat," I whisper, nudging her.

She's noticed it too, eyes wide. "Has that been here this whole time?"

Was it here during the scavenger hunt? I try and remember, but my mind draws a blank.

"We would have heard it, right?" I say, even though Esther is hardly an expert. "If someone had come here on that, we'd have heard the motor? Maybe it's always here for fishing or something."

Could someone have come to the island after all?

We head to the boat and find tarpaulin wrapped over it, protecting it from the storm.

Why would someone come here?

"It must be used for fishing," Esther says, but she looks stricken too. "Look, it clearly hasn't been moved in a while. There's no one else here but us."

"Robin was odd, wasn't she," I murmur. "Why is she all the way out here, thousands of miles from home? She's hiding something. What if she came back and it's been her all along?"

"Don't be ridiculous," Esther snaps, although her face pales at my words.

Something catches the corner of my eye and I let out a shriek. "What's that?"

The tide pushes in, masking it for a few seconds.

Esther frowns. "I don't see anything."

"Wait."

The tide eases back out again, the water turned black and shiny from the night sky. Finally, amidst the seaweed and debris, she appears.

Chloe.

"There!" I shout, taking off in a run down the sand. "It's Chloe!"

Esther follows me, and we pull her out to safety, away from the increasing tide.

She's drenched and pale. Her hair is stuck across her face, masking her features.

"Chloe, can you hear me?" I scream. I try shaking her. "Shit, she might have drowned. Maybe she fell in the water and got too tired to swim? Chloe—"

The words die in my mouth when I peel back her hair, ready to begin compressions in a desperate attempt to save her. My fingers come away red, the blood still wet, dripping down my hands and onto my dress. At first I'm confused. Her face shows no sign of injury. But then I turn her, and see the blow to the back of her head.

"Oh my God." In my shock, I drop her, and her head thuds onto the sand. I stumble backwards, falling onto my behind, scrambling to get up.

Chloe's body is already turning grey, mottled and affected by being out in the open like this. The blow is deliberate, not the result of an accident. She has been killed too.

My heart starts pounding.

"You," Esther hisses. "You did this. It was you all along."

"What?"

I lift my head, and to my astonishment, Esther brandishes a knife in front of her, aiming it directly at me. Where did she get that? When? Has she always had it on her?

My vision turns blurry for a second, and there are two Esthers, two knives, both gleaming at me.

Esther. I can't believe it.

"What are you talking about?" I say. "What are you doing, Esther? Calm down."

"I knew from the beginning," she says. "I really did. You've been spiralling out of control for months. All your shoplifting, your pretending to live a lifestyle that wasn't yours, even clearly ignoring the fact Andrew has been cheating on you your entire marriage. You had to have known. And you've been compensating for it ever since. We can't have Annabel Hannigan be the one suffering, after all. Not the leader of our gang."

My own knife presses in my back, the blade no longer cold but warm and moist with sweat.

Here we go. The truth is finally coming out.

"You've always resented me, haven't you, Esther?" I say. "You're the smart one, the one from a well-off family. But no one really liked you for you. They only gave you the time of day because I was your friend."

Her eyes flash with anger, and I know I've hit a raw nerve. "Is that what this has all really been about?"

"I don't know what you're talking about," I say.

"You can't even admit it to yourself, can you? You pretend everything is okay, and when your secrets begin to spill out—you have to stop it. You have to control everyone again. You're lying to yourself."

Lying to myself? That's rich, coming from her. She's been lying and keeping everyone's secrets for months.

I open my mouth to protest, but she carries on, clearly enjoying herself.

"Except this time, Poppy was the one in control, wasn't she? Your secrets were coming out, and you had to put a stop to it."

I want to tell her she's wrong, but I would be lying if I said one of my first feelings after the initial discovery of the blood in Poppy's room wasn't relief.

"And then Tanya? Planting the knife in her room like that?" Esther shakes her head. "You made us believe it was her. And then—what? Did she stumble on you getting rid of the body or something? Did she find something out? Was that why you had to do it?"

I realise what she's getting at. What she's trying to do.

"As for Chloe . . ." Her body still lies between us, a barrier. "Was she just too unpredictable? Too unreliable? Did you think she was going to panic and blame it all on you in front of the police? Or was it simply because she fucked Andrew and he enjoyed her more than he ever did you?"

"You bitch," I say quietly.

She steps back, and has the grace to actually look afraid.

"You killed them," she says. "It was you, Annabel. Trying to throw me off by mentioning that boat. Trying to insinuate it could be anyone but yourself."

I could almost laugh. It's come to this, has it?

What a clever, clever game.

I remove the knife from behind me. She startles at this; she hadn't expected me to come prepared. Which is stupid of her. She should know me better by now.

If this is how she wants to play, I'm ready for her.

TWENTY-NINE

Esther

MAY 22, 2023

Annabel has a knife too, pointing it at me with both hands, trying to keep herself steady.

This, if anything, is added confirmation to my words. Let her have one. It will make it far easier to explain to the police why I had to do it.

"I knew it," I say. "I knew it was you. I should have known. You killed them, didn't you?"

I am not going to die here, not like them. I have been through too much for that.

"I know what you're doing," Annabel shouts. "Stop pretending. There's just the two of us left."

"Why did you do it?" I ask. "You still haven't answered me."

Annabel laughs. "I can't believe this. I can't believe you're doing this."

"This is why you were sneaking around last night, isn't it?" I shout. "I saw you, heading out in that storm. What other reason would there be to do that? You went and found Chloe and killed her!"

She looks bewildered, clearly puzzled how I saw her.

"You're not pinning this on me." Annabel drops one hand from the knife, the other becoming steady on its own now, her grip strong. "I trusted you. I thought we were friends."

"We are friends." I'm trying to sound as soothing as possible, but my voice comes out in a nervous tremor. "All of your issues with shoplifting, stealing off your friends. The credit card debt. I kept it all a secret, didn't I? For years. Even my necklace. I forgive you. It's alright. You don't have to do anything. Put the knife down."

"You put the knife down," she says. "You're the one who should be explaining things to me. Why did *you* do it? Was it really jealousy, is that it? Something as basic as always being jealous of me?"

I'm lost for words. Jealousy? She really thinks that I would kill everyone on this island because I'm *jealous* of her?

"If that were the case, why are you still alive?" I snap.

"I know what you're trying to do," she says. "It won't work with me. It's me and you now, Esther. We don't have Chloe pulling her silly stunts for attention or mopey Tanya who only really became our friend because we were bored and took pity on her. It was always going to be me and you left, wasn't it? You wanted this."

"Annabel, I don't know what kind of game you're playing, but it needs to stop now."

She looks baffled for a moment, and I genuinely think she's lost it, but then a gleam appears in her eyes. A knowing look.

She is messing with me. I knew it.

"Esther," she says. "Put the knife down."

I hold it closer to my chest instead and step backwards. "Annabel, you need to calm down."

"Stop bleating my name like that," she snaps. "I know what you're doing. It's a common tactic, using the person's name to make them feel like you're someone they can trust. I'm not an idiot, remember. I did two degrees in Psychology."

Yes, she did.

It's easy to forget, a lot of the time, that Annabel has brains. Looking like she does, blonde and doe-eyed and dressed in the latest fashions, she comes across like a typical Barbie doll. But she was smarter than the rest of us at school, as smart as Poppy herself. When Poppy was a no-show on our A Level Results Day, it was Annabel who took centre stage, posing for all the photos. And I hated it. I was meant to be the smart one, not her. And she took all the glory, with barely any effort whatsoever.

Our little ringleader, Annabel Hannigan. Who out of everyone would have most resented Poppy's new interference, her suggestion that we were anything but perfect? Apparently, Annabel has become a consummate actress herself. All her horror and disgust at Poppy's and Tanya's deaths, her weakness, her pathetic pleas for us all to do the right thing. All an act. It's impressive really.

And the rest of us fell hook, line, and sinker. Still Annabel's toys, even ten years on from everything.

I risk a glance at the horizon. The sky remains dark, no sign of an impending sunrise. God damn it, what time is it? Robin needs to get here before there's only one of us left.

"Did you really think Poppy deserved to die?" Annabel asks.

I shake my head at her. "No, of course not. What we said before . . . we were just being dramatic."

"What about Tanya? Chloe?"

Chloe remains between us. I focus my gaze at Annabel, and begin to circle around Chloe's body, drawing us closer.

"No," I say. "No one deserved to die."

"So why are we here?" she says. "I don't understand."

I don't understand either. But I can't trust her to do the right thing. Annabel's already killed three people, why would she stop at the fourth? I need to put an end to it.

Even if that means killing her myself.

The thought comes surprisingly easily.

Adrenaline pumps through my veins, making me more alert than I have ever been. The knife's handle begins to make an imprint in my hand, I'm holding it so tight.

Perhaps she senses something in my resolve change, because her expression darkens. Out in the elements like this, both in thin white dresses, we look like a disturbing mirror image.

"If you would just put the knife down, this could all end," she pleads, sounding almost desperate.

"Never."

"Then what are we going to do?"

"If you won't put the knife down I'm going to have to make you." Before I get too tired, before you can overpower me.

I'm exhausted enough as it is. I've barely slept. The after-effects of the gin are still in me, sending my stomach into knots. I might be stronger than Annabel on a normal day, but this isn't normal.

How has it all gone so wrong?

"Please, Esther." She sounds so sad.

But then I look down at Chloe's body, and my determination returns. I am stronger than her. I can do this.

"I'm sorry, Annabel," I say, and before she can respond, I charge at her.

The ocean around us.

The sand gripping between our toes.

Yes, fight with everything you have. I certainly am. I've been fighting my whole life and it's led to this moment, here on the beach against the moon, the rumble of the sea behind us, the storm turned from an external force to an internal one, as each of us knows this is the last time.

Kill her.

THIRTY

Annabel

S he charges at me with a strangled cry, racing forward and throwing herself on top of me. My own knife is dropped as I grab at hers with both hands, screaming as the blade slices into my palms. We roll around on the sand, wrestling with the knife as she tries to tear it back away from me and I grip down hard despite the excruciating pain. Sand gets in my mouth, my eyes, down my dress, but I can't relent.

There are more screams, from both of us, I think, and we start kicking at one another. At one point she seems to pull back, so I lift my head and collide it with her own, sending her flying backwards. She scrambles to get up, but by that point I'm on top of her, knife now in my grasp.

"Get off me!" she snarls, gripping my neck with both hands.

The force of her hold makes my breath come out in choked gasps, and I have to drop the knife. She releases me to reach for it, and I manage to hurl myself up and away, heading across the sand.

Where is the other damn knife? I gaze around wildly, but there's no glint on the beach. The tide must have washed in and taken it, or buried it in the wet sand. Stumbling away, I find a hard rock and pick it up, grateful for anything.

It's wet with blood.

Some of Chloe's hair is sticking to it.

"Oh, fuck!"

Part of me wants to drop it, keel over and throw up. But Esther is charging behind me now, so I have to let go of my inhibitions and turn quickly, smashing the rock against the side of her head.

She falls back, screaming.

I lift the rock and hit her with it again, kneeling astride her, gasping. She tries to squirm away but it's impossible. As a last-ditch effort, she tries to stab me, but her grip is weak. Her strength is fading.

It's the final look she gives me: shock, fear, pain, all rolled into one, that makes me pause for a second, makes me doubt.

But it has to be Esther. There is no one left.

She senses my hesitation, and reaches out for the knife. I'm able to pull it away before she can, and her hand reaches my face instead, scratching me down my cheek.

I have no choice.

I stab her, again and again, enough times that she stops struggling underneath me.

"Annabel . . ." she gasps, and that is all she can say. Blood spits from her mouth and lands on my face. Her eyelids flutter, and she goes still.

She's dead.

I ease myself up, knees shaking, and then run into the ocean and throw up.

Part of me wants to fall into it myself, just drown in the waves.

I still don't understand *why*. That is what is driving me forward, what keeps me standing on my feet. Why did Esther do it? Poppy, I understand. Poppy ruined her life. Got her fired from her job, embarrassed her with those naked pictures that now might be anywhere. But Tanya? It doesn't make any sense. Out of anyone, Esther had the most grudge with me. So why was I left until last? Why did we explore the island together looking for Chloe?

More thoughts spring to mind. Chloe's horrible injury to the back of her head. The blood around her.

Esther's white dress. Until we fought, there wasn't even a drop of blood on it. How could that be? She hasn't changed outfits. How could she kill Chloe and not end up with a mark on her?

Doubt begins to creep into my mind. Everyone else is dead. She had to have done it.

The little motorboat remains on the beach, taunting me in the corner of my eye.

Pull yourself together.

I look down at my own dress now, the devastation across it. There are two deep cuts in my palms as well, from where I had to grab the blade. They're still bleeding. I wash my hands in the sea but it makes little difference, the water turning red around me. Even the sharp sting it causes doesn't offer me anything but further reminder that the pain is almost overwhelming. My nose is bleeding too, and when I feel around my face it's sore to touch.

None of it makes sense.

I stare out at the horizon, the smallest smudges of pink and orange. Dawn is coming, at last.

Why was Chloe left on the beach?

I don't know why the thought comes to me now, but it does.

Tanya, that made sense. It was the daytime and whoever killed her would have been discovered moving the body.

But Chloe is right here. She's on the beach. All it would have taken was for Esther to drag her in, and Chloe would have been swept away with the tide, never to be seen again. Why leave her body here, when she went to the effort of moving Poppy from the main lodge?

Why is Poppy's body the only one that vanished?

Oh my God. I clutch my forehead as a headache bursts into me, violent and throbbing.

Behind me, I hear clapping.

"Bravo."

Shaking, I turn, my whole body in slow motion. I'm covered in blood. My mouth tastes of vomit.

Poppy stands by Esther's body, hands on her hips.

She grins when she sees me.

"Quite the show," she says. "Well done."

THIRTY-ONE

Annabel

MAY 22, 2023

Poppy is alive. She's *alive*. There's just no way. She can't be standing in front of me.

I can't take my eyes off her. Even as I walk forward, out of the sea, I keep my gaze on her, as if she might vanish at any moment. Maybe I've fallen down somewhere and hit my head, and this is all one big hallucination.

"You can't be here," I say. "You're dead." I'm trembling. Did Esther kill me after all, and this is some kind of afterlife?

"Am I?" she asks. She feels for her pulse in her neck, giving it a couple of seconds. "I feel alive to me. Perhaps you'd like to come and check?"

How can she be so calm? So mocking?

Esther and Chloe are on the sand near us, lifeless.

"I killed Esther," I say. "I thought she was—I thought she had—"

Poppy smiles. "Oh, I know, you thought she was the murderer. I mean, who else was left? Just the two of you. It's funny, she thought the same thing about you."

My God. It wasn't Esther at all. Both of us, convinced the other was the guilty party because there was no other explanation.

"It was you," I whisper. "You killed Tanya and Chloe."

"Yes," Poppy says. "That was me."

I remember the sight of her room, the amount of blood there. How is she standing here? How is she alive?

"But how . . ." I can't finish my sentence. I've killed Esther. She's dead because of me. And Poppy has killed Tanya and Chloe. I'm next. I have to be next.

"I'll explain," Poppy says. "Come in here."

She gestures to her side, to the little green hut with its door open. The hut with the generator. That's where she was staying all this time?

She senses my hesitation. "If I wanted to kill you, I would have snuck up on you while you were in the sea."

"You don't want to kill me?"

"Oh no, Annabel," she says. "I have things I need to know. Things you need to tell me. And things I need you to hear. Consider it your duty as the last remaining bridesmaid—you can even call yourself my maid of honour, if you want."

I'm going to be sick again.

She smiles at me, raising an eyebrow. "Or maybe that should be maid of dishonour."

Is she expecting me to laugh? After everything?

"Come on." She's brisk, suddenly. "I want to get out of the cold. We haven't got much time."

It's only as she says it that I realise it has gotten colder, bitingly so, sending goose bumps across my arms. Now that the storm has died down, there's nothing to replace it, and the air sits fresh and exposed to the wide expanse of sea. Poppy turns her back on me and walks towards the green hut. I follow her, picking up the bloody knife from the ground as I go, debating whether or not to stab her and end it now.

As if she can read my mind, she turns, amused. "Thinking about stabbing me in the back, Annabel? It wouldn't be the first time." She lifts her dress and I notice she's wearing thick Doc Martens, unsuited to the beach. She bends down and takes something out from one of the boots, and as it glints in the early morning sky I can see she too has a knife.

Of course she's prepared. Why wouldn't she be?

"Don't make any silly moves," she says, as if we're discussing a game of chess. "Follow me and get inside."

I lower my own knife. Now is not the time. Poppy is taller and fitter than me. I have to have the element of surprise if I'm going to get out of this.

It only starts to feel real when she closes the door behind us, shutting out the outside world. The room isn't a generator at all, but more like a fishing hut, so perhaps Poppy was lying all along about that. There's a camp bed in here, I suppose for nights like this where it could be dangerous to trek back across the island to the main accommodation. Almost all of the space is taken up with equipment. There's fishing gear, as expected, but also diving gear, complete with flippers and scuba suits. In one corner of the room there's a carrier bag with some of the food from the pantry.

Poppy sits on the camp bed. When I study her face, I'm not sure if she's soaking from the storm or crying. She notices me looking and wipes her face urgently, which makes me believe it was tears after all. The horrible painting from the scavenger hunt is here too, sitting on the bed beside her. She catches me staring at it and smiles.

We're both on edge. I stand leaning against the door for some semblance of safety, the idea that I can wrench it open and run away if necessary. The knife feels slippery in my hand, and whether that's from blood or sweat I don't know.

How can she be sitting here? Her room was a massacre. All that blood.

"Explain yourself," I say, numb from everything. "What the fuck is going on? How are you alive?"

Poppy nods. There's no pleasure in her expression anymore.

"I faked my death," she says. "After I'd got my revenge on you all, destroying your lives back home, I knew you'd all be mad. Mad enough, even, to enact some revenge yourself. So I thought I'd jump ahead to the fun part, the aftermath. I covered the room in blood, even dragged my body from the bed to the floor in it so it looked realistic. Sprinkled spots of it in various places, including Tanya's window, the front porch, the doorframe. Put the shirt I was wearing in the sea, on that rock, to make it look like I'd been washed out. I'd already set up a little place here, stocked with food and a bed. And a live feed, of course."

She points, and there's a small screen split into four. Various cameras dotted about the area, prime viewing material.

"Of course, the storm spoiled the feed," she says. "That's why I was shocked to find Chloe at my door, seeking a way to turn the power back on."

My thoughts are flying all over the place. Part of me is still reeling from Poppy even being here at all. I had accepted her death. And now she's here, and I don't know what that means.

"So you killed her?" I say. "You killed Chloe?"

"Yes." She says this with no emotion. "Actually, it was sheer bad luck on her part that she happened to come this way. The storm had ruined my initial plan of picking you off one by one, but she did me a favour."

"How did you kill her?" The image of the rock covered in blood flashes in my mind, the same rock I used on Esther.

"It wasn't as easy as Tanya. She started running. It was dark. I picked up a rock and hit her over the head with it. I figured it was best to leave her there for you and Esther to find."

"How was there so much blood in your room, if you're not dead?" I ask, still picturing the grotesque bed with its dark bloodstains, the marks on the floor. "It was horrible."

"Pigs' blood." Poppy folds her arms. "From the mainland. I brought it over with me on the boat ride with Robin before you guys came, in a couple of large thermos mugs. I think the butcher thought I was some kind of cultist. He didn't ask too many questions."

"You did it just to mess with our heads."

"Oh yes. Making you all think one of the others was a killer was the best part."

In my panicked state, I try to recall the sequence of events. "So you're the one who got rid of the flares?"

"Of course. I couldn't have you alerting someone and ending the fun early."

"My top?" I think of it now, that awful sequined top that vanished so quickly.

She crosses her arms. "That, and smashing Chloe's makeup. Just small things, designed to trip you up a bit. I threw that top in the sea by the way. It's long gone."

"And you planted the knife in Tanya's room?"

"I wanted her to have the blame, at least for a little bit," Poppy says. "Before I killed her."

It's her nonchalant tone as she says this that finally breaks me.

"All of this is just a joke to you." I'm surprised by the force of my words as they tear out of me. "This entire holiday, this hen party. People have *died*, Poppy. You've killed them. Do you even understand what that means?"

Her eyes flash with anger, more incensed than I've ever seen her.

"Don't you dare say that to me," she says. "You have no idea. You don't know what you're talking about."

"Then *tell me*!" I shout. "You keep talking in riddles and I'm tired of them. If you want to kill me, then just go ahead and do it. I'm sure I deserve it according to you."

"I was trying to be the bigger person for so long," she says. "I've spent years trying to get over it, to move on. I went to Cambridge University, I became a bloody doctor. I should be living a happy life, a fulfilled life. But I'm not. No matter how far I tried to run, I always came back to you all. You ruined my life."

"We didn't ruin your life," I say. "You sound like you have a fantastic one! Like you said, look at you. It's better than ours. You're getting married, for Christ's sake."

"Oh, the beautiful fiancée?" Poppy sighs. "A lie, I'm afraid. As much as I might wish it were true."

I don't know why this surprises me, but it does. "You were lying about getting married?"

"I had to do something to get you all on this island, and a hen party seemed like the perfect excuse. This was all for you guys, and boy, did you deliver."

"But your Instagram!" It sounds pathetic even to my ears.

"Created so that you believed the story. Funny how all it takes is a few pictures of wedding dresses and a nice diamond ring and suddenly you're a bride-to-be no questions asked."

"Jesus Christ . . ." I don't even know how to respond. "But everything else—everything else in your life sounds wonderful. You still had no need to do this . . ."

"No." She raises a hand to stop me speaking. "I did all of that to try and prove to the outside world I was coping. To try and show my mum and dad I was happy. Because they aren't happy, as much as they pretend to be."

Sunlight begins to stream through the bottom of the door. At last, this horrible night is over.

But the day is just beginning.

There are tears in Poppy's eyes now. "Finally, I had to look the four of you up."

"When was this?" I ask.

"A year ago," Poppy says. "I've been watching you all for a long time. Investigating your lives. You were very easy to track."

"Chloe's burglary," I whisper. "That was you, after all?"

"She'll never know now," Poppy says. "That's a shame. I'd have liked to have seen her face knowing it was me. But doing that got me a whole load of access to everything about you all."

But Chloe did know. She'd figured it out.

And now I have the confirmation.

Does that mean Poppy really does have the video?

Here in the hut, without windows, the claustrophobic feeling seems to increase, everything closing in on me. "You tracked us for so long. Why?"

"To give you a chance," Poppy says. "It's as simple as that. If I saw that you were—I don't know, helping people, doing good deeds, living good lives, I think that would have been enough for me. I could have just taken what I needed and left you alone. But not even one of you could manage that. You were all still as selfish as always. You haven't even made any other real friends. That says a lot about who you are as people."

Taken what she needed?

"You all accepted my invitation," Poppy says, "and none of you apologised. You were more concerned with what I looked like."

Another awful truth.

"But faking your death?" I say.

"It was poetic justice," Poppy says.

"What's that meant to mean?"

Poppy sighs. "You all barely remembered the past. Or at least you pretended not to. Only Tanya was at least willing to bring it up. Did the rest of you forget?"

"We didn't forget," I say quietly.

"No." She looks me up and down, and the action makes me feel naked.

"It was ten years ago!" I can't tell her the truth: that even now, I still can't believe it was really that bad.

Poppy continues as if I haven't spoken. "The initial bullying, I could forgive perhaps. Kids bully other kids. That's an unfortunate fact of life. Kids can be nasty. But then you had to outdo yourselves."

I don't know what to say.

"You need to remember it," Poppy says. "Remember what you did ten years ago."

I shake my head. "This isn't the time. Everyone is dead, Poppy."

"This is the perfect time." Her voice sounds strangled. I can hear just how much this hurts her. "Ten years ago this very day, actually. May twenty-second, 2013."

The art exam.

"That was the worst day," Poppy says. "Why don't I take you back?"

I want to say no.

"You want an explanation for why I killed Tanya and Chloe and did this to you all?" she says. "Then you need to listen."

THIRTY-TWO

Poppy

Dear Diary,

I'm sorry if my writing looks shaky. My hands are still trembling from earlier. I've opened this notebook up and then closed it again a dozen times. How do I even process what happened?

I can't believe it. If I don't write it down I can pretend that nothing actually happened at all, and it was all some sick nightmare.

Except if I don't do something I think I'm going to fall apart.

Okay. I can write about this if I start at the beginning and pretend it's a story happening to someone else. That's the only way I'll be able to make sense of it. If I record everything, maybe I'll be able to deal with it. Maybe I'll be able to think about it all without crying.

This is a story about a girl who failed her art exam.

Our final piece for the Art A Level was an almost two-day-long exam in Miss Wersham's art room. We had this time, and this time only, to produce a project that showcased the very best of our ability. Everyone had been talking about it for months, even more than our portfolios, which were now done and waiting to be sent off to the exam board.

Before we got started, we were allowed to choose our own work spaces. I took myself immediately to the back of the room in the corner where no one else would be able to see what I was doing. I didn't want them to copy me at the last minute! My theme throughout my A Level has been isolation and the human body, and I've taken a lot of inspiration in my style from artists such as Frida Kahlo, Remedios Varo, and Gertrude Abercrombie, meaning my work has become much more surrealist.

"I can't wait to get started," Sally said after we'd all chosen our places and set up. I could see her easel and canvas from here and knew her work wouldn't be anywhere near as good as mine. She was just doing art for the fun of it. "I'm going to do a collage from all these newspapers I've collected and create an image of a bird to show my theme of spirituality really well."

How original. But I didn't say anything, I just nodded.

"I'm doing a sculpture within a sculpture," Jayla declared. Then she laughed nervously. "I hope it works. I've been practicing at home."

"What are you doing, Poppy?" Ebbie, another girl who was sitting closest to me, asked. "Your canvas is huge!"

I made sure to angle my easel even further towards the back to guarantee she couldn't see anything. "Something completely unexpected," I said with pride. "None of you will have ever seen anything like this before."

"Don't let Miss Wersham hear you say that," Jayla said. "She'll go mad thinking you're going to break the rules again."

"Miss Wersham isn't allowed in here," I said. It was true. As our teacher, she was seen to be biased and therefore couldn't be in the room whilst we were doing our exam. Instead, an external proctor had to come in and watch us. "And anyway, something can be edgy and controversial and still within the rules, you know."

"Right." Jayla wasn't convinced. "What's the idea you're going for, anyway?"

I put my finger to my lips to show I wasn't going to say anything more.

I wasn't the only one keeping quiet. Ollie had set himself up in the other corner and wouldn't engage in conversation at all, continuing to check obsessively that he had everything he needed.

At that point, the proctor, a rather dull-looking woman with grey hair and too-tight jeans on, stood up and called for quiet. She explained the exam rules (we weren't allowed to talk to each other, we couldn't look at each other's work, I mean duh) and then started a timer. We had eight hours in total for the exam, split across two days into four-hour slots. We were also allowed a break in between, so the timer was only for two hours each time. But it still felt like a huge task, and a lot of pressure to perform and produce something I'd be happy with in such a short period.

I almost don't want to write about my project. It hurts too much. But we're still pretending this is a story at the moment, right? This happened to a made-up girl. It didn't really happen to me.

Ebbie wasn't kidding—my canvas was huge. Almost as big as me. My plan was a self-portrait, but a surrealist one. The background was going to be full of objects that seemed positive, but on closer look were disturbing. Bright, colourful flowers that were wilting and growing upside down from the sky. Skulls as clouds. Apples with bites in them that revealed a rotten inside. Pomegranates spilling juice that looked like blood. Insects crawling between trees, as tall as them and with thousands of legs. Not ordinary trees—trees with mirrors for bark, shiny and reflecting sad fairy-tale figures trying desperately to reach out and escape. Finally, me in the centre, huge and crying, mouth open to scream, hair growing sideways as if I've been electrocuted. *There are silver lines on my arms and hands as I reach forward. I have no body; I float.*

Frightening. Edgy. Controversial. Surreal. Everything I wanted it to be.

Everyone was going to be stunned. And better—jealous they couldn't come up with something that so perfectly encapsulated their portfolio's theme and style like this. I was going to bring it with me to Slade. Show everyone what I was made of.

My ticket out. Like Charlie in Charlie and the Chocolate Factory, I was going to get my Golden Ticket and escape to a better place.

The first day I drew the scene out, making sure it was as perfect as possible in the timed conditions. The proctor got up and did a loop around everyone to make sure they had everything they needed at the beginning of the exam, and then spent the rest of it sitting at Miss Wersham's desk reading Vogue and Harper's Bazaar. Hardly a true professional. But everyone was equally as drawn into their work as I was, the room a hushed quiet, the only sounds those of pencils, paint brushes, paper rustling, and sculptures being melded.

The second day was more rushed, as I had to paint everything. Truth be told, I wanted to oil paint it, but I knew the drying would take too long. It had to be acrylic. The result was still the thick, sweeping surges of colour I wanted, bright in some places and horrifyingly dark in others.

"You have half an hour left," the proctor said, the first time she'd spoken since starting us up again after our break earlier in the morning.

I panicked, looking at what I had left. I'd painted my background, painstakingly carefully, making sure each part looked how I wanted it to, but I was only half through with myself in the centre. It meant painting faster than I intended, but the frenetic strokes and slight overlap of lines ended up looking deliberate, like I wanted my central figure to blend messily into the background and into herself.

I finished with barely a second to spare.

"Can you believe that's done!" Sally cried as we all walked out of the art rooms after we'd finished. "It felt like it would never end."

Last to leave, I turned back to look at the proctor. She was meant to go around and check our work, but she was busy fiddling with something in her bag and came out pretty much straight after us, clearly eager to get away. The door shut behind her with a buzz, locking automatically.

"I don't know how I did," Jayla mumbled. "I think I messed it up to be honest."

"At least you weren't sitting where I was," Ebbie said. "It absolutely stank. They keep saying they're going to do something about them and they don't. Boys are gross."

The art rooms share a wall with the boys' toilets, which are notoriously unpleasant, especially now in the summertime. Everyone tried to avoid sitting near that wall if they could. It wasn't great—but it had the most privacy, so I put up with it, choosing my corner knowing I'd have to grin and bear it.

"If it isn't the art buddies!"

Annabel, Chloe, Esther, and Tanya were standing together in the hallway as we all came towards them. Most people were intimidated by them. It was hard not to be when they looked like supermodels and the rest of us silly schoolkids. But since prom and the afterparty—I felt like I was okay. Not one of them. I'm not that crazy. But we'd had fun together. It was almost like we could be friends. So I didn't cower away like I would before.

"How was the art exam, Poppy?" Chloe asked.

As they all focused their attention on me, everyone else managed to carry on walking past. Chloe winked at Ollie as he went by, which

*made him blush furiously, and then he stopped near the corner, do-
ing something on his phone. Was he waiting for Chloe to chat to him
again? He couldn't be that delusional.*

*It was only me left standing there. I should have walked with
the rest of them, pretended I hadn't heard them. But I was just as
delusional as Ollie. I still thought they might actually want to be
friends with me, that they might actually have asked out of care for
how I did.*

I'm a sucker for punishment, clearly.

*"Hello? Is anyone in there?" Chloe said when I didn't answer
straight away, grinning. "I asked you a question."*

"It went fine." My voice was croaky from being unused for so long.

*"Huh?" Esther stuck a hand behind her ear and leaned forward.
"I didn't quite catch that. Did any of you?"*

"Nope," Tanya said.

"Honestly, Poppy," Chloe said, shaking her head.

*I laughed nervously, unsure whether they were joking or being
mean again.*

*"Guys, shut it." Annabel rolled her eyes, then smiled at me. "I'm
glad it went well, Poppy. You've been doing so great lately, haven't
you?"*

"What do you mean?" I asked.

*"The belle of the ball last Friday. Now smashing it in your exam.
Don't be modest! I bet you've done fantastic."*

My cheeks flushed with pride. "Thank you."

*"Something totally out there, right?" Esther said. "We've all seen
your art in the corridors. I bet you've gone totally experimental."*

*It was as if she'd read my mind, but I was confused when Tanya
elbowed Chloe and they both giggled.*

*"Exactly," I said. "I've tried to take all what I've learned so far
and put it into this one piece and really showcase something surreal."*

"I'm sure it's surreal," Tanya said. "Well done, Poppy."

It felt good hearing that from her. She looked sincere, a wide-open smile on her face and nodding encouragingly at me.

I should have remembered how good Tanya is at acting.

"Well, we can't wait to see it," Annabel said. "We'll be able to, right? They're going to show your artwork to people?"

"I think so," I said. "I can't wait for you all to see it too. Thanks for being . . . thanks for being cool this past week. It's been great."

"You certainly made yourself cosy at the party," Chloe said. "You really came out of your shell and we saw who you really were."

I frowned. I wasn't quite sure what Chloe was getting at.

Annabel cut across her smoothly. "Anyway, you should really get going. Mr. Edwards wanted to talk to you about your exam. That's what we came to tell you. Looking forward to seeing your art soon. It's going to be . . . surreal, for sure."

I hurried off, almost bumping into Ollie, who was still lurking on the corridor, ignoring them laughing behind me. They laughed at everything. They wouldn't be laughing at me, not now we were almost friends. It didn't matter that when I found Mr. Edwards he was confused, saying he hadn't told Annabel that at all.

I didn't understand at the time what was happening. But it soon became obvious later.

That afternoon, we were in a mock exam for Maths. Our last mock exam, in real exam conditions. I was the only person who took Art as well as Maths, so I was told it was unfortunate timing for me that I had had a real exam on the same day, but they couldn't change it just for me, and I had to still do it. Which was why I was stunned when Miss Wersham walked into the hall, murmured something to Mr. Holmes, and then came and told me to collect my stuff and come with her.

"Now?" I whispered. I became very aware of everyone looking up *from their exam papers, intrigued. Annabel and Esther were smirking, pleased with themselves, and I started to get a terrible feeling in the pit of my stomach.*

Miss Wersham nodded, face serious. "Now, please, Poppy."

I had to follow her out in the full view of everyone. It was so silent the only sound was our shoes as we walked out. As soon as the door to the hall closed behind us, I tried to find out what was going on.

"Has something happened at home?" I asked, horrified. "Are my mum and dad okay? Is it Wendy?"

"It's nothing to do with home," Miss Wersham clarified, but she still looked solemn. Even angry. "I'm so disappointed in you, Poppy."

"Disappointed in me?" I echoed with a squeak. "What have I done? Am I in trouble?"

"You'll see. I thought you knew better by now."

She said nothing else as we walked along together, and soon enough I realised where she was taking me. Back to the art rooms.

Had something happened with my exam?

Annabel, Chloe, Esther, and Tanya immediately appeared in my mind. Their cryptic comments. Their glee. Their proximity to our exam room.

Could they have done something?

To my shock, we arrived at the art rooms and found not only the proctor from earlier, but the head teacher, Mrs. Hargreaves, and one other serious-looking man in a suit with a visitor lanyard around his neck.

My face went pale. This was serious.

"What's going on?" I said, the tremble in my voice making it clear how scared I was.

Mrs. Hargreaves sighed, folding her arms. "When Miss Wersham came in to assign marks to the exam pieces this afternoon, she found yours in an unfit state. She had no choice but to inform me, and I called the exam board. Fortunately, they were able to send a moderator relatively quickly." She indicated her head towards the man in the suit, whose mouth was set in a thin line. "He confirmed what Miss Wersham suspected. Your final piece project is not only inappropriate and inconsiderate, but downright offensive, not only in its creation but also to poor Miss Wersham, who has worked so hard with you all these years. The moderator has had no choice but to disqualify it from consideration for the A Level."

My mind was racing. "What do you mean?" I barely understood what she said. "How is it offensive? I cleared it with Miss Wersham—"

"You most certainly did not clear this with me, Poppy," Miss Wersham cut in sharply. Her face was filled with disappointment. "I'm so surprised you would do this. After everything with your GCSE. I thought you had learned from that. You know full well I did not clear you to add those disgusting pieces to your painting. If only you had left it as it was, it would have been incredible."

Now I was even more confused. "What disgusting pieces? The painting of blood? The rotting fruit? You said that was fine!"

"Of course, the proctor should have been keeping a better eye on things," Mrs. Hargreaves said, glaring at the proctor, who at least had the grace to look ashamed, hanging her head and avoiding eye contact with anyone. "But it's ultimately your responsibility to produce something that follows the rules."

"Please." I started to cry, thick tears that clouded my vision. "I really don't know what you're talking about."

"For goodness' sake, young lady." Mrs. Hargreaves opened the art room door and stepped in. "Come and see for yourself and tell us why you think that's acceptable."

We all went in. My canvas had been turned around to face the front of the room. Everyone stood in a line behind me as I surveyed it, taking in the damage that had been done.

It was my painting.

Underneath the massacre on top.

Popped balloons hung, drooped and colourful, covered in needles and sticky with Capri-Sun, on each corner of the canvas. Their splashes had dried and looked like burst stained flowers that dripped down the sides.

Pieces of mirror were stuck onto the canvas in different areas, which caught the light and flickered like savage glitter. I could see myself within them, pale and horrified. Some were pierced into the canvas too and stuck out dangerously, their sharp edges jagged and threatening, just like the one I used to tear into my skin.

Worst of all were the bits of chicken skin that hung from the needles like a miniature butcher's shop and the smears of dog shit in brown swathes that looked like a deliberate creation of shadows in the painting. It was horrible. The way it had been smeared made me think of the red lipstick that I had smeared around my mouth, and it brought everything back.

It was all here. The Capri-Sun from my first day. Ruined birthday balloons to show all the birthdays I spent alone. And the pieces of mirror . . . they can't have known, but those most of all reminded me how ruined I had become. Not only because I could see my foul reflection, but because I had used a piece to destroy my body, and here they were on display as if I was proud of that fact.

I felt sick. This was brutal. It was beyond anything that had ever been done to me before. This was my art. It was meant to be safe. And now it had been twisted and taken out of my control, just like everything else.

"I don't understand," I whispered, taking a step back. "I didn't do this."

"There's no use pretending, Poppy," Miss Wersham said sadly. "This wouldn't be your first time stepping out of the box. We have had many conversations before about this."

My face must have gone very pale, and my legs wobbly, because she hurried forward to steady me. Mrs. Hargreaves brought me a chair.

"Don't start pulling amateur dramatics with me," Mrs. Hargreaves snapped. "Don't do something if you can't face up to the consequences."

The exam moderator cleared his throat. "Unfortunately, being disqualified from the final piece project means you have failed your A Level."

"Wait." My head snapped up to look at him, and my mouth fell open. "What do you mean? I can't have."

"What did you expect would happen?" Mrs. Hargreaves said. "Of course you've failed."

"But I can't have." Nausea began to bubble in my throat. "If I've failed, that means I won't go to Slade."

"You should have thought about that before you did all this." Mrs. Hargreaves shrugged, as if that was that. "For such insolent behaviour, you're going to be suspended from school for a week. I'll be phoning your parents now to let them know. You're only to come in if you have an exam."

I was barely listening to her at this point. My entire world was shattering. Ending. I had failed my Art A Level. That meant no Slade. That meant no getting out of here and achieving all my dreams.

I didn't do this. But I knew, in that moment, who had.

Annabel, Chloe, Esther, and Tanya.

I should have known the four of them would never be my friends.

But no one would ever believe me.

They were all starting to walk back out again, as if that settled it. I stood up shakily.

"I didn't do this!" I shouted. "It wasn't me!"

"These rooms were locked," Miss Wersham said. "No one else could have come in. Everyone, including you, returned their card key they got at the beginning of the exam at lunchtime. When the exam ended."

It didn't make any sense. But I knew those four had got in somehow. I knew it deep in my bones.

"You told everyone you were doing something unexpected," Miss Wersham continued. "And we've spoken to Ebbie, who was seated near you. She could smell something foul, but assumed it was the toilets."

"It was the toilets!" I protested. "Please, you have to listen to me. I don't know how this happened and I can't prove otherwise, but it wasn't me. I promise."

"Unfortunately, that doesn't change anything. You need to leave now. We'll be informing your parents, as Mrs. Hargreaves has said. I'm so disappointed in you, Poppy."

"Miss Wersham—"

But she simply shook her head. I was practically bundled out of the room, and the four adults walked with me without further comment, making sure I left the school building.

I was still crying, in complete shock at what had just happened. When I left the school gates and rounded the corner, everything was confirmed when I saw the four of them waiting for me, pure delight in their faces.

"Oh dear, Poppy, why are you so upset?" Esther asked. There was no sympathy in her voice.

"You know you're bright red and your mascara has run down your cheeks, right?" Chloe added. *"I couldn't even tell you were wearing makeup until I saw those big black splodges around your eyes like a panda. Talk about a cheap wand."*

"I thought we were becoming friends," I whispered. *"I thought you were starting to like me."*

"Friends?" Annabel repeated, as if the word disgusted her. *"Why the hell would you think that?"*

"Because . . . the prom . . ." Suddenly I was doubting my own memory. They had been nice, hadn't they? They'd invited me to their afterparty. I had danced with people. Drank. Had fun.

"You mean when we invited you to Esther's house and you tried to get with our boyfriends?" Chloe said. *"Yeah, you were getting real friendly, but not with us."*

My heart, already thudding from the shock of being disqualified, began to pound even harder. Part of me was scared I'd collapse there and then. *"I didn't! Aidan and Elliott were—they were being nice. I didn't think they were interested in me."*

Annabel scowled. *"Well, of course they weren't really interested in you. It was a joke. Chloe and I told them to, obviously. And you fell for it. You really would have betrayed us with them. Some friend you'd be!"*

They were twisting everything. She had to be lying. But in my panicked state, I didn't know what to say, or how to make it better. They'd already done their worst.

"Why did you get taken out of the Maths mock?" Tanya asked. *"Everyone was talking about it afterwards."*

Her question was innocent enough, but the gleam in everyone else's eyes confirmed what I already knew to be true.

"It was you four, wasn't it?" I mumbled. *"You messed up my art exam."*

"Us!" Annabel said, clutching her heart and swaying backwards dramatically. "Maybe if your art exam was messed up it's only what you deserved."

"I heard it was shit anyway," Chloe said, giggling. "Shit being your theme, apparently."

They knew. They knew it was smeared with dog poo.

"You can't prove it," Tanya said.

"I've been disqualified," I said. "I've failed my A Level. I'm not going to get to go to university now."

"Oh boo-hoo." Annabel rolled her eyes. "Did you think that was going to be a fresh start for you, is that it? A place where no one would know about poor little Poppy Greedy?"

My voice was choked with sobs. "Yes."

Annabel grinned. "Well, I have good news for you. It wouldn't have mattered anyway. You'd have got there and they'd have treated you the same as we did. Because you radiate desperation, Poppy. You're pathetic."

Something in me finally snapped. I raised my head, which had been staring at the ground, too scared to look, and I screamed at them all.

"I don't deserve to be treated this way! I haven't done anything! All I've ever wanted is to do my art and have some friends. Is that so bad? Is that so terrible?"

I darted forward, trying to slap Annabel, but tripped, crashing to the ground and into the hard gravel on my knees. The surge of pain only matched the turmoil on the inside.

"She tried to hit you!" Chloe screeched. "Oh my God! She's a lunatic!"

"You should get her back for that," Tanya said.

Annabel stood over me, then bent down and grabbed my chin

none too gently. "Don't ever touch me again, you freak. Enjoy spending another year in this dump." She turned back to the others. "Let's go."

"Bye, Poppy," Esther called as they began to walk away. "Sorry the whole art thing didn't work out."

I stayed on my knees, not caring how badly it hurt, listening to their laughter and jeers getting quieter and quieter as they disappeared into the distance. Fat tears fell from my eyes onto the ground, so big I could see them leaving brief wet imprints on the ground. For a moment I considered curling up into a ball and staying where I was, hoping for a cold night that would kill me and get all of this over with.

But I lifted myself up, shakily. My knees were burning, and my tights had torn, creating ladders on both legs, but there was nothing I could do about that. I walked home slowly, taking my time both because of the pain and because I knew my family would be waiting for me well aware of what had happened.

I'll spare you the details. But Mum and Dad were okay at first. They had received the phone call, obviously, but when they saw the state I was in when I got home they held back. Mum put me in the bath like I was six years old again with lots of bubbles and washed my hair and face and told me everything was going to be alright. Dad cooked a lasagne and we sat at the dinner table talking about anything except what had happened. Wendy was surprisingly quiet and well-behaved, which meant she must have known what had gone on.

It was after dinner when they finally sat me down, telling Wendy to do something in her room for an hour, and asked me to explain.

I told them it wasn't me. That someone else had to have come in and messed with my painting deliberately. They listened and made all the right noises, but I could tell they didn't really believe me. If they did, they would have contacted the school and tried to sort something.

I was too scared to tell them the truth. They'd think I was just pointing the blame at anyone, and I didn't have any proof.

Wendy was the only person I wanted to tell. I was so close to doing it as well. When we went to our rooms for the night, just as I was about to write in here, she knocked on my door and came inside. She didn't even say anything at first, just sat on my bed with me and hugged me tight.

We stayed like that for a long time.

"I love you, Poppy," Wendy said eventually, releasing me. "You know that, right?"

Wendy hardly ever said that. Only when she was practically forced to. She knew how serious this was.

This wasn't just a case of me failing my art exam because I wasn't good enough. This was me deliberately flouting the rules and making a fool of myself, being stripped of my grade. Slade won't even look twice at me now, not when they hear the reason why I've had to take another year. I'll be stuck here. Alone. Again.

"I love you too," I said.

"Things will get better," she said. "I believe you when you say it wasn't you."

But I don't think she did. She was just trying to comfort me.

No one truly understands how I feel. How could they?

The next time they're all out I'm going to go downstairs and steal a kitchen knife. I know the exact one. Small, sharp, only used rarely and shoved right at the back of the cutlery tray underneath two spatulas. No one will miss it.

It'll be easier to use than the mirror piece, the one I should never have thrown away. What was I thinking? Of course things weren't going to work out for me. Not that I would want to use that now anyway, not after similar shards were used to destroy my painting.

I could focus on my old scars. Open them up again. But I think I'll need more than just that. I need to feel something. Anything. As much as possible.

I'm not going to Slade. In the summer my application will update and it will tell me my offer conditions were not met, and my place has been withdrawn. All my plans, all my dreams, have disappeared in an instant, and it's all their fault.

Those four.

Those bitches.

I hate them. I hate what they've done to me.

THIRTY-THREE

Annabel

MAY 22, 2023

The art exam," Poppy says. "I had to do this because of the art exam."

I stand in the hut in absolute silence after Poppy's retelling of what happened that day.

"I just don't understand why," she continues, shaking her head. "Why would you do that to me? None of you cared about art. It didn't affect you at all."

I open my mouth to say something, then close it again.

I was angry with Poppy. I'll be honest. She looked so stunning that night, despite everything, and everyone was so interested in her. It wasn't fair. I'd spent years trying to be popular, maintaining a certain image, but I was never met with that reception. I couldn't afford to spend hundreds on that sixth form prom, so no one complimented my hair and outfit. I didn't want the last impression of her to be better than mine.

Even Aidan, my own boyfriend, seemed to prefer Poppy to me that night, not to mention all the other boys too. Chloe's boyfriend, Elliott. But Aidan was the worst. I can still remember the way he leaned over her, whispering in her ear, complimenting her, and then afterwards on the way to the party at Esther's house doing nothing but talk about her. Why had I been so mean to her in the past? She was so hot. She really needed to come to more parties.

So maybe I snapped. I was a teenager, for Christ's sake. She had been flirting with my boyfriend. Her! Of all people. I wasn't about to lose my boyfriend to someone like her. She wasn't about to upstage me at one of our final events of school and get away with it.

I know it sounds petty. And it was. But after all these years . . . why does it matter to her so much? Why is she so upset?

The day comes back to me so clearly. Sneaking into the art room (should I feel bad for still being proud of how we accomplished that, being able to get in there?), the four of us entering armed with as many rule-breaking items as possible. I came holding balloons and a box of needles, Chloe clutched bits of chicken skins we'd bought from KFC and even a couple of Capri-Sun pouches as a callback to when we first met Poppy, Esther had smashed a mirror and carried its broken pieces in a box, and Tanya had even gone to the trouble of collecting up some of her dog's shit in a bag. It absolutely reeked. Even now, the smell of everything is what I think of first.

Chloe took out her phone, a Motorola Moto X that at the time was the coolest possible phone to have. Turning on the video camera, she waved it around at us all and turned it on herself, grinning, then set it up on one of the tables near Poppy's project.

The whole room was full of exam pieces, but we knew which one was Poppy's straight away. It was this absolutely huge canvas, painted in incredible detail. A self-portrait. For someone who was only seventeen, even we could see the genuine talent on display, but that just made us even more determined to spoil it.

She looked beautiful in the painting, practically like she did at prom. Unacceptable.

"Let's start with the balloons!" I said. "Poppy was trying to go for a sad celebration look, I reckon. Let's each blow one up and pin it across the top, then burst them with these needles."

Esther laughed. "Wait, I have a better idea. Let's fill them with Capri-Sun first, *then* pop them. It'll explode everywhere."

"Oh yes, and that'll look deliberate too," Chloe said. "Those balloon-paint-popping pictures, like the ones Mia's mum does on *The Princess Diaries*."

We filled them and fastened them carefully to the painting in each of its four corners, and then threw a needle each at them. Chloe and Tanya took a couple of goes, but Esther and I got ours on the first try, the needles piercing the balloons and splattering Capri-Sun all over, its sticky orange residue creating a splash pattern that did look planned, as if Poppy had painted it on herself. The ones in the top corners dripped down the canvas, creating long marks that made the painting look like it was crying.

"This is so funny," Chloe said. "Now let's put loads of needles on the balloons, sticking out."

"And hang the chicken skins off them!" Tanya suggested.

"That's brilliant!" I said. "It's starting to look like some horrible avant-garde experiment gone wrong."

I brought out the mirror pieces, taking one and dragging it down the canvas so it tore, then stuck it in so it protruded dangerously, a sharp edge much bigger than the needles.

Chloe, Esther, and Tanya added their own pieces of mirror to the painting, sticking some with glue to lay them flat so we could see snippets of our reflections grinning at our efforts.

"Finally, the pièce de résistance," I declared, taking the bag of dog shit. "Shall we smear it all over? God, it's so disgusting! It stinks."

"Not all over," Esther said. "Look, where she's painted shadows in—we could add it there."

"Oh, that's brilliant!" Chloe grinned. "Thank God there's a sink in this room so we can wash our hands after. This is so vile."

We set to work, making retching sounds as we applied the shit to the canvas, like we were little kids doing finger-painting. It was disgusting, but it was worth it when we were done. And after we washed our hands, we stepped back to admire our masterpiece.

"Finished!" Chloe screeched, picking up her phone and filming the completed project at a closer angle. "Poppy's artistic talent!"

The whole thing looked like a twisted rebellion of an art project. The original painting was still visible underneath our destruction, but now with our additions it seemed like a satire, a mockery of a serious piece of work.

It was perfect. It was grotesque.

At the time we thought it was such a laugh. She wasn't meant to take it so seriously.

Okay. Maybe that's not fair. We did mean for her to take it seriously and get upset. But we didn't know she'd harbour a grudge about it for ten years. We just didn't think it was that bad.

Yeah. How wrong we were.

"Poppy." My voice is nothing more than a whisper, like I'm trying to calm a wild animal.

"All these years you've had to think about what you did, and you did nothing to amend your ways," Poppy says. "You tortured me throughout secondary school, never letting me have a moment's peace. Except for my art. And then you took that too. You destroyed the one thing that gave me joy in my life—my artwork. And then you agreed to this jolly little hen party, all expenses paid—and said *nothing* about it."

"I know I can't change what happened, but I'm so sorry," I say. "If there is anything, anything at all, I promise you, I will do it. Please don't . . ." I'm embarrassed at the way fear makes my voice break.

"It's too late," Poppy says.

"It's never too late," I say. "You're here in front of me, talking. We can make this okay. Whatever it is you want me to do."

I silently beg her: Please don't kill me. I don't want to die. My fingers tremble as they wrap further around the knife handle.

"Tanya knew the moment I walked into her hut I was going to kill her," she murmurs. "I'd knocked on the door—polite, unsuspecting. I came in and locked it behind me. She gave a good fight. I'm sure you saw that, practically everything was knocked over. But it's funny, do you know what she said to me as she lay there dying?"

My body is so preoccupied with terror it takes me a second to realise she wants a response. I shake my head.

"She said she was sorry. That she deserved it. That she'd been struggling for years with the guilt. But she never tried to reach out to me. Never tried to make amends. I think she was using her guilt as an excuse for everything that had happened to her."

"She wanted to make it up to you," I whisper. "She said as much when we got the invitations. She felt worse than the rest of us. I think because she had been your friend when you were little."

"I told her the truth in the end. And do you know what she said?"

"What?" The truth?

"She said, 'Then I really do deserve this.' Tanya deserved to die for what she did. Chloe and Esther, and you too."

"You're alive," I say, aware of her standing up, terrified of what she might do next. "You're here. I'm sorry. We can fix this somehow. We'll tell Robin Chloe died after hitting her head, and that Esther killed Tanya, and it was self-defence on my part. You don't have to do this."

Poppy shakes her head at me. "It is too late."

"It's not!"

"It is."

"We can fix this," I continue desperately.

"There is no fixing this. I'm not Poppy. Don't you see? Poppy is already dead."

"What?"

"She died almost ten years ago," she says. "Poppy killed herself."

THIRTY-FOUR

Poppy

AUGUST 21, 2013

Dear Diary,

It's A Level Results Day today and I want to die.

What is death like? I went to my granddad's funeral, almost ten years ago now. He was old and ill and very nearly a hundred, so even though people were sad they kept saying what a great long life he lived. I don't really remember him. All I kept thinking about was whether his favourite books were in the coffin with him, and whether it was cold. Now I know that's silly, obviously he isn't cold, he's dead. But maybe you are cold when you're dead.

I guess I'll find out soon. If things don't go to plan.

I didn't show up to any of my exams, but that shouldn't come as a surprise. My art portfolio, which I had spent months carefully preparing, was now worthless after I failed in my final project. I burned it in the garden, watching it melt away into nothing. I burned the Slade portfolio too, the one that had got me my interview in the first place. It was worthless now after all. Mum and Dad begged me to sit my other exams. Even Wendy begged me. They said I was throwing my future away. That I shouldn't let failing Art impact my entire life.

Today, I looked at the school website and saw everyone celebrating the exam successes. There was a photograph of Annabel and a couple of smart boys named Oscar and Lucas opening their results and jumping in the air, smiles on their faces. The title read: "Top Marks for Top Students!" I, of course, wasn't mentioned, even though I knew if I had done my exams as planned I'd be right there with them.

Underneath, there was a passage about the art department, and a picture of Ollie with his final piece project.

My painting was better. Well . . . it was. Before they destroyed it.

It said Ollie had managed to get a place at Slade after all. Was that my place? Did me getting kicked off enable him to get in? I remembered him saying he was on a reserve list. He had been so upset when I got in and he didn't. Look who would be laughing now.

Facebook showed the celebrations that were continuing into the evening, parties being planned. Annabel had gotten all A grades. Esther had done really well too, while Tanya passed reasonably enough. Chloe had failed her A levels, getting all Ds, but from the pictures she didn't seem to care. Other than Chloe, who was starting some kind of hairdressing apprenticeship, they would be off to university and whole new horizons, just like I was meant to be.

None of what had happened had affected them at all.

I mean, of course it didn't. I was just a big joke to them.

Even though they were disappointed with what happened, Mum and Dad grew increasingly worried about me. They tried talking to me, and when that didn't work, they forced me to the doctor's, so now I have a weekly therapist. And antidepressants. But I don't take them. I pretend to, then I store them in my bedside drawer inside a jewellery box, along with the knife I stole from the kitchen. That knife has become my constant companion.

They're both waiting for me to be ready. But I have a plan first.

I haven't been completely useless. I've seen people on Facebook, commenting about what happened with me and my art exam. Apparently there might be a video. Chloe filmed them all in the art room. So some people say anyway. No one has actually uploaded it, so it might not be true at all. But imagine that—a video, exonerating me. It could mean I get my place back if they actually showed it to anyone.

At the time I was too upset, but I realised there was an important missing piece of the puzzle I wasn't focusing on.

Those four couldn't have done it without someone to let them in. Each of us doing the exam was given a card key in order to access the room. Anyone not doing Art couldn't have got through the door. So someone had to have helped them. Maybe even joined in. If I can just find out who that is, maybe I can change things. Slade will offer me my place after all.

But in order to do that, I have to speak to one of them. And there's only one I ever could, even after how she treated me on that last day.

And if it doesn't work?

I guess it'll be time. Because there's nothing left for me here.

AUGUST 25, 2013

Dear Diary,

I am ready.

I might as well write down what happened here. It gives me a little bit longer to—

I need to pull myself together. Just because I can't write it down doesn't mean I'm not ready. Back to yesterday.

Mum and Dad couldn't know I was going out, not when I hadn't since it all happened. They'd have too many questions. I waited until they went to work.

It's so hard, thinking about those two. What I'm going to do to them. If they ever read this—I'm sorry. I'm so sorry I wasn't strong enough. You couldn't have done anything, I promise. None of this was your fault.

It was theirs.

My last hurdle was Wendy.

She was washing the dishes from breakfast, well-behaved as she always was nowadays, when I gave her a hug too. She turned, still with soapy hands, and hugged me back.

"What was that for?" she asked, eyes narrowing in suspicion immediately. Wendy, always so intelligent.

She's going to be so amazing when she's older.

"I'm going out today," I said.

"Out?" she repeated. "You?"

I hadn't showered in weeks. My hair was hanging lank and greasy past my shoulders, and my face was shining with sweat. The most I did anymore was wash at the sink when the smell got too much to bear. I'd been wearing the same pyjamas for four days now; any more than that and Mum would quietly place a new pair at the foot of my bed.

"I'm having a shower," I said, as if that wasn't obvious. "I'm going out for the day."

"You're what?"

"Don't tell Mum and Dad," I said quickly. "It's just something I have to do. Please."

"So you're the one who gets all the attention at the moment and I'm still doing favours for you?"

Yeah, that one hurt, I'll admit. Because it was true. Wendy has been practically forgotten about, Mum and Dad are so worried for me. And it makes me feel awful. But it won't be for much longer now, and then she can have all their attention.

"Please, Wendy."

She weakened at that. "Fine, whatever. Go. But you need to make sure you're back before Mum and Dad get home. I can't cover for you then. They'll go crazy at the thought of you out of the house."

"Oh, thank you!"

"Poppy . . ." She chewed her lip. "You are going to be alright, aren't you? This isn't going to be how you are forever, is it?"

I didn't know what to say to that. I couldn't lie to her.

"Please tell me what's going on," she said.

I'm sorry, Wendy. You deserve better than a sister like me.

By the time I stepped out of the house, nerves had tightened my belly. I didn't know what to expect when I got there. But I knew where I was going.

Tanya's house looked the same as ever, an ordinary Victorian terrace with an overgrown front garden. The lights were off as I walked up and for a terrible moment I thought she might be out and the entire journey a waste, but when I knocked on the door I heard movement from inside.

She opened the door herself, mouth falling open in shock at seeing me standing there. Even though I was washed and dressed, I knew that couldn't hide the months of damage I'd done to myself. My jeans had had to be tightened with a belt to the smallest loop, as everything was hanging off me. I'd lost so much weight, and I looked tired too. Defeated.

Oh, Tanya.

Sorry. I had to take a break and calm myself down. It's hard to write in a diary when you're crying so hard you can't see.

It's funny how clear my memories are of these horrible moments. Well, not funny ha-ha, more like funny tragic. But all I have to do is *close my eyes and think for a second, and it all comes flooding back. Each stabbing word, each terrible gesture or action.*

"Jesus. Poppy?" she said when she saw me standing there. "What are you doing here? Are you ill?"

"I've been better," I replied.

She shook her head, still in disbelief. "I can't believe it."

"Can I come in?" I asked.

I don't think she wanted me to, but she nodded, opening the door for me. She was so different on her own, without the influence of the others. We went into her living room.

"Is anyone else home?"

"My parents are at work." Tanya did not look happy. "Why are you here?"

"I need to talk to you."

"About what?"

"About the exam."

She closed her eyes at my question. Then, just when I gave up expecting her to answer, she said, "It's only an Art A Level. Nobody died."

"Only an Art A Level . . ." I echoed. "You know *being an artist has been my dream ever since I was little. We used to talk about it together. You being an actress, me being an artist. You all knew I got into Slade. I was going to make my dream happen."*

"It's not a big deal. You'll get into somewhere else."

"No, I won't. They think I broke the rules. There's no chance of me getting in anywhere. And it was—Slade." My voice broke, threatening tears.

She rolled her eyes at that. "Whatever. You'd have had to join the real world at some point. As if you were ever actually going to be a famous artist."

I gasped at her attack. "You don't know that. I could have made it. And instead now I have nothing. No A levels at all."

"Well, that's your own fault there."

"I think Chloe recorded it. What you four did. I've seen people saying online there was a video."

"Did she?" Tanya pulled a face, as if it was nothing. "That's such a Chloe thing to do. I don't know anything about that."

I tried not to let the hope I was feeling shine through in my tone. "But if there was a video it would prove I didn't do it. Maybe I could get my place back."

She didn't deny it. "What do you want from me, Poppy?"

It burst out of me. "I want you to take responsibility. Help me get the video from Chloe and take it to the teachers. Maybe I could get my place back and we could forget this ever happened. I could still get to go to London and we'd never have to see each other ever again."

"Chloe has probably deleted it," she said dismissively. "It wasn't that interesting."

"But we could just check—"

"And then we'd get in trouble," Tanya says. "No chance. I'm not helping you do that."

I tried a different tack. "Someone had to have let you into the art room. None of you take Art, you wouldn't have had access. You can blame it on them, say it was their idea. Who was it?"

She looked smug. "You wouldn't believe me even if I did tell you. It was their idea, you know. They let us in with their card key, returned it to Miss Wersham whilst we were still in the room and then kept watch while we did it."

It was hard to breathe when I heard what she said. I had my confirmation.

"Who was it?" I whispered, barely able to speak.

"You'll never hear that from me."

"Tanya, I'm . . ." Out of everyone, it was her in the end who I said everything to. And I need to write it down here. "I think I'm going to kill myself. I can't do this anymore. I need you to help me, or there's no other way out from this."

"Kill yourself?" She tried to hide her shock, but it was there, I'm sure of it. "You wouldn't do that."

"Look at me. I can barely function. You thought I was sick. I am."

"Sick in the head," she said. "Don't talk about killing yourself, that's stupid."

"I mean it," I said. Tears spilled from my eyes so easily, and soon enough I was sobbing my heart out. "Please tell me who helped you get into the art room. If I just knew who they were, I might be able to do something. Okay, you don't have to show the video. I get that. But if you told me who they were, the school could investigate. They might be able to prove something. Please."

She turned on me, anger coming in a flash. "You must be joking. I won't tell you who helped us. You're on your own."

"Tanya . . ."

"Get out, Poppy. Get out and don't come back. And if you're going to kill yourself, you might as well just get on with it and do the whole world a favour."

I had my answer.

"We haven't been friends since we were eleven," she said bitterly. "Stop pretending we had anything resembling a real friendship. We were children. Your dramatics don't fool me."

Tanya. My only friend in the whole world.

I don't know why it hurts so much, why I'm still surprised.

So where does that all leave me? Here, writing in you, diary. I never did give you a name. Probably for the best, otherwise you'd turn into someone else I'd feel guilty about leaving.

Oh, Mum. Dad. Wendy. I'm going to miss you.

The antidepressants are next to me on the bed. There's so many of them.

The knife is there too. I have to make sure.

In ten years, will those four even remember me? Annabel, Chloe, Esther, Tanya.

I don't think they'll remember me in ten months.

And whoever that mystery person was. The one who let them into the art room. Who was it? Sally? Jayla? Ollie? It could have been any of them. I thought the people who did Art liked me. We weren't friends, but I thought they at least saw me as a good person. I know I did with them. And yet one of them had to have betrayed me. Maybe they were all laughing at me behind my back with those four for years. I've been such a fool. Even art has failed me in the end.

I'm scared.

I don't want to die.

Yes, I do.

I have to do this.

And I'm really sorry.

THIRTY-FIVE

Annabel

MAY 22, 2023

Everything swims around me. "What are you saying?"

"I'm not sure why you're pretending to be so surprised," she says.

"You're Poppy! You're standing right in front of me! You just faked your death."

"I wish Poppy faked her death," she murmurs. "You're so stupid. I'm not Poppy at all."

"You're not . . ."

My vision clears and I look at the woman we all thought was Poppy Greer. The drastic change in appearance, but there was still Poppy underneath it all. I don't get it. She looks so much like her.

"She killed herself," she says simply, "in the summer after the exams. She never recovered from it. From everything you did."

I can picture her—Poppy, as a teenager. Her braces. Her mousy hair. Her smile even when we were vicious.

"We would have known," I say, determined not to accept this. "We would have found out about her suicide. Someone would have told us."

"It was kept quiet," Poppy's impersonator says. "Poppy's parents didn't want people finding out. It was a very small funeral. Family only. After all, she had no friends."

"But surely it still would have come out. People would have known."

"Of course. If someone had bothered to actually ask after Poppy, find out what happened to her. But none of you did. You didn't *care* to know." Her words are further daggers.

She stops for a moment, gathering herself.

"That's why you burgled Chloe," I say. "You were looking for the video of us ruining her exam."

The woman nods, closing her eyes. I don't dare; closing my eyes would take me back to it all.

"And I found it," she says. "I forced myself to watch it, the entire thing. What struck me most was the sheer joy you all got out of it."

"We didn't think it would be a big deal," I say. "It was just . . . a bit of fun."

Poppy's impersonator laughs, a hollow sound. "A bit of fun! None of you knew just how much hope Poppy was hanging on that Slade place. On getting out and escaping from you all."

"We're sorry," I say. "I'm sorry."

She turns on me, the laughter dying on her lips. "I've already told you, it's too late for apologies."

"Who are you?" I ask.

"You haven't figured that out?" she snaps. "I thought you were supposed to be the smart one."

"I am . . . I . . ."

"You need to tell me their name," she says, folding her arms.

"Whose name?"

"The person who helped you get in that room," she snaps, viciously. "The one who enabled you to destroy her artwork. Your accomplice."

I'm about to blurt it out, just get it over and done with, when something stops me. "If I tell you his name, what are you going to do to me?"

"His name," she repeats, and I want to curse my mistake. "It was a boy. You really are something, Annabel, you know that?"

I need to get out of here. While I still have his name, she can't do anything to me.

But she's not done with me yet.

"Let me tell you why this isn't going to end well for you, no matter what stunt you try and pull," she says. "You killed her. There's nothing you can do now. I killed Tanya first because Poppy begged her for help, right at the end, the day before she killed herself. She told her she was going to commit suicide, and Tanya told her she was attention-seeking, and to get on with it."

Tanya had learned from me so well.

"Poppy left a diary which explained everything. Every tiny, horrific detail."

"How do you even know about all this? How did you read Poppy's diary?" I ask. "Who are you?"

Poppy—who I thought was Poppy—nods at me. "Take a good look, Annabel. Who could I possibly be?"

I consider her, staring her up and down. She was able to get access to Poppy's diary. She knows personal details that someone who wasn't there couldn't just pretend.

I stare at her sad, angry eyes and at last the final detail clicks into place.

"You're Wendy," I say. "You're Poppy's sister."

THIRTY-SIX

Annabel

Wendy. Of course.

My mind strains to remember Poppy's sister, and sure enough, images return to me: dark hair, dark eyes, completely different from the woman standing in front of us now. A mixture of triumph and fury rests in her expression. I don't want to believe any of what she's said. I want her to be Poppy more than anything.

"You look nothing like her," I say. "I remember Wendy. You're totally different. You're . . ." Like Poppy, I want to say. A new and improved version of her.

My head is a mess.

"Poppy killed herself the day after Tanya told her she deserved to die." I open my mouth to speak, but Wendy lifts a finger to silence me and carries on. "She had stored the antidepressants she was on somewhere, and took them all after we had gone to bed. I don't know if she doubted they would work—but she also had a knife." Her voice becomes strained as she struggles to continue. "By the time I found her, she had been dead for hours. There was blood everywhere. The funeral was weeks later, after the autopsy."

She takes a breath, steadies herself. I wait.

"Her room stayed as it was for so long. None of us could bear to go in there. It took a whole year before Mum and Dad decided we needed to move. It was like we had her grave in the middle of our house. When we were packing everything up, I found her diary. But I didn't read it for so long. I was so angry at her, for what she had done to our family."

What the hell do I do?

"It wasn't until my own A Level Results Day, almost two years since she'd died, that I decided to look at it. And I found out . . . everything. But I tried to forget about it, to focus on my own life. To make Mum and Dad proud, because they were so broken. Still are, really, though they pretend they're fine. I went to university, I became a doctor."

"The hen party?" I whisper.

She shakes her head. "Wishful thinking. It wasn't fair that Poppy never got to have a wedding of her own, a life of her own."

"You're right, it wasn't fair." I'm burbling now, buying time whilst the sun continues to rise. What time is Robin coming? She said the morning, but what does that mean?

"None of you even considered what it might be like from her perspective. So I had to make you see."

"The artwork in the huts," I whisper, remembering their unsettling imagery. "We thought Poppy had painted them."

"I hired someone," Wendy explains. "A talented artist. Not as emotional as Poppy's work. But I showed her what was left of Poppy's art and had her reproduce classic pieces in her style, as close as possible. It wasn't quite the same, a bit too polished. But it had the effect I wanted." Her tone becomes wistful. "I wish I could have seen how Poppy's paintings would have developed. She was going to be so great. But you cut that short. Just like her life."

"You want to know who helped us into that room," I say.

"Oh, Annabel, clever as always," she says. But her face grows serious. "Yes. I want you to tell me the name of your accomplice."

It's all I have. My only bargaining chip.

"And if I do?"

"The better question is what if you don't," Wendy says. "Do you really want to try me? Really?"

The cold strength in her voice makes my mouth dry and my hands tremble. I believe her completely.

"Okay," I say. "His name was Ollie Turner."

Ollie Turner.

It was the Monday after our prom, a gloriously sunny afternoon the four of us were spending sunbathing on the field behind the back of the music rooms. We hadn't really interacted with Ollie much before this; he was in my biology class and we'd worked on a project together, which had involved me going to his house a couple of times a week for a month or so, but that was about it. The others barely knew him at all. He was quite good looking in a gawky artist kind of way and Chloe had secretly fancied him for ages, but then she fancied anyone with a pulse and a crooked smile.

"Did you see the way Poppy was eyeing up Aidan?" I said. I was still furious. Aidan and I had actually argued about it when everyone else had left and we were walking home. He'd even offered to walk Poppy! There was no chance I was letting that happen, so I splashed a bit of water on my dress and pretended I'd been sick in one of Esther's bathrooms so he had to stay.

It was meant to be a joke, inviting Poppy to the party. I had even slipped an ecstasy pill in her drink in the hopes she'd make a total idiot of herself, but if anything it just made her lose her inhibitions and become the friendly, confident person she clearly could have been if we'd left her alone. Every guy at that party was staring at her, enchanted.

"What about Elliott as well?" Chloe said. "Esther, you were lucky to catch them when you did. Cheap slut."

Esther nodded. "I couldn't believe it when I went out there and saw them both, practically hanging off each other. They denied it but I knew."

"It's all her fault." Chloe scowled. "What was Elliott meant to do if a girl was throwing herself at him? She was definitely trying to make him cheat."

"She tried talking to me about my acting," Tanya put in, looking annoyed. "Clearly she was showing off about her stupid art school place and wanting to make me feel bad."

"She needs to get what's coming to her," Esther muttered. "Trying it on with your boyfriends like that. Acting like she's somebody all of a sudden."

"Are you talking about Poppy Greer?"

We turned, startled, and found Ollie had crept up behind us without our realising it.

He looked a bit uncomfortable, standing awkwardly there whilst we were sitting down, but none of us offered for him to join us.

"So what if we are?" Chloe asked, rolling onto her stomach and sitting with her chin resting on her palms. She used her elbows to push her boobs together so Ollie got a good view of her unbuttoned shirt, revealing cleavage and a neon pink bra underneath. "Aren't you, like, artsy buddies?"

He scowled. "Definitely not. She's done nothing but go on and on about how she's got into Slade. It's this fancy art university in London. She really thinks she is it."

Tanya rolled her eyes. "Yeah, she won't shut up about that, even to us."

"Poppy Greer swanning off to London in a few months," I said. "It seems so unfair."

"Poppy Greedy always takes what she wants," Chloe murmured. "It'd be funny if we could mess that up for her."

"Well, what if you could?" Ollie mumbled.

"How exactly?" I frowned.

"She'll go off to Slade and forget about us," Tanya said.

"Not if something happened to her Art A Level," Ollie said. "If she failed, she'd be taken off the course."

We considered this for a second.

"As funny as that would be," I said, "how would we even do that? None of us do Art A Level and we wouldn't even know how she'd be able to fail."

"I do. Our exam starts tomorrow." Ollie looked strangely excited by his idea. "On the second day, when everyone else has left, I could let you four in. We're not allowed to do certain things with our art. You could bring that stuff in and put it on her painting, and then she'd fail."

"Is that not a bit much?" Tanya asked, a worried expression on her face. "She loves her art. It's everything to her."

"She could retake it," Esther said. "It's not that big of a deal."

"It *would* be funny," I said, warming to the idea.

"How do we make sure we're not caught?" Tanya wondered, still uncertain.

"I'll keep watch," Ollie said. "If anyone comes down the corridor, I'll tell you and give you a chance to make a run for it. But no one should be, they're not being looked at until the afternoon."

"Sounds perfect, then," I said. "Let's do it. Don't look so glum, Tanya. It's only a bit of fun. It'll make up for you not getting into that drama school, won't it!"

"Fine, fine," Tanya said. She had auditioned for some snooty drama school also in London and hadn't even got an interview. "I guess you're right. It would be good for her to see her art isn't as amazing as she says."

"Great," Ollie said. "It's a plan, then."

"Why are you so keen?" I asked, raising my eyebrow.

He blushed, but his voice came out sounding more forceful than I'd ever heard it before. "I want to go to Slade. She stole my place. I'm just getting it back."

His answer made me smile and Chloe cackle with delight.

"This is going to be so funny," she said. "I can't wait to see her face."

Now, Wendy stares at me after I say Ollie's name, mouth open.

"Ollie Turner?" she echoes, looking stunned. "The one who got into Slade when Poppy's place was taken away from her?"

"Yes, him."

"If you're lying about him, that would be a very stupid thing to do."

"I'm not. It was Ollie."

"Ollie Turner," she whispers, more to herself than to me.

Ollie's uncertainty when we were finished flashes back in my mind. His shock at just how far we went. He regretted it the moment we were done.

I don't tell Wendy this.

"He wasn't her friend," I say.

"I know that," she hisses straight back. "I'm just glad—I'm just relieved Poppy never knew it was him. Now head outside. It's about time we finish up here."

I open the door and head out onto the beach, aware of Wendy close at my back, constantly turning round to check she isn't about to stab me. It's morning now, the sky blue all around us, a gentle whisper of a breeze. Other than the debris on the beach, there's no sign of the storm last night. Chloe and Esther remain, of course, and I turn my back to them and face the horizon.

Wendy comes to my side, but she looks out too.

"Why leave me until last?" I ask, though I think I know the answer.

Wendy confirms my suspicions. "Annabel, you were always going to be the last one standing. You've always been the one in control, the leader of the gang. You weren't going to lose."

I'm distinctly aware that Wendy is distracted talking about all this, her knife still in her hand but lowered to her thigh. I'm still holding the knife that killed Esther, her blood long dried on the blade.

But I must have done something to give my thoughts away. Wendy indicates her head towards my knife. "Even right now, after everything, you're still thinking about how you're going to kill me before I can kill you. Isn't that right?"

"I'm not—"

"Even after being reminded of what you did. You're still ready to kill me." She sighs, as if this disappoints her. "A survivor trait for sure. It would be admirable in anyone except you, because you don't deserve to live. And yet, I am going to let you."

"What?" I'm thrown off guard.

"I said I'm going to let you live."

"Why?"

"Because someone needs to go down for these murders. And I'm not planning on it being me."

"You're insane." I lift the knife up, point it at her. "You can't just get away with this."

"I already have," she says. "*I* was never here, after all."

I can feel the blood draining away from my face. "What do you mean?"

"I must admit I was dying to hear about Robin's mix-up," she says. "But none of you brought it up. Perhaps Robin didn't let slip that you were actually our bride all along, Annabel? It was your hen party, not mine."

The memory flashes back to me so clearly. Robin thinking I was the bride. Esther going to correct her and me laughing her off. Enjoying the mistake. Thinking it was all a great joke.

Something must have revealed itself in my face, because Wendy grins. "Oh, so she *did* tell you that you were the bride. Clearly you didn't bother correcting her. Why would you? Any excuse to be the centre of attention."

"So what?" Her utter delight in this baffles me. "So Robin thought I was the bride. What does it matter?"

Wendy turns to look at the island behind us. Even though the storm has settled and a soft morning glow has hit the place, it still seems dangerous. It knows everything that has happened here. It hides Tanya's body and offers Chloe's and Esther's as tributes at our feet.

"You booked this holiday," Wendy says. "Not me. If anyone—say, the police—were to look into the records of this trip, they would find it booked under the name of Annabel Dixon."

"What are you even talking about? I didn't book this!"

"You're not very sensible with money, are you, Annabel?" Wendy says. "You have so many credit cards you didn't even notice when one of them went missing for a few days—ample time to book a holiday."

"How did you steal my credit card?"

"It's amazing what private investigators can do. They give so much information. So many juicy secrets."

For one mad moment I'm considering throwing myself at her and killing her.

"You taught me well," Wendy says. "I learned from the very best after reading Poppy's diary. All your nasty little schemes. It always came down to you, Annabel. No, you don't get the luxury of dying. I want you to suffer in prison for the rest of your life, for you to lose your cheating husband and fancy home and fake friends."

"You can't think I'm just going to let you get away with this," I say, shaking my head. "You're crazy. I'm going to tell the police this was all you, and I was acting out of self-defence. You're going to be the one going down for this, not me."

"You're going to tell them what exactly?" Wendy says. "That you—you who orchestrated this entire trip—don't have money problems? A dozen credit cards, one of which bought this holiday? Don't have an entire wardrobe of stolen goods at home, some probably even with the security tags still on them? That you didn't have a huge falling-out with your friends on this trip? Maybe this falling-out became violent. Everything was starting to come out and you snapped."

My mouth falls open.

"Poor Esther, stabbed to death trying to get you to stop murdering Chloe," she continues. "And what of poor Poppy? The fourth bridesmaid?"

I can't listen to any more of this. My fingers grip the handle tightly, and I ready myself to run at her.

But she's quicker than me. She smacks down on my arm, causing me to lose my hold of the knife. It falls to the sand and she picks it up quick as a flash, then comes even closer and rests it against my throat, her own still firm in her left hand.

"Who knows what happened to poor Poppy?" she whispers, as if nothing just happened. Her breath is so close it tickles my neck, filling me with nothing but dread. "Poppy Hall, that is. It wouldn't do well to use Poppy's real name on the booking form. I guess you must have drowned her. Her body will never be found."

She steps back and throws the spare knife into the trees. It disappears in a second, too far for me to attempt to reach it.

"The police will find that knife. They'll find you covered in blood." She shrugs. "It's hardly rocket science."

This bitch. This *bitch*.

It was all her. This is all her fault. Hers, and her pathetic sister's. I will not allow myself to go to prison. This can't be happening.

Wendy gestures to the motorboat. "I am going to go back to the mainland on this. And then I'm going to get on a plane home, and find Ollie Turner. Goodbye, Annabel. Enjoy your life in prison. You truly deserve it."

She doesn't wait for a response, and I don't give her one; she walks over to the fishing boat. Never once does she break eye contact with me, never once does she lower her knife, even placing the handle between her teeth to push the boat out onto the sea. As soon as she's in and away, starting the engine, only then does she finally put the knife down, giving me a final smug smile and even a small wave.

I watch her go, the boat starting to move out into the wider ocean. There's no stopping her. I have to figure out what I am going to do from here.

THIRTY-SEVEN

Annabel

MAY 22, 2023

The boats start to disembark. The emergency services come rushing towards me, medical kits in hand that won't have any use here.

I step forward, ready to greet the police, working up a few more tears.

I've had hardly enough time to come up with a proper plan. Robin arrived and summoned the police within moments. But I'm not going to go down without a fight.

One of the male police officers comes towards me. He's rather tall and delicious, and he isn't wearing a wedding ring. If I didn't look in such a state I could probably use him to my advantage, but instead I'm going to have to play the damsel in distress card.

"What's happened?" he says, trying to sound intimidating but failing miserably.

As if I cannot hold my own weight, I gingerly move closer to him, wobbling, keeping my hands spread wide so he can see the gashes in them, so he knows this wasn't a simple case of a woman gone mad. This was self-defence at worst. At best I'm going to get away with it all.

He reaches out his hand and I jerk backwards, as if I'm too frightened to come near him. The alarm in his eyes pleases me immensely; I must be doing a pretty good job of this.

"Where are the others who came on this island with you?" he asks.

Ah, here we go. The other police officers have rushed by me, heading into the rest of the island. It won't be long before they find Tanya, at least. Chloe and Esther might take a while longer.

What can I do?

There will be DNA, of course. Fingerprints. Proof that Wendy was here and that she killed Chloe and Tanya. But my DNA and fingerprints will be everywhere too. I touched Chloe. I touched Tanya. And not only that—the evidence of dozens, hundreds of people who have stayed here before. Not to mention the storm, which will have definitely interfered with Chloe's body. Esther's too, left out on the beach like that. And Wendy didn't go anywhere near her.

It's my name on the credit card. I supposedly booked this place.

Calm down. You can figure this out.

Robin saw Wendy. There's at least one person other than myself who knows there was a fifth woman on this island. That there is another suspect in all of this.

Except . . .

A sudden chill air hits my body, sending goose bumps across my arms. I draw myself into a hunch, wrapping myself in an embrace.

It's just like Wendy said. Robin saw *Poppy*. And Robin thought I was the bride. It was my hen do. And I was the one left standing.

"Sarge!"

One of the other police officers comes hurrying back down the path.

"We've got a body," she says. "In one of the huts."

The sergeant turns back to me. He takes out of his handcuffs. "Call for backup," he says to his colleague, and then grabs me roughly by the arm and turns me around. "What is your name?" he asks.

"Annabel Dixon," I say, because there's no use pretending otherwise.

"Annabel Dixon, I am arresting you on suspicion of murder," he says, locking my hands into the cuffs behind my back. "You do not have to say anything..."

Poppy Greer's freckled face dances in my mind.

She had to go and kill herself, didn't she? Over nothing. Over less than nothing.

Soon enough Poppy's face changes into Wendy's, that smug smile she had as she powered away in the boat, thinking she'd won.

Well, she hasn't.

I'm not stupid. I'll keep quiet for now. Get myself a good solicitor. I'll think of a plan.

"Two more bodies!" I hear over the sergeant's radio as he forces me into the speedboat. One of the paramedics from the ambulance starts to check me over, cleaning my wounds and wrapping bandages across my hands.

Game on, Wendy. I'll be seeing you sooner than you think.

THIRTY-EIGHT

Wendy

Well, well. That went rather successfully, didn't it?

Talk about getting what I came for and more.

Sitting in the airport lounge, hot coffee to keep me going before I can sleep on the long flight home, I can't help the smile that rests on my face at last. The airport is loud, hundreds of people waiting for flights for all over the world. Even in the early morning, the light is artificially bright, no doubt exposing my wind-swept hair and tired eyes. It doesn't matter. Soon I'll be able to wash the stink of that island off me for good and leave those bitches behind.

As people chatter around me, I can't help but wonder. Am I sitting with good, honest people going about their day, happily leaving a pleasant holiday? Or people concealing terrible secrets?

Naturally, I'm sure it's both. And maybe those terrible secrets are worth having.

I take a sip of my coffee, considering everything.

How do I feel? "Exhausted" is the first word that comes to mind. Drained. A part of me has forgotten what Poppy was really like before this. It takes looking at photos from when we were little kids to find the Poppy I barely remember now.

No, mostly I remember that awful night when I woke up with the sense that something was terribly wrong. I crept into Poppy's room, the open window allowing the moon to showcase her dead body to me in all its brutality. Blood was everywhere. She had slit her wrists with a knife. Not only that, but her arms were covered in old scars. Ones she had clearly inflicted on herself months or even years before. I picked up that knife with trembling hands, and all I could think was that I had failed her. Me. Her sister, her oldest friend. I had failed her. I might as well have stabbed her with the knife myself. The others are to blame, but a part of me killed her too, because I didn't notice what was happening. I knew those girls picked on her, I knew that sometimes things were truly awful, but I didn't realise just how bad it was. Seeing her there, helpless and lifeless, I wanted to hide her away and pretend it wasn't happening. But in the end, all I could do was scream.

Mum and Dad are never going to be the same. Mum tries hard. I don't think I've seen her cry since those first few weeks, but I know she does in private. I found a pile of tissues stashed under a pile of magazines in the bathroom cabinet once, covered in her mascara. The strain of pretending to be fine has taken its toll on her: she's not even sixty, but she's wrinkled and shrunken like a woman twenty years older. She can't even bring herself to say Poppy's name. That's how she gets by: pretending Poppy only exists on birthdays and Christmas, and the day she died. Dad is more obviously destroyed. I don't think a single day has gone by where he hasn't cried. It happens in the evenings, when he's watching television, or it can happen during the day when he's gardening. All of a sudden he'll gasp, as the memory of his dead daughter hits him, and he'll be gone.

For years afterwards, I hated Poppy. I'll admit it. She was the one who did this to herself, and she left me to pick up the shattered pieces, too broken to ever become whole again. My teenage years, rather than being full of fun and rebellion, were a conscious effort to be the perfect daughter, to never worry my parents, and it was never enough.

It wasn't until I read her diary that I knew I had to do something.

But it worked out better than I ever could have imagined.

I touch the tattoo on my wrist, Poppy permanently inked into my skin. In the end, I got the last piece of the puzzle I was after. My notepad balances on my lap. How satisfying it is to take my pen and draw a line through each woman. Then I turn to the newest page.

One more name.

One more target.

Does he ever still think of Poppy, the girl who was meant to have his life? Did he go to Slade that September and think about whether she was doing okay? Or did he simply arrive and begin his life anew, with no thought or care to the mess he left behind?

Well. Someone will soon be coming to remind him.

The overhead speaker sounds.

"Flight BA 2256 to London Gatwick is now boarding. Please proceed to Gate 6."

I close the notepad with a snap and press it into the side of my bag.

No one's coming for me.

Annabel is going to go down for it all, as much as she's going to try and manipulate her way out of it. She's out of her depth this time.

As I head to the gate, I can't help but catch my breath at the sight of a family ahead of me. The parents are distracted, looking around at the shops, the father lumbered with dragging two large, wheeled suitcases. Behind them, pinching and poking at one another, are two sisters, a matching pair of mousy, freckled girls. The younger one is sulking, unhappy at her sister's upper hand. Just when I think she's going to burst into tears, the older sister reaches out again, but this time puts her arm around her and cuddles her close.

My hand wipes away at my eyes. It won't look good to start randomly crying in an airport.

After all, what are sisters for?

Those bitches might have started it, but I sure as hell finished it.

ACKNOWLEDGMENTS

———

There are so many people I would like to thank for helping to make my dream come true.

Firstly, to Helen Heller, not only the best literary agent in the world but someone who has changed my life completely. You believed in this book and in me and offered such valuable feedback. Thank you for everything.

To Saliann St-Clair, Katie James, Sarah McFadden, and everyone at the Marsh Agency. To Joe Veltre at the Gersh Agency.

Thank you to my editor, Rachel Kahan, for loving *She Started It* and helping to make it what it is today. You're brilliant! To the amazing team at William Morrow, including Ariana Sinclair, Kim Lewis, Olivia Lo Sardo, and Ali Hinchcliffe, for everything from copyediting to cover design to marketing—you are all phenomenal.

E. A. Aymar became my mentor through Pitch Wars, an experience I will never forget. You were the very first person outside of family and friends to read my work, and not only that, you thought it was halfway decent! With your guided support and feedback, that manuscript became something I could query confidently to agents. But you didn't stop there—no matter how many times I call or message with a question or worry, you're there to help me. I've never met someone so selfless and dedicated to seeing other people succeed. And when you felt your advice wasn't enough (which it always was!) you introduced me to some generous and kind authors who helped me and whom I'd like to thank as well: Susi Holliday, Jennifer Hillier, Bruce Holsinger, Hannah McKinnon, and Alex Segura.

My fellow Pitch Wars mentees—thank you for being so supportive! Special shout-out to Kelly Mancaruso, who cry-laughs with me whenever I need it!

Freddie Valdosta, you read a very early draft of this and gave me fantastic feedback. Not only that, you're the best friend in the world and you never doubted for a second that this book would get published.

To my mum and dad, who are my absolute number one champions. Ever since I was little you have supported my dream of being an author. From buying hundreds (probably thousands!) of novels, to painting my very first writing desk an amazing pink and getting me endless notebooks and pens, you have never stopped believing in me and I wouldn't be where I am today without you. I did it! My brother Lewis, the best older brother anyone could ask for. Not normally a book person, you have been excited and supportive every step of the way with me on this journey and that means so much! (I'll be cracking open that champagne on release day!) To my wonderful old cat, Toby, who has been on my lap many times over the years when I've been writing.

My whole extended family has been so remarkable ever since I told them about this book, and I hope you all know how much I love and appreciate you for taking such an interest.

My partner, Joe, could not have been more incredible. From reading endless drafts and offering your opinions to helping me with characters to simply running me a bubble bath after a long day, you are wonderful. Thank you so much. There would be no book without you.

If you have read this book—thank *you*.

Finally, this book is dedicated to the memory of my grandmother, Marie Blackmore. She passed away a few days after I found out William Morrow had bought *She Started It,* and it meant everything to me that she was able to know before she died. She and I bonded so much over books and our love of reading, and she always believed I could be an author. I hope I have made her proud. Thank you, Granny. I love you.